THE TROUBLE WITH DUKES

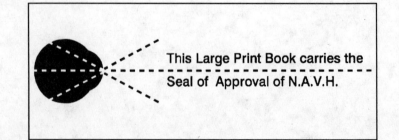

This Large Print Book carries the
Seal of Approval of N.A.V.H.

THE WINDHAM BRIDES SERIES, BOOK 1

THE TROUBLE WITH DUKES

GRACE BURROWES

THORNDIKE PRESS
A part of Gale, Cengage Learning

Farmington Hills, Mich • San Francisco • New York • Waterville, Maine
Meriden, Conn • Mason, Ohio • Chicago

LIBRARY OF CONGRESS CATALOGING-IN-PUBLICATION DATA

Names: Burrowes, Grace, author.
Title: The trouble with Dukes / by Grace Burrowes.
Description: Large print edition. | Waterville, Maine : Thorndike Press, 2017. |
  Series: the windham brides ; #1 | Series: Thorndike Press large print romance
Identifiers: LCCN 2016055575| ISBN 9781410498526 (hardcover) | ISBN 1410498522
  (hardcover)
Subjects: LCSH: Large type books. | GSAFD: Love stories.
Classification: LCC PS3602.U7687 T76 2017 | DDC 813/.6—dc23
LC record available at https://lccn.loc.gov/2016055575

Published in 2017 by arrangement with Grand Central Publishing, a division of Hachette Book Group, Inc.

Printed in the United States of America
1 2 3 4 5 6 7 21 20 19 18 17

To my late, red-haired, blue-eyed mother

ACKNOWLEDGMENTS

I'm so very happy to be writing in the Windham world again, and I have to thank my editor, Leah Hultenschmidt, at Grand Central/Forever, for giving me this opportunity. The book you're holding is the result of an entire village's hard work and goodwill, from our cover model (who is really and truly named Megan), to the art department that made a stunning image into a luscious cover, to the unseen heroes in copyediting and proofreading, as well as marketing and sales representatives whose diligent efforts are responsible for the book finding its way to many shelves. I have the kindest readers in the world (no bias here), and this book has had the nicest team in the world supporting it. Thanks to one and all — it's good to be the author!

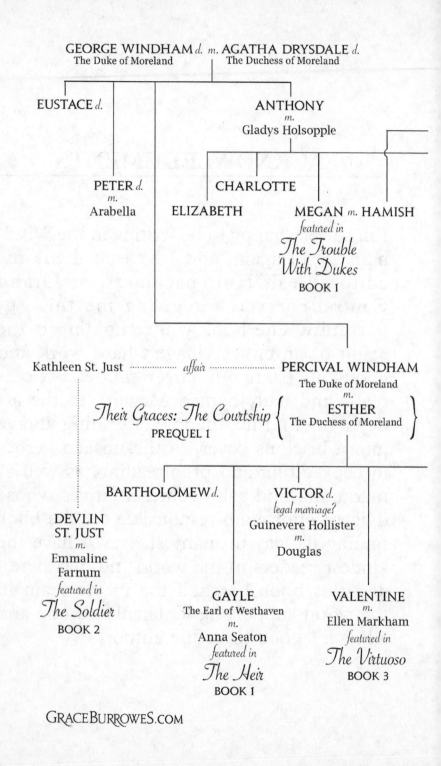

GEORGE WINDHAM *d.* *m.* AGATHA DRYSDALE *d.*
The Duke of Moreland   The Duchess of Moreland

EUSTACE *d.*

ANTHONY
m.
Gladys Holsopple

PETER *d.*
m.
Arabella

ELIZABETH

CHARLOTTE

MEGAN *m.* HAMISH
featured in
The Trouble
With Dukes
BOOK 1

Kathleen St. Just ⋯⋯⋯ *affair* ⋯⋯⋯ PERCIVAL WINDHAM
The Duke of Moreland
m.

Their Graces: The Courtship
PREQUEL 1

ESTHER
The Duchess of Moreland

BARTHOLOMEW *d.*

VICTOR *d.*
legal marriage?
Guinevere Hollister
m.
Douglas

DEVLIN
ST. JUST
m.
Emmaline
Farnum
featured in
The Soldier
BOOK 2

GAYLE
The Earl of Westhaven
m.
Anna Seaton
featured in
The Heir
BOOK 1

VALENTINE
m.
Ellen Markham
featured in
The Virtuoso
BOOK 3

GRACEBURROWES.COM

WINDHAM *Family Tree*

JAMES MACHUGH *m.* SUSAN MALCOLM

ALASDAIR   MAGNUS   RHONA

ANGUS   EDANA

ANWEN *m.* COLIN
featured in
Too Scot to Handle
BOOK 2
WINDHAM BRIDES

·········· *affair* ·········· Cecily O'Donnell

The Duke And His Duchess
PREQUEL 2

MAGGIE
m.
Benjamin Portmaine
featured in
Lady Maggie's Secret Scandal
BOOK 5
WINDHAM FAMILY

SOPHIE
m.
Vim Charpentier
featured in
Lady Sophie's Christmas Wish
BOOK 4
WINDHAM FAMILY

EVE
m.
Lucas Denning
featured in
Lady Eve's Indescretion
BOOK 7
WINDHAM FAMILY

LOUISA
m.
Jos. Carrington
featured in
Lady Louisa's Christmas Knight
BOOK 6
WINDHAM FAMILY

JENNY
m.
Elijah Harrington
featured in
Lady Jenny's Christmas Portrait
BOOK 8
WINDHAM FAMILY

CHAPTER ONE

"I don't want any damned dukedom, Mr. Anderson," Hamish MacHugh said softly.

Colin MacHugh took to studying the door to Neville Anderson's office, for when Hamish spoke that quietly, his siblings knew to locate the exits.

The solicitor's establishment boasted deep Turkey carpets, oak furniture, and red velvet curtains. The standish and ink bottles on Anderson's desk were silver, the blotter a thick morocco leather. Portraits of well-fed, well-powdered Englishmen adorned the walls.

Hamish felt as if he'd walked into an ambush, as if these old lords and knights were smirking down at the fool who'd blundered into their midst. Beyond the office walls, harnesses jingled to the tune of London happily about its business, while Hamish's heart beat with a silent tattoo of dread.

11

"I am at Your Grace's service," Anderson murmured from his side of the massive desk, "and eager to hear any explanations Your Grace cares to bestow."

The solicitor, who'd been retained by Hamish's late grandfather decades before Hamish's birth, was like a midge. Swat at Anderson, curse him, wave him off, threaten flame and riot, and he still hovered nearby, relentlessly annoying.

The French infantry had had the same qualities.

"I am not a bloody Your Grace," Hamish said, thanks be to the clemency of the Almighty.

"I do beg Your Grace's — your pardon," Anderson replied, soft white hands folded on his blotter. "Your great-great-aunt Minerva married the third son of the fifth Duke of Murdoch and Tingley, and while the English dukedom must, regrettably, fall prey to escheat, the Scottish portion of the title, due to the more, er, liberal patents and peregrinations common to Scottish nobility, devolves to yourself."

Devolving was one of those English undertakings that prettied up a load of shite.

Hamish rose, and for reasons known only to the English, Anderson popped to his feet as well.

12

"Devolve the peregrinating title to some other poor sod," Hamish said.

Colin's staring match with the lintel of Anderson's door had acquired the quality of a man trying to hold in a fart — or laughter.

"I am sorry, Your — sir," Anderson said, looking about as sorry as Hamish's sisters on the way to the milliner's, "but titles land where they please, and there they stay. The only way out from under a title is death, and then your brother here would become duke in your place."

Colin's smirk winked out like a candle in a gale. "What if I die?"

"I believe there are several younger siblings," Anderson said, "should death befall you both."

"But this title is Hamish's as long as he's alive, right?" Colin was not quite as large as Hamish. What little Colin lacked in height, he made up for in brawn and speed.

"That is correct," Anderson said, beaming like a headmaster when a dull scholar had finally grasped his first Latin conjugation. "In the normal course, a celebratory tot would be in order, gentlemen. The title does bring responsibilities, but your great-great-aunt and her late daughter were excellent businesswomen. I'm delighted to tell you

13

that the Murdoch holdings prosper."

Worse and worse. The gleeful wiggle of Anderson's eyebrows meant *prosper* translated into "made a stinking lot of money, much of which would find its way into a solicitor's greedy English paws."

"If my damned lands prosper, my bachelorhood is doomed," Hamish muttered. Directly behind Anderson's desk hung a picture of some duke, and the fellow's sour expression spoke eloquently to the disposition a title bestowed on its victim. "I'd sooner face old Boney's guns again than be landed, titled, wealthy, and unwed at the beginning of the London season. Colin, we're for home by week's end."

"Fine notion," Colin said. "Except Edana will kill you and Rhona will bury what's left of you. Then the title will hang about my neck, and I'll have to dig you up and kill you all over again."

Siblings were God's joke on a peace-loving man. Anderson had retreated behind his desk, as if a mere half-ton of oak could protect a puny English solicitor from a pair of brawling MacHughs.

Clever solicitors might be, canny they were not.

"We simply tell no one about this title," Hamish said. "We tend to Eddie and Ron-

14

nie's dress shopping, and then we're away home, nobody the wiser."

Dress shopping, Edana had said, as if the only place in the world to procure fashionable clothing was London. She'd cried, she'd raged, she'd threatened to run off — until Colin had saddled her horse and stuffed the saddlebags with provisions.

Then she'd threatened to become an old maid, haunting her brothers' households in turn, and Hamish, on pain of death from his younger brothers, had ordered the traveling coach into service.

"Eddie hasn't found a man yet, and neither has Ronnie," Colin observed. "They've been here less than two weeks. We can't go home."

"*You* can't," Hamish countered. "I'm the duke. I must see to my properties. I'll be halfway to Yorkshire by tomorrow. I doubt Eddie and Ronnie will content themselves with Englishmen, but they're welcome to torment a few in my absence. A bored woman is a dangerous creature."

Colin slugged Hamish on the arm, hard. "You'd leave tomorrow?"

Anderson flinched, while Hamish picked up his walking stick and headed for the door.

"Your pugilism needs work, little brother.

15

I've neglected your education."

"You can't leave me alone here with Eddie and Ronnie." Colin had switched to the Gaelic, a fine language for keeping family business from nosy solicitors. "I'm only one man, and there's two of them. They'll be making ropes of the bedsheets, selling your good cigars to other young ladies again, and investigating the charms of the damned Englishmen mincing about in the park. Who knows what other titles their indiscriminate choice of husband might inflict on your grandchildren."

Hamish had not objected to the cigar-selling scheme. He'd objected to his sisters stealing from him rather than sharing the proceeds with their own dear brother. He also objected to the notion of grandchildren when he'd yet to take a wife.

"I'll blame *you* if we end up with English brothers-in-law, wee Colin." Hamish smiled evilly.

A staring match ensued, with Colin trying to look fierce — he had the family red hair and blue eyes, after all — and mostly looking worried. Colin was softhearted where the ladies were concerned, and that fact was all that cheered Hamish on an otherwise daunting morning.

Hope rose, like the clarion call of the pipes

16

through the smoke and noise of the battle-field: While Eddie and Ronnie inspected the English peacocks strutting about Mayfair, Hamish might find a peahen willing to take advantage of Colin's affectionate nature.

Given Colin's lusty inclinations, the union would be productive inside a year, and the whole sorry business of a ducal succession would be taken care of.

Hamish's fist connected with his brother's shoulder, sending Colin staggering back a few steps, muttering in Gaelic about goats and testicles.

"I'll bide here in the muck pit of civilization," Hamish said, *in English,* "until Eddie and Ronnie have their fripperies, but Anderson, I'm warning you. Nobody is to learn of this dukedom business. Not a soul, or I'll know which English solicitor needs to make St. Peter's acquaintance posthaste. Ye ken?"

Anderson nodded, his gaze fixed on Hamish's right hand. "You will receive correspondence, sir."

Hamish's hand hurt and his head was starting to throb. "Try being honest, man. I was in the army. I know all about *correspondence.* By correspondence, you mean a bloody snowstorm of paper, official documents, and sealed instruments."

Hamish knew about death too, and about

sorrow. The part of him hoping to marry Colin off in the next month — and Eddie and Ronnie too — grappled with the vast sorrow of homesickness, and the unease of remaining for even another day among the scented dandies and false smiles of polite society.

"Very good, Your Grace. Of course you're right. A snowstorm, some of which will be from the College of Arms, some from your peers, some of condolence, all of which my office would be happy —"

Hamish waved Anderson to silence, and as if Hamish were one of those Hindoo snake pipers, the solicitor's gaze followed the motion of his hand.

"The official documents can't be helped," Hamish said, "but letters of condolence needn't concern anybody. You're not to say a word," he reminded Anderson. "Not a peep, not a yes-Your-Grace, not a hint of an insinuation is to pass your lips."

Anderson was still nodding vigorously when Hamish shoved Colin through the door.

Though, of course, the news was all over Town by morning.

"My dear, you do not appear glad to see me," Fletcher Pilkington purred. *Sir*

18

Fletcher, rather.

Megan Windham ran her finger along the page she'd been staring at, as if the maunderings of Mr. Coleridge required every iota of her attention.

Then she pushed her spectacles halfway down her nose, the better to blink stupidly at her tormentor.

"Why, Sir Fletcher, I did not notice you." Megan had smelled him, though. Attar of roses was not a subtle fragrance when applied in the quantities Sir Fletcher favored. "Good day, and how are you?"

She smiled agreeably. Better for Sir Fletcher to underestimate her, and better for her not to provoke him.

"I forget how blind you are," he said, plucking Megan's eyeglasses from her nose. "Perhaps if you read less, your vision would improve, hmm?"

Old fear lanced through Megan, an artifact from childhood instances of having her spectacles taken, sometimes held out of her reach, and sometimes hidden. On one occasion they'd been purposely bent by a bully in the church yard.

The bully was now a prosperous vicar, while Megan's eyesight was no better than it had been in her childhood.

"My vision is adequate, under most cir-

cumstances. Today, I'm looking for a gift."
In fact, Megan was hiding from the madhouse that home had become in anticipation of the annual Windham ball. Mama and
Aunt Esther were nigh crazed with determination to make this year's affair the talk of
the season, while all Megan wanted was
peace and quiet.

"A gift for me?" Sir Fletcher mused.
"Poetry isn't to my taste, my dear, unless
you're considering translations of Sappho
and Catullus."

Naughty poems, in other words. Very
naughty poems.

Megan blinked at him uncertainly, as if
anything classical was beyond her comprehension. A first year Latin scholar could
grasp the fundamental thrust, as it were, of
Catullus's more vulgar offerings, and
Megan's skill with Latin went well beyond
the basics.

"I doubt Uncle Percy would enjoy such
verse." Uncle Percy was a duke and he took
family affairs seriously. Mentioning His
Grace might remind Sir Fletcher that
Megan had allies.

Though even Uncle Percy couldn't get her
out of the contretemps she'd muddled into
with Sir Fletcher.

"I wonder how soon Uncle Percy is prepared to welcome me into the family," Sir Fletcher said, holding Megan's spectacles up to the nearby window.

Don't drop them, don't drop them. Please, please do not drop my eyeglasses. She had an inferior pair in her reticule, but the explanations, pitying looks, and worst of all, Papa's concerned silence, would be torture.

Sir Fletcher peered through the spectacles, which were tinted a smoky blue. "Good God, how do you see? Our children will be cross-eyed and afflicted with a permanent squint."

Megan dreaded the prospect of bearing Sir Fletcher's offspring. "Might I have those back, Sir Fletcher? As you've noted, my eyes are weak, and I do benefit from having my spectacles."

Sir Fletcher was a beautiful man — to appearances. When he'd claimed Megan's waltz at a regimental ball several years ago, she'd been dazzled by his flattery, bold innuendo, and bolder advances. In other words, she'd been blinded. Golden hair, blue eyes, and a gleaming smile had hidden an avaricious, unscrupulous heart.

He held her glasses a few inches higher. To a casual observer, he was examining an interesting pair of spectacles, perhaps in anticipation of considerately polishing them

21

with his handkerchief.

"You'll benefit from having my ring on your finger," he said, squinting through one lens. "When can I speak with your father, or should I go straight to Moreland, because he's the head of your family?"

That Sir Fletcher would raise this topic at all was unnerving. That he'd bring it up at Hatchards, where duchesses crossed paths with milliners, was terrifying. Other patrons milled among the shelves, and the doorbell tinkled constantly, like a miniature death knell for Megan's freedom.

"You mustn't speak with Papa yet," Megan said. "Charlotte hasn't received an offer and the season is only getting started. I'll not allow your haste to interfere with the respect I owe my sisters." Elizabeth was on the road to spinsterhood — no help there — and Anwen, being the youngest, would normally be the last to wed.

Sir Fletcher switched lenses, peering through the other one, but shooting Megan a glance that revealed the bratty boy lurking inside the Bond Street tailoring.

"You have three unmarried sisters, the eldest of whom is an antidote and an artifact. Don't think you'll put me off until the last one is trotting up the aisle at St. George's, madam. I have debts that your

22

settlements will resolve handily."

How Megan loathed him, and how she loathed herself for the ignorance and naivety that had put Sir Fletcher in a position to make these threats.

"My portion is intended to safeguard my future if anything should happen to my spouse," Megan said, even as she ached to reach for her glasses. A tussle among the bookshelves would draw notice from the other patrons, but Megan felt naked without her glasses, naked and desperate.

Because her vision was impaired without the spectacles, she detected only a twitch of movement, and something blue falling from Sir Fletcher's hand. He murmured a feigned regret as Megan's best pair of glasses plummeted toward the floor.

A large hand shot out and closed firmly around the glasses in mid-fall.

Megan had been so fixed on Sir Fletcher that she hadn't noticed a very substantial man who'd emerged from the bookshelves to stand immediately behind and to the left of Sir Fletcher. Tall boots polished to a high shine drew the eye to exquisite tailoring over thickly muscled thighs. Next came lean flanks, a narrow waist, a blue plaid waistcoat, a silver watch chain, and a black riding jacket fitted lovingly across broad shoulders. She couldn't discern details, which only made the whole more formidable.

Solemn eyes the azure hue of a winter sky and dark auburn hair completed a picture both handsome and forbidding.

Megan had never seen this man before, but when he held out her glasses, she took them gratefully.

"My most sincere thanks," she said. "Without these, I am nearly blind at most distances. Won't you introduce yourself, sir?" She was being bold, but Sir Fletcher had gone quiet, suggesting this gentleman had impressed even Sir Fletcher.

Or better still, intimidated him.

"My dear lady," Sir Fletcher said, "we've no need to ignore the dictates of decorum, for I can introduce you to a fellow officer from my Peninsular days. Miss Megan Windham, may I make known to you Colonel Hamish MacHugh, late of his royal majesty's army. Colonel MacHugh, Miss Megan."

MacHugh enveloped Megan's hand in his own and bowed smartly. His grasp was warm and firm without being presuming, but gracious days, his hands were callused.

"Sir, a pleasure," Megan said, aiming a smile at the colonel. She did not want this stranger to leave her alone with Sir Fletcher one instant sooner than necessary.

"The pleasure is mine, Miss Windham."

Ah well, then. He was unequivocally Scottish. Hence the plaid waistcoat, the blue eyes. Mama always said the Scots had the loveliest eyes.

Megan's grandpapa had been a duke, and social niceties flowed through her veins along with Windham aristocratic blood.

"Are you visiting from the north?" she asked.

"Aye. I mean, yes, with my sisters."

Sir Fletcher watched this exchange as if he were a spectator at a tennis match and had money riding on the outcome.

"Are your sisters out yet?" Megan asked, lest the conversation lapse.

"Until all hours," Colonel MacHugh said, his brow furrowing. "Balls, routs, musicales. Takes more stamina to endure a London season than to march across Spain."

Megan had cousins who'd served in Spain and another cousin who'd died in Portugal. Veterans made light of the hardships they'd seen, though she wasn't sure Colonel MacHugh had spoken in jest.

"MacHugh," Sir Fletcher broke in, "Miss Windham is the granddaughter and niece of dukes."

Colonel MacHugh was apparently as

bewildered as Megan at this observation. He extracted Megan's spectacles from her hand, unfolded the ear pieces, and positioned the glasses on her nose.

While she marveled at such familiarity from a stranger, Colonel MacHugh guided the frames around her ears so her glasses were once again perched where they belonged. His touch could not have been more gentle, and he'd ensured Sir Fletcher couldn't snatch the glasses from Megan's grasp.

"My thanks," Megan said.

"Tell her," MacHugh muttered, tucking his hands behind his back. "I'll not have it said I dissembled before a lady, Pilkington."

The bane of Megan's existence was *Sir Fletcher,* but this Scot either did not know or did not care to use proper address.

Sir Fletcher wrinkled his nose. "Miss Megan, I misspoke earlier when I introduced this fellow as Colonel Hamish Mac-Hugh, but you'll forgive my mistake. The gentleman before you, if last week's gossip is to be believed, is none other than the Duke of Murdoch."

Colonel MacHugh — His Grace — stood very tall, as if he anticipated the cut direct or perhaps a firing squad. With her glasses on, Megan could see that his blue eyes held a bleakness, and his expression was not merely formidable, but forbidding.

He'd rescued Megan's spectacles from certain ruin beneath Sir Fletcher's boot heel, so Megan sank into a respectful curtsy.

Because it mattered to her not at all that polite society had dubbed this dear, serious man the Duke of Murder.

CHAPTER TWO

"I've changed my mind," Hamish said, touching his hat brim as some duchess sashayed past him on the walkway. "We're leaving at the first of the week."

"You can't change your mind," Colin retorted, "and you just greeted one of the most highly paid ladybirds in London."

Colin was being diplomatic, for Hamish had committed his blunder in public — where all of his best blunders invariably occurred. Three days ago, Hamish had come upon Sir Fletcher Pilkington, but at least that unwelcome moment had transpired in a bookshop.

"The lady's clothes were expensive," Hamish said, "and not the attire of a debutante. She smiled at me, and she had a maid trotting at her heels. How was I to know she wasn't decent?"

"Because of *how* she smiled at you, as if you're the answer to her milliner's prayers for the next year."

Hamish tipped his hat to another well-dressed lady who also had a maid but lacked the smile.

"The damned debutantes look at me the same way. As if I were a hanging joint of venison, and they a pack of starving hounds."

"You aren't supposed to greet a woman unless she acknowledges you," Colin said as they came to a crossing.

"That last one scowled at me as if I were something rank stuck to the sole of her dainty boot. That's the sort of acknowledgment the Duke of Murder can expect."

A beer wagon rattled past, barrels stacked and lashed to the bed. Hamish owned two breweries, and in his present mood, he could have imbibed the inventory of both establishments and started on the distillery Colin had inherited upon coming of age.

"You need a finishing governess," Colin said. "Or a wife."

Oh, right. "I'm guessing among polite society they're much the same, which is why we'll all be heading home by this time next week."

Though Colin had a point. The young ladies ogling Hamish's title all knew how to make their interest apparent without blundering. They waved their painted fans, they simpered, they smiled, but not like *that*. They cast lures across entire ballrooms and formal gardens, without once setting a slippered foot wrong.

The battlefield of the London season had rules. Hamish simply hadn't grasped those rules yet.

He'd sooner grasp a handful of blooming nettles.

"If we go home now," Colin said, "you will never hear the end of it. Ronnie and Eddie have been invited to several balls, and depriving them of those chances to husband-hunt will earn their enmity until the day you die."

A Scotswoman was a formidable enemy, and two Scotswomen were the match of any mere mortal man.

"When is the next damned ball?" They were all damned balls, and damned musicales, and damned Venetian breakfasts, for where Ronnie and Eddie waltzed, either Hamish or Colin must follow.

"Next week. We take the street to the left."

Hamish did not ask how his brother knew the address of one of the most expensive modistes in a very expensive city. Colin was a good-looking fellow, and he had independent means. He'd taken to the bonhomie and challenge of army life like a sheep to spring grass, and his occasional sorties to London were just so many more bivouacs to him.

"How can two otherwise intelligent women spend half the day choosing fabric?" Hamish avoided meeting the eye of an older blonde woman accompanied by a younger lady with the same color hair. "I swear Ronnie and Eddie left their brains back in Perthshire."

"And there," Colin murmured, "you just snubbed the Duchess of Moreland and her youngest daughter, who happens to be a marchioness."

Hamish came to a halt. "We're going home, ball or no ball. I'm behind enemy lines without a map, a canteen, or a sound horse, Colin. One of my blunders will soon see me married or dead in a ditch."

Or worse, killing somebody. When Hamish had first mustered out, he'd been provoked into challenging one man to a duel, but fate had interceded to prevent serious harm to either combatant. Hamish and his former dueling partner — Baron St. Clair — were even cordial now when their paths crossed.

The Baroness St. Clair was a different and less forgiving article.

"That's why I'm here," Colin said, tipping

31

his hat to a flower girl. "To make sure you stay alive. I owe you that, and the last thing I want is a dukedom complicating my life. As long as you don't call anybody out — anybody else out — an apology ought to cover most of your missteps, and you'll soon have the lay of the land."

Hamish resumed walking, because standing still in the middle of the walkway was enough to draw the notice of passersby.

Perhaps wearing his kilt hadn't been an inspired notion. He'd hoped if any ladies were attracted by his title, they might be repelled by the sight of his bare knees. London women were apparently a stouthearted lot, because so far, Hamish's experiment had been a failure.

His entire visit to London had been a failure, but for that single moment when quick reflexes had spared a lady's spectacles from harm. Hamish hoped somebody would come along to spare that same young lady from Fletcher Pilkington's company.

That somebody wouldn't be Hamish, more's the pity. Miss Windham either hadn't known or didn't care that Hamish was the least appropriate man to hold a lofty title. Pilkington had doubtless remedied *that* oversight posthaste.

"Do you get the sense that Ronnie and

Eddie are enjoying all this waltzing and shopping?" Hamish asked.

He and Colin had alternated coming home on winter leave, and every two years, Hamish had returned to Scotland to find taller, prettier young women wearing his sisters' smiles. By the time he'd sold his commission after Waterloo, he'd hardly known Rhona or Edana.

They doubtless preferred not to become too well reacquainted with their oldest brother now, though they seemed to like his new title just fine.

"Our sisters are delighted with London so far," Colin said. "The shop is down this street. Tomorrow you're due for another fitting at the tailor's."

"Bugger the tailor," Hamish said. "He wants only to increase his bill. Aren't there any Scottish tailors in this blighted city?"

"English tailors are the finest anywhere," Colin replied, walking faster. "They're the envy of every civilized man the world over. You'd bash about in your kilt and boots, swilling whisky, and embarrassing your siblings instead of taking advantage of the privileges of your station."

Guilt assailed Hamish, the same guilt he'd felt as a captive in French hands. When he'd been led away from the scene of the ambush, bleeding in three places, his vision blurred, his head pounding, and his hearing mostly gone, he'd been in the clutches of an enemy more deadly than the French.

Shame had wrapped chains around his heart — for leading his men into an ambush, for succumbing to capture rather than dying honorably, for leaving Colin unprotected. In London, half pay and former officers abounded, and the sooner Hamish was away from them, the better.

"My station is all the more reason for me to leave this cesspit of privilege," Hamish said. "I do not now, nor will I ever, fit in, Colin. If you didn't want me wearing the kilt, then you might have said so before we left the house."

Colin's complexion was lighter than Hamish's, and thus when Colin blushed, his mortification was apparent to all. His ears were an interesting shade of red by the time Hamish paused outside an establishment called Madame Doucette's.

"You're known for wearing the kilt now," Colin said. "Once you showed up at that card party in the plaid, your fate was sealed. I'm having the full kit made up for myself."

"London shops have the most ridiculous names," Hamish said, hand on the door latch as foot traffic bustled past them. "Take this place, for instance. If I didn't know better, I'd think from the name it was a whorehouse."

Colin made an odd noise.

"Don't act as if I'd just kneed you in the balls," Hamish went on, peering through the door's glass. "Madame Doucette, my handsome kilted arse."

Immediately behind Hamish, a throat cleared.

A battle-hardened soldier grew accustomed to the way time expanded, or the mind's perceptions contracted, so that when faced with a mortal threat, the soldier could weigh options, calculate trajectories, and assess risks in the blink of an eye.

That same sense came over Hamish in the instant necessary to perceive that the blonde duchess and the little marchioness were regarding him curiously, as if not a Scotsman but a kilted great ape had appeared on the streets of Mayfair.

"My husband has often made similar remarks about milliners' establishments," the duchess said. She had a smile no duchess ought to possess — wise, kind, lovely, and a hint naughty too. If Hamish lived to be a hundred, his smile would never approach this woman's for complication, dignity, or attractiveness.

Blood would tell.

"I beg Your Grace's and your ladyship's pardon," Hamish said. "I apologize to you both. In the military, I developed a sadly unguarded tongue."

The young marchioness looked to be stifling a case of the giggles, while Hamish wanted to thump his head against the nearest wall.

"You might not have guarded your tongue, but you guarded your country," Her Grace said, patting Hamish's cheek as if he were a tired little fellow in want of a nap. "One has to admire your priorities, Your Grace, despite your colorful observations."

The duchess swept into the shop, Colin snatching the door open at the last instant. The marchioness curtsied prettily, winked at Hamish, and followed her mother into the modiste's.

"I think I'm in love," Colin muttered when the door was once again safely closed.

"It's nearing noon. You were overdue," Hamish replied charitably.

Colin smiled the slightly lost smile of a man who'd appreciated the fairer sex in six different countries, and Hamish, while not in love, certainly knew himself to be in trouble.

Deeply, deeply *in trouble.*

36

■ ■ ■ ■

"We're in trouble now," Elizabeth Windham whispered, peering through the window curtains. "Aunt Esther and Cousin Evie are upon the doorstep, and we've yet to choose your fabric."

Madame Doucette was still fluttering about with the pair of Scottish sisters Megan had met somewhere between the silks and the velvets. Miss Rhona and Miss Edana were both tall, merry redheads, though they lacked a fashionable sense of color.

"Not that one," Megan said, leaving Beth's side to take the bolt of yellow silk from Miss Edana's grasp. "Yellow is a difficult color to wear well, though it can be a lovely accent. Say you choose this pale green, for example. A yellow lace edging to your handkerchiefs would suit, or golden-yellow bonnet ribbons and a matching parasol."

Miss Rhona ran a hand over the yellow silk. "You even coordinate bonnet ribbons and handkerchief borders when you're concocting an outfit?"

Didn't everybody? "Bonnet ribbons must be some color. Why not choose a shade that

37

suits you?"

A look passed between the sisters, as if this was a question they'd store up to fire off in some other circumstances known only to them.

Aunt Esther and Cousin Evie swept into the establishment, though mostly Aunt Esther, who was as tall as the Scottish ladies, did the sweeping.

"My dears," Aunt Esther said, "I considered sending out the watch in search of you. What can you be thinking, dawdling here with the ball only a week off?"

The *watch* was a familial euphemism for Eve's older brothers: Lord Westhaven, Lord Valentine, and the oldest Windham cousin, Devlin St. Just, who'd soon be visiting from his earldom in the north. Megan loved her male cousins as much as she dreaded their fussing and lecturing.

The shop bell tinkled again, and all movement, all talk, ceased. Two sizable gentlemen stood immediately inside the door. They blocked enough of the light coming in the front windows to dim the sense of a happy feminine retreat.

"This green," Miss Edana said, shoving an entire bolt of silk at Madame. "I've made up my mind, I'll take the green."

"Yes, Miss," Madame said, scurrying to

38

the back of the shop without even acknowledging the gentlemen.

Men came into modiste's establishments, sometimes with a wife, a sister, or a daughter, more often with a mistress. A shrewd shop owner scheduled those visits, and used fitting salons in the back to ensure no awkwardness developed between patrons of different social strata.

These men did not belong in this shop in any capacity. The less tall fellow — he was in no wise short — was exquisitely attired in morning clothes, and bore a resemblance to the Scottish sisters.

The other fellow . . .

A queer feeling came over Megan, shivery and strange, but also happy, as if she'd recognized a friend from childhood whose features had altered with time, but whose countenance evoked precious memories . . .

In this shop of velvets, silks, and delicate lace, the larger man wore tartan wool. His kilt was a pattern of greens and blues, like lush pastures and summer sky woven about him, topped off with a dark blue velvet waistcoat, green wool jacket, and lacy white cravat.

His looks were like the textures he wore. Different, intriguing, and to Megan, attractive for their contrasts, like an arrangement of flowers in an unexpected vase.

He was not handsome, though. Too much sorrow lurked in his blue eyes, too much wariness. His features lacked refinement but were suited to those eyes. That jaw hinted of stubbornness, and his chin reinforced an impression of implacability. Granite cliffs stood as this man did, against howling winds, crashing seas, and centuries of marching seasons.

Though at the moment, the granite-strong man was apparently felled by indecision.

"I recognize you," Megan said, going toward him, her hand outstretched. "You rescued my spectacles the other day in Hatchards."

The gentleman's expression went from wary to dismayed, as Megan took him by the arm and tugged him forward in Aunt Esther's direction.

"You must meet my family," Megan went on, though the gentleman was apparently not used to being led about, for he remained unyielding, despite Megan's attempted guidance. "They will certainly want to make the acquaintance of so gallant and polite a fellow."

Hamish knew how to survive this ambush. He must snatch Colin by the elbow, duck back out the door, and wait a safe distance down the street until Edana and Rhona were finished beggaring him.

But the bespectacled young lady with the soft voice had already taken Hamish prisoner, and to free himself, he'd have to lift her hand away from his arm. Such a maneuver required touching her, and even Hamish knew that taking liberties with a proper woman's person was the equivalent of social suicide.

"Come along," the lady said, patting Hamish's hand. "Aunt is perfectly lovely, as a duchess is supposed to be."

The perfectly lovely duchess apparently had a sense of the absurd, for she extended a gloved hand in Hamish's direction.

"His Grace of Murdoch," she said, "if I'm not mistaken. A pleasure, and this must be your brother, Captain Colin MacHugh."

Colin bowed, while Hamish took the duchess's hand and scrabbled desperately for what a man was supposed to say to a graciously smirking duchess.

"Your Grace," Hamish said, bowing. "A pleasure to meet you, and you are correct, this rascal has the honor to be my brother, Colin MacHugh."

A flurry of curtsying and bowing and damned introducing went on for half the

41

day. The Marchioness of Mischief was Lady Deene. The ranks of officers on the Peninsula had included a Lord Deene. The man had been a fool if he'd preferred war to remaining by his marchioness's side.

Edana and Rhona elbowed their way into the queue, as did a pretty little thing named Miss Elizabeth Windham, another niece of the duchess.

Hamish's sense of impatience worsened, because he had no pencil and paper with which to sketch these relationships, and he'd probably forget them before he was out the shop door. The person responsible for this trooping the color was off in a corner, half-hidden by a bolt of flowery and expensive-looking fabric.

Megan Windham would be difficult to forget.

"Your Grace will pardon me," Hamish said, "but we neglect a member of your party in our exchange of pleasantries."

Hamish had sisters, he had battlefield experience, and he had keen eyesight, even in low light. Across the shop, Miss Megan went still, as if she'd heard a twig snap in a forest she'd thought to enjoy in solitude.

"Megan," Her Grace called in tones both pleasant and imperious. "Come make your farewell curtsy to His Grace, and then we must be on our way. Madam, twenty yards of the green silk for Miss Edana, and twenty of the blue for Miss Rhona. Maroon trim for both, maroon silk shawls and slippers, maroon stockings. The young ladies will send you an additional order for petticoats and so forth at their convenience."

Hamish was too glad for the duchess's sense of command to quibble at the death blow she'd dealt his budget.

Miss Megan glided over to offer Colin and Hamish a curtsy. From her, the gesture wasn't an awkward bob but rather an exercise in deference and grace. Everything from the drape of Miss Megan's skirts, to the inclination of her head, to the tempo at which she raised her hand, was . . . lovely.

Colin whacked Hamish's back.

"Miss Megan," Hamish said. "A pleasure." A blessing, more like, to behold such feminine dignity, and also a sorrow. Blond, handsome Pilkington was on familiar terms with Megan Windham. For that alone, Hamish wished he'd shot the bastard when he'd had a chance.

"Your Grace," Megan said as Hamish let her hand go. "Your sisters' company has brightened our morning considerably, and now that we've been introduced, I hope they will come to call soon and often."

"Oh, of course," Edana said.

"We'd love to," Rhona added.

"We'll look forward to it," the duchess replied, linking her arm with Miss Megan's.

For an instant, Miss Megan appeared to resist her aunt's gentle attempt to drag her to the door, and in that instant, Hamish locked gazes with a woman who'd provoked him to wishing.

Very bad business, when a battle-scarred soldier got to wishing for anything more ambitious than a good ale or a well-cooked joint.

"Do come by," Megan said, her gaze unreadable behind the blue of her spectacles. "The preparations for the ball have turned our home into a madhouse, and sane company will be very welcome."

A hint of the duchess infused Megan's parting shot. Not *would you please come by,* or *I hope you'll come by,* but the imperative: *Do come by.* Hamish had given and received enough orders to know one when he heard it.

"I am sorry, Miss Megan, but my family and I are soon to depart for the north."

If the words hurt the lady as much as they hurt Hamish, she gave no sign of it. Those spectacles were wonderful for disguising emotions. Perhaps Hamish would find a pair

44

for himself. In Scotland, no lovely, kind, soft-spoken women peered at Hamish with honest curiosity, but nobody called him the Duke of Murder either.

"Don't be ridiculous," the duchess said. "You are a duke, sir, and your sisters must be presented at court if they haven't been already. I'll not hear of you leaving Town until that courtesy has been attended to. You will call upon us to discuss that matter, if nothing else."

"But Your Grace, I have responsibilities, and we've tarried in London some while already," Hamish replied, even knowing that arguing with a senior officer was folly.

"Sir, I have raised five daughters," Her Grace said, *most* pleasantly. "Your sisters are entitled to enjoy London in every respect. You will please come to the ball on Tuesday next, and bring your siblings. Do I make myself clear? A written invitation will be in your hands by sunset."

Rhona and Edana stood like recruits quivering to be chosen for a choice assignment, but unable to speak out of turn while they awaited their captain's direction. In their yearning silence, Hamish saw them not as his pestering, expensive, bewildering sisters but as two pretty young ladies who'd endured as many Scottish winters and plain wool cloaks as they could bear.

"Your invitation is most gracious," Hamish said, suppressing the urge to salute the duchess. "We will be honored to attend, Your Grace."

Honored being the prettied-up English term for doomed, of course.

CHAPTER THREE

Gayle Windham, Earl of Westhaven, was too self-disciplined to glance at the clock more than once every five minutes, but he could see the shadow of an oak limb start its afternoon march up the wall of his study. The remains of a beef sandwich sat on a tray at his elbow, and soon his youngest child would go down for a nap.

Westhaven brought his attention back to the pleasurable business of reviewing household expenses, though Anna's accounting was meticulous. He obliged his countess's request to look over the books because of the small insights he gained regarding his family.

They were using fewer candles, testament to spring's arrival and longer hours of daylight.

The wine cellar had required some attention, another harbinger of the upcoming social season.

Anna had spent a bit much on Cousin Megan's birthday gift, but a music box was a perfect choice for Megan.

"You haven't moved in all the months I've been gone," said a humorous baritone. "You're like one of those statues, standing guard through the seasons, until some obliging brother comes along to demand that you join him in the park for a hack on a pretty afternoon."

Home safe. Devlin St. Just's dark hair was tousled, his clothes wrinkled, his boots dusty, but he was, once again, *home safe.*

The words were an irrational product of Westhaven's memory, for his mind produced them every time he saw his older half-brother after a prolonged absence. Westhaven crossed the study with more swiftness than dignity, hand extended toward his brother.

"Good God, you stink, St. Just, and the dust of the road will befoul my carpets wherever you pass."

St. Just took Westhaven's proffered hand and yanked the earl close enough for a quick, back-thumping hug.

"I stink, you scold. Give a man a brandy while he befouls your carpets, and good day to you too."

Westhaven obliged, mostly to have something to do other than gawk at his brother. Yorkshire was too far away, the winters were too long and miserable, and St. Just visited too infrequently, but every time he did visit, he seemed . . . lighter. More settled, more at peace.

And if ever a man was happy to smell of horse, it was Devlin St. Just, Earl of Rosecroft, firstborn, though illegitimate, son of the Duke of Moreland.

"I have whisky," Westhaven said. "I'm told the barbarians to the north favor it over brandy."

"If you had decent whisky, I might consider it, but you're a brandy snob, so brandy it is. How are the children?"

Thank God for the topic of children, which allowed two men who'd missed each other terribly to avoid admitting as much.

"The children are noisy, expensive, and a trial to any sentient being's nerves. Our parents come by, dispensing a surfeit of sweets along with falsehoods regarding my own youth. Then Their Graces swan off, leaving my kingdom in utter disarray."

Westhaven passed St. Just a healthy portion of spirits, though being St. Just, he waited until Westhaven was holding his own glass.

"To kingdoms in disarray," St. Just said,

touching his glass to Westhaven's. "Try uprooting your womenfolk and dragging them hundreds of miles on the Great North Road. Your realm shrinks to the proportions of one unforgiving saddle. Rather like being on campaign."

St. Just could do this now — make passing, halfway humorous references to his army days. For the first two years after he'd mustered out, he'd been unable to remain sober during a thunderstorm.

"Her ladyship is well?" Westhaven asked.

"My Emmie is a saint," St. Just countered, taking the seat behind Westhaven's desk. "If you die, I want this chair."

"Spare me your military humor. If I die, you and Valentine are guardians of my children."

A dusty boot thunked onto the corner of Westhaven's antique desk, the same corner upon which Westhaven's own much less dusty boots were often propped, provided the door was closed.

"Val and I? You didn't make Moreland their guardian?"

"His Grace will intrude, meddle, advise, maneuver, interfere, and otherwise orchestrate matters as he sees fit, abetted by his lovely wife in all particulars. Putting legal authority over the children in your hands

50

was my pathetic gesture toward thwarting the ducal schemes. You will, of course, oblige my guilt over this presumption by giving me a similar role in the lives of your children."

St. Just closed his eyes. He was a handsome fellow, handsomer for having regained some of the muscle he'd had as a younger man.

"I can hear His Grace's voice when you start braying about what I shall oblige and troweling on verbs in sextuplicate."

"Is that a word?" St. Just asked.

"Trowel, yes, a humble verb. Probably Saxon rather than Roman in origin."

Westhaven pretended to savor his brandy, when he was in truth savoring the fact that his older brother would — in all his dirt — come to Westhaven's establishment before calling upon the ducal household.

"Where is your countess, St. Just? She's usually affixed to your side like a very pretty cocklebur."

"Where's yours?" St. Just retorted. "I dropped Emmie and the girls off at Louisa and Joseph's, though I'm to collect them —"

The door opened, and a handsome, dark-haired fellow sauntered in, Westhaven's butler looking choleric on his heels.

"I come seeking asylum," Lord Valentine said.

St. Just was on his feet and across the room almost before Val had finished speaking. The oldest and youngest Windham brothers bore a resemblance, both dark-haired, and both carrying with them a physical sense of passion. Valentine loved his music, St. Just his horses, and yet the brothers were alike in a way Westhaven appreciated more than he envied — mostly.

"You come seeking my good brandy," Westhaven said when Val had been properly embraced and thumped by St. Just. "Here."

He passed Valentine his own portion and poured another for himself.

"We were about to toast our happy state of marital pandemonium," St. Just said. "Or so Westhaven thinks. I'm in truth fortifying myself to storm the ducal citadel."

Valentine took his turn in Westhaven's chair. "I'd blow retreat if I were you."

Westhaven took one of the chairs across from the desk. "What have Their Graces done now?"

Valentine preferred to prop his boots — moderately dusty — on the opposite corner from his brothers. This put the sunlight over Val's left shoulder.

None of the brothers had any gray hairs

yet, something of a competition in Westhaven's mind, though he wasn't sure whether first past the post would be the winner or the loser. They were only in their thirties, but they were all fathers of small children — small *Windham* children.

"His Grace is sending Uncle Tony and Aunt Gladys on maneuvers in Wales directly after the ball," Valentine said, "while Her Grace will snatch up our lady cousins, doubtless in anticipation of some matchmaking."

They had four female cousins: Beth, Charlotte, Megan, and Anwen. They were lovely young women, red-haired, intelligent, and well dowered, but they were Windhams, and thus in no hurry to marry.

A situation the duchess sought to remedy.

"So that's why Megan was particularly effusive in her suggestions that I come south," St. Just mused, opening a japanned box on the mantel. "Emmie said something untoward was afoot."

A piece of marzipan disappeared down St. Just's maw.

"Goes well with brandy," he said, offering the box to Val, who took two. "Westhaven?"

"How generous of you, St. Just." He took three, though the desk held another box, which his brothers might not find. His

53

children hadn't.

Yet.

"Beth and Megan have both been through enough seasons to know how to avoid parson's mousetrap," Westhaven said.

"I wondered what Their Graces would do when they got us all married off," Valentine mused, brandy glass held just so before his elegant mouth. "I thought they'd turn to charitable works, a rest between rounds until the grandchildren grew older."

He tossed a bit of marzipan in the air and caught it in his mouth, just as he would have twenty years earlier, and the sight pleased Westhaven in a way that he might admit when all of his hair was gray.

"Beth is weakening," Westhaven said. "She's become prone to megrims, sore knees, a touch of a sniffle. Anna and I do what we can, but the children keep us busy, as does the business of the dukedom."

"And we all thank God you've taken that mare's nest in hand," St. Just said, lifting his glass. "How do matters stand, if you don't mind a soldier's blunt speech?"

"We're firmly on our financial feet," Westhaven said. "Oddly enough, Moreland is in part responsible. Because he didn't bother with wartime speculation, when the Corsican was finally buttoned up, once for all, our finances went through none of the difficult adjustments many others are still reeling from."

"If you ever do reel," Valentine said, "you will apply to me for assistance, or I'll thrash you silly, Westhaven."

"And to me," St. Just said. "Or I'll finish the job Valentine starts."

"My thanks for your violent threats," Westhaven said, hiding a smile behind his brandy glass. "Do I take it you fellows would rather establish yourselves under my roof than at the ducal mansion?"

Valentine and St. Just exchanged a look that put Westhaven in mind of their parents.

"If we're to coordinate the defense of our unmarried lady cousins," St. Just said, "then it makes sense we'd impose on your hospitality, Westhaven."

"We're agreed, then," Valentine said, raiding the box once more. "Ellen will be relieved. Noise and excitement aren't good for a woman in her condition, and this place will be only half as uproarious as Moreland House."

"We must think of our cousins," St. Just observed. "The combined might of the Duke and Duchess of Moreland are arrayed against the freedom of four dear and determined young ladies who will not surrender their spinsterhood lightly."

"Nor should they," Westhaven murmured, replacing the lid on the box, only for St. Just to pry it off. "We had the right to choose as we saw fit, as did our sisters. You'd think Their Graces would have learned their lessons by now."

A knock sounded on the door. Valentine sat up straight, St. Just hopped to his feet to replace the box on the mantel, and was standing, hands behind his back, when Westhaven bid the next caller to enter.

"His Grace, the Duke of Moreland, my lords," the butler announced.

Percival Windham stepped nimbly around the butler and marched into the study.

"Well done, well done. My boys have called a meeting of the Windham subcommittee on the disgraceful surplus of spinsters soon to be gathered into Her Grace's care. St. Just, you're looking well. Valentine, when did you take to wearing jam on your linen?"

Moreland swiped the box off the mantel, opened it, took the chair next to Westhaven, and set the box in the middle of the desk.

"I'm listening, gentlemen," the duke said, popping a sweet into his mouth. "Unless you want to see your old papa lose what few wits he has remaining after raising you lot, you will please tell me how to get your cousins married off posthaste. The duchess has spoken, and we are her slaves in all things, are we not?"

Westhaven reached for a piece of marzipan, St. Just fetched the brandy decanter, and Valentine sent the butler for sandwiches, because what on earth could any of them say to a ducal proclamation such as that?

The Duke of Wellington had expected all of his direct military reports to know how to waltz, and thus Hamish had made it a point never to learn. His Grace had also preferred officers with titles and aristocratic lineages. When conversation in the officers' mess had turned to women, war, and wagering, Hamish had brought up breweries, distilleries, and commerce.

Trade in all its plebeian glory.

As a result, Hamish had no idea what sort of small talk was expected when calling on a duchess.

"Colin, you'll accompany our sisters inside," Hamish said, while Rhona and Edana perched on the very edge of the coach's forward facing seat. The vehicle was more properly a traveling coach than a town coach, because four MacHughs did not fit comfortably in the toy carriages favored by polite society.

"Hamish, Miss Megan invited *you*," Rhona said.

"And the duchess ordered *you* to come along with us," Edana added. "The Duchess of Moreland, who can ruin somebody with the lift of her eyebrow."

Hamish knew exactly which duchess, though the woman would probably be bored merely ruining somebody. If she took a man into dislike, there'd be nothing left of him to *be* ruined. She was the worst variety of foe — the worthy sort in full command of her foot, horse, and cannon.

Colin opened the carriage door and sat back. On the cobbles, Old Jock stood by, chest puffed out, doing his best to uphold the dignity of the house of MacHugh.

Shamed by an arthritic coachman.

Hamish climbed out of the carriage, which undertaking rocked its inhabitants. Edana followed, but remained half in, half out, her gloved hand extended.

"Eddie, for God's sake," Hamish said, hauling her the rest of the way out. "You've been getting in and out of coaches since you were a wee pest. You could drive this coach better than Old Jock" — an indignant breath sounded at Hamish's elbow — "when he's been swimming in the whisky barrel. Stop hanging on me."

Her eyes narrowed in a fashion that would have sent the last wolf in Scotland fleeing into the sea.

Colin emerged from the coach and turned to assist Rhona. "Let's bicker away the morning on the duchess's very doorstep," he suggested, "knocking on her door being tediously predictable."

"You were supposed to send a footman in with your card," Rhona said, smoothing her hand over skirts that had probably cost more than the coach.

Now she bothered to inform her own brother of the niceties? "Why get trussed up in my finest, put up with you lot, trouble the horses — and our Jock — just to send around a stupid card for which the bloody printer seeks to charge daylight robbery rates, which I am not about to pay?"

Edana's grip on Hamish's arm dug into the tender spot in the crook of his elbow. Knew all a man's vulnerable points, did Edana, because Hamish had taught them to her.

"You left the house without your calling cards? Hamish, how could you?"

He thrashed free of her grip. "It's like this, Eddie. If you let the trades know they can steal from you, they steal from you. Rules of battle, plain and simple. If the enemy retreats, you rout him. If the enemy stands his ground, you engage him. You do not hand over your hard-earned coin with a superior smile like some infernal, mincing duke who hasn't got a brain in his idiot English head."

Somebody shut the coach door with a *bang.* "I make it a point never to mince, not even when private with my duchess."

Colin's features went blank, Rhona studied her slippers — pink, of all the useless colors — and Edana for once had nothing to say.

A tall, lean, older gentleman in riding attire stood beside Hamish's coach — blocking any retreat back into the coach, in fact. The fellow had shrewd blue eyes, and his hair was the pale gold of an aging Saxon warrior.

Hamish had likely insulted the man on his own doorstep. "My apologies for bickering with my siblings on the very street." He ought probably to have bowed, for this fellow was doubtless a damned duke, but taking his eyes off the gentleman seemed ill-advised.

"Percival, Duke of Moreland, at your service. I have a small but precious cohort of grandchildren, and eight grown children, sir, all of them wed. Bickering is the music of a family with nothing serious to fight about."

Also the music of a family that hadn't progressed to the breaking-furniture-and-hurling-oaths stage of a difference of opinion.

Colin's elbow jabbed at Hamish's ribs.

"Hamish, Duke of Murdoch, Your Grace."

Edana's elbow hammered him from the other side, which made no sense. A duke was a "Your Grace," of that, Hamish was certain.

"You're paying a call on my duchess," Moreland said, striding up the walk. "We can continue the introductions inside and prevail upon Her Grace for some sustenance. The social season can be exhausting, but I assume you've already found that out."

Introductions.

Well, of course. Polite society apparently had nothing better to do than exchange an endless lot of tedious introductions. Even in the military, which had been polluted with titled lords and aristocratic younger sons, protocol had wasted as much time as polishing weaponry.

Edana took Hamish by one elbow, Rhona got him by the other, and thus he was press-ganged into the ducal mansion, Colin trailing behind.

"Alert the ladies," Moreland said to the footman who opened the door. "I found a stray duke wandering about on the walkway, with his two lovely sisters and a handsome brother, no less."

"Of course, Your Grace. The ladies are in the green parlor, and I'll let the kitchen know more guests have arrived."

"Come along," Moreland said, setting off at a brisk pace. "Her Grace is doubtless expecting you, though I warn you: She's in the throes of planning a ball for our nieces. I tread very lightly at such times, and I'm a veteran of His Majesty's Canadian campaigns."

That a military veteran and a duke, no less, was daunted by an upcoming ball comforted Hamish not one bit.

Neither did the Moreland dwelling. The ducal mansion was a monument to fanciful plaster work, with porcelain vases tucked into alcoves, hothouse flowers arranged with artless grace, and light glinting off gilt pier glasses. The carpets were thick enough to muffle the duke's boot steps. Hamish was reduced to silently towing his sisters forward, lest they become transfixed by the sheer wealth on display.

Wealth *and* good taste. Hamish recognized good taste mostly because he hadn't any himself. He had breweries and battle scars, and now several awestruck siblings.

The Moreland mansion was hell with an English accent, at least for Hamish.

"Murdoch, you'd best introduce your family to me before we brave the gauntlet within," the duke said. "Her Grace will have all in hand, but a fellow likes to impress his duchess whenever possible."

Moreland's tone was genial, and the smile he turned on Edana and Rhona hinted at the handsome young officer who'd strutted around in regimentals decades before. And yet, Hamish would comply with His Grace's request, and not because manners required him to.

He'd oblige Moreland with a rehearsal of the introductions because Moreland had campaigned in Canada years ago — a place as beautiful as it was dangerous — and because the officer in Hamish respected competent command when he saw it.

He'd seen plenty of the other kind, and been guilty of it too.

Two minutes later, the duke flourished the parlor doors open and led his guests into another room full of light, lovely, priceless appointments. The golden-haired duchess perched among four red-haired young

63

women, two of whom Hamish didn't recognize.

Miss Elizabeth Windham sat to the right of the duchess, who brightened visibly at the sight of Moreland, as if a rider bearing dispatches had come safely through the lines.

Opposite them was Miss Megan, and right beside her sat Sir Fletcher Pilkington, like a spider idling about in the middle of a gossamer web.

Aunt Esther had explained to Megan long ago that introductions followed a set pattern so a woman had time to memorize names and titles. When Megan had met Sir Fletcher for the first time, she had silently repeated a silly rubric: His name is Sir Fletcher, he could never be a lecher.

A man so goldenly gorgeous, graceful, and charming would not have to press his attentions on a woman. She'd hand over her entire evening to him, and half of her dignity, without being asked.

Alas, Megan had handed over even more than that.

"Ah, Moreland!" Aunt Esther said, beaming at her duke. "You have brought friends to enliven our day."

Uncle Percy assisted his duchess to her

feet, beaming right back at her.

Some of Their Graces' effusive mutual regard was for public consumption — Uncle Percy did love to make an entrance — but much of it was genuine.

"My dear," Uncle Percy said, bowing over Aunt Esther's hand, "the Duke of Murdoch has come to call and brings his siblings. We will need a larger parlor at the rate you're collecting gallants this season."

Sir Fletcher was on his feet, muttering polite greetings over the hands of the Mac-Hugh sisters, while their oldest brother hung back, his blue-eyed gaze watchful.

"Anwen," Aunt Esther said, "might you have the kitchen send us a fresh pot and some sandwiches to the terrace? The morning is lovely, and the gardens are coming along nicely."

Anwen shot Megan the barest glance of sympathy and scampered off, likely not to be seen for hours.

"Good morning, Your Grace," Megan said, taking the Duke of Murdoch by the arm before Sir Fletcher could attach himself to her side. "Shall we repair to the garden?"

His expression could have frozen the Thames in July. "Aye."

Sir Fletcher offered an arm to Lady Edana, Uncle Percy escorted Lady Rhona, and Colin MacHugh was left to accompany Her Grace. All very friendly and informal, and so tediously gracious Megan wanted to shriek.

"Uncle Percy is proud of his roses," she said, leaning closer to the Scottish duke. "It's too early for them, but if you compliment the gardens generally, he'll be pleased."

Murdoch glowered at her. "Your uncle hasn't held a pair of pruning shears since Zaccheus climbed down from the sycamore tree. Why would I compliment Moreland on gardens he never tends himself?"

The question was appallingly genuine, maybe even a touch bewildered.

"You are a new duke, he's a duke of great consequence. His favor could benefit you," Megan said, starting from simple premises. "Uncle is responsible for these gardens, for hiring the gardeners and supervising their progress. If the gardens prosper, Uncle Percy has managed them and those who tend them well."

"Meaning no disrespect, miss, but that's not the way of it."

Sir Fletcher laughed at something Lady Edana said. He probably practiced laughing before his shaving mirror, he looked so charming and elegant when overcome with mirth. He tossed back his head, injected just the right quantity of merriment into his laughter, angled his smile with a calculated degree of warmth —

"I beg your pardon," Megan said, hauling her attention back to her escort. Murdoch looked like the word laughter had yet to find its way to his vocabulary. "I believe I grasp how Uncle Percy's household works quite well, Your Grace. Shall we find a seat?"

A bench, so Megan could sit on one end and put the duke on her only available side.

"Firstly," Murdoch said, keeping his voice down, "your uncle loves the gardens because they make his duchess happy. I suspect these gardens hold memories too, mostly the cheerful sort. The gardener is likely some old fellow who's been on the job since His Grace was in leading strings, and the duke has little to say about any of it. Couldn't turn the old blighter off if he killed every posy on the premises. Wealth only looks like it gives a man power. In truth it makes him less free."

The gardener was a fixture by the name of Murray. Megan had no idea whether that was a first name, a last name, or a nickname. He was simply Murray, and regarding the garden, he was an absolute, if kindly, dictator.

"What's secondly?" Megan asked as Murdoch led her across the terrace and down the steps into the garden proper.

"Secondly, Miss Meggie, if you hate a man, you mustn't do it so others take notice."

Miss Meggie. Oh, how Murdoch transgressed the bounds of decorum, and how she liked his familiarity.

"I don't hate you. I barely know you."

"I refer to Sir Fletcher. Maybe you're jealous of the attention he shows my sister, but you needn't be. I will gut the varlet where he stands if he thinks to take anything approaching a liberty with my Eddie."

Megan wished Sir Fletcher would take liberties with Lady Edana, with *any* young woman in a position to hold him accountable for his scoundrel ways. She wished all men were as given to honest speech as Murdoch, and she wished she'd met this gruff Scotsman much sooner.

"Your notions of family loyalty are quite violent," Megan said. "Is that why you've been dubbed the Duke of Murder?"

CHAPTER FOUR

The Duke of Murder?

Miss Megan's gaze was merely curious. She couldn't know how that sobriquet twisted in Hamish's gut like a rusty bayonet wielded by enemy hands.

"That's what they're calling me, aren't they? I suppose it fits."

She patted his arm. "You were a soldier. My cousins Devlin and Bart were soldiers. Devlin came home the worse for his experiences, Bart lost his life in Portugal. War results in a lot of ugly death. Even ladies grasp that unfortunate reality."

Ladies — a few ladies — might grasp the generalities, but no lady should have to hear the details as Hamish had lived them.

"Tell me about this ball, Miss Meggie. I've been to a few of the regimental variety, but they're mostly about staying sober until the womenfolk go home, and cutting a dash in dress uniform."

Her gaze went to Sir Fletcher, who was courting death by standing too close to Edana. Colin was monitoring the situation from the duchess's side, and Rhona stood nearby with Moreland.

Sir Fletcher was surrounded, did he but know it. If he thought to offer for Edana, he was a worse fool than Hamish knew him to be.

Miss Megan was a calm sort of lady, or maybe those blue-tinted spectacles gave her a calm air. She trundled along beside Hamish, preserving him from all the small talk and silliness transpiring on the terrace.

"A ball is a test of endurance," Miss Megan said. "Think of it as a forced march. You provision as best you can, but traveling lightly is also important. Dress for comfort, not only to impress. Eat little beforehand, for there will be abundant food and drink, and study the morning's newspaper so you'll have some conversation to offer your dinner partner."

Hamish had carried men on his back through the snow on the retreat to Corunna. Not merely a forced march, but a complete rout, the pursuing French promising death for any who faltered. He'd sooner endure another such march than the London season.

"It's that sort of ball, with dinner partners?"

"One dinner partner, usually, though
people congregate in groups too. Your
partner for the supper waltz is generally
your dinner companion, and the supper
waltz tends to happen around midnight."

She peered at him, a man facing doom.
"Shall I save my supper waltz for you, Your
Grace?"

Sir Fletcher would hate that. Hamish had
studied the assembled company as the
introductions had plodded on, and Major
Sir Fletcher Pilkington was an accepted
friend of the Windham household. He'd
been sitting practically in Miss Megan's lap,
and she'd tolerated that presumption.

And yet, in the bookshop, Sir Fletcher had
been bullying the lady.

"Sir Fletcher hasn't spoken for your
waltz?" Hamish asked.

Miss Megan had led them to a fountain
that featured a chubby Cupid with an urn
on one shoulder and a slightly chipped right
wing. She took a seat on a bench flanking
the fountain, which meant Hamish could sit
as well — as best he could recall.

"Sir Fletcher is much in demand as a
dancing partner," Miss Megan said.

The dashing knight had been a slobbering

hound where the camp followers were concerned, until they became acquainted with his temper.

"Sir Fletcher is a jackass," Hamish replied, perching on the edge of the fountain. "If that insults your intended, I do apologize, but you deserve better." Any woman deserved better than Sir Fletcher Pilkington.

"He is the son of an earl, a decorated war hero, and considered handsome," Miss Megan said. "Uncle Percy has assured me Sir Fletcher's prospects are sound enough."

Then Uncle Percy hadn't bothered to ask the moneylenders who watched the comings and goings at Horse Guards. Too busy flirting with his duchess, perhaps. He'd be better off protecting his niece's flank, as it were.

"So you'll waltz with your Knight of the Sound Prospects," Hamish said, not liking the idea at all. "You'll make a fetching couple. That matters to some." Though Miss Meggie didn't strike him as a lady to be taken in by a handsome face or a lot of flirtatious blather — and those were Sir Fletcher's best qualities.

"Please sit beside me," Miss Megan muttered.

"I beg your — ?"

She got a grip on Hamish's sleeve and

hauled stoutly. He took the place to her right.

"You're a determined woman. Edana and Rhona are too, but they've had to be."

"They are Lady Edana and Lady Rhona now," Miss Megan said. "You have become a duke, so your siblings' status has changed as well."

Hamish's bank balance had certainly changed. "My pismire of a solicitor said something about this, though he claimed it would cost considerably and take some time. I haven't mentioned anything to my sisters about acquiring the title *lady*."

Miss Megan slipped her glasses down her nose to peer at Hamish. "Your brother also becomes a courtesy lord. All it takes is a warrant of precedence signed by King George. I think you must ask for my supper waltz, Your Grace."

As if the king was about to extend favors to the Duke of Murder? "Miss Meggie, there's no point to my asking for your supper waltz."

If Hamish were to waltz with any woman, though, it would be Megan Windham. She didn't put on airs, she was quiet, and in an understated, easily overlooked way, she was lovely.

"Ask me anyway." She sounded much like

73

her auntie, the Duchess of Doom.

"Miss Meggie, though it pains me to admit it, I'm nearly famous for not knowing how to waltz. I'd embarrass us both and likely end up on my kilted arse before all of polite society."

This time, she patted his hand. "Nonsense. If I can learn to waltz, so can you. Tomorrow afternoon should suffice. Bring your sisters, I'll round up a few of my cousins, and we'll have an impromptu tea dance at my cousin Westhaven's townhouse."

Moreland was teasing Rhona, who was a shy soul when she wasn't threatening mayhem for want of a few dresses. *Lady* Rhona, according to Megan Windham. Hamish needed to know more about that warrant of whatever, and for his sisters' sakes, he needed to learn to waltz.

"Name a time, and promise me this gathering will be private," he said. "I'll not be falling on my backside for the entertainment of half of Mayfair."

Sir Fletcher was sauntering up the path, Edana beside him. Damned if she didn't look half-smitten, more's the pity.

"You'll not be falling on your backside at all," Miss Megan said, "but you are to remain by my side so long as Sir Fletcher is about, do you understand, Your Grace?"

Hamish did not in the least understand, though he hoped Miss Megan's order — for it was an order — meant she had a few reservations where Sir Fletcher was concerned. What Hamish knew for certain was that he had somehow been talked into letting this little, bespectacled blueblood teach him to waltz, and worse, he was looking forward to that ordeal.

"A word with you, Your Grace."

Hamish looked about, wondering when somebody had let a bloody damned duke into the conversation. Across the music room, Megan Windham was sorting through music at the piano, Edana and Rhona by her side.

The three fellows surrounding Hamish were Miss Megan's cousins, and by some sleight of hand known only to English dukes, all three cousins were titled.

"Beg pardon," Hamish said. "The 'Your Grace' bit will take some getting used to. You might as well know I can't waltz for shite."

"Language, Murdoch," the biggest of the three muttered.

The one with all the lace at his throat and wrists took to studying the parquet floor in

75

the manner of a gunnery sergeant trying not to murder his own recruits on the first day of target practice.

"I honestly cannot waltz," Hamish said, hoping Miss Meggie could at least play the piano. Rhona and Edana had a few passable tunes memorized, but they were no substitute for an orchestra.

"If Megan has decreed that you're to learn to waltz," the auburn-haired fellow said, "then you shall learn to waltz. She is soft-hearted, and we will not allow you to disappoint her."

Lord *Shall and Allow* must be the ducal heir.

"That's good," Hamish replied, making sure his sporran hung front and center. "You ought to be protective of her, because she'll have no toes left if she dances with me." Very pretty toes they likely were too.

"She will have all of her toes," the nancy brother said. "Can your sisters waltz?"

"I expect so. They've had a dancing master coming around for the past three years. Expensive little shi— blighter."

"Then let's be about it," Lord Nancy Pants said. He wore as much lace as a French colonel intent on impressing the ladies, but had a good set of shoulders too. "Ladies, if you'd choose your partners, the

76

entertainment portion of the afternoon is about to begin."

Edana took the heir, Rhona made her curtsy to the big fellow cousin, and Hamish was left . . .

"You're not wearing your specs," he said as Miss Megan rose from a graceful curtsy.

"The year I made my come out, they went sailing off my nose in an energetic turn and landed in the men's punch bowl. I haven't worn them on the dance floor since. Shouldn't you bow, Your Grace?"

She offered her bare hand — this was a practice dance, after all — and Hamish executed the requisite gentlemanly maneuver.

"Now what?"

"Now Lord Valentine will play the introduction. . . ."

God above, the nancy bastard knew his way around a keyboard. This was not the tortured thumping Hamish associated with country dances and overheated ballrooms, this was *music.*

"Slower!" Miss Megan called, and the speed of the music calmed, though the melody acquired more twiddles and fara-diddles along the way. "We'll need a lengthy introduction as well."

"More introductions?" Hamish muttered.

Her eyes were truly lovely without the spectacles, large, guileless, the blue of the Scottish sky over high pastures in spring.

"The waltz is in triple meter, like the minuet," Miss Megan said. "One-two-three, one-two-three, and all you need to do is feel the downbeat."

Scotsmen were born to dance. They had no particular defenses against being handled by determined women, though. Miss Megan put one hand on Hamish's shoulder and grasped his hand with the other.

"Your free hand goes above my waist, toward the middle of my back, but not quite. You want it where you can guide me. Your Grace, it's customary to assume waltz position when contemplating the waltz."

Hamish longed to touch her — to assume this genteel, slightly risqué, elegant dance pose with her — and he didn't dare.

"I might knock ye over," he said, hoping the twiddles and faradiddles kept his words from her cousins' notice.

"You cannot possibly. I'll simply turn loose of you and step back should your balance become questionable. The simplest way to learn the waltz is to pattern your steps like a square. . . ."

Hamish's balance had become questionable back in Hatchards bookshop, when

78

he'd heard Pilkington sneering and strutting through a conversation with a lady. He'd lost his balance all over again at the dress shop, and pitched it into Moreland's prize rose bushes in the ducal garden too.

Miss Megan nattered on, all the while the other couples twirled and smiled around them, the music lifted and lilted, and Hamish wanted to kill Sir Fletcher Pilkington. The ability to flirt in triple meter had seen the younger son of an English lord elevated to the point where he got good men killed, and men only half-bad flogged nearly to death.

"You look so fierce," Miss Megan said when they were on their second lurch about the room. The lady, fortunately, was more substantial than she appeared, and determined on Hamish's education.

"I'm concentrating. Anything more complicated than a march and a fellow gets confused." Her perfume was partly responsible, half spice, half flowers. Not roses, but fresh meadows, scythed grass, lavender and . . .

He brought the lady a trifle closer on a turn, the better to investigate her fragrance, and between one twirl and the next, Hamish's instructress became his every unfulfilled dream on a dance floor. She had the

79

knack of going where a fellow suggested, as if she read a man's intentions by the way he held her.

Megan Windham made Hamish feel as if spinning about in his arms sat at the apex of her list of delights, the memory she'd recount in old age to dazzle her great-nieces and granddaughters. She danced with the incandescent joy of the northern lights and all the feminine warmth of summer sun on a Scottish shore.

To her, he was apparently not the Duke of Murder or the Berserker of Badajoz. He was simply a lucky fellow who needed assistance learning to dance. The relief of that, the pleasure of shedding an entire war's worth of violence, was exquisite.

For another turn down the room, Hamish wallowed in a fine, miserable case of heartache, for this pleasure was illusory — he had killed often and well — and the lady could never be his. Worse yet, she apparently belonged to that walking hog wallow of dishonor and guile, Sir Fletcher Pilkington.

The sooner Hamish waltzed his own titled, homesick arse back to Scotland, the better for all. The Duke of Murdoch was all grace and power, and his protestations about not knowing how to waltz must have been for his sisters' sakes. Soldiers could be shrewd like that. St. Just, Westhaven, and Valentine would surely beg a set from the ladies as a result of this informal rehearsal, and Murdoch had probably known as much.

"A couple usually converses during a waltz," Megan said as they started on another circuit of the music parlor. "How do you find London, that sort of thing?"

Murdoch's sense of rhythm was faultless, but he'd apparently misplaced the ability to smile — at all.

"Find London? You go down the Great North Road until you can't go any farther, then you follow the noise and stink. Can't miss it. I prefer the drovers' routes myself. The inns are humble, but honest."

Megan's mother was Welsh, so a thick leavening of Celtic intonation was easily decipherable to her. She switched to Gaelic, as she occasionally did with family.

"I meant, does London appeal to you?"

Nothing had broken His Grace's concentration thus far. For dozens of turns about the room, despite Westhaven's and St. Just's adventuresome maneuvers with Murdoch's sisters, and Valentine's increasingly daring tempo, the duke had become only more confident of his waltzing.

One simple question had him stumbling.

And when a large fellow stumbled and tried to right himself by grabbing on to a surprised and not very large woman, and that woman stumbled . . .

Down they went, though Megan landed on His Grace, an agreeably solid and warm place to find herself. His sporran had twisted itself to his hip, and his arms remained about her.

"Miss Megan," Lady Edana cried. "Are you all right? Hamish, turn loose of her, for pity's sake, you'll wrinkle her skirts, and break her bones, and tramp on her hems, and *get up,* you can't simply lie there, a great lummoxing lump of a brother."

"Get up now," Lady Rhona chorused. "Oh, please do get up, and promise you'll never attempt to waltz in public again. Wellington might be at Her Grace's ball, or the king. Oh, Ham, *get up.*"

His Grace could not get up as long as Megan luxuriated in the novel pleasure of lying atop him.

"I'm fine," she said, kneeling back after enjoying two more instants of His Grace's abundant warmth and muscle. Westhaven hauled her to her feet by virtue of a hand under each elbow, glowering at her as if she'd purposely yanked fifteen stone of Scottish duke to the floor.

St. Just extended a hand to Murdoch and pulled him upright, but not fast enough to hide a flash of muscular thigh from Megan's view, not fast enough by half.

The duke righted his sporran, bowed, and came up . . . *smiling.* "Miss Meggie, my apologies for hauling you top over teakettle. You speak the Gaelic."

All the rainbows in Wales, all the Christmas punch brewed at the Windham family seat, couldn't approach His Grace's smile for sheer, charming glee. That smile dazzled, intrigued, promised . . . oh, that smile was quite the weapon against a woman's dignity.

Megan fired off a shy, answering volley of the same artillery. "My mother is Welsh, and I enjoy languages. Welsh and Gaelic aren't that different to the ear."

In fact, each Scottish island and region had its own dialect, some sounding nearly Irish, others approaching a Scandinavian flavor, and Megan didn't pretend to grasp the proper spellings, dialect by dialect. But she could manage well enough in casual conversation to take a Highland duke very much by surprise.

"Nobody speaks the Gaelic in an English ballroom," Murdoch said. "Not since the Forty-Five, probably not ever." He made a few words of Gaelic sound like a great feat of courage, not a simple courtesy to a new-comer.

St. Just and Westhaven watched this exchange like a pair of oversized pantry mousers placing bets on the fate of a fugitive canary.

Bother the glowering pair of them.

Nobody smiled at Megan Windham the way Murdoch was smiling. Even without her glasses, she could see the warmth and approval in his eyes, see all the acceptance and admiration a woman could endure from one man.

"Nobody ends the waltz by falling on his partner," Westhaven snapped. "Lord Valentine, if you would oblige. The duke is in want of practice, assuming Cousin Megan is none the worse for her tumble."

Megan had tumbled hopelessly, right into a pair of bottomless blue eyes, a pair of strong arms, and . . . those thighs. Ye manly waltzing gods.

"I'm fine," Megan said, putting her hand on Murdoch's shoulder. She was apparently becoming a proficient liar, because having seen his great, beaming benevolence of a smile, she might never be fine again.

Cousin Valentine struck up another introduction at the piano, the pace moderate, the ornamentation minimal, and Megan

84

wished someday, ages and ages hence, she might tell her granddaughters about the time the dashing Scottish duke had waltzed her right off of her feet.

Hamish would fight across Spain, scale the mountains, and march through the whole of France all over again for a waltz like the one he was sharing with Megan Windham.

He danced with the same passionate abandon formerly reserved for when the swords were crossed after the fourth dram of whisky, and the camp followers had acquired the airs and graces of every soldier's dreams.

Miss Megan beamed up at him, her hand clasped in his, her rhythm faultless, her form starlight in his arms.

When the music came to a final, sighing cadence, Hamish's heart sighed along with it.

"My thanks for a delightful waltz," he said as Miss Megan sank into a deep curtsy. She kept hold of Hamish's hand as he drew her to her feet and bowed.

"The pleasure was entirely mine, Your Grace."

While the sorrow was Hamish's. To her, this was just another waltz, a charity bestowed on a reluctant recruit to the ranks of the aristocracy.

To Hamish it had been —

"Now you lead her from the dance floor," the big cousin barked. "Parade march will do, her hand resting on yours."

On general principles, Hamish stood his ground. This fellow had begun to look and sound familiar, and one thing was certain: Hamish had the highest-ranking title in the room.

"You served on the Peninsula?" Hamish asked.

Megan's cousin spoke with an air of command, and he had the watchful eyes of the career soldier. Hamish put his age at about mid-thirties, and his weight about fourteen stone barefoot and stripped for a fight. His waltzing had been worthy of a direct report to Old Hooky himself, his scowl was worthy of a captain, possibly a major.

"You behold Colonel Lord Rosecroft," Miss Megan said, patting the fellow's cheek. "Cousin Devlin is quite fierce, but he has to be. He's the father of two daughters and counting, and the oldest of ten siblings. Her Grace contends that he joined up in search of a more peaceful existence."

Rosecroft shot Hamish a glance known to veterans the world over. *Let her make light of me,* that look said. *Let her make a joke of the endless horrors. We fought so that our womenfolk could pat our cheeks and jest at our nightmares. They remained at home, praying for us year after year, so that some of us could survive to make light of their nightmares too.*

Miss Megan tugged at Hamish's hand. "Now you return me to my chaperone or help me find my next partner, the same as any other dance. We make small talk, greet the other guests, and look quite convivial."

"That's three impossibilities you've set before me, Miss Meggie."

Hamish had amused her, simply by speaking the truth. "I saw you smile, Your Grace," she said, leading Hamish over to the piano. "Your charm might be latent, but it's genuine."

He leaned closer. "I won't know your next partner from the crossing sweeper, I have no patience with small talk, and looking convivial is an impossibility when you're known as the Duke of Mur—"

"A gentleman never argues with a lady," the colonel observed, hands behind his back, two paces to Miss Megan's right. He bore a resemblance to Moreland in his posture and about the jaw, and yet he was apparently not the ducal heir.

"Does a gentleman lie to a lady, Rosebud?

87

My sisters will tell you I can't keep social niceties straight, I lack familiarity with those of your ilk, and I've no gift for idle chit-chat."

"None at all," Edana said.

"He's awful," Rhona added, russet curls bobbing, she nodded so earnestly. "We despair of him, but one can't instruct a brother when he won't even try to accept one's guidance. We tell Hamish to inquire about the weather, and his response is that any woman who can't notice the weather for herself won't notice a lack of chatter in a man."

They meant well, and they were being honest, but a part of Hamish felt as if he'd been knocked on his arse again, kilt flapping for all the world to see.

"I've made the very same point to my countess," the auburn-haired Earl of Enunciation said. Hamish forgot his name. "Why must we discuss the weather at tedious length when there's nothing to be done about it and its characteristics are abundantly obvious? Better to discuss . . ."

Edana, Rhona, and Miss Megan regarded him curiously.

"The music," said Lord Nancy Pants rising from the piano. He was a good-sized fellow, for all his lace, and he had that ducal jaw too. "Ask her if she prefers the violin or the flute, the piano or the harpsichord. Ask her what her favorite dance is, and then ask her why."

"That is brilliant," the earl said. "A lady can natter on about why this or why that for hours, and then why not the other."

"You didn't unearth that insight on your own," the colonel interjected. "Ellen put you on to it, and you're taking the credit."

Nancy Pants grinned, looking abruptly like Colin — a younger sibling who'd got over on his elders, *again.*

"Gentlemen, please," Miss Megan said. "Valentine's smile presages fisticuffs, and we've already obligingly moved the furniture aside. The point of the gathering is not to indulge your juvenile glee in one another's company but rather to make certain that His Grace of Murdoch acquits himself well at Aunt Esther's gathering."

Three handsome lords looked fleetingly abashed.

Women did this. They wore slippers that could kick a man's figurative backside with the force of a jackboot. Their verbal kid gloves could slap with the sting of a riding crop, and their scowls could reduce a fellow's innards to three-day-old neeps and tatties.

To see three English aristocrats so effectively thrashed did a Scottish soldier's heart good.

"Small talk can be learned," the ducal heir said, entirely too confidently. "You're good with languages, Megs. Teach your duke the London ballroom dialect of small talk. If my brothers could learn it, it's not that difficult."

"If you hadn't had my example to follow —" the colonel growled.

"Would you please?" Edana asked. "We've tried, but Hamish . . . he's stubborn."

"And slow," Rhona added. "Not dull, but everything must make sense to him, and that is a challenging undertaking when so much about polite society is for the sake of appearance rather than substance."

They were being helpful again, drat them both. "I manage well enough in the kirk yard."

"Church yard," all three cousins said at once.

"Where I come from, *where I am a duke,* it's a kirk yard," Hamish said. "And to there I will soon return, the sooner the better."

Edana's expression promised Hamish a violent end before he could set a foot on the Great North Road. Rhona looked like she wanted to cry, however, and that . . .

that shamed a man as falling on his arse before English nobility never could.

"Walk in the park," Lord Nancy Pants said. "Tomorrow, if the weather is fair, Megan can join His Grace for a walk in the park. Joseph and Louisa are in Town, Evie and Deene are as well. Take Lady Rhona and Lady Edana walking, Murdoch. Megan will be attended by a pair of cousins-in-law, both of them titled, and you can rehearse your small talk."

"Excellent tactics," the colonel muttered.

"Her Grace would approve," the earl said. "I like it. Megan?"

She'd rather be called Meggie by those who cared for her. Hamish would rather sneak off to Scotland that very moment. Hyde Park was a huge place, crammed full of bonnets, parasols, ambushes wearing sprigged muslin, and half-pay peacocks in their regimentals.

Rhona looked at her slippers — peach-ish today, more expensive idiocy.

Studying his sister's bowed head, Hamish located the reserves of courage necessary to endure another battle.

"If Miss Megan can spare me the time to walk in the park, I would be grateful for her company."

"Oh, well done, Your Grace," she said,

smiling at him. Not the great beaming version he'd seen on the dance floor, but an even more beguiling expression that turned her gaze soft and Hamish's knees to porridge.

"Two of the clock, then," the earl said. "Assemble here. I'll make the introductions, and Her Grace's ball will be the envy of polite society, as usual."

Within five minutes, Hamish was bowing over Miss Megan's hand in parting, though he'd committed himself to tomorrow's skirmish in defense of MacHugh family pride — or something. The Windham cousins seemed genuinely, if grudgingly, intent on aiding the cause of Hamish's education, probably for the sake of their own family pride.

And Miss Megan was smiling.

Hamish was so preoccupied with mentally assembling metaphors to describe her smile that he nearly missed the low rumble of the pianist's voice amid the farewells and parting kisses of the ladies.

"He's a disaster in plaid," Lord Nancy Pants muttered.

"He provoked Megan into trotting out her Gaelic," the colonel added. "Not the done thing."

Well, no, it wasn't. Falling on one's arse

was not the done thing, arguing with a lady was not the done thing. One ball, however, for the sake of Ronnie and Eddie's pride, one little march about the park, and Hamish could retreat with honor, which sometimes *was* the done thing.

Hamish got Rhona by one arm, Edana by the other, and hauled them bodily toward the door, which was held open by a fellow in handsome blue livery.

"My thanks for the dancing lesson," Hamish called, because expressing sincere gratitude was also the done thing where he came from. "Until tomorrow."

Miss Megan waved to him. *"Mar sin leibh."* A friendly farewell that fortified a man against coming battles and provoked both the colonel and the musician to scowling.

And as the liveried fellow closed the door, another snippet of clipped, masculine, aristocratic English came to Hamish's ears.

"You give up too easily. I think Murdoch has potential, *Rosebud.*"

Chapter Five

London's weather was abominably change-able. Megan's eagerness to walk with the Duke of Murdoch was abominably fixed.

She was all but engaged to Sir Fletcher, a problem for which she could see no resolu-tion, and yet, three-quarters of an hour tramping the familiar confines of Hyde Park was all she could think about.

"I hear you spoke a bit of the Gaelic with His Grace of Murdoch," Mama said. *In English.* She sat at the piano and leafed through music in the chamber designated as the music library.

"I suspect Gaelic is His Grace's first language," Megan replied, extricating a fad-ing daisy from the bouquet on the window-sill. "I merely asked a question that was easier to understand in Gaelic."

Mama, being Welsh, had music in her blood and bones, in her very vowels and consonants. When she got out her violin and

94

Valentine accompanied her at the keyboard, magic happened, and Papa's eyes took on a particular gleam.

"You don't aid the man's cause by provoking him to speak Gaelic," Mama said, paging through some Mozart chamber works. "His reputation is that of a savage, one who delighted in bloody murder for king and country, if the talk is to be believed. No wonder Lord Tarryton's daughter cried off from her engagement to Murdoch all those years ago. Then he must wear his heathen attire on the very streets of Mayfair, argue with no less person than your dear aunt before one of the biggest gossips ever to open a modiste's shop . . . You aren't listening."

Megan was listening, to the memory of a Scottish burr apologizing for sending her top over teakettle.

"Sir Fletcher also took up arms in defense of his country," Megan said, finding another dead specimen amid the blooms. "Nobody calls him a murderer." He was willing to murder a young woman's future, though.

"Sir Fletcher comes from an excellent family, he dresses appropriately to his station, he has the look of a man who's considering making an offer for you. Your attentions to Murdoch, while exactly the sort of kindness a true lady demonstrates in all circumstances, will not advance your situation, my dear, *or your sisters' situations.*"

A third wilted daisy went onto the cloth Megan had laid out beside the bouquet.

"I see your point, Mama, but Westhaven suggested this walk in the park, and Westhaven promised titled escorts for Murdoch's sisters."

Westhaven, as the ducal heir, was the cousin who could do no wrong. In Megan's estimation, Gayle Windham, Earl of Westhaven, Viscount Common Sense, Baron Dutiful, was also hard-pressed to have any *fun.* Uncle Percy agreed with her, which suggested the Almighty should consider documenting the same sentiment on stone tablets.

Mama's warning — all of Mama's many warnings — were well meant, but simple logic plagued Megan nonetheless.

Aunt Esther extended a gesture of welcome to the new duke and was commended for her graciousness. Megan supported the duchess's overture and was now risking her sisters' prospects? Had Sir Fletcher not been parked on Megan's figurative doorstep, Mama wouldn't think twice about this walk in the park.

Anwen was painfully shy, Beth painfully

on the shelf, and Charlotte painfully determined to marry when she was good and ready, not one instant before.

"There's the coach coming 'round," Mama said with the acuity of hearing known only to mothers. "Find your parasol, lose your Gaelic, and try not to let the duke develop any expectations. Charitable impulses are commendable, but we know who Sir Fletcher's people are, and that's a fine thing as well."

Mama pinched Megan's cheek gently, as she'd been pinching that same cheek since Megan's infancy, and marched off toward the front door, Herr Mozart forgotten.

Megan pitched her dead flowers, cloth and all, into the nearest waste bin. They'd soon stink, a servant would find them, and this minuscule, impulsive rebellion in the park against Mama's expectations would do no harm.

And it might accomplish a scintilla of good.

"You both look exceedingly fine," Hamish snapped. "Stop fretting, and let's get this over with."

Edana's mouth firmed, and Hamish prepared for another sibling skirmish on a Windham walkway.

Ronnie put a hand on Eddie's arm. "He's paying us a compliment, Eddie. Ham, you're supposed to knock. If the knocker's up, the household is receiving. Give it a tap, please."

"When we're scouting unfamiliar territory, Murdoch will do," he said, rapping the knocker against the brass plate. The result was louder than pistol shots reverberating across the Mayfair street.

"Knock genteelly," Ronnie hissed through a fixed smile. "Not as if you're the excise man searching house to house for contraband whisky."

Colin would have known how to knock, but Colin had not been invited on this sortie, and Hamish hadn't known whether a spare sibling was permitted or not. Numbers apparently had to match on social outings, as was the case with a fair fight.

"Your Grace, ladies, welcome. You are expected." Another fellow in blue livery was bowing them into the house. "I'll announce you, if you'd be so good as to wait here a moment?"

Ronnie and Eddie did look quite fetching. Their red hair was brushed to a shine and styled atop their heads, accentuating height and the good bones of which MacHugh women were justifiably proud. Feathers and

flowers adorned their coiffures in confec-
tions too colorful to be called bonnets. Their
dresses might have beggared the dukedom's
exchequer, but in green and maroon, they
made a fetching pair.

"I meant what I said, about you both looking fine," Hamish muttered. "A bit of the
plaid, and you'd be ready for any proper
gathering."

They exchanged That Look, the one that
said he'd Done It Again, though nobody
ever bothered to tell a man what *It* might
be.

"Murdoch, Lady Edana, Lady Rhona,
welcome," their host said. "If you'll join me
in the family parlor, I'll make the introductions."

Oh, raptures abounding! More introductions.

Their host was Gayle, Earl of Westhaven.
Over a few drams last night, Hamish had
sat Colin down, got a diagram from him,
and then memorized the relationships as
any competent commander memorized a
map of the terrain for an upcoming battle.

Making *sense* of that terrain was a more
complicated undertaking.

If Edana and Rhona were nicely turned
out, Miss Megan was perfectly attired. She
wore toast-brown velvet trimmed with deep
red and the occasional dash of cream.

Hamish bowed over her gloved hand. "You put me in mind of a perfectly baked scone, slathered with raspberry jam and fresh butter." He'd offered this compliment at a point when the general conversation had paused, and that pause became a silence.

An awkward silence.

"Well done, Murdoch," growled some earl or other. "Now we're all famished."

Megan Windham was apparently related to half the titles in Mayfair. This earl fellow was dark-haired, not exactly handsome, and had no pretensions to charm. Hamish liked him on sight. He had blunt features and the swooping scowl of an officer who didn't waste his troops, horses, or shot, and waltzed at Wellington's command and no other's.

He also looked familiar, but Hamish could not place him, not with Megan Windham's perfume stealing into his senses. She did look good enough to eat, and her fragrance . . . her fragrance was lovely enough to dream about.

"We're to work on our small talk," Miss Megan said as the party marched out into the afternoon sunshine. "Have you thought up any questions suitable for the dance floor, Your Grace?"

He'd made a list after he'd studied Colin's

battle map. "Who is madam's favorite composer? Does the lady have a preferred musical instrument? What is her favorite season of the year? What scent recommends itself to her on a gentleman's person?"

Thanks to the pianist, Hamish knew to append "Why?" to each of those inquiries. *Why* not only kept the lady talking but probably revealed more tactical intelligence than all the foregoing questions put together.

Meaning Hamish would not underestimate Megan's pianist cousin, despite his lace.

"That last one might be risky — the one about a gentleman's scent," Miss Megan said. "Late at night, the typical ballroom can be . . . close."

"Rank, you mean? I've smelled worse."

"You mustn't say that, Your Grace. When I made my come out, I developed a list of bachelors whom I dubbed the Parsley Princes — gentlemen who ought to spend more time freshening their breath before they ask to stand up with a lady. Call upon your thespian skills if you must, but try to exude equable good cheer, pleasure in the lady's company, and gentility at all times."

The very qualities that would have got Hamish's men killed on the Peninsula. "I'm known for exuding rage, Miss Megan. I'm the Berserker of Badajoz, the Terror of Toulouse. You needn't spare my sensibilities."

"Why?" She'd fired off her question quietly, so the rest of the party would not have heard her over the rattle of passing coaches and clip-clip of hooves.

Honesty was a relief, but a sad one. "Why not bother with delicacy? Because I haven't sensibilities to spare." Not the polite variety, at least.

"No, I meant, why are you the Terror of Toulouse and the Berserker of Badajoz. Why are you the Duke of Murder? There were other soldiers at all those battles, doing what soldiers do."

Across Park Lane lay the green beauty of Hyde Park, relatively quiet at this hour, though it would fill up with carriages soon. The high flyers and their escorts, polite society, and everything in between assembled on fine days in the late afternoon for parade inspection.

To Hamish, veteran of too many battles, Hyde Park's hedges and wrought-iron fences prevented orderly retreat. The towering maples might hide snipers, the Serpentine could drown recruits unable to swim, and firing at water turned the trajectory of bullets unpredictable.

"If I discuss the war with you, I will commit a great breach of etiquette," Hamish said, though kissing Miss Megan would be a greater breach — and a far lovelier memory.

"I'll just put my questions to Keswick, Deene, or St. Just. They'll tell me."

Keswick was apparently the cranky dark-haired earl, while the Marquess of Deene was the little marchioness's husband, and Devlin St. Just was the Earl of Rose*croft*.

"They won't tell you much, Miss Meggie. Wartime memories are best not shared in genteel company."

She marched along at a good clip until they'd crossed the street and entered the park through a pair of imposing gates.

"I can't deflect the gossip if I don't know its source, Your Grace. Forewarned is forearmed, and my cousins will so tell me. One will let something slip if I'm persistent, probably Keswick because he's so softhearted. I'll take that morsel to Lord Deene and imply that I know more than I do. Deene will let one more fact slip, which I'll stitch together with the first to create an inference. The process takes patience and timing, but my family numbers several veterans. On Mama's side, they can be quite garrulous in the right mood."

When tipsy, in other words. The London season involved a fair amount of tipsiness, apparently.

The park was quiet, which meant Hamish had to lower his voice. "I notice you do not solicit the assistance of Sir Fletcher."

Pilkington would be happy to explain the particulars of Hamish's military record to her in all their gory ignominy, and his version of Hamish's history would be ignominious indeed.

"I wouldn't start with Sir Fletcher."

They'd put some distance between themselves and the rest of the party, which was fortunate. Miss Megan should have been instructing Hamish about small talk, not digging tunnels under his defenses.

"You'd go to Sir Fletcher if your cousins refused to oblige? Very well, then, I killed people."

The words . . . hurt. They brought to mind the horrendous noise and stink of battle, but also the surprise and bewilderment of men who'd got up that morning never expecting to end the day — *or their lives* — on the end of Hamish's bayonet.

In Hamish's eyes, they would have seen apology, regret, and a determination to kill again.

"You were a soldier," Miss Megan said. "I

suspect you were a very good one, maybe too good."

He nearly went stumbling onto his arse again. This woman was capable of wielding words with more deadly skill than any sniper could fire a weapon.

"Let's leave the matter there, shall we? I would not want to argue with a lady. Why do you suppose ladies are not prohibited from arguing with gentlemen?"

Miss Megan showed him mercy, and allowed the change of subject. "Because an argument takes two parties at least. If one refuses to engage, then there can be no argument. Ladies might attempt to provoke a fellow to a disagreement, but if he thwarts their efforts with his charm and politesse, then no argument will ensue. Who is your favorite composer, Your Grace?"

Rabbie Burns, closely followed by Robert Tannahill, a pair of brilliant fellows who'd died too soon and worked too hard.

"That Beethoven seems to know what he's about."

Hamish had apparently surprised her, but Eddie and Ronnie had dragged him to a few musicales. Highland winters were long enough that even Hamish had dawdled about on the keyboard a bit.

"Do you have a favorite among Beethoven's works, sir?"

The soft, sweet, tender ones appealed, though they could be deceptively difficult to learn. "The Third Symphony is a thumping good air. What of yourself? Have you a favorite?"

"I like the music my mother sang to me when I was a child, though much of it is in Welsh and may not be written down anywhere. For chamber music, Mozart will do. He's very elegant."

Boring, he was. Never got together enough instruments to really shake the rafters. One set of pipes on a battlefield produced more sheer sound and fury than all Mozart's fiddles and twiddles combined.

"Elegant is fine." Elegant music provided covering fire for gossip and flirtation, which was, after all, the very business of polite gatherings. "Which of Mozart's operas do you prefer?"

Miss Megan prattled on with the ease of one born to Mozart and Haydn, Hyde Park, and symphony concerts. By the time their party returned to the gates facing Park Lane, they'd been conversing amiably, to appearances, for more than half an hour.

"I think you'll do, Your Grace," she said as they waited to cross the street. "I've enjoyed taking the air with you."

Hamish wanted to ensure she'd not go asking Pilkington about Spain — or Portugal, or France, or Waterloo — and was about to raise that impolite topic when the man himself came trotting down Park Lane on a fashionably underweight bay.

The moment Miss Megan spotted Sir Fletcher, her posture changed. Her chin came up, her shoulders went back, her smile wilted into a strained caricature of good cheer.

Sir Fletcher caught sight of them and trotted closer, the moment putting Hamish uncomfortably in mind of when the French cavalry came pounding out from behind their artillery. The English infantry in their squares had waited as those big, deadly animals trotted closer, their riders ready to slash a man's head from his body. . . .

Hamish nearly shoved Megan behind him, for as Sir Fletcher came ever closer, he aimed a pointed inspection at them. At the last moment, Pilkington switched his reins to one hand and touched his hat brim with a gloved finger.

He hadn't been smiling, and now neither was Miss Megan. If Hamish didn't know better, he would have said the woman who could inquire bluntly about sieges and murder looked . . . afraid.

She wouldn't be asking Sir Fletcher difficult questions if she could help it, and that was . . . that was a relief.

Troubling too, but mostly a relief.

"Why do you suppose Mama and Papa are haring off to Wales just as the season is getting under way?" Charlotte asked.

Charlotte, veteran of many seasons, wasn't as daunted by the upcoming weeks as Megan was, but then, nothing much daunted Charlotte. *Ever.*

"Perhaps they're leaving London after the ball because another spring in Town is tedious, expensive, and boring," Beth muttered from behind her embroidery hoop. Beth did exquisite close work, which Megan couldn't attempt without bringing on a megrim.

"Perhaps Mama and Papa retrace their wedding journey because they are in love," Anwen said. "They know Aunt Esther will happily look after us, so Mama and Papa can have one of their honeymoons when Wales is looking gorgeous."

Wales was always gorgeous. Half-wild, relentlessly green, music in the very names of the villages, magic in the hills, and lovely, fluffy sheep more plentiful than Mayfair dandies.

The sheep were often better mannered than the dandies too.

Maybe that was why Anwen loved yarn, knitting, crocheting. . . . Anything that put soft wool in her hands would remind her of summers spent near Cardiff. She wound a pile of sea-green merino into a ball, her movements graceful and rhythmic.

"I don't care why Mama and Papa are leaving for Wales," Megan said. "I wish them safe journey and many rainbows."

So to speak. Mama and Papa could be shamelessly demonstrative. Worse even than Uncle Percy and Aunt Esther, whose waltzing still turned heads.

"How did your outing with the Duke of Murdoch go, Megs?" Charlotte asked. "He's quite dashing in his Highland finery."

Anwen's winding paused. "Kilts are a lovely fashion."

Kilts were made of wool, while Megan's fancies lately had been made of moonbeams and mischief.

"Our outing was prosaic," she said. "His Grace, contrary to all gossip, is a charming man who acquits himself well on the dance floor and in conversation. He should do very nicely at Aunt's ball, and his sisters are delightful."

When they weren't berating their brother

in public.

"But what?" Charlotte demanded.

Beth stabbed at her hoop with a silver needle. "Leave her alone, Charlotte. Megan has a kind heart, and it won't hurt for Sir Fletcher to know other men find her attractive."

"Sir Fletcher found Hippolyta Jones attractive until her papa's bank collapsed," Charlotte replied. "The year before that, wasn't he chasing after Sally Delaplane — or her grandfather's sugar plantations? Too bad for Sir Fletcher that Sally caught the eye of a French comte."

"And when Sir Fletcher first mustered out, he was dangling after the Barington heiress," Anwen added. "Or that was my impression. I could be mistaken."

"You're not mistaken," Beth said, "but you're kinder than I am. Sir Fletcher is a younger son trying hard not to look like a fortune hunter. He's not my first choice of husband for anybody."

All of Megan's joy in her Hyde Park outing, all of her curiosity regarding the Terror of Toulouse, shrank back to the girlish fancies from whence they'd sprung. Sir Fletcher had not been pleased to see her on Murdoch's arm.

"I do wonder about Murdoch's wartime

reputation," Charlotte said. "Lady Melodia Tarryton was engaged to him at one point, but she broke it off when His Grace mustered out. Nobody ever said why she changed her mind."

"Perhaps she found someone else while Murdoch was away," Megan offered.

"Or maybe she found out his true nature. One gathers Murdoch was very fierce in battle. And there are stories. . . ."

"You'd like a fierce husband, Charl," Anwen said, winding faster. "You need that, in fact, but I'd hate to watch you whisked off to Scotland. We'd only see you once every five years, and never get to spoil your babies."

Anwen mentioned babies rather a lot and was passionately devoted to bettering the lot of orphans.

Megan pushed her spectacles up her nose. "I doubt Murdoch is looking for a bride, though his sisters might be inspecting the eligibles. What else have you heard about him, Charlotte?"

"The Duke of Murdoch hasn't a reputation for bravery per se," Charlotte said. "I'd say it's more a reputation for savagery. One hears that when he challenged Baron St. Clair, the weapon of choice was bare fists, and Murdoch intended to beat the baron to death. Only the timely intervention of third parties prevented the next thing to murder."

Charlotte had the ability to sit at a table playing whist, to every appearance puzzling over her next discard while in fact she was listening to a trio of men gossiping over at the window. Growing up, she'd made a formidable spy on the male cousins, and now she was simply formidable.

"Baron St. Clair is a substantial fellow," Megan said, "and was a soldier himself. Why does one assume he'd be defeated, much less killed, in a fair fight?"

"We shouldn't speak of such things," Anwen said, setting her yarn into her workbasket.

"Why not?" Beth asked, knotting off a golden thread. "If Charlotte didn't tell us what she overhears, we'd never get any of the best gossip. I heard that Murdoch had a dreadful temper in battle, and was always to be found in the thick of the fighting."

The duke's eyes, so glacially distant when he spoke of war, suggested the same. He'd doubtless fought with everything he had, every time, and the battles haunted him. Megan, by contrast, was facing defeat at the hands of a knighted weasel and had offered the merest whimper of protest.

"Murdoch's years of soldiering will get

him through Aunt Esther's ball," Charlotte said. "The matchmakers will overlook a little savagery in a man with a dukedom and two lucrative breweries. His brother will be considered quite the catch too. They won't be so keen on the sisters, though. Very pretty, and gentlemen do seem fascinated with red hair."

They shared a sororal moment, for all four Windham sisters had red hair. Beth was a glossy titian, Charlotte more auburn. Megan tended to strawberry blonde, while Anwen — quiet, shy Anwen — had hair that could be described only as blazingly red.

"Megs, have you saved your supper waltz for Sir Fletcher?" Anwen asked. "He's a very fine dancer."

Oh, wasn't he just? "He hasn't asked me for it. I thought I might dance the supper waltz with the Duke of Murdoch."

Though *he* hadn't exactly asked her yet either.

"Those roses should never have been cut," Charlotte said, frowning at the bouquet wilting on the windowsill. "The hothouse varieties simply do not fare well off the vine. Giving Murdoch your supper waltz is quite generous, Megs. Do you think Sir Fletcher will mind?"

He'd mind awfully. "Murdoch, like Mama

and Papa, will be decamping directly after Aunt's ball. I can give His Grace a single dance before he returns to Scotland, and there's nothing Sir Fletcher can say to it."

Sir Fletcher would say a great deal. His chilly glower on Park Lane assured Megan she was already due for a lecture. She moved to the sideboard to give the roses a drink from the pitcher, a futile gesture of compassion for the already doomed.

"You don't want to marry Sir Fletcher, do you?" Anwen asked, noiselessly closing the lid of her workbasket. Everything she did was calm, graceful, and ladylike — almost everything.

"Sir Fletcher hasn't proposed." Not in the usual, proper sense. *Thank God.*

Megan's sisters became absorbed in not looking at her or at each other.

"As long as Papa is off cavorting with Mama in Wales," Charlotte said, "Sir Fletcher can't very well propose, can he? All he can do is court you and escort you. The season is long, and the ballrooms are full of bachelors. Sir Fletcher had best not grow overconfident of your affections."

Megan harbored *no* affection for a man who'd exploit a young woman's missteps, no matter how handsomely he turned down the room. The idea of fulfilling her wifely

114

duties with Sir Fletcher made her ill, though all over England, women were doubtless enduring worse in the name of family honor or simple survival.

Besides, Sir Fletcher had no need for Megan's affections. He had her letters — dozens and dozens, all clearly signed by her, and that was awful enough.

CHAPTER SIX

Old, doomed feelings welled as Hamish heard himself announced as "the *Duke* of *Mur*doch!" above the heaving sea of gossip, fashion, and music filling the Windham ballroom. The herald — may he be damned to a permanent case of piles — had even thumped his pikestaff three times to ensure everybody got a good gawk at the new duke.

Edana and Rhona used the moment to preen before the entire assemblage, and well they should, for their finery was exquisite. Nevertheless, in the ballroom below, ladies whispered to their escorts, mamas drew their daughters closer, and former officers exchanged knowing smirks.

Hear ye, hear ye, the Duke of Murder has arrived.

"Now what?" Hamish muttered.

"Now," Colin said, "we lead the ladies down to the dance floor, fetch them some punch, and glower at any who presume to

116

approach without an introduction."

In the past week, between perambulating about in the park, receiving callers, and paying calls, Edana and Rhona must have met half of Mayfair.

"Rather like defending the garrison," Hamish said, escorting Rhona down the grand staircase. He knew better than to rush. Ronnie was enjoying herself, and her smile was . . . well, the garrison would need a good deal of defending, based on the loveliness of that smile.

"Rather like being a brother," Rhona corrected him. "Oh, there's Miss Windham and Miss Megan, and I see Lady Deene. We met her in the modiste's."

"I see Sir Fletcher over by the punch bowl," Eddie chimed in from Colin's side. "He is such an attractive fellow."

They were nervous. Hamish sensed this the same way he'd known his recruits were nervous the night before a battle. Sane men were terrified going into battle, but masculine pride insisted that the only sensible reaction to impending death was to clean spotless weaponry, compose maudlin letters, or reread notes from sweethearts.

"You both look stunning," Hamish said, reaching for a paraphrase of his pre-battle speech. "I will dower you down to my last farthing if you see a fellow who takes your fancy, provided he's worthy of you. You are the equal of any person here, if not superior to them all. You're as well educated as Colin or I, you know every dance, you could sing the entire ballroom to tears. You're the daughters of Clan MacHugh, and the blood of a hundred generations of warriors flows through your veins. Victory has been in your hands since you left the coach. Stop fretting and prepare to show mercy to your prisoners, even as you put your foes to shame."

They'd reached the bottom of the world's longest staircase, and just in time, for Rhona stumbled on her hem.

Hamish caught her, caught the look of bewildered surprise in her green eyes.

He winked. She started to grin, smoothed her brow, and offered the room that glowingly attractive smile she'd fired off from the top of the steps.

All right, then.

"Shall we charge?" Colin muttered. "Repair to the punch bowls, rather?"

Where Sir Fletcher lurked waiting to ambush the unwary, no doubt.

"A glass of punch would suit," Rhona said. "The first sets will form soon, and I'm promised to Sir Fletcher."

She attempted to haul Hamish off to the

118

left side of the battlefield — ballroom, rather.

"Be careful with Pilkington, Ronnie," Hamish said. "Colin and I know him from our army days, and he did not distinguish himself as a leader of men." More than that, somebody who'd been taken captive by the French, leaving his own men without any leader at all, could not say.

"Sir Fletcher has shown favor toward Miss Megan Windham," Eddie murmured. "But my gracious, evening attire does show off a man's attributes, doesn't it?"

Colin snorted, and Hamish maintained a commanding officer's silence.

Sir Fletcher sparkled, laughed, and bowed over the ladies' hands until Hamish wanted to shove the brave knight's head under the nearest fountain. Colin took up a flirtation with some viscountess, and the hands of the tall clock near the orchestra stopped moving.

Rather like taking a watch as sentry, when the night acquired pitiless permanence. For four interminable hours, the moon would hang unmoving in the sky, while unseen creatures rustled in the undergrowth and a French picket a few hundred yards away listened desperately for the shuffling and munching of his own horses at grass.

As long as the beasts remained relaxed and calm, no midnight raiders approached.

"You might consider looking bored rather than dyspeptic, Your Grace," said a voice at Hamish's elbow. "Or you could indulge a flair for adventure and ask some widow to dance."

Joseph, Earl of Keswick, stood to Hamish's left. Keswick had been among the Windham relations recruited for escort duty in the park, and true to Hamish's hunch, his lordship had served on the Peninsula.

With notable distinction.

"My lord," Hamish said, offering a bow. "Good evening. I look dyspeptic because I am dyspeptic." The stomp and thump of the dancers' feet too closely matched the rhythm of an army on the march, and the pounding of the megrim radiating from Hamish's left temple.

Keswick was dark-haired, and tonight at least, dark-humored. "*Good* evening, indeed," he said. "While I watch my countess flirt, flatter, and charm her way through hours of interminable dances and pretend I would not rather be anywhere else —"

He fell silent, and the look that came over his saturnine features was transfixed, almost pathetically so, except such benevolence infused his expression, such quiet joy, that in that moment, Hamish would have said Keswick was capable of effortless charm, grace, and every virtue to which a gentleman aspired.

"My love," Keswick said, holding out a gloved hand to a dark-haired lady. "Introductions are in order. . . ."

Merciful powers. Not more introductions . . . Except what else could the evening hold but an endless parade inspection for the Duke of Murder? Miss Megan had warned Hamish it would be so, and Keswick — married to one of Megan's battalion of cousins — ensured she was right.

For the next two hours, Hamish was thwarted from returning to his siblings' sides. Barons and viscountesses, honorables and eligibles, Hamish was subjected to more bowing and curtsying in one evening than he'd endured in any year in Scotland. He danced with half of the Duchess of Moreland's daughters and daughters-in-law, was teased and flirted with by the other half, and still, the hands of the clock advanced at only a crawl. . . .

While Hamish considered pelting through a window before his head exploded and his two cups of punch made an unscheduled reappearance.

"You see now why the terraces and card

rooms are necessary," Keswick said as the hour neared midnight. "Even the bravest officers are permitted winter leave."

"The terrace appeals." The ballroom was positively stifling, Edana and Rhona did not lack for dance partners, and Colin was practicing his flattery on the wallflowers.

Time to fall back and regroup.

"You're through the worst of it." Keswick gestured Hamish past a set of double doors. "The duchess has seen that the rest of the hostesses will have to invite you to their social functions, and all will fall into place."

They were in a gallery separating the ballroom from a torchlit terrace, and the air was cooler and quieter. The stomping still reverberated through the floor and hammered against Hamish's skull.

"There will be no 'falling into place,' Keswick," Hamish said, abandoning any pretense of good manners. "I'm leaving for Scotland in a few days' time." He'd make that the dukedom's motto, considering how often he repeated the words in his head.

"You must do as you see fit," Keswick replied, marching out into the night, "though leaving so many invitations unreturned would be insufferably rude and redound to your eternal discredit. I'm nearly always rude, but my countess keeps me on the social side of insufferable. I believe you're to dance the supper waltz with Miss Megan Windham?"

Foreboding swamped Hamish, and foreboding was a familiar companion. He'd found himself lost in a hostile wilderness once before, one infested with French patrols, French sympathizers, and no reliable landmarks. Hamish shook off the memory, which invariably ambushed him at the worst possible moments.

"Keswick, I haven't time to kick up my heels in London much longer. I have lands to see to, tenancies to look over, and some damned manor house or seat or ruin, which, as duke, I must inspect and pretend I'm pleased to acquire."

The solicitors had explained that the dukedom's seat actually straddled the border — the location of which had been somewhat fluid in centuries past — putting Hamish in possession of English land.

Of all the curses.

Keswick's gaze in the flickering torchlight was both amused and pitying. The amusement was welcome, for after two hours of chit-chat, false civility, and a pounding head, that amusement infuriated Hamish, while the pity . . . the pity threatened his reason.

"Stop feeling sorry for yourself," Keswick shot back. "The damned earldom of Keswick, and the barony lurking beneath it, came to me upon the loss of my only living relation. A dearer old fellow you never met. Sixtus was jovial, generous, the best of men, and his faith in me when I decided to buy my colors was the greatest asset I might have had in battle. *One soldiers on,* Murdoch."

Even out on the terrace, Hamish could hear violins screeching above the marching army of debutantes and dandies. Laughter floated on the night breezes, along with a noxious blend of lamp oil, exertion, perfume, and tobacco.

Then somebody — some tipsy, gossiping, unsuspecting soul — murmured a bit of gossip *in French.*

Hamish's French, like that of most British military officers, was proficient.

"Murdoch has such a brutal air," a woman said in titillated Parisian accents. "One can't help but wonder, given all the talk . . ."

"He was taken captive, you know," a bored male voice replied in the same language. "His men never said exactly how that happened. Not held prisoner for very long, by all accounts. Perhaps the French haven't your appreciation for savagery, my dear."

124

Somebody was speaking — in English — but Hamish could not grasp the words. He was under another moonlit sky, in the foothills of the Pyrenees, exhausted, furious, his heart pounding in time with the blows falling on him from all directions.

Go down fighting. You've the blood of a hundred generations of warriors . . . the blood of a hundred generations of warriors . . . a hundred generations of warriors. . . .

Self-defense begged for expression. A compulsion to destroy panicked its way past the part of Hamish that watched from a vantage point above his head.

This again, this mindless surrender to despair. This clamoring demand to salvage a shred of honor with a tidal surge of violence.

This loss of all control, of all hope, and he'd been doing so well . . .

While the Hamish choking in his evening finery raised a hand to strike out at the next fool who sought to subdue him. His ears roared, his vision misted red, his breathing came in great, soughing bellows.

He knew what was happening, and yet he could not preserve himself from the disgrace bearing down from all sides. *Go down fighting. Die hard . . . make them die harder.*

"There you are." The soft words came from

Hamish's right. "I'm so glad I found you. Our dance approaches, and I've been looking forward all evening to my waltz with you."

Between the part of Hamish preparing to wreak havoc without mercy and the part of Hamish collapsing in defeat at the hands of violent memories, a rational thought emerged, like the ringing of church bells over a battlefield.

Gently spoken Englishwomen did not participate in moonlit ambushes. He could trust that conclusion as a fact grounded in a soldier's experience.

Hamish lowered the fist that had been raised to the level of his heart, while the tittering couple moved away, and the violins lilted along, spreading gracious melody over the tramping of the dancers' feet and the pounding of Hamish's heart.

Keswick's watchful stillness suggested Hamish might have been a horse beaten too many times, crowded against the walls that had prevented flight to safety. The animal could strike out at the very person who sought to tend its wounds and lead it to freedom.

"Miss Megan," Keswick said, not taking his gaze off Hamish. "Good evening. Is it time for the supper waltz?"

126

The scent of lilacs came to Hamish as a gentle grip wrapped around his elbow.

"The next set should be the supper waltz," she said. "You may entrust me to His Grace's care, Keswick, and find your countess."

Saved. Saved not by Keswick's fist plowing into Hamish's jaw, not by Colin tackling his older brother and slamming his head against the paving stones. Saved, not even by a certain baroness storming onto the dueling grounds and hurling scolds in all directions.

Saved by a quiet question and a hand on Hamish's arm. He nearly collapsed at Miss Megan's feet, as a man will when battle-madness eases its stranglehold on reason.

"Murdoch," Keswick said. "Shall I leave you and Miss Megan to find your own way back to the ballroom?"

Hamish managed a nod. "Aye."

"Thank you, Joseph," Miss Megan added. "I'm sure Louisa is looking for you."

After another pointed visual inspection, Keswick bowed to the lady and departed.

"Joseph is fierce out of habit," Miss Megan said, leading Hamish to a shadowed bench. "His children take shameless advantage if he doesn't put up a show of gruffness, but he is a much loved man. Louisa, of all people, was smitten to her toes and remains in that blessed state to this day.

"Do sit down," she went on. "I overheard Lady Viola's speculations, Your Grace. She's a tart, of course, and you're not to spare her a moment's thought. My feet ache, by the way. We're sitting out the supper waltz. Please say something, for I'm babbling."

The sound of Megan's voice, with its hints of Wales and heart-deep goodness, soothed Hamish. Her proximity, her invitation to sit with her beneath the torches, to rest for a moment in the shadows, calmed his spirit, like a well-aged dram on a bitter night.

Hamish said the first words that came to mind. "I'm glad you found me too, Miss Meggie. Very glad."

Megan's heart was still pounding, her belly was in an uproar, and all she could think was that with the Duke of Murdoch, she'd find sanctuary. He was a good man, honest, honorable, all the things Sir Fletcher was not. For the length of an entire minuet, Megan had endured Sir Fletcher's smiling, bowing assurances of ruin, should she fail to yield to his proposal posthaste.

"We can waltz if you insist," Megan said. "It's not that I'm ashamed to be seen with you." Though she was very ashamed of herself.

"You should be." His Grace sat immediately beside her, not the polite twelve inches away propriety demanded.

The ballroom had grown very warm, while out on the terrace the late night air was chilly, typical of early spring. One could not be comfortable anywhere, in other words. And yet, the duke gave off a lovely heat, and his very bulk sheltered a lady from chilly breezes.

"Ashamed to be seen with you?" Megan asked. "Why would you say such a thing?"

"You heard that Lady Viola. I was taken captive and held by the French, I lost a fiancée somewhere along the way. I'm a savage. Five years from now, no matter how well I waltz or how harmlessly I natter on about the weather, the talk will still follow me. Any woman seen in my company will be the subject of unkind speculation."

He sounded so matter of fact that for a moment, Megan's own troubles receded. "You were imprisoned by Baron St. Clair. He's apparently been forgiven for joining the French Army as a youth, though nobody will say why."

The duke patted Megan's hand. "He was a youth, that's why. Stranded in France

129

when visiting his mother's people during the Peace of Amiens. St. Clair's a good sort, in his way, though I'd not like to meet his baroness in a dark alley. Do your feet truly ache? My head is killing me and I'll not venture near the punch bowl again."

The change of subject was less than deft and that pat to Megan's hand had been . . . *off*. Murdoch didn't strike her as the patting kind. Perhaps Megan's own upset was responsible, or perhaps Lady Viola's gossip was to blame.

"Shall we stroll, Your Grace? Many people do at the supper interval."

"Stroll." He made the word sound suspect. "Aye, though I'm sure finer points attach to strolling, and you will please instruct me in them." He rose and offered his arm, quite correctly.

Megan stood, though such was the difference in their heights that she could have climbed onto the bench itself and not been much taller than her escort.

"You are not a savage," she said softly. "You are a soldier, or you were."

"And now I'm a duke. Feels like being taken captive all over again. One minute I'm on patrol, consumed with my missing brother's whereabouts, cheered to think we've spotted his horse's tracks. The next

130

all is chaos and noise, mayhem, and blood-shed."

Did Lady Viola know that Murdoch had been looking for his missing brother when the French had descended upon him? Did anybody?

Megan slipped her arm through the duke's. "We'll find quiet down by the fountain. I'd like a moment of quiet."

"God knows, I would too."

Megan discarded a handy conversational inanity about the ballroom decorations, for even with an escort, making her way in the dark required focus.

"Lady Viola gave you a bad moment, didn't she?" Megan asked when the steps had been safely negotiated. "Keswick was worried, and he doesn't worry easily."

"Lady Viola merely spoke the truth, but yes. I wanted to thrash her and whatever fawning dandiprat was with her. My reputation for violence was not lightly earned, Miss Meggie, though I should not speak of such things to one so fine as you."

Megan and her escort moved down the path, past white-clad debutantes doubtless trying to look bored on the arms of their brothers' friends. In the low light, Megan could see only ghostly shapes and shadows, and the duke's escort became a matter of

131

necessity rather than social convention.

"*I* wanted to thrash Lady Viola," she said, "and when it comes to soldiering, who can you speak with about it? Carrying a secret hurt only makes the ache worse, in my experience. It paces about in your mind, like a lion in a menagerie. Miserable, far from home, burning to escape. Until you know, you just know, no matter how stout the fence, how high the gate, or how danger-ous the choice, that poor, crazed animal, trapped so far from home, will risk all —"

Murdoch's hand closed over Megan's where it rested on his arm.

"We'll talk," he said gently. "It can't be so bad as all that."

His understanding was a chink in the wall of misery surrounding the rest of Megan's life. "If I talk, I'll start to cry." And possibly never stop.

"If you talk, I'll listen. I came armed for skirmishes." He brandished a white hand-kerchief. "Do you know how much the rogues on Bond Street want to charge to have my coat of arms embroidered on this little bit of cloth? Now *that* is a scandal worth gossiping about. Worse, I do not doubt the poor ladies ruining their eyes to create such finery are paid a pittance com-pared to the tailor's profit from their labor."

132

"Your sisters might take on such a project." Beth could manage it easily.

"That pair. Have they tried to sell you any of my cigars? Enterprising of them, but ye gods, Miss Meggie. I pity the fellow who stumbles into their gunsights. They know how to make a rope of bedsheets, though you mustn't tell anybody I said that."

He teased, he complained, he wandered the garden with Megan until almost everybody else had gone in for the supper waltz and Megan could hear the soft splash of the fountain as water poured over the fingers of a perpetually smiling shepherdess.

"Have I made enough small talk, Miss Meggie? I confess my store is about exhausted. I'm down to asking why, you see, which is my question of last resort. Why are you so upset, and why must you deny me the pleasure of the only waltz I've anticipated with any joy?"

Megan sat not on the bench flanking the fountain, but on the stone wall surrounding the fountain's sunken square. Because she'd been here by day, she knew that heartsease had been planted on all four sides, and lampposts sat at each corner of the square. Three of the lamps needed relighting, rather like Megan's hopes.

"I'm in trouble," she said around a lump

in her throat. "I have been rash, silly, and stupid, and I must pay for my foolishness with the rest of my l-life."

The tears came, but true to his word, Murdoch was prepared. He sat right beside her, lent her his handkerchief, rubbed her back, and waited. When she'd cried not nearly enough, Megan rested her forehead against his arm, feeling so weary, she might have gone to sleep right there on the hard stones.

"Could be worse," His Grace said. "Could be you wake up in a French garrison, chained to the wall, your head throbbing like ten devils are trying to get out of your skull. You know my shameful past, Miss Meggie. Why don't you tell me of your great silliness?"

His Grace made confession sound so reasonable, a mere trifle between friends, and he followed up his invitation with a companionable arm around Megan's shoulders. She rested her cheek against his biceps, wishing she'd met him years earlier, before he'd gone in search of his missing brother.

Before she'd written those damned letters.

"I fell in love," she said, "or thought I did. In truth, I fell . . . I don't know, into stupid-

134

ity. Infatuation, rebellion, boredom. I met Sir Fletcher at a regimental ball and struck up a flirtation with him. I'd made my come out and had a few seasons. I knew everything and was soon to make a fabulous match with a dashing, wealthy, titled, kind, handsome, witty, interesting, princely gentleman as yet unknown. One with estates in Kent, preferably, nice family, and no need for acute vision in his wife."

"This unknown paragon sounds like one of your cousins," Murdoch said, his hand moving soothingly on Megan's back. "One of those cousins who should have warned you: Regimental balls are responsible for much mischief. The most dangerous creatures in the military are newly commissioned officers. The enlisted men see a spotless uniform on a young gent wearing new boots, they put in for a transfer. If his horse is high strung, his hair always combed, so much the worse."

Well, yes. War wasn't a fashion magazine come to life, was it? Insightful, though, to notice that Megan's manly ideal was based on Westhaven, Valentine, and St. Just.

"You've described Sir Fletcher the evening we were introduced," she said, "though he was wearing dancing slippers and had one unruly curl gracing his brow. He was all

135

manners, charm, and daring kisses."

"Rutting, bedamned varlet."

Megan smiled her first genuine smile in days. "You're being polite, aren't you?"

"I'm being saintly compared to what I'd like to say, and here I thought all my stores of self-restraint blown to bits. You're a good influence, Miss Meggie."

Another squeeze of her shoulders. Perhaps she'd misread Murdoch and missed a latent capacity for affection. Megan slipped her arm around his waist, for that seemed the logical place for her arm to go — though perhaps not the most sensible. His back was lean, and even through his evening attire she could feel the strength and warmth of him.

He smelled good too. Heathery, of all things.

"So Pilkington took liberties," Murdoch said. "You're not the first young lady he's kissed, and I hope he's not the only fellow whose charms you've sampled."

Megan sat up and peered at her companion in the shadows, though she could not make out much of his features.

"I'm not . . . I'm not fast, Murdoch."

Though here she was, *nestling* against him. Nestling *and* nuzzling.

"Of course you're not fast," he said.

"We're more practical in Scotland than you are in the south. We expect a woman to make an informed choice about a matter as serious as marriage. If she doesn't like a fellow's kisses, the wedding night is rather too late to find that out, and the fellow will be all the more miserable for it too. You've heard of handfasting?"

A couple ended up handfasted when they'd agreed to marry, then anticipated the vows. The union was legal and binding, and unlike Sir Walter Scott's portrayal of it, usually considered permanent.

"My mother waxes eloquent about the mischief engendered by the custom of handfasting," Megan said.

"Oh, right. As if dueling, scandal, or shaming a pair of lusty young people for indulging in the joys of nature is a better plan? Meanwhile, your London tailors kit a fellow out so snugly that the ballroom becomes one giant game of 'show me yours' while the ladies pretend ignorance. But back to your kisses, please. Somebody will soon be out here, insisting you dance with him, lucky toad."

Show me yours? Megan had grown up among five healthy male cousins. She'd eavesdropped with no less than three sisters and five female cousins, and then there were

Charlotte's reports from various card rooms, archery contests, and race meets.

Megan knew very well what "show me yours" alluded to, and perhaps she ought to have been scandalized by such blunt speech . . . except Murdoch was right. Some people's idea of evening attire — some ladies' and some gentlemen's both — was nearly indecent.

"I wrote Sir Fletcher letters," she said, "recounting his kisses, swearing eternal devotion, longing for his embrace, and . . . so forth. The terribly scandalous sort of so forth."

The so forth part was especially mortifying. *Show me yours,* indeed.

The duke rose, and Megan felt bereft, chilled, and — all over again — stupid, stupid, stupid. His Grace would be polite, for in his way he was gallant, but he'd explain to her that he had to return to Scotland that instant, and she mustn't spend too much time around his sisters in the coming weeks, please. He would not judge her for her lapses, of course, but . . .

But.

"You have cousins," he said, puzzlement in his voice. "At least one of them was a soldier, another will be a duke, and the nancy one has the shoulders of a stevedore

138

and is no fool. Why haven't they simply asked for the return of these letters? If they call on Sir Fletcher as a group, he'll likely wet himself he'll be in such a hurry to surrender the contraband."

"I adore your honest speech," Megan said. "You think in terms of logic and honor, and that is . . . that is the very problem, you see."

Murdoch took off his evening glove and trailed his fingers through the shepherdess's endless waterfall. "I *see* that adoring a fellow got you into this mess, Miss Meggie, but I thank you for the compliment. I am . . . considered unsophisticated, and rightly so. Simple logic, right and wrong. Those I can keep straight even in a noisy, stinking ballroom. Why won't your cousins confront Sir Fletcher?"

Murdoch assumed the problem was with Megan's cousins. How she treasured him for his reasoning.

"I won't ask my cousins to confront Sir Fletcher because he'll call them out, of course," Megan said, scooting on her perch, though finding a comfortable seat on cold, hard stone was a hopeless undertaking. "I couldn't bear that, and a duel would ruin my reputation anyway, bring scandal down upon my sisters, and disappoint my parents.

For two years after Rosecroft mustered out, he had to consume spirits to endure thunderstorms. The idea of subjecting him to gunfire or swordplay, for any reason, is beyond me."

"What was Sir Fletcher doing for those two years and more, and why is he only now making a pest of himself to you?"

His Grace asked a shrewd question.

"I've concluded I'm Sir Fletcher's fiancée of last resort." Another hurt, to be any man's last resort. "First, he paid his addresses to a banker's daughter, but her family's fortunes declined sharply and they no longer come to Town. Then, he became devoted to a sugar heiress, who moved to the West Indies. I was relieved to see him pursuing other women, when it became clear he wasn't at all as interested in me as I had been in him. I considered I'd had a near miss, a bitter but important lesson."

"Rotten luck, that he still has your letters."

"I don't think it's luck, Your Grace. I think Sir Fletcher is that good at scheming. He's turned the entire season into enemy territory for me. I never know when he'll accost me at the punch bowl, demand a dance, or inflict himself on me at a musicale. I understand better now, why Rosecroft was so

140

unsettled when he came home from Water-loo."

His Grace took a seat on the rim of the fountain, his evening glove peeking from his jacket pocket like a white flag. He brushed his fingers over the wool of his kilt, drawing attention to a pale male knee.

Oh, for spectacles and blazing torches by which to appreciate the picture he made.

"Soldiers generally don't discuss their peacetime challenges," His Grace said, "but Rosecroft is not the only man in England having difficulty — or in France, Germany, Spain, Poland, Portugal. Thunderstorms, nightmares, and stupid duels too, of course. We all have near misses, Meggie Windham, and they haunt us."

He clearly included his own history in that category. Such a past would bedevil a commanding officer long after the war ended.

"I can't tell my cousins about these letters," Megan said. "I've thought of telling Uncle Percy, but he's the worst of the lot when it comes to protectiveness, save for my own papa. Uncle Percy might not call Sir Fletcher out, but he'd ruin him all the same, and it would still be a scandal. A ruined man has no reason to keep his mouth shut."

Murdoch rose, and Megan felt tears

threatening all over again. He'd bow, he'd tell her Sir Fletcher wasn't the worst option, and she had to marry somebody, after all.

She'd told herself some version of those same lies many times.

Murdoch crouched before her and took her hand. "You can't marry Pilkington, Miss Meggie. He has a cruel side; ask any man who served under him. Sir Fletcher delighted in lifting the lash, even on boys whose only crime was stupidity. The scandal of a few passionate letters would provide you sanctuary from a life tied to such a man."

Megan's free hand went to her middle. "I want to say you're exaggerating, that you don't like him because he's English, and golden, and did not fall into French hands."

Though had Sir Fletcher fallen foul of the French, he'd have done so in uniform. Charlotte had reported that Murdoch had been captured *out* of uniform, which accounted for him having been handed over to a French officer notorious for his skills at . . . interrogation.

"Sir Fletcher is golden and English," Murdoch said, rising and remaining before her. "I don't like him, I never have, and I won't lie about that. Other people would say he's a good catch."

Megan closed her eyes. "Other people would be wrong. If Sir Fletcher will take advantage of me, he's not a gentleman. He cannot be trusted to protect those weaker than he, if he instead exploits them when it's to his advantage."

She was revealing more than she'd intended to, brushing up against memories she'd sworn she'd never revisit.

A foot scraped on the flagstone, the scent of wool and heather came closer, then warmth, then an embrace so gentle, so enveloping and secure, adoration was too tame a word for the emotion that inspired Megan to rise, slip her arms around Murdoch's waist, and rest her forehead against his chest.

Sanctuary, indeed. Blessed, heather-scented, impregnable sanctuary.

CHAPTER SEVEN

War was so damned seductive. Nobody warned a lad as he took the king's shilling that he was risking not only his life, but also part of his soul, his sanity, and certainly his heart.

As Hamish held a weeping Megan Windham in his arms, his emotions lurched close to grief, for all he'd left on the battlefields of Spain and France.

Camaraderie without limit.

Affection for his men and even for some of his fellow officers.

Shared memories of valor, squalor, violence, victory, and everything in between.

Bad rations that had tasted ambrosial.

Haggard women who should have been canonized for their part of the war effort.

A worthy enemy, even including St. Clair, who'd held Hamish's life in his hands.

Homesickness and horror that went deeper than the soul.

Hilarity only a soldier could grasp and only at the time.

Holding Megan, Hamish could acknowledge all of those losses and injuries, and even treasure them for the proof they offered that not all of his military memories were of shame and indignity.

He saw too, though, that war seduced a man's reason by promising him that what he had to offer, what he had to give, mattered desperately. He would not live, die, march, moan, retch, itch, sweat, or swear in vain. *He mattered.* Every soldier, regardless of how stupid, clumsy, bumbling, or venal, mattered indispensably, and thus his future was forfeit and he was glad to surrender it.

Being a duke did *not* matter. Waltzing, social calls, riding in the park . . . so much wasted time and foolishness. Being oldest brother to a lot of unruly siblings hadn't mattered as much as Hamish had hoped, for he'd been absent two years at a stretch, and his family's life had gone on without stumbling.

Holding Megan Windham, though, *that mattered.* Holding her confidences, that mattered terribly. When all of polite society saw Hamish as some kind of titled bear perfect for baiting in a ballroom, she relied on him to come to her aid.

"About Sir Fletcher," Hamish said, when the lady's bout of tears had ebbed. "I canna kill him for ye, Meggie, though for once, the notion of murder has some appeal."

She was luscious to hold. Soft, sweet, warm . . . her hair under his bare hand was the lambent warmth of candlelight and the cozy fire in the hearth, and silky too. Hamish wanted to gather her closer, but didn't dare.

She gathered *him* closer. "You are no killer, Hamish MacHugh. You needn't posture for my sake."

Society probably saw him as nothing but a killer — or a coward. Hamish made himself step back, resuming his place beside her on the bench, and to hell with propriety. He tucked her close, and she bundled against him.

The rightness of that, the sublime absolution of it, made the souls of the hundred generations of MacHugh warriors rise up and dance up across the heavens.

"I have promised a certain baroness I will never again call a man out," Hamish said. "Her ladyship was most insistent, and the consequences she threatened me with motivate me to keep my word. Dueling is ridiculous, in any case."

Inside the Windham mansion, the orchestra struck up the introduction to the waltz.

Hamish had wanted to dance with Meggie Windham, but this conversation beneath the guttered torches was far more precious.

"If you can't call Sir Fletcher out, what does that leave?" Megan wailed softly. "I can't call Sir Fletcher out, and he's pressed me again to set a date. My parents depart for Wales next week, and Sir Fletcher said either he'll talk to Papa before then, or take other measures to ensure our engagement must be announced."

Hamish considered calling on the Baroness St. Clair and asking for one small dispensation from the promise he'd made her, but no. That would mean calling on St. Clair as well. The baron still featured in Hamish's nightmares, and in all honesty, the idea of a duel turned Hamish's stomach. Then too, he did not want to explain Megan's situation to anybody, for her confession had been given in confidence to Hamish.

And only to Hamish.

"I won't let you do murder," she said, stroking a hand over the pleated drape of his kilt. "Your conscience forbids you from dueling with Sir Fletcher, and yet, he has my letters. Thirty-one of them. He brags about taking them out and reading them before the fire in his library of an evening.

Keeps them in his desk drawer, where he can enjoy them at any time. He finds them wonderfully entertaining too."

In the privacy of his mind, Hamish fashioned foul epithets for Pilkington in English and Gaelic, both. The moment, however, wanted practicality, despite Megan Windham's hand on Hamish's thigh.

"I could bribe him," Hamish said. "Buy the letters from him."

"You are paying for two sisters to make their come outs," Megan said. "Your wealth is in Scotland, I'm guessing, and Sir Fletcher will want his money before Mama and Papa leave next week."

Sir Fletcher would also learn, if paid once, that he could demand more payment in the future, until all of Megan's sisters were safely married. Megan would never know peace, and she'd have to confess her missteps to any fellow who sought her hand.

"The objective here is not to win a skirmish, then," Hamish said as his thigh endured another soft, slow caress through a single thickness of wool. "We must win the war."

"You hated war."

How he loved hearing those words from her, for they were the truth a soldier, much less a disgraced soldier, never quite admitted to another.

"I do not hate that a man who plunged an entire Continent into twenty years of endless, pointless carnage, ended up sitting on his rosy arse in the middle of the south Atlantic, Meggie. Napoleon's own troops were weary of him by the time we engaged them at Waterloo, but they'd lost their taste for being ruled by a king. Boney left them nothing to do but fight until not a Frenchman under the age of eighty remained to hold a gun."

And God help the army that faced the surviving French women, much less the mothers of all those men who'd died in service to an emperor's bloodthirsty delusions of glory.

"I do not want to marry Sir Fletcher Pilkington," Megan said. "I've considered running off."

So had Hamish. "Running doesn't work, Meggie. You only look guilty of whatever charge you're trying to avoid. You turn a retreat into a rout when you run, and you hand over the field to your enemy. The English learned that lesson on the way to Corunna. We fight to win, and we fight dirty."

Battle talk felt oddly invigorating, for once. Megan's hand stroking Hamish's thigh, though likely nothing more than a nervous gesture on her part, was invigorating too.

"What does that mean, Your Grace? I'm a half-blind spinster-in-the-making, and I don't know how to fight at all."

Megan was neither half-blind when it came to what counted, nor a spinster of any sort. Every woman had weapons, provided somebody showed her how to use them.

But Megan Windham was *good,* and good people did not recognize the face of evil when it smiled at them from their own ballrooms. A man outcast and disgraced among his fellow soldiers had occasion to know who was good, and who was merely posturing.

Megan Windham did not study Hamish's face when he spoke, she instead aimed her gaze at her slippers, the fountain, the darkened border of posies. She relied on her hearing to deliver a conversation's meaning to her, rather than the evidence of her eyes.

Truly, her vision was impaired.

For such a woman to labor over more than thirty letters, each word painstakingly chosen, full of her hopes and recollections, each epistle risking everything she valued . . . For her to commit her sentiments to paper, over and over, had been a labor of enormous magnitude and trust.

For Sir Fletcher to betray that trust was an equally enormous wrong.

Hamish picked up her hand rather than let it wander over his thigh even once more, and kissed her knuckles.

"Fighting dirty means, Meggie Windham, that we simply steal the letters back."

"I don't see Megan among the dancers," Devlin St. Just, Earl of Rosecroft, growled. "Her Grace assigned *you,* Keswick, to ensure Murdoch got through the evening without a mishap, and he's not even participating in the supper waltz. How could you lose track of a man that large, particularly one wearing a deal of blue and green plaid?"

Joseph, Earl of Keswick, had married into the Windham family because nothing in heaven, earth, or any other realm would have prevented him from spending the rest of his life with Louisa Windham by his side. Her brothers were unavoidable nuisances, the type of collateral obligations a man endured when his heart's desire slept next to him every night.

Rosecroft, Westhaven, and Lord Valentine were also the biggest mother hens in Mayfair — excepting possibly their own father.

Also quite dear.

"Megan and His Grace are taking a bit of air," Keswick said. "I see you aren't dancing either, Lord *Rosebud.*"

Valentine Windham had shared the misnomer for his eldest brother, which epithet, Keswick suspected, had been intentional on Murdoch's part. Keswick had observed Scottish regiments in action, and a Scottish soldier's humor was as wicked as his temper.

"Shall I dance you over the balcony, Keswick?" Rosecroft replied. "Her Grace likes these gatherings to be memorable."

They stood at the railing of the ballroom's minstrel's gallery, for as any competent general knew, control of a battlefield's high ground was necessary to make the best use of the artillery. On the dance floor below, anybody who was somebody went swaying past in triple meter, looking their best, smiling their most dazzling.

But no Megan Windham, and no Duke of Murdoch.

"This gathering will be memorable," Keswick replied.

"What aren't you telling me?" Rosecroft muttered. "You left Megan in the garden with a man we don't know well, and now she's missing in action. Not well done of you."

"What have you heard regarding Hamish MacHugh?"

Louisa twirled about among the dancers, partnered by some kilted earl. Titled Scotsmen seemed to be the featured bachelor of the season, may God help the poor bare-kneed sods.

"Regarding MacHugh — Murdoch, rather — I haven't heard enough," Rosecroft said. "Sir Fletcher implies that Murdoch was a problem even before the French hauled him off that mountainside. To hear Sir Fletcher tell the tale, Murdoch disobeyed direct orders, was never honorably mentioned in the dispatches, had a murderous temper in battle, and disappeared back to the Highlands within weeks of Waterloo."

Rosecroft had clearly been gathering intelligence, a role at which he'd excelled during the war.

"Most any man with sense mustered out after Waterloo," Keswick replied, "and we *all* disobeyed direct orders. We misunderstood them, misconstrued them, pretended they hadn't been timely received. My thespian skills were sometimes the better part of my military successes. Do you truly accord Sir Fletcher Pilkington's word any weight?"

A telling silence ensued, during which

Rosecroft's gaze followed the progress of a lovely blonde dancing with the Duke of Moreland. She was the Countess of Rosecroft, and the salvation of Devlin St. Just's soul.

"Megan is interested in Sir Fletcher," Rosecroft said. "They were in earnest conversation throughout the entire minuet, which is an interminable penance of a dance."

Gayle Windham, Earl of Westhaven, sauntered up from the direction of the stairs. "Awake past your bedtimes, my dears? Or wouldn't the wallflowers spare you any pity dances?"

In his evening finery, Westhaven looked every inch the ducal heir, though Keswick knew exactly what the earl was about. He was checking on his older brother, making sure Rosecroft, who'd traveled down from Yorkshire with no less than a wife and two small *female* children, was bearing up under the strain of civilized socializing.

Keswick had daughters and sons in quantity. He knew all about bearing up and about checking on family.

"We're discussing Keswick's dereliction of duty," Rosecroft said. "He's lost track of Murdoch, who was last seen disappearing into the hedges with Megan in tow. You will recall that we were dragooned into an impromptu tea dance without tea cakes, the object of which was to ensure that Murdoch, known among his fellow officers as —"

Westhaven was studying his brother as if Rosecroft had burst forth into an aria in praise of spotted unicorns.

"You sound like our papa," Westhaven said. "Though the privilege of imitating Moreland ought properly and exclusively to belong to *me,* you sound *exactly* like His Grace lecturing on the subject of Whig politics. If you ask me, Megan is the one doing the towing."

He nodded discreetly — Westhaven was *always* discreet — toward the end of the ballroom closest to the supper buffet. Megan Windham led a brawny, kilted fellow toward the stairs to the minstrel's gallery. Both Megan and her nominal escort held plates of food. Murdoch wore the bemused expression of a prizefighter who'd been rendered unconscious in the first round, but had no recollection of the blow that had felled him.

"All present and accounted for," Keswick said. "Nobody missing in action, but two people apparently wise enough to take advantage of Her Grace's practice of opening the buffet before the supper waltz ends.

Perhaps you should do likewise, Lord Rose-*bud*. My countess claims hunger can make a man irritable."

Dark brows swooped down while Westhaven took a sip of his champagne — or pretended to.

"If somebody doesn't tune that violoncello, I will not answer for my behavior." Lord Valentine, looking lacily resplendent, had emerged from a card room. "Who else is pleading a teething child, breeding wife, or aching head to leave immediately after supper?"

"You will not leave until Her Grace says you can leave," Westhaven said as Lord Valentine plucked the champagne from his brother's hand. "All appears to be going well, but then, this is the Duchess of Moreland's ball."

Benevolent providence, fate, and a sensible Deity knew better than to thwart Her Grace's wishes on the matter of her seasonal ball. Mere grown sons and sons-in-law would dance until dawn if the duchess required it of them.

"It's early for you to start whining," Rosecroft said, swiping the glass from his youngest brother.

"Ellen sent me on my own tonight," Lord Valentine replied, looking stoic in the face of such a miserable fate.

A moment of fraternal sympathy ensued, with nobody looking anywhere in particular, for a Windham fellow attending a ball without his lady was a pathetic specimen indeed. Other exponents of good breeding might pretend they barely knew their spouses socially, not so the Windhams.

"Megan and Murdoch not only took a deal of fresh evening air in the gardens together," Rosecroft said, "they have dodged the supper waltz in favor of more conversation. Gentlemen, I believe we have a situation brewing. They were surpassingly devoted to their shared waltz at Westhaven's tea-cake-less tea dance."

Keswick considered taking a turn stealing the champagne, but the glass was nearly empty.

"My very point," he said, "which is why I asked what we know of Hamish, Duke of Murdoch, before you went off into some pout about missing your sweets."

Rosecroft turned a glower on Keswick. "My countess ensures I'm kept well supplied with *sweets,* I'll have you know, very good tea cakes among them. Iced tea cakes by the dozen, with filling, and —"

"Somebody get the poor old thing to the buffet," Lord Valentine muttered, before his expression arranged itself into a charming smile. "Megan, good evening. You look lovely, as usual. Murdoch."

The conversation fell into a lull as the music below came to an end, and even Westhaven seemed to need a moment to muster yet another polite, proper verbal sally. Murdoch peered over the balcony at the dancers now assembling into a very long line that stretched into the ballroom itself.

"Miss Megan, you had the right of it. Sitting out the waltz in favor of a dash through the buffet line was a brilliant strategy." He peered at the Moreland heir. "You're accounted a canny fellow. If you intended to sit out the supper waltz, I wonder why you weren't down there, choosing the tastiest morsels for your countess, Worsthaven."

Lord Valentine fell prey to a spate of coughing, while Rosecroft passed *Worsthaven* the empty glass, and began thumping his baby brother soundly on the back. Very soundly.

Miss Megan murmured something about finding a seat before they were all taken, and led her kilted duke off among the potted palms.

Lord Valentine recovered from his coughing fit and bowed to his older brothers. "*Rosebud, Worsthaven,* I bid you good night. I'm off to find a piano with which to entertain Her Grace's guests during supper. I can't wait to hear what verbal artillery that Scot will aim in my direction, or yours, Keswick. I confess, I begin to like the fellow."

He bowed to Keswick and strolled away, smirking handsomely.

"Valentine has always carried something of a burden regarding his name," Westhaven remarked, finishing the champagne. "Perhaps we ought not to have teased him quite as much."

"We're his older brothers," Rosecroft said. "We had a duty to tease him or our sisters would have tormented him even worse than we did. He turned out well enough, after all."

Rosecroft was a fine strategist, and after Keswick had consulted with Louisa regarding the evening's developments, he'd probably consult Rosecroft as well. One thing was clear, based on what Keswick had overheard while lurking among the honeysuckle. Megan Windham could not marry Sir Fletcher.

Murdoch's plan for salvaging Megan's situation was — like many good plans — expedient, discreet, and did not require displays of violence. That it was illegal and dangerous was Murdoch's challenge to meet.

Megan had not come to the ball expecting to recruit an ally in the person of Hamish, Duke of Murdoch, and yet, his worthy qualities were as obvious as the plaid on his kilt.

He *did* listen. He did *not* judge. He was practical, kind, honorable, had a subtle sense of humor — and a sense of the absurd — and, of all things, his nature was, indeed, affectionate.

"Shall we find a table in the portrait gallery, on the terrace, or up here, Your Grace?"

Megan had purposely brought Murdoch to greet her titled cousins, for the more polite society saw the duke accepted by his peers, the less anybody would dare speak ill of him.

"I like to be near greenery," His Grace said. "*Camouflage,* to use the French term."

"Or the pleasure of natural surroundings," Megan replied, leading the way to a table situated among enormous ferns.

The minstrel's gallery ought to have been the warmest location on the premises, but Her Grace ordered the highest window-panes opened before a ball even began. The result was warm air with a hint of move-

160

ment in the most private of possible locations. Card rooms opened off the gallery as well, so foot traffic typically came and went in the direction of the stairs. The crowd in line for the buffet meant for the present, Megan could enjoy relative seclusion with her escort.

"Do you like all this folderol?" His Grace asked. "I'd honestly rather be home in my library reading Wordsworth or Burns."

"At this hour, my head usually aches too much to read anything," Megan said. "My spectacles help me see, though wearing them all day takes a toll."

Megan arranged herself side by side with Murdoch at a small table, both of them facing out across the gallery. The effect was like being behind a hedge, with a view of the fields and gardens beyond.

"Can you see the portraits across the ballroom?" Murdoch asked.

What ensued was a quiz of sorts, the result of which was to reveal that Megan could see clearly without her glasses at only a specific, middle distance, something she hadn't realized before.

"For the most part, I make guesses," she said, offering the duke a bite of pineapple.

Aunt Esther was permitted one truly extravagant entertainment at the height of each season, complete with ice sculptures, pineapple, and hothouse flowers. In a few weeks' time, her second, less formal gathering would mark the beginning of the season's end, after which the summer exodus from the capital would ensue.

How many letters would the budget for this ball have ransomed if Murdoch couldn't steal them back in the next few days?

"You guess at faces?" Murdoch asked, taking the pineapple from her fingers.

"I guess at everything. Faces, expressions, moods, innuendo. If I know a person, then seeing his face clearly isn't as important. For strangers, I'm quite at sea unless I peer at them closely, or they speak with particular emphasis."

The pineapple met its fate, though His Grace had delicate manners. "Sir Fletcher likely slipped past your guard, in part because you weren't wearing your specs and didn't know him well. Took me a while to realize English ways are different from Scottish ways, not only English speech, but English mannerisms. Got me in some trouble when I first bought my colors."

Nothing about this conversation was particularly remarkable — Megan's eyesight had never been good, Sir Fletcher *had* slipped past her guard — and yet, Megan could only have had these exchanges with a friend.

A true friend, who saw *her* clearly, who was willing to be seen *by her* just as clearly.

"What was different about the English officers?" she asked.

"Not only the officers, the whole bloo—blessed lot of them. Their humor is different, meaner, more sly, not as plainly funny to a Scotsman, while I suppose they think our jests childish. Englishmen consider it more dignified to ignore minor insults, though to a Scotsman, no insult is minor. If I know I've been insulted, then my brothers expect me to *do* something about it, not merely utter a few equally nasty words in response, and go prancing on my way."

"Is this why the Scottish typically fought in their own regiments, the English in theirs?"

Murdoch sat back. "And the Irish in theirs? I suppose it is. Best to go into battle alongside fellows you understand, but it's also true you fight hardest for your own." Then more softly, "You'll fight to the death for your own. The generals know that."

Megan squeezed his hand, and because they were dining, her gesture was bare fingers to bare fingers. Murdoch's grasp was warm and firm, in contrast to some others she could name.

"Sir Fletcher would fight hardest to preserve himself," Megan said, considering a forced strawberry. "Though I suspect he found a way to avoid the worst of any battle. How will we steal back my letters?"

She asked in part because Murdoch's gaze had gone so bleak at the mention of *fighting for his own,* suggesting he'd lost men in battle — every officer did — or something even worse.

"*I* retrieve the letters by gaining access to Sir Fletcher's library in the dark of night and reaving them from his desk drawer. *You* assist by providing the intelligence for this undertaking and drawing me a map of his house, right down to the positioning of the furniture in his library and the location of each window."

"I can't draw you anything at the moment," Megan said. "I haven't my glasses."

Murdoch helped himself to a strawberry from her plate. "Then talk to me, Meggie. Tell me what you recall of Sir Fletcher's home, and draw me a map tomorrow when you have broad daylight, a fresh mind, and your spectacles. I'll take you driving if the weather's fair, and you can pass along your sketch, then. A week from now, you can burn those letters one by one, and sleep secure in victory over a wily foe."

Which delightful notion, Megan could not have contemplated a single minuet ago.

She described not only the floor plan of Sir Fletcher's family home, but also the placement of the furniture as best she recalled it.

"What will you do if the desk is locked?" she asked.

"Pick the lock," Murdoch replied, putting a few candied violets on Megan's plate. "Don't tell me you're scandalized. You have a platoon of sisters, and you grew up with older boy cousins, and they have another platoon of sisters. You're probably a better lock picker than I am."

Megan was quite proficient with a hairpin. "Why do you say that?"

"Because you don't see as well as I do. You likely listen more closely, and your sense of touch would be more acute. Many of the best harpers in the Highlands have been blind. We have blind fiddlers, blind pipers. Seems only fair, if the Almighty withholds the boon of sight, that other gifts are given fuller expression."

A queer pang assailed Megan at that bit of philosophy. She popped a sweet, crunchy violet into her mouth.

"I like to sing Mama's songs from Wales

or the occasional drawing room piece with my sisters, but I'm not the musical prodigy Lord Valentine is."

Another pat, to her shoulder this time. Murdoch really was an affectionate man. Megan could still feel the pleasure of his embrace, warm, sheltering, fragrant, and . . . masculine. So very masculine.

"The harper's gift isn't only the music, Meggie. I love music, my sisters have beautiful voices, Colin plays a wicked fiddle. My blind uncle Leith excelled us all in skill because he was determined. His strength wasn't only the music, but also the sheer, unrelenting stubbornness to learn despite a lack of sight."

The queer feeling spread, a chill followed by warmth. Megan suspected she'd just been complimented, not as an Englishman would render a compliment — to the pale blue shade of her dress, to the sprigs of violets woven into her coiffure, to something easily *seen* — but as a Scotsman gifts a lady with a compliment.

"Sir Fletcher is stubborn," she said. "Also mean." He was no sort of kisser either, all rough, fumbling hands, thrusting tongue, and haste.

"Does the food not agree with you?"

She pushed aside the memory and took a

sip of punch. "The food and the company are very agreeable. I can't say when I've enjoyed a supper break more. Tell me about your home, Your Grace."

"You must visit someday. The landscape is wilder, the light sharper, the air more invigorating. You'd like it."

Megan would love it, for Murdoch clearly did. The longer he spoke of Scotland, and Perthshire in particular, the more heavily accented his English became, until Megan slipped into Gaelic, and he did too, and the orchestra resumed its graceful, measured dances without Megan even noticing.

Their plates were empty and their glasses as well by the time Murdoch assisted her to her feet.

"You have ruined me for socializing, Meggie Windham. My expectations for a society ball have been raised to include excellent conversation, a dash of intrigue, and the company of a lady whose well-reasoned opinions aren't in the common way. My thanks for taking pity on a home-sick Scotsman."

He'd taken her hand and enfolded it in both of his, though neither he nor Megan had put their gloves back on, for they yet lingered amid the ferns.

She did not want to let Murdoch go.

Didn't want to let her hand slip from his, did not want to lose him among the throng below, did not want to fill her ears with violin melodies and gossip when she could instead be arguing economics and poetry with him.

Alas, Megan was without spectacles, and thus when she went to kiss Murdoch, she had to cup his cheek against her palm, the better to perfect her aim. An hour ago, she might have contented herself with his cheek — a friendly kiss.

But somewhere between a pat on the arm, and a compliment to her stubbornness, friendly had become inadequate. Murdoch was championing her cause, routing a scoundrel, and putting himself at risk on her behalf simply because he was a gentleman.

Megan put her mouth to his, lingering for a moment, so he'd know she'd hit the target she couldn't quite see clearly but could enjoy wonderfully even with her eyes closed. He was warmth and wonder, a hint of lemons, a whiff of heather.

And she was in love.

Longing sharper and more desperate than homesickness shot through Hamish as he cradled Megan's hand against his cheek.

"You must not, Meggie."

Such was her determination that a man might easily mistake it for a lack of comprehension. Megan Windham's gestures, her speech, her responses were all characterized by hesitation, a moment in which she appeared to be choosing words, deciding how to reply, or casting about for answers.

Hamish knew better. As a Scotsman among English officers, as the head of his family, as a former soldier outcast among his fellow veterans, he knew what her lowered lashes truly signaled.

She was marshaling her self-restraint, being prudent. Being relentlessly self-controlled and at a cost only another passionate soul behind enemy lines might suspect.

A frisson of the battle lust pierced the warmth Megan's kiss brought, an irrational conviction that Hamish alone could free her from that moment of hesitation she brought to even a stolen kiss. She'd cupped Hamish's cheek first, a tender gesture that cut him to the marrow of his lonely soul.

And then she fixed bayonets and charged his lines.

Megan pressed her mouth to Hamish's more firmly, and he swung her about, so his sheer bulk would block from view the

169

identity of the woman who had dared kiss the Terror of Toulouse.

Megan Windham was a terror in her own right, sending Hamish's common sense teetering on the brink of oblivion. She went at him with everything — wrapped her arms about him, leaned into the kiss, and into a man contemplating the complete surrender of his wits.

"Meggie, no. You needn't kiss —"

Her breasts pressed against Hamish's chest. Her hand slid around his waist to anchor him more closely. A damp, sweet warmth swiped against the next protest Hamish would have made. Strawberries and tart lemons, daring and desire.

Arousal leapt into the affray, and that — that delightful, damnable, male reaction — fortified Hamish's honor. He lifted his head, but cradled Megan's jaw, so her cheek was pressed against the lace and linen of his cravat.

"Ye daft woman, you needn't kiss me to get your letters back. It's no' like that."

"You daft man, I'm not kissing you because I have to. I'm kissing you because I want to. Let me go."

She spoke through clenched teeth.

Hamish held Megan a moment longer, because *he* wanted to, because he had to,

170

because a brief demonstration of self-possession on his part was a good idea all around. When he was sure she wouldn't resume kissing him — and sure he wouldn't resume kissing her — he let her go but did not step back, lest somebody catch sight of her.

"Your hair," he said, passing Megan the long evening gloves folded on the table. "You'll want to see to it." He wanted to see to it — see to destroying what remained of her coiffure.

She ran her fingers through his locks, brisk, presuming gestures such as Hamish's sisters might have made but never had.

"You're presentable enough," she said, tugging on the right glove. The undertaking was . . . ach, God help him, *erotic.* Megan was careful, smoothing out the wrinkles by caressing her own arm, until only a few inches of flesh between her shoulder and her elbow remained exposed.

Skin that Hamish abruptly wanted to get his mouth on. "I'm thanking the Highlander who started the fashion of wearing his sporran front and center on a stout belt, Meggie Windham. You plunder a man's reason."

The second glove went on even more slowly. A woman who'd eavesdropped on her male cousins and picked locks knew exactly why Hamish was so thankful to that randy Highlander.

"From one kiss?" she asked, looking entirely too intrigued with her evening glove.

"From thinking about one kiss. With you. I'm for Scotland after your letters are retrieved. If you're not careful, I'll kidnap you and steal you for my own."

She passed him his gloves, and when Hamish would have snatched them from her grasp, she held on to them.

"I'd like that, Your Grace. You've said the Highlands are beautiful."

They both kept hold of his gloves for a moment, not a tug of war, but some variant of the old May dances that connected a couple by the decreasing length of a colorful scarf.

"You would not like being ruined, gossiped about, and disgraced," Hamish said. "I spoke in jest — poor jest. Scottish humor, there you have it."

He'd spoken from the heart.

She released his gloves. "Take me driving early tomorrow," she said. "Don't wait for the fashionable hour. Tomorrow night is the Hendersons' soiree, and the next night I'm promised to Lady Leighton's musicale. Monday is the Halstrops' ball, and Sir

Fletcher has already claimed my supper waltz."

She fixed her hair while she spoke, her movements competent despite her gloves as she rearranged pins without benefit of a mirror. She would not need a mirror, for without her glasses, she probably could not have seen her own reflection.

"Monday night I'll retrieve your letters, then," Hamish said. "By Tuesday afternoon, I'll be on my way to Scotland and your troubles will be over."

Megan paused, a hairpin tipped with gold in her grasp. "Must you sound so eager to depart?"

Hamish took the pin from her, surveyed the possibilities, and his *sgian-dubh* was in his hand in the next moment.

"Hold still, Mad Meggie." Before he could think better of it, four inches of russet curl lay across his palm. He stashed the knife back in his stocking, and pinned Megan's hair in a soft loop over her ear. "Ye'll do for now. More than do."

She glowered at Hamish — though her glower had a bit of a gloat to it — then patted her hair, while he tucked the lock into his sporran and donned his gloves.

"Until tomorrow," she said, slipping the loop of a painted fan over her wrist. "I thank you, Murdoch, for a very pleasant supper break. I ask that you not depart for the Highlands without personally conveying those letters into my own hand. The last thing I need is an intermediary losing them for me all over again."

"I'll turn over the letters to you and no other." Meaning Hamish would leave for the Highlands by Tuesday noon, which would allow the turnpikes to clear out, after all.

And allow his heart to break, at least once more before he blew full retreat up the Great North Road.

CHAPTER EIGHT

"Even for you, that's a nasty scowl, Keswick," Devlin St. Just, Earl of Rosecroft, said.

"Wait until you have sons," Keswick replied as the party below reassembled itself for dancing. Long lines this time, a reel or country dance to work off the supper offerings. "No scowl on earth is nasty enough to quell the irreverence of adolescent boys. Were it not for the fortitude of my countess at my side, I'd be a fearful wreck at the prospect of the coming years."

"We'd all be fearful wrecks, but for our countesses. How's the leg?"

Louisa waved from across the ballroom with her left hand. Keswick made her an elaborate bow. That was their signal for "this will be the last set."

Thank God. "My injuries pained me far worse before your sister took me in hand," Keswick said. "She sees to it that I eat properly, I move about when I might instead remain at my desk for hours. I ride out on fine mornings — you're joining us tomorrow, right?"

Rosecroft assayed a scowl of his own. "It *is* tomorrow. Leave without me if I'm not at the gates by the appointed hour. Emmie has fixed opinions about the folly of grown men staying out all night and neglecting proper rest. If it should storm tomorrow evening, I will inevitably be required to read the children their bedtime stories, and need I remind you, Keswick, one does a poor job of subduing dragons and witches at one's peril."

"I was slaying dragons, witches, *and* sea monsters before you learned your first cure for excessive drink." And yet, the dawn ride after Her Grace's grand ball was a tradition — a *family* tradition — and not to be ignored lightly.

A smiling Megan Windham wafted past them, pretending to examine the pattern on her fan.

"If she can't see us," Rosecroft muttered, "how does she expect anybody to believe she's admiring the flowers on her fan?"

"She saw us. She simply ignored us," Keswick replied. "If we remain at this balcony, we should soon spot the Duke of

Murdoch stumbling by, his kilt pleating in odd places, his expression bemused. Megan rather kissed the poor fellow into submission not ten minutes ago."

While Keswick had stood about, his back to the combatants, trying to look inconspicuous by the ferns, and praying Louisa would soon take him home.

Though what had Murdoch expected, when he'd allowed a Windham lady to lead him behind the greenery?

"I recalled something about Murdoch," Rosecroft said as the orchestra started the introduction. "Something I'd heard years ago, before all that nonsense about disobeying orders, getting separated from his men, and being held by the French."

Being held by the French, particularly after being captured out of uniform, was not nonsense.

"What did you hear?"

"At Corunna," Rosecroft said, his voice conveying the dread every British soldier associated with that episode in hell. "His men made it to the ships. I heard it said every single one of his men and their families made it to the ships."

Which meant through exhaustion, privation, deadly winter storms, with the French promising death to any stragglers, Hamish

177

MacHugh had somehow safely led hundreds of soldiers, their wives, and even a few children to the evacuation ships.

"I'd forgotten that," Keswick said, as Mac-Hugh — Murdoch, rather — went sauntering past with a nod in their direction.

He was tidy and calm, when by rights he ought to have crawled out from behind those ferns, given the formidable passion of a Windham female intent on kissing a fellow witless.

"I wonder what else we've forgotten about him," Rosecroft said. "I hear he plans to leave for the north, so perhaps we'll never have a chance to find out."

Rosecroft strode off, which meant Keswick was free to call for his coach and take his lady home. First, he'd stop by the card room and make a few casual inquiries of those who'd served with him on the Peninsula, also a few *very* casual inquiries.

Murdoch might plan to leave soon for the north, but as Mr. Burns had written, the best laid schemes o' mice and men, gang aft agley.

War had become more entertaining the day Sir Fletcher Pilkington had overheard a gunnery sergeant explaining to a recruit that the business of an army was to advance. The fighting, the marching, the besieging was all in aid of advancement. When a man became a necessary article to that continued advancement, he was expected to do less fighting.

Thus the regimental cobbler never saw frontline action, for an army needed boots. The artificers who repaired harnesses, belts, pistols, and holsters were never deployed to the fore either. The scribe, though he occupied an informal position, was also kept out of the worst fighting so he might pen more wills, letters to sweethearts, or the occasional forged requisition.

Regimental politics had made more sense from that day forward, and situations Sir Fletcher could make sense of, he could manipulate for his own benefit.

"I hardly expected to see you out and about today," remarked a fellow on a rangy chestnut gelding. The horse was fit rather than sleek, somewhat like his owner. The saddle and bridle were spotless, though worn, as were the rider's boots and gloves.

"Puget," Sir Fletcher said, offering the mounted version of a bow. "If I make an appointment, I keep it. Shall we be off? I've no need to get caught up in the carriage parade today."

The Honorable Garner Puget, third son

of the Earl of Plyne, nudged his horse forward. "How are your sisters?"

Sir Fletcher's four sisters were beyond the reach of a mere third son, at least in the opinion of their wealthy, titled papa. Rather than dash Puget's hopes regarding the oldest of those sisters, Sir Fletcher turned his horse toward one of Hyde Park's less used bridle paths.

"My sisters continue to thrive, thank you. Lady Pamela was asking after you just this morning. She wondered why you missed the Windham do last night."

"I didn't miss the Windham do. I was present until the good-night waltz."

Doubtless hoping Sir Fletcher would finesse the poor fool one of Pamela's dances. But for a moment's distraction with a buxom widow in an unused parlor, Sir Fletcher had been too busy keeping an eye on various Windhams and inebriates.

"Pamela must have missed you," Sir Fletcher said. "She's much in demand among the nabobs and cits. They do favor a lady with a title."

Puget remained silent in the face of that goading. He was not a loquacious soul, but his skill with a pen was considerable.

"I need you to write me up a few vowels," Sir Fletcher said as the horses ambled

180

along. "Nothing extravagant. A few pounds here and there."

"You said you were all but engaged to a Windham. Why not do as other younger sons do and trade on your expectations?"

Had they been in the army, Sir Fletcher could have ordered Puget into the thick of the fighting, and Puget would have had no choice but to go, such was the discipline of the British military. Alas, the war had ended, more or less, and vague threats on a leafy bridle path were the best Sir Fletcher could do.

"You are a discerning fellow, Puget," Sir Fletcher said. "Think about it: A man from good family with a spotless reputation and excesses of charm and sophistication might be given leave to pay his addresses to a woman of suitable station. This is generally not a matter of public proclamation, though the lady will know she's been claimed."

Sir Fletcher had been given that leave first with Sally Delaplane and then with Hippolyta Jones. In both cases, he'd traded on his expectations rather exuberantly, and required his father's assistance to avoid the sponging house. The earl had made it plain no further aid would be forthcoming, and the merchants had been growing impatient. Sir Fletcher had come across Megan Windham's old letters in the very nick of time.

"I'm familiar with courting protocol, Sir Fletcher." Puget sent his horse ahead through a narrowing in the path, and rather than hold back a slender oak branch that blocked the way, he allowed it to slap against Sir Fletcher's chest.

That minor rudeness gratified Sir Fletcher as a bout of swearing from Puget would not have.

"I've every confidence you shall soon have need of courting protocol yourself, Puget. In any case, between obtaining leave to pay Miss Megan Windham my addresses, and plighting my troth with her, inquiries will be made."

"You're an earl's son. The inquiries will be made mostly regarding your family's situation, and their contribution to the settlements."

Sir Fletcher rather hoped that was the case, but hoping was for fools when a man could plan instead. The business of an army was to advance.

"The family finances will be quite in order," Sir Fletcher replied. "The expenses of a social season, however, exceed a bachelor's means, and thus I have immediate needs to see to."

More debts in other words, most of them

to the trades, others in the form of markers and notes of hand. The Duke of Moreland, his brother, and his squadron of sons and sons-by-marriage would learn of those all too easily.

"All gentlemen have debts, and you have one to me," Puget said. "I haven't so much as danced with Lady Pamela since last month, and you said she wanted for partners. She sat out four times last night, Sir Fletcher."

That was rather a lot, even for Plain Pammy.

"Strategy, my good fellow. When you dance with her next, my step-mama will have become desperate to keep Lady Pamela on the dance floor. Even my father would overlook a penniless younger son's presumption when Step-mama explains it to him that way."

This was pure tripe, but Sir Fletcher knew Puget's circumstances, and had engineered some of those circumstances in fact. Tripe was as much consideration as Puget would get from his former commanding officer.

"How much and from whom?" Puget asked.

"Fifty pounds should do it," Sir Fletcher said. "Perhaps fifteen or twenty each, from Quimbey, Barchester, and, say, Hancock.

The usual approach will serve. The gentlemen played a bit too deep when in their cups, and I happily benefitted from their bad luck at cards. My man of business will discreetly pass an IOU complete with signature before their men of business, and my finances will come right."

"You're daft," Puget snapped, taking the left fork in the bridle path. "Quimbey was never seen drunk in public even before he married. Barchester is a sot, I'll grant you, but he hasn't twenty pounds to pay you with. Hancock never plays deep and I've never seen a sample of his handwriting."

Here was the moment Sir Fletcher enjoyed the most, when arrogance led the righteously unwary further in the very direction Sir Fletcher intended them to bumble.

"You're the penmanship expert. You tell me whose notes of hand can be most credibly duplicated."

Not forged. Puget grew rabid at the mention of the word, and well he should, for forgery remained a hanging felony.

"Why not a Windham? They're obnoxiously well fixed, you have to have played against some of them from time to time. As duke's sons they'll write in typical Etonian copperplate."

Puget had an odd ability to assess character based on handwriting, and handwriting based on character.

"I'll avoid them because they are *Windhams*," Sir Fletcher replied. "Moreland will manage the settlement negotiations as head of the Windham family. That's as close to an overprotective duke as I'd like to come."

Sir Fletcher let Puget parse possibilities in silence. Far better for the forger himself to suggest who the next victim should be.

"Lieutenant Lord Hector Pierpont," Puget said. "Drinks rather more than he ought, former soldier, typical education, and he frequents the same coffeehouse off Grosvenor I do. I've seen his notes of hand often enough to be able to replicate his penmanship."

"You've hit on a brilliant solution, as usual. I don't doubt that come Monday night, Pamela will bask in your clever company for at least the duration of a minuet."

"I want a waltz, Pilkington, preferably the supper waltz."

Sir Fletcher, though fools in love must be allowed their petty dramas. "You will write the IOU for the full fifty pounds?"

Puget's expression became gratifyingly hopeless, then determined. He was the best kind of felon, being both reluctant and

185

highly competent.

"Pierpont can stand the expense," Puget said, "and if you bilk him for the entire amount, he might be less inclined to drunkenness when he gambles in the future."

A reluctant, competent felon with a troubled conscience. What could be better? "I'm sure you're right. You're doing him a favor, when you put it like that. Poor wretch ought to be thanking you for warning him off even greater excesses of vice."

Such was Puget's skill, the poor wretch would never know he'd been robbed. Sir Fletcher would send his man of business to call on Pierpont's. Pleasantries would ensue, a bank draft would be handed over in exchange for an exquisitely forged IOU.

And thus, a problem solved. The army would advance without a drop of bloodshed.

"Lady Pamela will look with favor on your request for her supper waltz at Monday night's ball," Sir Fletcher said.

A single waltz was small consolation for the years Pamela would spend marching through various formal parlors and ballrooms in aid of some gouty old baron's interests, much less the nights she'd spend in his bed.

Geneva, as the indulged youngest, might look forward to a happier fate. If she were lucky, the present earl would expire before she came of age — cheering notion.

"Isn't that your intended?" Puget asked as the horses emerged onto a broader thoroughfare.

Through the hedgerow and across a green, Megan Windham sat on the bench of a phaeton side by side with a large man in a kilt. She made a pretty if somewhat nervous picture, but then Megan was as timid as a smooth-chinned navel ensign shipping out for Cathay.

"Poor thing has apparently drawn charitable duty again," Sir Fletcher said, "for that's the new Duke of Murdoch at the reins. I do believe His Grace is pulling that phaeton with draft stock."

The beasts put to were at least matched, both chestnuts with four white socks, but they were far from the sleek Dutch trotters one expected a duke to drive.

"Hamish MacHugh owns two thriving breweries," Puget said, again turning his horse to the left. "He fought like a demon for Britain, no matter what the mess hall gossip was about conduct unbecoming an officer or desertion. As far as I'm concerned, he can drive any pair he pleases to drive."

"Megan isn't wearing those ghastly spectacles, so she can't see you, Puget," Sir

Fletcher said gently. Puget had seen a great deal of Megan's handwriting, and for him, that was tantamount to peering at a person's soul — a curse, when a man was plagued with a conscience.

"She's sitting rather close to the duke for a woman doing charitable duty," Puget said. "But then, Murdoch takes up a lot of the bench. I saw them walking out last week with some of her cousins. Does that make you nervous?"

Puget would enjoy the thought that Sir Fletcher's marital prospects were tenuous. "Megan will never play me false." Sir Fletcher need not say more, not to Puget.

The phaeton rattled past twenty yards away, an incongruously delicate vehicle drawn by enormous horses with the hairy feet and coarse heads of the least refined specimens ever to qualify as equines. The sight should have been laughable, but with a duke at the ribbons, nobody would offer public ridicule.

"Don't underestimate yonder Scot," Puget said. "Hamish MacHugh disobeyed direct orders and the generals left him alone because the French were terrified of him. My men said when the French caught him, they let him go because he was too danger-ous to hold. Every Scotsman in the army

188

would have personally avenged MacHugh's death ten times over had the French let him come to harm."

If an army could advance on the strength of soldiers' gossip, Wellington would have flown over the whole of Spain in a week.

"Scotsmen like to kill things, Puget, and if nobody else obliges them, they kill each other. The French exaggerate, and should anybody need a reminder of Hamish Mac-Hugh's violent nature, I — who witnessed his brutality firsthand — will happily provide same."

Sir Fletcher had done some of that reminding in the card rooms last night. Never hurt to reminisce about old times with fellow veterans, after all. MacHugh's younger brother was tagging along on this London trip, and Sir Fletcher had a nagging sense that one would cause trouble.

Sir Fletcher had once sent Colin Mac-Hugh from camp on a goose chase — typical prank among bored officers — and the whole business hadn't ended well. Everybody in the officer's mess had agreed that the Scots were singularly lacking in gentlemanly humor.

"Miss Megan might be too good for the Scot," Puget said, "but she deserves better than you."

"Of course she does," Sir Fletcher replied, for the time had come to end this outing. "All the ladies deserve better than the fate life hands them, which is why I will make her an excellent husband. I'm mindful of the good luck that's coming my way."

Megan hadn't been exactly smiling from her perch beside Murdoch, but such was her refinement that she hadn't looked grim either. Without the dreadful glasses, she was pretty enough, despite that red hair.

"You're very sure of your future," Puget said as they drew nearer to the noise and bustle of Park Lane. "Very sure the Windhams will look favorably on your suit."

"I'm to meet with the lady's papa on Monday afternoon, and I hope to convince his lordship that I offer Megan a love match, in the great Windham tradition. She's a shortsighted, plain spinster with red hair. She knows she could do *much* worse."

Particularly if she attempted to refuse Sir Fletcher's proposal.

Megan's Monday afternoon had not gone well, and her evening was turning into a disaster.

"You will please spare a dance for Garner Puget," Sir Fletcher said as he bowed over her hand. "If he's seen dancing with a Wind-

190

ham, then he won't look as presumptuous for standing up with Lady Pamela."

Megan curtsied, though fatigue weighted her limbs. The social season was exhausting, and for the past few nights she'd slept miserably. Garner Puget was a good dancer, though he had an unhappy mien and little conversation.

"The hostesses and matchmakers generally see to apportioning the bachelors among the wallflowers," Megan said as the orchestra struck up the introduction for the supper waltz. "Lady Halstrop and her sisters are conscientious in that regard."

As conscientious as hungry raptors flying over a freshly scythed hayfield. No single gentleman would sit out a dance if the matchmakers could arrange it otherwise. Megan had seen the Duke of Murdoch twirling down the dance floor earlier in the evening, though not for the past hour.

"If your attention were any more fixed on that clock," Sir Fletcher said, "I'd think you had an assignation, Megan, my dear."

Megan did have an assignation. Tomorrow morning, she desperately hoped to entertain Murdoch in her mama's best parlor, and to retrieve from His Grace every single letter she'd written to Sir Fletcher Pilkington.

"I'm tired," she murmured. "Meaning no

disrespect to present company, but my feet ache." As did her head and her heart.

The waltz began, Sir Fletcher pulled Megan too close, and they moved off. To anybody observing, Sir Fletcher would be a dashing, besotted fellow, quietly enraptured by the lady in his arms. He smiled sweetly, his gaze was devoted, and his partnering only a bit presumptuous.

Megan wanted to presume her last cup of punch all over his snow-white cravat.

"Poor darling," Sir Fletcher crooned, loudly enough for the couples nearby to overhear. "Of course, you're exhausted. If you'd rather leave the dance floor we can enjoy the gardens instead."

God, no. Megan knew what Sir Fletcher was capable of in a moonlit garden or a secluded alcove.

"If I were to sit out a dance, it wouldn't be the waltz." Not the waltz promised to Sir Fletcher in any case. "Is that Lady Pamela dancing with Mr. Puget now?"

"You truly can't see them?" Sir Fletcher asked, his tone quite un-besotted.

"Lady Pamela is carrying a blue fan and wearing a peach-colored gown tonight, so I assumed it was she. I cannot discern features at this distance." Megan could tell that her admission annoyed Sir Fletcher, though.

"See that you don't pass on this miserable eyesight to my children," he said. "As long as you bear me sons, my father will deal generously with me, but I don't fancy the notion of my offspring sporting about in blue spectacles."

Then marry somebody else. Megan couldn't say that, not until she had her letters back.

"I am the only Windham with any significant impairment of vision or any other faculty, Sir Fletcher." Anwen was shy to a fault, but shy women bore healthy babies every day. "You needn't worry about the trait showing up in your progeny."

In Megan's progeny, perhaps.

"You do look fatigued," Sir Fletcher said, turning Megan under his arm. "You're not thinking of dodging off to Wales with your parents, are you?"

Well, yes, she had been. When Sir Fletcher had closeted himself with Papa for a half hour earlier in the day, Megan had been ready to dodge off anywhere rather than risk appearing for tonight's ball.

"My parents prefer to make those journeys without benefit of their daughters' company." She used the next turn to reestablish a proper distance from her partner.

"Is it my imagination, or are there more

193

Windhams in evidence this season than in previous years?" Sir Fletcher was brandishing his smile again, while his gaze remained calculating. "I've seen more of Keswick, Rosecroft, Deene, and your cousins these past two weeks than during last year's entire season."

Megan had her suspicions regarding what Murdoch had called a gathering of the Windham clan. Her theory ought to make her sisters nervous, for it was certainly no comfort to her.

"I am not the only unmarried Windham," she said. "Their Graces take matchmaking seriously, and have likely assembled the family with that situation in mind."

Sir Fletcher laughed the golden, public laugh that made Megan's insides curdle, especially when she'd said nothing humorous.

"You will not remain unmarried much longer, my dear. I met with your papa today."

And Papa, the wretch, hadn't even warned Megan the appointment had been made.

"Papa has yet to apprise me of the nature of your exchange. Had my sisters not told me of your call, I'd have no notion you'd come by."

Sir Fletcher steered Megan too close to

the edge of the dance floor, for she nearly bumped into Joseph, Earl of Keswick.

"Then you will find the time to speak with your papa privately," Sir Fletcher said, "and before he chases your mama into the Welsh countryside. It's disgraceful, a couple that age making an annual wedding journey. You and I will have more decorum, once you provide me with a few sons."

Oh, yes, Sir Fletcher. At once, Sir Fletcher. Three healthy boys by Christmas, Sir Fletcher.

He would happily see Megan die in childbed, if it meant he bested his brothers in the race to provide the old earl a potential heir. As Megan had tossed and turned last night away, she'd concluded that Sir Fletcher's impetuous wooing years ago had been more about that race than preparing for this subsequent courting-by-blackmail.

Westhaven went twirling by, his countess in his arms. Megan knew them by how they danced as a couple, by their absolute unity of movement.

"I do not speak for my father's schedule, Sir Fletcher. I have been available to him, but you must allow for the notion that his lordship has a mind of his own. He's a duke's son, after all."

The relevant truth was even simpler. Papa and Mama were partners in all matters of significance, and Papa would not have given Sir Fletcher leave to court Megan without first consulting Mama.

And Mama, bless her soul for all eternity, was preoccupied with preparations for the upcoming journey.

"Lord Anthony will consult *you* regarding the acceptability of my addresses?" Sir Fletcher seemed puzzled by such consideration.

Of course Papa would. "Mama might have you in mind for one of my sisters, or have another arrangement under consideration for me. If Papa didn't give you a direct answer, he had reasons of his own."

Sir Fletcher studied Megan for the duration of two eight-measure phrases. The waltz was in a minor key, which made the dance more dramatic and haunting. She'd never hear this tune again without feeling a sense of dread bordering on panic.

"You will approach your father at breakfast tomorrow," Sir Fletcher said. "Demand to know why I met with him, express your rapturous support for my suit. An announcement must be made soon, and a date set not long after that if I'm to put a babe in your belly before the shooting begins in August."

Lovely. First take aim at the wife, then at

the grouse. A fine set of priorities. Sir Fletcher would be *at Megan* incessantly once he married her, and no earthly power could preserve her from his demands.

"I will do my best to accost Papa at the very next opportunity." Megan would also do her best to ensure no such opportunity arose.

The waltz built toward its final crescendo, which afforded Sir Fletcher an excuse to lean closer. He smelled of roses, but beneath that Megan picked up old sweat and stale tobacco. His breath was foul, and dancing this closely, Megan could see that Sir Fletcher's artfully styled golden locks had already begun to recede.

"I have considered compromising you," he said, "in the interests of dispensing with all of this posturing and preening. I still might. My creditors are not a patient lot."

Panic became real for an instant, a sense of all the air disappearing from Megan's lungs, all the reason deserting her mind. Blind flight from the dance floor and even from England loomed as the only solution to the problems her lack of judgment had created.

She was on the point of jerking out of Sir Fletcher's arms — what a scandal that would cause! — when sanity reasserted itself. At that very moment, Murdoch might already have retrieved her letters. She might have won free through the good, stealthy offices of an ally she could never have anticipated relying on even two weeks ago.

"You have already compromised me, Sir Fletcher," Megan said. "Announcing that fact now will reflect on *your* family as well as mine. You have unmarried sisters as well as older brothers who need wives, and you are one dance away from being branded a fortune hunter. Show yourself to be the scapegrace younger brother, and your papa might well cut you off. Moreland could send me to the country to repent of my supposed sins rather than grant us leave to marry."

The dance came to an end, and Megan dropped into the expected curtsy. Sir Fletcher drew her up, and waited while other couples filed off the dance floor.

"Such a sensible little thing you are," he said, patting her hand. "I have, of course, already weighed those factors, which is why I await your father's leave to court you. See that my patience is rewarded, my dear, or it will go the worse for you. I can spread enough rumor to ruin you without creating scandal outright."

His smile was indulgent, his caresses to

Megan's hand made her skin crawl. She sent up a prayer for Murdoch's skills at thievery, and smiled right back.

CHAPTER NINE

Megan Windham's recall of the Pilkington townhouse had been blessedly accurate. She'd drawn Hamish a map, right down to where a portrait of dueling fencers hung and on which side of the library fireplace the hearth tools stood.

Noisy business, when cast iron pokers went clattering against the bricks.

The third window Hamish tried — the family parlor — had been carelessly closed, so the latch had been easy to coax open. The rest had been a matter of hoisting, twisting, and silently cursing while praying the floorboards wouldn't creak.

The library desk was locked, which gave Hamish hope that, indeed, Megan's letters were secreted therein. He'd inserted a pick into the keyhole and begun the delicate process of easing the mechanism open when a question rang out through the darkness.

"Are you a thief?"

Hamish straightened slowly, searching the shadows of the darkened library. "Of course not, miss."

The girl shifted her doll from one hip to the other. Hamish would put her age at about seven. Too old to suck her thumb, too young to be entirely fearless in the dark. Her nightgown was a pale swath in the gloom, and her blonde hair caught the moonlight coming through the library window.

A fairy sprite, and every Scotsman knew fairies were the embodiment of mischief.

"If you're not a thief, what are you?"

Hamish was *in trouble*. Great, awful trouble. "I'm the new footman. Name's Thomas. Just started today."

The girl skipped into the library, smiling hugely. "Why aren't you in livery?"

A bright child — confound the luck. "I'm too big. Had to have a new kit made up, and it's not back from the tailor's yet. That's a lovely dolly. What's her name?"

"Harold. She's contrary, like me. I'm Lady Geneva. Why is it dark in here, Thomas?"

"Saves coin to leave the candles unlit when the family's out. Is wee Harold up past her bedtime, milady?"

Delicate lashes lowered. "Will you peach on us?"

Before Hamish had been a soldier, before he'd been head of the family, a brewery owner, a duke, or *anything,* he'd been an older brother.

Thank the kind powers, he knew what this child wanted.

"I could be sacked for not doing my duty and reporting your wanderings," he said, crouching to address the girl at eye level. "I shouldn't like to be sacked. My family would be disappointed that I'd lost my new job already, but Harold ought not to wander the house by herself."

Lady Geneva climbed onto a sofa, standing barefoot on the cushions. "Do you have older sisters?"

"Younger sisters, milady. Your sisters are older?"

She heaved such a sigh as ought not to come from one so small. "They get to go out dancing, and my brothers go out too, but they play cards and sometimes they get sore heads. Do you know how to play cards?"

"I've played a game or two. Someday you'll go out dancing too, Lady Geneva. You'll have pretty dresses and adventures."

Dresses alone wouldn't do for this one, God help her parents.

She swung Harold in a wide arc, as if

sweeping around a dance floor, and nearly knocked a lamp over.

"I want to waltz at Almack's," she said. "So does Harold. I'm very pretty. Papa tells me so all the time. Mama used to be pretty, and my sisters have pretty dresses. They want to get *married.*"

"Does Harold want to get married?"

"No!" Geneva punctuated her reply with a few emphatic bounces on the sofa cushions. "She wants a pony of her own, so she doesn't have to wait until Fletcher takes her up on his horse, and walks up and down the mews with her. Fletcher is my spoiled brother. Frank is lazy, and Theodore is a disappointment. Martin is the heir. I'm to call him Lord Paltrow."

Hamish caught the child mid-bounce and affixed her to his hip. "Spoiled brothers are the very devil. I haven't any, and I'm grateful for that. I hope you aren't spoiled?"

"Not yet. Neither is Harold, but she's cross sometimes." Geneva fiddled with the lapel of Hamish's coat — a dark garment for a dark errand. "Fletcher forgets. He says he'll take me up on his horse, and then he rides off and forgets. He's busy."

Now there was an understatement. "Hadn't you better take Harold back up to bed before any of your brothers or sisters come

203

home and find you've left the nursery?"

"You smell good. Do you know how to tell time, Thomas?"

"One of few skills I can claim with confidence, your ladyship, and I know it's time you were abed."

A large, long-haired black cat came strutting into the library, tail held high. The animal sniffed here and there, in the manner of cats.

"That's Lucifer. He's Pamela's cat. Fletcher says Lucifer is her family."

"Her familiar, you mean. He's a grand fellow. Seems everybody worth knowing is awake past their bedtime in this house."

Geneva rested her head against Hamish's shoulder. "I like you, Thomas. Harold likes you too. Will you read me a story?"

Well, damn. "Is that why you came down to the library? To find a story?"

On the street before the house, a coach went clattering past, the sound isolated at an otherwise quiet hour.

"I can't read in the dark," Geneva said, "but I like to have a book with me, to put under my pillow. Harold likes knowing our stories are close by too."

The cat stropped itself against Hamish's stockings, and if the damned beast could have spoken, it would probably have asked to have a tray sent up from the kitchen, and a fire lit in the hearth.

The sound of shod hooves against cobbles slowed, then faded as the coach reached the corner.

"I must insist you return to the nursery, milady. The hour is quite late, and you need to set a good example for Harold. Perhaps tomorrow, she can go riding on Lucifer's back if he's in an obliging mood."

"Lucifer doesn't like that game. I got scratched the last time we tried to play, and Fletcher said it serves me right. My nurse tipples. I think that means she snores."

"Something like that," Hamish said, setting the child on her feet. "I must stay here at my post in the library until your family comes home, and you must warn Harold not to wander the house late at night. She might stub her toes, bruise her shins, or come tumbling down the stairs."

"Harold and I slide down the bannister."

"I'm sure you do."

The hoofbeats that had faded abruptly sounded more loudly, as if the coach that had just passed the house was now coming up the alley.

"That's our coach," Geneva said, running to the window. "I know the sound of our coach."

"Then up to bed with you and Harold this instant."

"My sisters will tell me all about who danced the waltz and who was a fox," she said, spinning around again. "Good night, Thomas! I hope your new livery comes soon."

She scampered off with one more pirouette, Harold held by one wrist. Harold's feet whipped past the hearth, and clipped the top of the stand that held all of the cast iron fireplace implements, sending the lot teetering toward the bricks.

At the same moment, Lucifer decided to strop himself against Hamish's wool stockings again, and as Lady Geneva and her doll disappeared through the library doorway, Hamish made a dodge for the hearth stand, only to overbalance as the cat tangled between his feet.

"Murdoch!" Megan couldn't shout across the garden, lest she wake a sister still sleeping in the house, but the dratted man did not respond to his title. "Hamish Mac-Hugh!"

That got his attention, just as he was about to swing into the saddle. "Miss Megan. Good morning. I was told you were not at home."

Megan looked both ways to ensure no inconvenient neighbors, sisters, or parents were strolling up the alley, then crossed the cobbles to steer His Grace through the garden gate.

"Please walk the duke's horse," Megan said to the groom. "We'll be but a few minutes."

The groom, who'd known Megan since she'd fallen off her first pony, didn't so much as blink before flipping the gelding's reins over its head and leading it away.

"Don't look as if your only means of escape has just been closed off," Megan said. "I told the staff I was indisposed because I'm dodging my papa. Why are you limping?"

"Had a wee mishap. Took a tumble onto my, er, hip, and some disobliging bricks broke my fall."

He was being stoic, or Scottish, or simply male. "You're probably bruised halfway to next Christmas, and I divine this is my fault. I am doomed to land you in awkward situations. Does this latest injury pain you very much?"

Nothing short of serious discomfort could have robbed His Grace of his military bearing. Megan closed the garden door behind him, and led him to the sunken fountain in the back corner. Hedges bordered the fountain — one side each given to honeysuckle, privet, lilacs, and trellised roses. The privet stood between the fountain and the house, which ensured a measure of privacy.

"Time will put me to rights," Murdoch said. "I have your letters, Miss Meggie, and that's what matters." He extracted a packet of folded papers from an inside pocket and held them out to her. "I did not count them or so much as glance at them, so you'd best make sure they're all here."

Had King George, the entire Eighty-Second Foot, and the biggest gossips in Mayfair been peering over the garden hedges, Megan could not have stopped herself from wrapping her arms around the duke.

"Thank you," she said against the wool of his riding jacket. "Thank you, thank you, thank you. Thank you isn't enough, it doesn't convey — Oh, drat, I hate to cry."

"So do I," Murdoch said, his arms enfolding her. "Sometimes, the tears must have their moment."

Megan wept for shame carried too long and too close to her heart, and for relief, and for sheer joy, to have found a champion who'd defeated Sir Fletcher so handily.

"I want to stand outside Sir Fletcher's

house and shout rude taunts," Megan said, accepting a plain linen square from the duke. "I never shout."

"And you're never rude," Murdoch replied, his hand glossing over Megan's hair, "but when you've broken a siege you thought would never end, only rude shouting will do — or worse."

For an odd moment, Megan had the sense that the embrace had become mutual, as if she'd lashed her arms around Murdoch in an excess of emotion and provoked some answering sentiment in him. She eased her grip, but did not let him go.

"Rosecroft claims the sieges were awful," she said, "and what followed was even worse. I can understand a little bit why. I have my letters, and now I want to steal something from Sir Fletcher to get back the rest of what he tried to take from me."

Murdoch stepped away. "Brutality in victory would only give you cause for regret, Miss Meggie. I'd rather endure the march to Corunna all over again, than live two minutes of the aftermath of Badajoz."

Megan could hardly reconcile that gently spoken admonition with the handsomely attired gentleman before her. Murdoch's eyes said he knew all about brutality in victory, and in captivity, and every place in between, and she hated that more than she hated Sir Fletcher Pilkington.

The duke's embrace had said other things — sweet, precious sentiments Megan wanted to savor as much as she wanted to enjoy besting Sir Fletcher.

"Please sit with me," she said, choosing the bench behind the highest hedge. "You must count the letters for me, because my hands are shaking."

Murdoch scooped up the packet from the bench where Megan had tossed it, and produced a flask from an inside pocket.

"A wee dram to steady your nerves."

The flask was warm from his body heat, and embossed with a rampant unicorn wreathed in thistles.

Megan unscrewed the cap and passed the open container under her nose. "This is whisky." Soldiers drank whisky.

"Colin owns a fine distillery. Don't stop to admire the flavor or get acquainted. Just down the hatch."

"*Slàinte!*" Megan muttered, tipping the flask up. She hadn't tried whisky since she and Charlotte had got hold of Papa's hunting flask ten years ago. After one sip, Charlotte had pronounced all men mad. Megan had been coughing too hard to speak.

"*Do dheagh shlàinte,*" Murdoch rejoined.

Your good health.

Megan took the tiniest sip, and braced herself for fire and mayhem but got only . . . warmth. Lovely, delicious, bracing warmth. A kiss from within, a hint of brilliant sunshine and scouring sea breezes with the barest traces of heather and spice beneath.

"Lovely," she said, patting the place beside her. "Read me the dates of the letters and I'll keep a count."

Murdoch helped himself to a dram, put the flask away, then lowered himself gingerly to the bench.

"You took more than a tumble, Your Grace. First we'll count the letters, then you'll tell me exactly what happened."

He read over a series of dates, thirty-one in all, and as the total climbed closer to the number that had haunted Megan since Sir Fletcher had first threatened her, the day shifted from pretty, to promising, to glorious.

"They're all there," she said. "Every one, present and accounted for. You have done the impossible, and made short work of it. Anything you could possibly ask of me is yours to command, Murdoch."

Though what had she, a shortsighted, retiring, red-haired spinster-in-training, to offer a titled, wealthy, seasoned soldier?

He patted her knee and passed her the letters, which Megan set aside rather than hold in her hand one moment longer than necessary.

"I'm off to Scotland tomorrow," he said. "I'd be most obliged if you'd keep an eye on Ronnie and Eddie in my absence. They are new to fancy society and might not see the ambushes they're riding into. They'll need friends, and you know what you're about when it comes to the London season."

More rude words popped into Megan's head, for she did not want her friend and champion leaving for the north now, when she was finally free to be his friend too.

"You ask nothing for yourself," she said. "Your sisters did not retrieve these awful letters, you did. Have you no wishes or wants of your own that I might aid before you travel on?"

He shifted, suggesting a hard bench was an uncomfortable perch — or that he was preparing to prevaricate.

"I have wishes and wants," he replied, "and my family's happiness figures prominently among them. You understand about wanting family to be safe and happy, else those letters would not have been a problem, Miss Meggie."

True. "I want you to be safe and happy

too." And she did *not* want him to be hundreds of miles away in Scotland. "Was it difficult to retrieve the letters?"

Another shift. "I made the acquaintance of the youngest Pilkington, a wee lass by the name of Geneva. In about ten years, she'll set the town on its ear, but she was hospitable enough to a bumbling footman who hadn't any livery yet. Unfortunately, I also made the acquaintance of Lady Pamela's cat, who did his best to knock over the hearth set and myself as well."

"You had an adventure," Megan said, though it sounded as if His Grace's adventure had also been a perilously close call.

He rose stiffly. "All's well. You have your letters, and I can be on my way."

Megan had no choice but to see him to his horse. "Will you fetch your sisters home at the end of the season?"

"Colin can see them home, assuming they don't find English gentlemen to take to husband. The novelty of this excursion will soon pale for them both, I'm guessing, and they'll be glad to get back to Scotland."

"You are homesick." What could Megan offer to compete with home? Mama still missed Wales decades after marrying Papa, and despite claiming that where her family was would always be her home.

"Homesick? That, I am. Have been for half my life," Murdoch said. "I would like you to promise me something, Miss Meggie."

"Of course." Maybe he'd ask her to write to him, and of all gentlemen, Hamish MacHugh, Duke of Murdoch, was the one to whom Megan would feel safe putting any sentiment on paper.

"You must not be writing to any gentlemen in the future," he said as they approached the high wall at the back of the garden. "Mind your reputation closely, because once Sir Fletcher discovers the letters are missing, he'll not accept defeat easily. He'll waylay you if he can, he'll spread rumors without any basis in fact, he'll try to compromise one of your sisters. Be more careful than ever, try to think of the worst he could do, and then what's even worse than that."

"You want me to be a soldier, to approach this season as a military campaign. I can warn my sisters, and I'll be careful."

Megan would also be homesick, for this man, for his company, for his kisses.

Beyond the wall, the steady clip-clop of hooves sounded in the alley, nearer and nearer.

"Then good-bye, Miss Meggie, and God

keep you." He smoothed his hand slowly over her hair, a tender caress that wasn't nearly as presuming as Megan would have preferred.

"You won't allow me to give you even the smallest boon?" she pressed. "I feel as if I ought to tie a ribbon to your sleeve at least. You've been a friend, an ally, and a confidant. I will be in your debt always, and you're simply riding off, never to be seen again, when but for you, I might never —"

He cupped her cheek against the warmth of his palm. "You'll have me in tears, Miss Meggie. Good-bye."

He drew her closer and touched his lips to hers.

Hamish stole a kiss, of parting, of rejoicing, of thanks. Megan was safe now, and he'd send along a note to one of her cousins — Rosecroft or Keswick — warning them of the threat Pilkington might pose. Hamish would add Colin to her honor guard; Megan would alert her sisters, and soon, she'd be beyond Sir Fletcher's schemes.

Sir Fletcher had the combination of characteristics that made for competent line officers. He was smart and lazy. What he couldn't delegate, he'd dodge, and when it became clear that further troubling Megan

Windham was more risk than reward, he'd find other quarry to pursue.

Megan was safe. Hamish's heart, however, was not whole. He'd leave a piece of it in her keeping, for what woman ever — for any reason — had thrown herself into his arms, and wept on his shoulder, as if he alone held her trust?

So his kiss bore an element of regret, that he'd not met Megan before war had stolen his innocence, and left him incapable of maneuvers among the very people Megan called family.

That regret somehow shifted closer to passion, to a yearning for what could not be. He gathered Megan in his arms, as if he'd imprint the feel of her on his memory, and to hell with gentlemanly everything. For one moment, for the duration of one kiss, Hamish could admit that he craved this woman every way a man longed for his heart mate.

When she should have stepped back, Megan wrapped herself close to Hamish in a manner that had nothing of parting and everything of welcome about it. She got him by the hair, tucked a leg between his knees, and — God have mercy upon a poor soldier — where was Hamish's sporran when disaster threatened?

"Meggie, you mustn't —"

"Don't go," she whispered against his mouth. "Please don't ride away, as if —"

As if her tongue weren't besieging the stout walls of Hamish's best intentions. As if her breasts weren't softly crushing the breath from Hamish's common sense and self-restraint. As if every particle of him wasn't clamoring to toss her into his saddle, and reave her from beneath the noses of —

She slid a hand around his hip, and gave Hamish a gentle squeeze on a part of him that had recently acquired a large purple bruise.

The pain was a welcome recall to common sense. Hamish ended the kiss, but remained in a loose embrace with the woman who'd haunt him clear back to the Highlands.

"Meggie, I'll never fit in here. I'm followed by gossip and rumor everywhere I go. I nearly struck Keswick in public for no reason, and that's not the worst of it. You don't truly know me, which is for the best. Burn the letters, and think of me fondly, but I must go."

She pressed her forehead to the middle of his chest. "I *know* you. I know the parts of you that matter, and I'll never forget you. I'll look after Edana and Rhona, and I'll look after Colin, but it will be a long, long time before I stop looking for you to enter the ballrooms with them or come calling at their side."

A mutual haunting, then. Hamish pressed his mouth to hers one more time when he should have made the parting real. He was on the verge of that very display of heroism when the garden gate swung open, and the Duke of Moreland stood before them, one hand braced on the gate, his hat in the other.

A moment of silence passed, but neither Megan nor Hamish stepped back, for they were wedged beneath the arch of the doorway in the garden wall.

"If it isn't Murdoch and my own dear Megan," Moreland said. "Megan, perhaps you'd be good enough to tell your parents I've come to call? Murdoch, don't look so hopeful. You aren't going anywhere until I've had a private word with you."

CHAPTER TEN

The Code Duello was cited in officers' messes, gentlemen's clubs, bordellos, and every masculine venue in between. Wellington had taken part in duels, and Percival Windham, duke, former cavalry officer, and father to five sons, had seen more than his share of the field of honor.

He'd also seen every one of his children happily wed, and knew that what looked like dishonorable behavior to a doting uncle might be a harbinger of true love — or disaster.

Murdoch was a duke, however, and the trouble with dukes was that they required respectful, delicate, but firm handling — Percival's own duchess had assured him of this — and one crossed a duke at considerable peril.

Especially a duke in love.

"Has a custom sprung up in Scotland," Percival began, "of accosting young ladies in their own gardens and making spectacles of them with passionate overtures? Is this an accepted practice where you come from, Murdoch, when no understanding has been established with the young lady or her family?"

Murdoch assumed the posture of an officer at attention, his gaze unnervingly flat. "I do apologize, Your Grace. My behavior was inappropriate and ungentlemanly. I meant the young lady no disrespect, nor will I ever."

As stirring declarations went, that would do nicely, but what had Murdoch truly been about?

Moreover, what would Percival's duchess make of those gruff admissions? They were the right admissions — heartfelt apology, acceptance of all responsibility, assurance of future good conduct — and offered with convincing probity, but the nuances, like the Scot's gaze, bore an impenetrable quality.

Percival assayed his best ducal glower. "I should call you out, Murdoch." Esther would never tolerate that nonsense.

"Again, I apologize, Your Grace, to you as head of Miss Megan's family, and I will happily apologize to Miss Megan and her parents, as well. I have no excuse and I've

220

behaved wrongly."

Megs was quiet, sweet, unassuming, and exactly the type of young lady the head of the family most fretted about. Esther had been quiet and unassuming, as had Percival's daughters — when they were hatching up schemes of a sort to turn a duke's hair gray.

"Do you know, Murdoch, just this morning, my duchess charged me with getting you to the next court levee, where I'm to present you for a royal introduction. When I've dealt with that exercise in tedium, I'm to procure a warrant of precedence for you that will see your sisters officially established as ladies and your brother as a lord."

A nose some might call impressive wrinkled. "I'm a debutante duke now?"

"You might well be a dead duke for this morning's work. I am quite proficient with both pistols and swords."

"Again, Your Grace, I tender a sincere apology. I will put my sentiments in writing if need be. Moreover I can assure you that by this time tomorrow, I'll be bound for Scotland, never to trouble you again."

The Code Duello required that if an apology was offered in good faith, and no blow had been struck, then bloodshed ought not to follow. Murdoch apparently knew the rules and was relying on them to avoid a violent confrontation.

Was this gallantry or cowardice? Esther would have a useful opinion on that question.

"I'll not call you out," Percival conceded. "Somebody should, though, and Megan's cousins and papa have not the counsel of my duchess to stay their hands in rash moments."

Murdoch — wisely — said nothing. He had sisters, and sisters had a way of educating a fellow in the art of discretion. As did children, and yet, Percival's hearing was excellent.

Don't go . . . please don't ride away as if . . . Megan, pleading with this oversized, taciturn, rough-hewn Scot.

And the Scot's response: *"Meggie, I'll never fit in here . . ."* And something about burning letters. All very dramatic, and then . . . two young people locked in a desperate embrace where they might have been chanced upon by any passing duke.

Or gossip.

"Megan has attached the interest of Sir Fletcher Pilkington," Percival said. "I've been summoned here to discuss that situation with Lord Anthony before my brother departs for Wales. Sir Fletcher is from a fine family, served his king loyally, and has been respectful of Megan in every regard."

More silence, and Murdoch widened his stance, as if bracing for the bite of the lash.

"My duchess has advised caution where Sir Fletcher is concerned." Esther had taken the poor fellow into positive dislike, accusing him of bowing too low, never passing a mirror without glancing at his own reflection, chasing after heiresses, and other dreadful transgressions.

"Caution is always warranted where suitors are concerned," Murdoch said — growled, more like.

"I can still call you out, Murdoch."

Those blue eyes went flat again. Not merely chilly or hostile, but devoid of any human sentiment. Percival had seen eyes like that in the aftermath of battle, usually on the faces of those taken prisoner.

"Call me out if you must, Moreland. I would decline to meet you."

Decline to meet? "Are you impugning my skill now, young man? Claiming I'm too enfeebled to hold a weapon?"

"Of course not, Your Grace. But Meggie — Miss Megan, rather — would be the subject of our disagreement, would she not? No matter how carefully we chose seconds, her reputation would be at risk of harm, and that I cannot allow."

Oh-ho. When a fellow went from kissing to cannot-allowing where a young lady was concerned, all in the space of five minutes, a prudent duke took notice.

"My duchess would scold us both into next week at the very mention of the field of honor," Percival said. "You do not want to chance upon Her Grace in a scolding mood, Murdoch."

And yet, a challenge was in order because Murdoch was right: Suitors of any stripe deserved close scrutiny, and the duchess's odd notions should never be lightly dismissed.

Percival paced across the alley, weighing strategy, letting the prisoner anticipate a dire fate.

Damned interesting time for Gladys to haul Tony off to the wilds of Wales. "I have every confidence that Sir Fletcher's suit will meet with Lord Anthony's eventual favor, but Sir Fletcher likely enjoys that same confidence."

Murdoch refused to rise to that bait.

"You, however," Percival went on, "have graduated to the kiss-stealing stage. Without excusing your behavior in the slightest, I must admit your attentions were not forced upon my niece."

224

If anything, Murdoch's expression cooled further, from a man without hope, to a man without a heart.

"Nor will my attentions *ever* be forced on any young lady, lest Your Grace mistake that matter." Such a mistake regarding Murdoch's gentlemanly honor would be fatal, based on the young man's tone, Code Duello be damned.

Abruptly, Percival knew what opinion his duchess would pronounce on the entire situation. Esther approved heartily of protective fellows, and she approved of fierce young women too.

"Just so," Percival said, again pacing the width of the alley. "I also hold to the quaint notion that young ladies ought to have final say regarding which fellow they wed, provided the fellow has been deemed worthy of the lady's interest. I'm according you that honor, Murdoch. Within the bounds of discretion, and assuming my brother agrees with me, you are free to pay your proper addresses to Megan, though you will doubtless have competition from Sir Fletcher."

Murdoch's brows came down. He opened his mouth, but no words emerged.

Esther would be delighted.

"I don't approve of *you*," Percival said, which was not entirely accurate. "I merely think Sir Fletcher will esteem more highly a prize he must work to win. If Megan decides she'd prefer an unpolished Scot who steals kisses — well, that Scot is a duke, he's reputed to be more than solvent, and Megan was engaged in a bit of amatory larceny too. Best of luck, in other words, because you'll need it."

"I was supposed to leave for Scotland tomorrow, Your Grace. I'm aware of the honor you do me, but I must in all candor —"

"You're reciting the wrong speech, Murdoch. I'm not proposing marriage to you. I'm using you to goad Sir Fletcher into courting Megan the way she deserves to be courted. You will join me for next Tuesday's levee, and we'll take my town coach. I'll send my solicitors around to have a chat with you regarding the warrant of precedence, and my tailors will be by this afternoon to ensure you have adequate attire for the occasion."

The poor fellow looked bewildered, which was a vast improvement over his earlier, bleak expressions.

"But sir, traveling north has become —"

"One doesn't interrupt a duke, Murdoch, *or* a duchess. Don't forget that." Unless one was family to same, in which case interruptions came from every direction. "I have two further points in need of elucidation."

"Yes, Your Grace."

"I heard you mention letters to Megan. I'll not have heated correspondence between you and my niece. Firstly, reading is difficult for Megan because of her eyesight, so your passionate effusions are likely wasted on the page. Secondly, any man who indulges in literary fancies toward his lady risks his sentiments becoming public, and if that happens, I won't have to call you out. My sons and sons-by-marriage will line up for the privilege."

Well, no, they wouldn't — the entire lot of them were married to very fierce women — but the threat sounded impressive.

"Understood, sir. Was there anything more?"

Megan's Scot was looking so serious, so willing to be chastised. The longer Percival considered the situation, the more he approved of his decision. He patted the younger man on the shoulder.

"Don't fret too much about the levee. Five minutes of chatting about the Highland scenery or discussing the fox pelt dangling from your reticule, and —"

"*Sporran,* Your Grace, and that's a badger pelt."

"— and I'll have you out of there. One other thing."

Megan's Scot had interrupted a duke. Moreland liked the man for that, because national dress with the Scots had become a matter of pride. Avoiding harm to a lady's reputation was gentlemanly prudence, but avoiding all confrontation was spineless cowering, which would not do.

"My apologies for the interruption," Murdoch said, "but Your Grace was goading me."

"So I was. Now I'm chastising you. Not for sharing a stolen kiss with a willing and winsome young lady — once upon a long ago time, I did likewise a time or two." Or two hundred. "This is for getting *caught* stealing that kiss and putting Megan's reputation at risk."

Moreland clipped Murdoch on the jaw, a good, stout blow such as would appease a young man's guilt and a mature duke's pride.

"Tell the groom to put up your horse, and I'll introduce you to my brother," Percival said. "And again, best of luck." In all likelihood, Sir Fletcher was the one who'd need some luck.

For as Percival let himself into the back garden, the Scot remained behind, smiling

228

such a smile as would make a certain duchess quite pleased with her duke.

"Megs, do you fancy this Scottish fellow?" Papa asked, pacing across the morning room.

Uncle Percy had been all congenial good cheer when he'd come upon Megan kissing Murdoch in the garden, but Uncle Percy was at his most civilized when he was plotting the downfall of some encroaching member of Parliament or unmannerly viscount.

"I like Murdoch exceedingly, Papa."

His lordship was pretending to peer out the window, though his objective was doubtless to give Megan a measure of privacy.

"Murdoch hasn't . . ." Papa clasped his hands behind his back. "That is to say, he's not a refined fellow, and I'd take a very dim view of any presumption upon the good nature or the person . . . Megs, do you *truly* like him, or are you trying to spare a clueless swain a sound thrashing at the hands of your cousins?"

What on earth had Uncle Percy said to Papa? "Both?"

Papa left off staring at a garden he'd seen in bloom every morning for weeks. "Your Uncle Percy has taken it into his head I

should allow Murdoch to pay you his addresses, though not because Murdoch is my
ideal son-in-law."

Pay you his addresses.

Megan had come into the morning room
expecting to be chastised for forward behavior. In the alternative, she was braced for a
command to pack her things, because she
was being sent to the rural family seat in
disgrace, or worse, she was to accompany
Mama and Papa on one of their annual
honeymoons.

While Hamish rode north to his much-
missed home in the Highlands.

In all the English language, the four words
Megan would have least expected her father
to put together in the same sentence with
"Murdoch" were "pay you his addresses."

Her insides rearranged themselves such
that her heart was wedged more closely
against her ribs.

"Murdoch's addresses would be welcome," Megan said, her voice shaking only
a little. "Very welcome, in fact." The most
welcome addresses in the entire history of
addresses the world over.

Papa was not merely distinguished, he was
handsome. His features bore the patrician
stamp of Saxon nobility — blond hair gone
gold, blue eyes, bold nose, firm chin — but

he also had a quickness, a perceptivity and subtlety that he usually covered with charm. He was a ducal spare, no threat to anybody.

Megan knew better. Papa was shrewd and kind, both, and Megan loved him dearly. She did not, however, entirely trust him.

"Murdoch's addresses would be *very welcome,*" Papa said, moving away from the window to inspect a drawing Charlotte had done of Mama several years earlier. Mama smiled a naughty smile, which Charlotte had caught to the life. "Megs, your mother and I love you very much. Is there any reason you might want us to put off this trip to Wales?"

Any reason . . . ? "To plan a wedding, you mean?"

Papa remained by the portrait. Megan couldn't make out his features that clearly, nor Mama's smile, but she knew from her father's posture that his casual tone belied a certain tension.

"It's no secret your Mama and I were a love match. I happen to approve of affection between spouses, within reason. Marriage is hard enough without trying to make a go of it with a complete stranger. I also know you're your mother's daughter, and a Windham. Either legacy would tempt you to a certain impetuosity where matters of the heart are concerned, but both together, well, a father worries."

A father also — for the first time in Megan's memory — blushed.

"Murdoch is a *gentleman,* Papa." Unlike Sir Fletcher.

Who no longer had possession of Megan's letters.

"They can be the worst transgressors, which is why Murdoch has been set loose among the pigeons, so to speak. Sir Fletcher paid a call on me yesterday, also intent on asking permission to pay you his addresses."

Megan fluffed her skirts. "Sir Fletcher Pilkington?" *The worst rotter in all of Mayfair?*

"Of course, Pilkington. Megs, he comes from good family, and Percy seems to think Sir Fletcher might mature into a worthy article, as husbands go. I thought you fancied him."

On the walkway beyond the window, Murdoch escorted Mama past the sundial. As chance would have it, they occupied the exact distance necessary for Megan to see their expressions. Mama was all earnest discussion — Mama was usually earnest — and Murdoch was the attentive young gentleman at her side.

He was such an attractive man. Not handsome in the pretty, golden sense, but stalwart, honest, durable. Thirty years from now, his looks would have changed little, and he'd be just as well mannered, just as —

"Megs?"

"Yes, Papa?"

"What about Sir Fletcher?"

Sir Fletcher no longer had Megan's letters, that was *what about* Sir Fletcher. "I would not be marrying his good family, Papa, I'd be marrying him, and he's done nothing to earn my particular esteem in all the time I've known him." Not one damned thing. Turn her head, yes. Manipulate her into granting liberties, certainly. Make a complete fool of her — beyond doubt.

But Megan's esteem had been earned by the Scotsman who might still be planning to leave for his homeland in the next twenty-four hours.

"You hardly know this Murdoch fellow," Papa said. "He's only recently come into his title, and hails from so very far away. Percival has spoken on Murdoch's behalf, but I'll not discourage Sir Fletcher just yet. Consider your options while your mama and I are in Wales, but Megs?"

"Yes, Papa?"

"Be careful. Percival endorsed Murdoch's suit, but my brother has a taste for matchmaking that I don't share. I rather like hav-

233

ing my ladies about me, where I know they are safe and well loved. If you decamped with your Highland laddie, I would miss you awfully all the rest of my days."

Megan hadn't seen that ambush coming, a genuine expression of paternal sentiment right in the middle of lectures and awkward warnings.

"Papa, I haven't gone anywhere, and you are the one leaving for Wales."

"Wales makes your mama happy, and that makes me happy. You are all a-quiver to accost your Scot in the garden again, but Megs, no more kisses where any visitor, gardener, or parent peering out an upper window might see you. Moreland caught you too — he fancies himself quite the intelligence officer, does Percival — so I had to act surprised. A bit of discretion will go a long way toward sparing me my brother's preening in future."

Gracious, Megan loved her Papa terribly.

"Yes, Papa. I do understand." Megan understood that Murdoch had been given permission to *pay her his addresses,* which was even better than having her letters restored to her — provided Murdoch had given up his fixation on returning to Scotland.

Papa kissed her forehead and Megan offered him a curtsy. As soon as she reached the privacy of the corridor, she picked up her skirts and ran full tilt for the garden.

The only experience Hamish could bring to bear on the morning's developments was the aftermath of a blow to the head. A fellow's hearing was sometimes affected, or his balance, but more than that, reality took on a distant, storied quality. Everything happened at a mental remove, as if instead of Hamish himself wandering around the garden on the arm of Megan's mother, some other dazed fellow enjoyed that honor and made small talk about . . .

Robert Tannahill, a contemporary of Mr. Burns who'd also died young and left a beautiful legacy.

"But the songs that aren't written down are my favorites," Lady Anthony was saying. "You should ask Megan to sing some for you. She's quite talented, and here's our Megs now."

Our Megs.

Megan had come out onto the back terrace. She stood at the top of the steps, no glasses, no gloves, just a swatch of lovely blue muslin, a white shawl, and glorious red hair in a simple twist. At this distance, she'd have difficulty seeing him clearly so Hamish waved. The movement apparently caught her attention for she waved back. Her smile beamed across the roses, hedges, and dewy grass, so that all of Hamish's awareness was focused on her, the most perfect blossom in the garden.

In a few awkward moments with her father and her uncle, Hamish had been granted permission to offer the lady his heart. He wanted to sprint across the grass, scoop her up, and whirl her around in his arms like a prize secured.

He also wanted to haul her by the hand back to the secluded fountain, and there inspect her entire inventory of kisses, before inventing a few more with her nobody had yet thought of in all the history of kissing.

And he wanted to weep, because for all Megan's family had made it possible for him to court her, he was still bound for Scotland.

"Your smile when you behold my daughter is . . ." Lady Anthony bent to sniff at a precocious sprig of honeysuckle. "You put me in mind of my husband when we were courting. We feared our union would not meet with the approval of our parents, and we were making plans . . . Well, that's a tale for another time. You have exactly thirty minutes, Murdoch, before Megan will be summoned to take tea with her Papa and me. Use your thirty minutes wisely."

"Yes, your ladyship, and safe journey, ma'am."

Lady Anthony kissed Hamish's cheek — the Windhams were an affectionate family, when they weren't violent — and glided away. She said something to Megan, squeezed her daughter's hand, and disappeared into the house on an elegant rustle of green velvet.

Megan lifted her skirts, as if she'd descend the steps in imitation of her mother's dignity, but then she sprinted across the garden and smacked into Hamish's waiting embrace.

They were visible from the house, so Hamish merely held her, and treasured the lovely, luscious feel of her in his arms. Her crown fit beneath his chin, her breasts —

He stepped back. "Megan Windham, I owe you an apology. I ought not to have been kissing you where anybody could chance upon us. I ought not to have —"

She kissed his cheek. "I ought not to have taken such a risk either, but I'd love to kiss you all over again. Will you court me, Hamish MacHugh, or will you flee to Scotland?"

He wished she were wearing the blue

spectacles, or maybe that he could wear them. Anything to obscure the hope in her eyes, and the trust.

"Meggie, nothing has changed. I'm not the man for you. I'd take you away from everything you know and care for, to a place where winter can start in September and go on until May. My siblings do nothing but bicker. You'd grow bored —"

She wound her arm around his. "My siblings bicker and I've been bored for years. What aren't you telling me? The truth, Hamish, for I would very much like you to court me."

The truth — the most dangerous weapon ever turned on a man's good intentions. "We will talk, and you will listen, and then you'll bid me farewell."

Silence was another weapon an intelligent woman wielded with great skill, and Megan was a very intelligent woman. She wandered with him to the benches around the sundial, and took a seat, pulling him down beside her. His hip was throbbing, but the bench was warm — some consolation, that.

"Why would you want a man like me for a husband, Meggie? I'm not . . . I'm not polished. I'm not English. I don't intend to be very good at this duke-ing business, and I am fond of a good Highland whisky."

"My mother is not English, Sir Fletcher is very polished, and as for the duke-ing, you've done a fine job of being a gentleman, so what does the duke part matter? I rather enjoyed sampling your whisky myself."

Logic should be forbidden to marriageable women. "Meggie, you think because I pilfered a few letters from a desk drawer that I'm some sort of knight errant. I'm nothing like a knight errant."

"You learned to waltz so you wouldn't embarrass your sisters. That's the behavior of a gallant fellow, Murdoch."

"I like to dance — most Scots do — and waltzing isn't complicated."

She raised her face to the sun, which would have set Ronnie and Eddie running for their bonnets and parasols — or ordering Hamish to fetch them.

"Am I so awful, Hamish? I thought you liked me."

"You are lovely." Her eyes closed, her chin tilted up toward the sun's warmth, her freckles on view for any man within kissing distance to see . . . Hamish's chest ached, and something like rage stirred at the thought of leaving her alone on that bench in . . . about twenty-three minutes, according to the sundial.

"What are you trying to protect me from?" Megan asked, opening her eyes and peering at him with the merciless sagacity of a cat. "That's the only reason I can think of for you to abandon me now. You believe whatever retaliation Sir Fletcher will seek, whatever risks I'm facing now, your hand in marriage somehow trumps those fates for awfulness. You owe me an explanation, Hamish. Friends are honest with each other."

Friends. Friends did not skewer each other with impossible demands for truth.

An inconvenient voice in Hamish's head insisted friends didn't ride off to Scotland without an explanation either.

"I'm trying to protect you from me, Meggie," Hamish said. "Ask your soldier cousins, and they'll tell you I have a reputation for violence and cowardice, both. I dodge the battles I ought to wage, and yet, once engaged, I'm a savage. I kill for pleasure according to some, and when I should have died fighting, I surrendered myself into enemy hands instead. I'm no kind of soldier, and they're right. I hated the whole business, and you'll hate being my duchess too."

My duchess. The words alone brought him delight when he associated them with her.

She took his hand, which in a courting

situation was permitted.

"I'm glad you didn't die fighting. Your siblings are glad you didn't die fighting, as are all those people up in Perthshire who depend on you. Who are these *blind idiots* that think death is such a wonderful accomplishment? Death is within anybody's grasp. The greater challenge is to live, and to love despite our errors and failings. Be glad you didn't die, Hamish MacHugh. Maybe you had some bad moments, or you harbor regrets — I surely do. But be very glad you didn't die."

Between one quiet moment and the next, a queer feeling suffused Hamish, as if without Megan's hand to hold, he might have lifted into the air and dissolved into the sunshine. As if Megan's words had lit some taper inside him that longed to join with the greater warmth of the sun's light.

I'm glad you didn't die fighting.

"You are a woman of original and passionate sentiments."

She said nothing, but kept a fierce hold of his hand. The words errant and error had the same root, both meaning to wander. Hamish's heart had been wandering since he'd bought his commission, and for the first time, he had a sense of homecoming. Not coming back to familiar territory, but

241

coming home.

He sat beside her for eleven more minutes, his backside throbbing, wonder suffusing his every breath. The sense of benediction would not leave him, the sense of an insight granted when most needed, the sense that Megan would not fail him.

I'm glad you didn't die fighting.

"My superior officers called me an animal," he told her. "They said the French should have put me down like a rabid dog."

She rested her head on his shoulder. "Your fellow officers said this?"

"I've killed with my bare hands, Meggie." He'd never said those words to another, he should not have said them now. They hurt in a whole new way, leaving sorrow and bewilderment where disgrace had been. "In the heat of battle, true, but half the regiments on both sides saw me do it, and I think the British were more horrified than the French." Hamish forced more words out, lest Megan think society's view of him was in error.

"We were to be gentlemanly about our warfare, if you can believe that. Wellington insisted. No plundering the countryside, no firing on the French pickets, and they didn't fire on us. Battles were orderly in their way — artillery, cavalry, and infantry, in that sequence. You might shoot a man, even an unarmed man, take him down with a weapon, but you didn't . . . you didn't put your hands around his neck, and end his life in an instant when he's thrown his weapon aside."

Megan said nothing, so Hamish soldiered on. "I did exactly that. He had no gun, not even his bayonet to defend himself, but he wouldna get out of my way. I put my hands on him, and then he was dead."

Now, Megan would get up, shake out her skirts, and wish Hamish a safe journey to Scotland. She'd look at him with horror, or worse — unbearably worse — pity. Hamish would spend his entire journey trying to out-gallop the temptation to drink himself to death.

Megan gave him more of her weight, as if exhaustion afflicted her, even so early in the day.

"Does one go to war hoping a fellow officer is proficient at the minuet?" she asked in the same tones she might have inquired about tuning the bagpipes. "Would waltzing have defeated the Corsican? Fine manners? An excellent tenor aria? Skill at whist, for God's sake? Your fellow officers were likely afraid of you and of their own demises. Their cowardice is not your problem. The

243

war is over, Hamish."

That queer feeling washed over Hamish again. Part shiver, part warmth, part bewilderment. Wellington had preferred that his officers know how to waltz. On that bit of military lore, Hamish's resolve to leave the lady to enjoy the rest of her London season without him caught, snagged, stumbled, and . . . collapsed.

Waltzing had *not* vanquished Napoleon. Many said the entire victory at Waterloo had turned on one Scottish officer's willingness to plunge headlong through French fire to save the British forces holding a strategic chateau.

The war is over, Hamish. Nobody had said that to him either.

"I hated the battles," Hamish murmured, kissing Megan's fingers. "Hated the sieges, the false bravery, the stink of fear, the smell of blood. I hated the noise and the violence. I hated every minute of it."

But he loved her. Hamish loved that Megan Windham, who was brave in ways his fellow officers would have failed to see, could hear this confession.

"Any sane person should hate war," Megan said.

Hamish had hated war with a passion,

244

though no soldier admitted that to his fellows.

"Meggie, if I court you, it will be in complete earnest. Not for show, not for a lark. I will offer you my wealth, my title, my family." And because she inspired courage in him, "I'll offer you my heart — yours, and yours alone, forevermore. If that's what you want?"

She sighed a soft, happy sigh and smoothed a hand over his thigh. "I give you permission to pay me your addresses, Hamish, and I will accept nothing less than a courtship in complete earnest."

He'd never court another. Megan had heard the worst that would be said about him, and was still right there at his side.

"The war is over, Meggie Windham. You're absolutely right about that. Let the courtship begin."

CHAPTER ELEVEN

"You're very decorous about this courtship business," Anwen observed. "If I had that much Scottish duke to cast longing glances at, I'd be bribing my sisters to lose sight of me while picnicking at Richmond Park, or to suddenly need a book from the library when my suitor came to call."

Longing glances had been the sum of Megan's amorous undertakings where Hamish MacHugh was concerned. Ever since he'd been caught kissing her in the garden, he'd been maddeningly proper, never dancing with her more than once an evening, never holding her an inch closer than propriety allowed.

At Richmond, his brother Colin had been more flirtatious than he had.

"I'm torn," Megan said, pushing the cover back from the piano keys. "Part of me wants to gobble him whole, Anwen. Another part of me wants to stand absolutely still and marvel that not only do I have a suitor, but I have one I admire greatly." One who treated her with every evidence of esteem.

Megan would rather a bit more passion and less esteem, though.

Anwen came down beside her on the piano bench. "You truly fancy him?"

Truly, passionately, endlessly — and intimately. "You don't like Murdoch?"

"He's impressive," Anwen said. "Not pretty, not fancy, not clever, not . . . ornamental. I approve of him all the more for being in want of charm, sharing that characteristic myself. He'll do for you, but I wish he didn't live so far away."

What mattered charm?

Hamish was clever enough to steal back letters undetected, but more than that, he was honest. *I've killed with my bare hands, Meggie.* This battlefield violence appalled the man who'd committed it, while the charming Sir Fletcher had been proud of a scheme that reduced Megan to marital chattel.

"London is hard for Hamish," Megan said. "Did you notice that when we went out to Richmond, his coachman avoided taking us past Horse Guards? Hamish doesn't belong to the clubs where former officers congregate, and he'll never attend

247

one of Wellington's dinners. I can't fathom exactly how or why, but I suspect part of Hamish MacHugh is still fighting the French."

Or his own officers, may a blight afflict the hypocritical lot of them.

"St. Just took years to come home," Anwen said. "I'll visit you in Scotland. That's a warning. You will marry Murdoch, won't you? You're not just using him to bring Sir Fletcher up to scratch?"

"Sir Fletcher is not what he appears to be, Anwen. Keep your distance from him."

Anwen played a right-hand C major scale, the one that used only the white keys. That seeming simplicity actually made it one of the harder scales in Megan's opinion, the fingers having no black keys to create a tactile frame of reference.

"This instrument needs tuning," Anwen said.

"It always needs tuning when Beth gets in a Beethoven mood. The season drags on forever when a woman approaches thirty."

A soft tap sounded on the music room door.

"Enter," Anwen called.

The season could drag on forever when a woman approached twenty-six too.

Hamish followed the butler into the room,

Lord Colin at his side. Anwen was off the bench and dipping curtsies mid-scale, though Megan would have gone musically mad rather than finish on any note other than C.

"Just the gentleman we were discussing," Anwen said, twining her arm with Colin's. "I've been meaning to ask your lordship's opinion regarding a certain volume of French poetry. Won't you accompany me to the library? I have difficulty reaching the highest shelves."

Anwen would cheerfully scamper up any ladder or climb the very doorjamb to get to a book of her choosing. She led Colin from the room, blathering about French and Latin and Megan hardly knew what, for Anwen — dearest of sisters — had left Megan alone with her intended.

Who did not look pleased to find himself alone with her.

"Lock the door, Your Grace," Megan said.

Hamish crossed his arms. "Meggie Windham, what are you about?"

Megan veered around him, rather like dodging behind an oak, and locked the door. "What are *you* about, Hamish? You've treated me like somebody's wallflower auntie this week. I can understand a man needing to polish his waltzing, but you are

249

wickedly skilled with kisses. Your embraces are fierce and tender, your very scent beguiles my knees into fluttering. If reducing me to begging for your favors is a foretaste of your husbandly stratagems, then we are about to have a very heated discussion."

His brows twitched down. "Beguiling, you say? My *scent* beguiles your knees?"

Megan got hold of the leather belt holding his sporran about his waist and tugged. "Spare me your maidenly vapors, sir. You carry the scent of heather and open skies, fresh sea breezes, and warm peat smoke. No gentleman has ever smelled as enticing as you do. I dream of your scent and wake up with my pillow between my knees."

"Blessed St. Andrew, Meggie. You mustn't tell me such things."

Hamish didn't smile often, but he was smiling now. A great beaming wonder of a smile — aimed at his boots.

Megan pushed him onto the settee, and he took a seat. Obliging of him, when he'd likely stood against entire French regiments.

"We are all but engaged," she said, straddling his lap. "Why aren't you stealing kisses? Why aren't you meeting me behind hedges and in the mews, sampling my charms?"

She stole a few kisses, lest he forget the

joy to be had in such larceny.

Hamish tasted of mint and patience. The mint was lovely, while the patience . . . Megan had had enough of patience.

"Meggie, dearest darling, you're setting a match to a powder magazine." He had a hand on each of her biceps, and that was not where Megan wanted his hands.

"Your sporran has to go," Megan said, kneeling up and working at his belt. "Sporrans are lovely in their place, and I understand they hold a flask, a comb, funds, but now is not the — Get this off, Hamish."

She wasn't accustomed to giving orders, but it occurred to her that Hamish was accustomed to *taking* orders. Why hadn't she grasped sooner that he was *waiting for her* to show some preference in the matter of his kisses?

He unfastened the sporran with a gratifying economy of movement. "Has anybody told you that you have a latent streak of ducal command about you?"

Uncle Percy had dragged Hamish to a levee two days ago, a ducal command Megan approved of.

"I am the granddaughter of a duke, and I'm about to become a duchess, I hope." She set the sporran aside and settled onto his lap. "That's better. I *am* about to become a duchess, aren't I?"

Hamish kissed her, sweetly, patiently, adoringly.

Megan wanted to smack him with his sporran. "That is not an answer, Hamish." Though his kisses were lovely. *Loving.* Decades of his kisses would not be enough, particularly not when paired with the slow, smooth glide of his palms over her back, or his hand, gently clasping her nape.

"Cease your nattering, Meggie mine. Kiss me a while, would ye please?"

She could kiss him forever, could melt into the warmth and tenderness of him, the sure sense that this man was her mate in all ways, and yet, he held back. Megan got a fistful of his hair, cupped his jaw, and plundered his mouth without mercy.

Plundering could be a mutual endeavor. Hamish was stealthy, was the trouble. Megan tasted, he teased. She tactilely shouted demands, he whispered back encouragement. Desire rose, along with frustration and determination, until Megan was so muddled, she declared a temporary ceasefire and curled against Hamish's chest.

"You have driven me daft, Hamish Mac-Hugh."

And Megan had driven him to desire, at least. Through her skirts and the single thickness of his wool kilt, she felt the unmistakable evidence of his arousal.

"Daft," he whispered, kissing her temple. "Witless, mad, trapped between longing and —"

He kissed her again, and over the beating of her heart, and the fire in her blood, Megan reached for the common sense that a plain girl who couldn't see clearly had learned to rely on before she could read.

Why would a man risk dishonor for her by stealing correspondence from the home of a peer, and kiss her *like that,* but deny her the words and deeds of a de facto fiancé? Megan sat up, which had the agreeable effect of putting certain of her parts in proximity with certain of Hamish's parts.

"You desire me," she said, brushing his hair back from his brow. "I desire you. You esteem me, and I esteem you. You've taken risks for me, and I'd protect you with my last breath."

"Don't say such things, Meggie."

She spoke only the truth, but another truth crowded up against her heart. "You are waiting for me to cry off. Waiting for me to change my mind, to bestow my favors elsewhere. You are waiting for me to send you one of those awful letters and claim my feelings have changed."

Waiting for her to abandon him, as he'd been abandoned by a previous fiancée, by his own men when he'd been taken captive, and by his fellow officers when he'd mustered out.

"I have been given permission to pay my addresses to you," Hamish said. "I make no presumptions, Meggie Windham. The choice goes to the lady, and unfair advantage was taken of you once before. I will not have it said your decision to wed me was anything less than —"

Affection, understanding, and joy all collided where uncertainty had been.

Hamish's reticence was not indifference or indecision, but rather, *respect.* Great, abiding, honorable respect. The trouble with dukes — with *her* duke — was that he was just a wee bit *too* honorable.

"You are daft," Megan said, "but you are *mine* in all your daft glory, and *I am yours.* I choose you, Hamish MacHugh, Duke of Murdoch. I am choosing you. You are the man I want for my husband, my champion, my friend, my lover. I will not unchoose you, I will not change my mind. We will argue, disagree, weather troubles, and possibly even quarrel, but you are mine now, and that door is locked. You can't escape, not ever."

Hamish tucked a lock of her hair over her ear. A simple gesture, but he imbued that small touch with reverence and caring.

"You're sure, Meggie? I'm stubborn, and I can't always find words when words are needful. I can't find the right words, at least. I'll go off fishing or rambling for hours, and you'll despair of me. I grow surly in late winter and snappish. I raise my voice when I'm frustrated."

"So do I. Kiss me. Better still, ravish me, for I certainly intend to ravish you."

Hamish's features were not clear to her, but she could feel him weighing, measuring, considering, and so she waited. Bless Hamish for the gentleman he was, he'd not have it said she was coerced into an engagement. For that alone, she fell in love with him all over again.

Megan would not have it said Hamish was merely following orders, though, or a guilty conscience, or Uncle Percy's pronouncements.

The silence went on. A bird thumped against the glass of the window and flew off. Across the corridor, a woman's laughter rang out from the library. Still, Megan waited, because waiting was part of listening, and listening was part — a large part — of caring for another.

"I'm trying to come up with a pretty speech," Hamish said, gathering her closer. "We'll be here until Doomsday before that happens. If it's a thorough ravishment you want, Meggie, I'm your man. I will always be your man, and you will be my duchess."

Our children would have red hair.

Anwen pushed aside that thought and led Lord Colin to the library. He was a sunnier version of his older brother — tall rather than enormous, handsome rather than striking. Her urchins would like him.

Given that the boys at the orphanage were pickpockets and street thieves in various stages of reform, this was not entirely a compliment.

"You intended to consult me regarding a volume of French poetry?" Lord Colin asked.

He wore the kilt, as his brother had. On him Highland attire was dashing, whereas on the duke . . . everything Hamish Mac-Hugh did was touched with boldness, while Lord Colin was more inclined to charm.

Urchins could be charming, when they wanted to steal your watch.

"If you're interested in poetry, we can certainly discuss it," Anwen said, opening the French doors. "Mostly, I sought to give my sister privacy with a man she adores."

"After a fashion, I adore Hamish too," Lord Colin said, "when I'm not exasperated with him. Siblings, ye ken."

His accent was soft, but always detectable. *Siblin's,* not siblings.

"I've wondered if older brothers are as burdensome as older sisters. My family is well-intentioned, but as the youngest, I enjoy a surfeit of instruction, lectures, examples, and cosseting."

Lord Colin came up behind her. "Smothering, you mean. You being so wee, they've probably been at it since you were born."

Well, yes, though lately, Anwen had been fighting back. She'd soon be five-and-twenty, and her health was quite sound.

"Shall we step outside for some fresh air, Miss Anwen?"

Lord Colin was much bigger up close, about the size of Anwen's male cousins, who were a lot of strapping, bothersome cosseters at large, where their female relations were concerned.

Blast the lot of them. "You're welcome to enjoy the garden. I'd need to fetch my bonnet."

"We'll keep to the shade," he said, winging his arm and winking.

Nobody winked at Miss Anwen Windham. She took his lordship's arm and let him lead her to a bench beneath the maple near the back wall.

"We're visible from the music room," she said. "In case you were worried about propriety."

"I don't think the occupants of the music room will be a reliable source of chaperonage, but you're safe with me, Miss Anwen. If my gentlemanly honor were to weaken in the face of your many charms, my brother's fists would soon see my priorities properly reestablished."

He bore the fragrance of freshly scythed meadows and soft sea air. Good scents, and they went well with the garden.

"Murdoch would beat you for stealing a kiss?"

"Aye, but if the lady were to do the stealing, that would be a different matter entirely."

Perhaps this was flirtation? "You're a frequent victim of such thievery, I take it?"

"Never frequently enough. Do you think they'll be happy?"

Anwen didn't know what to make of this flirting, if flirting it was, but she approved of a man who'd worry about his brother.

"Megan is easy to underestimate. If she's

enamored of your brother, then she'll do her best to make the union a happy one. If she's not enamored, then there shouldn't be a union."

Lord Colin folded his arms, fabric bunching over muscles. "You favor the love match, then?"

"You don't?" Scotsmen were rumored to be practical to a fault.

"I know a lot about infatuation, Miss Anwen, but very little about romance. A little diversion, a harmless frolic, what's not to like about that? But the great passion the poets write about? Not my cup of tea, as you English would say."

The morning was glorious, and to sit outside without a pestilential bonnet shielding half the world from Anwen's view was a surprising treat. She should enjoy the fresh air more often.

"If you're not an expert on romance, my lord, where does your interest lie?" She was honestly curious, and not because Lord Colin could become a family connection.

"Whisky," he said, lowering his voice and leaning near. "I own a distillery and have shares in a second whisky-making venture. I'm among that rare few who're willing to pay the damned excise man rather than have him constantly blowing up my stills. If you make a good product, people will pay for it, and the king's man needn't be avoided. Novel concept, but it's working so far."

If he'd made gin, Anwen would have had a lecture prepared about the evils of blue ruin. Half the population of her orphanage was the result of lives wrecked by inebriation.

He didn't make gin, so Anwen fell back on a simple scold. "Language, Lord Colin."

"My apologies, but there's no such thing as a blessed excise man. You want poetry, there's plenty likening him to the devil's familiar. Where do your interests lie, Miss Anwen?"

He assumed she had interests, other than bonnets and bachelors. How *novel.* "I am much absorbed with charitable work, Lord Colin. The plight of our poor children in particular concerns me."

"Plight?"

"To be homeless, friendless, and starving, with no hope of betterment is a plight. They are children, and entirely undeserving of such suffering." Anwen would argue with the archbishop of London himself on that score.

"To be free," Lord Colin replied, "to live by their wits, to come and go as they please, and take up with whatever mates they fancy,

260

that is a plight many a Highlander would love to share."

"They'd be free to starve on the streets of London," Anwen retorted. "To freeze, to endure diseases without number, and to — I'm arguing with you."

Or something. This discussion was like an unbonneted view of the garden, wider, more varied, not restricted to what was in sight directly ahead.

"We're no' arguin', lass. We're having a wee chat. Arguin' imperils breakables in my family. My sisters excel at it. What else holds your interest besides poor children?"

What would it be like, to *imperil the breakables* with Lord Colin? Anwen could hardly fathom the notion.

"Very little, if you must know. I'm passionate about my charitable work. Do you suppose we ought to wander past the music room windows?" The curtains were pulled, and the French door closed, so Megan's privacy should be safe enough.

"You'd risk *freckles.*"

Anwen rose, because that observation graduated from teasing to a challenge. "I can survive a few freckles, and you can tell me what interests you besides whisky."

He prosed on about medicinal uses of Highland herbs, Neil Gow's fiddle tunes —

whoever that was — and a surprising range of topics, most of which related to his native Scotland. He put Anwen in mind of her boys — curious about many things, collecting interests like a mud lark would collect buttons and coins on the tidal flats.

"You don't mean to tell me your every waking hour is concerned with a lot of dirty children," he said.

"Not my every waking hour, and the boys aren't dirty when I get through with them."

"Aye, they are. The moment your back is turned, they're off skinning their knees, tearing their trousers, and being boys. Getting dirty is part of it."

She loved that about them. Normal boys got dirty, and all she wanted for those children was some normality — meals, prayers, a home, a few years of stability. Not too much to ask.

A comfortable silence stretched while Anwen cast about for some other subject in which she could profess an interest.

Lord Colin's knees came to mind. Sitting on the bench in the shade, Anwen had resisted an urge to stare at his manly knees, exposed by his Highland attire. Who knew that a man's knees could be interesting?

Not that her interest signified anything.

Maybe the preachers had the answers after all. Maybe joy and pain balanced, and divine justice put matters right if a man were patient enough. Hamish would ponder philosophy later — maybe.

For now, he'd seize the joy with both hands and hold tight, for Megan Windham intended to hold tight to *him.*

"The past week has been an eternity," he muttered, burying his nose against her throat. "I've seen you fluttering by on the dance floor, smiling at this baron or that twit — you smell like lemons. I love lemons. Always have."

Lemons and cinnamon. The scent concentrated as he nuzzled lower, suggesting the lady had applied her perfume with an intent to entice. She need not have. Megan Windham fresh from a hog wallow would have scrambled Hamish's wits beyond recall.

"Blast this bodice," Megan muttered, shimmying. "Let me — That tickles. Do it again."

She squirmed, she fussed, she flung orders and suggestions at him. When Hamish undid the bow in the middle of her décolletage, she sighed, her breath warming his ear.

263

Instead of a corset, she wore old-fashioned country stays, which laced up the front, ending in another satin bow at the top.

"What is a mortal man to do when faced with such temptation?" Hamish mused, gliding his hands up the sides of Megan's breasts. She was well endowed, a fact he'd managed to mostly ignore until she'd taken up residence in his very lap.

"You pick locks in the dark," Megan said, untying his cravat. "Surely a pair of bows doesn't exceed your abilities?"

Her fingers glossed over his throat and chest, which Hamish took for Megan's version of an inspection. She might not be able to see him in detail, but she would know him as well as or better than a fully sighted woman could.

Hamish undid the second bow with his teeth. "Do you know, under Scottish law, a man and woman are considered married if they express an intent to wed, then consummate those intentions. Is that what you want, Megan?"

She paused, her palm resting over Hamish's heart. "I want you, now and always. I'm not without experience, you'll recall. You needn't fret over my maidenly sensibilities."

Megan certainly wasn't fretting, which reassured the part of Hamish that hesitated despite the bounty before him. Sir Fletcher had much to answer for, which Hamish would also ponder *later.*

"I wish your maidenly sensibilities had received the respect they were due, Meggie. I adore your passion, but —" How did a man with his lap full of half-undressed, willing, adult female express both regret for the loss of her virtue, and joy to be the recipient of her trust and generosity?

That man didn't express his gratitude with words, not if he was Hamish MacHugh. He instead pushed aside layers of linen and muslin, feasting his senses on shades of ivory, cream, and pink. Lovely, delectable, sweet, silky, luscious — lemony too — and wondrously pink.

"I wasn't ignoring you, Meggie. I was trying to be respectful," he said, switching from one breast to the other. "Trying to show you the restraint a proper gentleman — I was a fool."

Megan tugged at her skirts. "My fool."

"All yours, Meggie. You seem so confident and self-reliant. I never thought I was leaving you to doubt. I'm sorry. We'll learn, though. We'll get the knack — *merciful winged cherubs, Meggie Windham.*"

While Hamish had kissed and nibbled and

licked and teased, Megan had rearranged their clothing, so nothing came between them. Not a kilt, not a chemise, not a sporran, and not much gentlemanly restraint either.

"Enough blather," Megan said, fishing through all the petticoats and whatnot frothed around them, and wrapping a hand about the part of Hamish least inclined to any restraint whatsoever. Her touch was sure, possibly bordering on desperate.

He'd blundered, in other words. He'd tried to show the lady and the world that he'd never presume on her good will, and he'd left her uncertain of his regard. Hesitating now would only allow more doubt to plague her.

"You do it," Hamish said. "Take your time, and take *me,* however it pleases you to do so."

She tormented him, learning his contours, feathering soft, sweet caresses over him in locations that had gone uncaressed for too long. Somewhere amid sighs, kisses, curious explorations, and silent oaths, Hamish concluded that a special license was a fine custom, though not as fine as handfasting.

Because from this day forward, he considered himself committed to Megan in every way that mattered.

"Now?" Megan asked, fitting them together.

God, yes. Now. "I am in your hands, Meggie. Do as ye please."

She pleased to end one torment for Hamish in the interest of beginning another. One slow, cautious wiggle, push, retreat, glide, and advance after another, Megan Windham *pleased.* From the intensity of her focus, Hamish gathered that her previous experience had not been great, nor had it afforded her an opportunity to do more than endure Sir Fletcher's pawing.

"This feels . . . ," Megan said, taking more of him. "I like how . . . this is intimate."

She hadn't been sure, in other words. She hadn't been given any intimate confidence in herself.

"If you merely like it, then I've some convincing to do," Hamish said, adding a minute thrust to the festivities.

Megan went still. "Do that again. Exactly like that."

Hamish obliged, and before long, they'd established a glorious, urgent rhythm.

Megan kissed him and linked her hands at his nape. "This isn't like — Oh, that's lovely. More of that. Please, Hamish."

More attention to her breasts, while counterpointing the movement of her hips, and refusing the screeching need to *hurry.* Megan's breathing quickened to a soft pant, while Hamish closed his eyes, lest the sight of her in the grip of passion rout his self-discipline.

Closing his eyes didn't help. That only made the weight and warmth of her more compelling, only made the pleasure well higher and faster.

And yet, as Megan keened softly against Hamish's shoulder, and then went limp in the aftermath of her pleasure, he managed to hold off his own satisfaction. A man protected those who belonged to him, and that meant until vows had been spoken. Hamish might please his lady eight times a day, but his own gratification would have to wait until she'd taken not only his heart but also his name.

CHAPTER TWELVE

The morning was fair, while Sir Fletcher's mood was bloody awful. He'd snapped at Geneva for sticking her finger in the jam pot at breakfast, and then his lordship had snapped at Sir Fletcher, and the smirking from the harpies around the table had been unbearable.

"Let's walk, shall we?" Sir Fletcher said, rising from the bench along the perimeter of Grosvenor Square. Puget fell in step beside him, suggesting the former captain understood when an order had been given.

"I told you I wanted the supper waltz," Puget muttered. "Lady Pamela said all she could risk was the allemande. Your parents are negotiating on her behalf with some northern earl who seldom comes to Town but needs a nanny for his wards. I won't have it, Pilkington."

"*Sir Fletcher,* if you please. You shall have it, unless Pamela agrees to run off with you, and that she will not do." The morning air became perfumed with true love's frustration, about which Sir Fletcher did not care. "I need more money."

"You just came into fifty damned pounds. How can you spend fifty pounds in a week?"

Sir Fletcher tipped his hat to the new Duchess of Quimbey, who was accompanied by an enormous dog. A footman led a second, equally sizable canine a few yards behind her.

"A single gentleman of good breeding has needs, Puget, especially during the season. Your papa's an earl. Must I draw you pictures?"

"Fifty pounds would keep some families for a year."

"You don't say. Thank you for that fascinating revelation. I, by contrast, need an infusion of cash by this time next week."

Puget walked along in silence for a dozen yards. He wasn't a bad sort, but neither was he particularly clever, despite claiming a host of artistic abilities. A clever man with Puget's skills would have forged his way to the funds necessary to wed the fair Pamela by now. At the very least Puget could have been immortalizing aging duchesses on canvas — or their flatulent pugs. Sporting portraits might also have netted him a solid income, provided he wasn't offended by the stench of sweat.

"You have no intention of aiding my cause where your sister is concerned, do you?"

The only cause Sir Fletcher was interested in aiding was his own. While spreading rumors about a certain Scottish duke, Sir Fletcher had been drawn into a few card games, and luck had run against him. The result had been more than a week of dodging invitations, for debts of honor were to be paid promptly.

"I have supported your efforts where Pamela is concerned, else you'd not be permitted even an allemande. True love is supposed to be determined, Puget. I can't do all the work, nor can I remedy your fundamental unsuitability in my father's eyes. That will take coin or at least a gentlemanly means of support, which brings me back to the topic at hand."

"I won't do it," Puget said. "I've told myself that no sacrifice is too great if it means Lady Pamela and I can be together, but a dance here and there, while Lady Pamela is paraded like a prize mare before some bumpkin from Cumberland —"

Pammy was more of a heifer, sturdy and hale. "I'll have a word with the bumpkin, tell him Pamela is prone to megrims and

271

tantrums, which is nothing but the truth. She requires a fortune in bonnets and boots too, and puts a significant dent in Cook's larders. Leave the bumpkin to me, and have another fifty pounds in my hand by week's end."

Puget paused at the street corner, his gaze traveling back across the square. "She said she'd meet me here before noon."

Oh, for God's sake. Noon was at least a half hour away. "Puget, attend me. Find some other former officer to fleece by week's end, or you'll have danced your last allemande with my sister."

"There are no other officers, Pilkington. I've racked my brain, combed through my journals and old records. You've dipped into the pockets of the ones with both coin and a propensity for drink and cards. The list is shorter than you'd think."

Probably true, because many who'd mustered out were now leg-shackled, and that could cramp a man's social habits abominably.

"Who is in Town this year that normally ruralizes for the season?"

Puget paid attention to the social scene. A younger son without means had to. "More Windhams than usual, but Keswick and Rosecroft are neither gamblers nor drunks."

"What about MacHugh?" Sir Fletcher said. "He's new to the title, rumored to have means, and has two sisters and a brother in tow. You saw his handwriting on various requisitions or dispatches, and he's doubtless been welcomed into any number of gentlemen's clubs now that he has a title."

A Scottish savage waltzed into a fine old title, while an English earl's son was reduced to scheming to pay the tailor. Justice was a blind, deaf, poxy old whore, and relieving MacHugh of a few quid would rectify one of her more egregious missteps.

"MacHugh's — Murdoch's — penmanship is distinctive," Puget said, thin lips pursing, "but he never drinks to excess. I haven't seen him in the clubs either. For him, a stray gambling debt won't do."

Impatience flared, for a call on the household of Lord Anthony Windham had become a pressing priority.

"Then concoct a bootmaker, G. Puget and Sons, or something like it. Send an overdue bill around to the new Duke of Murdoch, payable by return post to your present lodging. Outfitting a family new to Town in a season's worth of boots ought to be at least fifty pounds of custom."

G. Puget and Sons might also serve as a vintner, butcher, or tobacconist. The scheme was simple and elegant, a great improvement over Puget's more complicated games.

At the far end of the square, Pammy's embonpoint figure came sashaying around the corner, her lady's maid trailing behind her. One street from her home, she'd be permitted to take the air with such a weak excuse for a chaperone, particularly if Stepmama had overindulged the previous evening.

"Fine," Puget said. "I'll send His Grace of Murdoch a bill for boots, but this is the last time, Pilkington. You put my neck in a noose with your requests, and that hasn't got me any closer to putting a ring on Lady Pamela's finger."

Nothing short of divine intervention would accomplish that aim. "Send word when you have the money, and don't despair where Pamela is concerned. She is a very determined young woman."

Particularly when a plate of tea cakes was involved.

Puget was already walking away, gaze intent on his lady fair. Sir Fletcher took off in the opposite direction — it wouldn't do for Pamela to spot him in company with her gallant swain — and soon arrived at Lord Anthony Windham's townhouse.

"If you'd please alert Miss Megan Windham to my presence," Sir Fletcher said, passing over his walking stick and hat to the butler. "And I'd like to bid her parents farewell before they leave for Wales too."

Lord Anthony had intimated that marital protocol required him to consult Megan's mother regarding potential suitors — a courtesy between parents. Sir Fletcher had murmured appropriate masculine commiserations, but no note had come from Lord Anthony, no quiet word had been offered on a shady bridle path, and thus no public courtship could ensue.

Without a public courtship, a bachelor had no solid prospects to trade upon, as every shopkeeper and merchant seemed to know.

"Sir Fletcher, good day." Anwen Windham smiled at him, a dark-haired kilted fellow at her side. Both brought an air of mischief with them into the foyer, as if they'd just got away with tippling in the library.

The kilted fellow looked familiar, suggesting Sir Fletcher had crossed paths with him in some drawing room or other.

"Miss Anwen, good morning. I don't believe I know your guest." All the kilted barbarians tended to look the same, which was doubtless why they distinguished themselves with different plaids — a family motto woven in fabric for the illiterate.

"Actually, you do know me," the fellow said. "We served together in Spain, and were introduced at Her Grace of Moreland's. Captain Lord Colin MacHugh, at your service, Sir Fletcher."

Ah, yes. The younger MacHugh, the one who'd nearly got his brother killed by the French, court-martialed by the English, and canonized by the Scots.

Instinct prodded Sir Fletcher's memory for more than a vague recollection of army days and a prank gone awry where Captain MacHugh was concerned, but why sort through that garbage — most of it preserved in bad wine — when a lady needed a call from her most devoted admirer?

"You have the right of it, Lord Colin," Sir Fletcher said, charming smile at the ready. "I stand corrected. A pleasure to renew my acquaintance with you. Miss Anwen, I'd hoped to see your parents off on their journey, and to pay my respects to Miss Megan."

Sir Fletcher beamed at her as sweetly as a smitten swain ever did beam.

She wrinkled a nose a tad on the unfortunate side. "Megan isn't at home, I'm afraid, and Mama and Papa have already departed.

You just missed them."

Damn and blast. Manners forbid inquiring as to whether "not at home" was a euphemism for "not at home *to you.*"

"I don't suppose your parents left their direction? I can wish them a safe journey by post."

"I'll send an address 'round once we've removed to Moreland House. So much upheaval involved in changing households, you know."

Miss Anwen needed to work on her gracious smile, for her expression had rather a lot of teeth to it and not much warmth.

"I'll bid you good day," Sir Fletcher said, casting a hopeful look up the main staircase. He couldn't very well chase Megan down across the nearest ballroom, not until he'd replenished his exchequer.

"Good day," Lord Colin said, taking Sir Fletcher's walking stick and hat from the butler and holding them out. "Enjoy the lovely weather."

The butler held the door open, and Sir Fletcher had no choice but to saunter back the way he'd come. What did it mean, that Lord Anthony had decamped for Wales — Wales, of all places — without giving permission for an eminently worthy suitor to pay addresses to Megan?

Though his lordship hadn't *forbidden* Sir Fletcher to spend time in Megan's company either, a heartening realization. Sir Fletcher swung his walking stick, decapitating the tallest specimen from among a bed of orange flowers.

Permission to court a lady was a formality, nothing more, and Megan would see that permission was granted directly. Puget would muster the coin needed to placate the greediest of Sir Fletcher's creditors, and soon, all would come right.

Sir Fletcher was halfway back to Grosvenor Square before he realized he might stray across Puget and Pammy making calf's eyes — heifer's eyes in her case — in public. That disagreeable thought sent his steps veering south, toward St. James's Street. Few would be about in the clubs at such an early hour and a fellow could always put a meal on his account.

Perhaps the bumpkin from Cumberland would be on hand and available for a quiet word regarding Pammy's many vices . . . except Puget had neglected to mention the bumpkin's name or title.

A pity, that. A rotten shame. Just another example of how the smallest details could send the course of true love top over tail right into the nearest reeking ditch.

278

■ ■ ■ ■

"His Grace is entirely too pleased with himself," Westhaven remarked. "Somebody's parliamentary bill is about to be defeated, somebody's canal drained. Whose turn is it to deal?"

The Windham menfolk gathered for cards at least weekly if no other familial gatherings took precedence. They met not at any club but in Westhaven's library. The card parties had become the social highlight of Keswick's week and he suspected his brothers-by-marriage viewed it similarly.

"Having our lady cousins underfoot means Her Grace is in alt," Rosecroft said. "If Her Grace is happy, His Grace is happy."

"And if Their Graces are happy, the kingdom must be secure," Lord Valentine muttered, appropriating the deck from Westhaven. "Unless, of course, one's children are teething, colicky, or fretful, or the baby won't sleep through the night, or —"

"— the housemaids are feuding," Westhaven added.

"Or your daughter has to write letters every day to her damned dog and her damned pony," Rosecroft said. "Valentine, you've shuffled the deck enough."

279

"Up past your bedtimes, the doddering lot of you," Lord Valentine said, dealing cards with the dispatch of a man who claimed a wealth of manual dexterity. "What's this I hear about Megan taking a fancy to the waltzing Scotsman?"

Glances were exchanged around the table, though Westhaven — ducal heir that he was — merely watched the cards piling up before him.

"Megan has taken a fancy to the Duke of Murdoch," Rosecroft said. "He's not what I would have chosen for our Megs."

Keswick glowered at his cards, though he held a decent hand. "Who would you choose for her?"

Keswick didn't know Megan Windham well, but he liked her. She was sensible, loyal as hell to her family, and patient with children and dunderheaded cousins. More to the point, Keswick's countess, Louisa, was fond of Megan.

"I'd prefer an Englishman," Westhaven said. "Scotland is too far away."

"I second that motion," Lord Valentine said, finishing the deal. "I also would have thought Megs better suited to a soft-spoken fellow, one who favors books, plays the violin, and smokes a pipe. Not some Highland warrior who wears a skirt and barely

280

knows proper forms of address."

"We weren't all born into ducal families," Keswick observed. "Are we here to play cards or matchmake?"

"Matchmake, of course," Westhaven replied, arranging his hand. "Does anybody have an objection to Murdoch? I thought Sir Fletcher Pilkington had caught Megan's eye, but my countess informs me I am in error."

"Countesses do that," Rosecroft muttered. "Valentine, why can't you deal a fellow any decent cards?"

"Because I'm after your pin money," Lord Valentine said. "My sisters expect me to keep you lot in line, and that thankless task requires that I relieve you of your valuables. Keswick, however, is apparently holding a decent hand."

The door opened, admitting Lucas Denning, Marquess of Deene, whose privilege it was to be married to Eve, the youngest of the ducal Windham children.

"Bring the decanters over," Rosecroft said as the players made room for an extra chair. "And condole dear Valentine on the impending loss of his last groat to his elders."

"Your arrival interrupted an interesting discussion, Deene," Westhaven said, topping up each man's drink as Lord Valentine dealt a fresh hand. "Cousin Megan has taken a fancy to the new Duke of Murdoch. We're wondering if Sir Fletcher's charms have paled, or if she's trying to bring Sir Fletcher up to scratch by showing favor to a competitor."

"Murdoch?" Deene considered his cards. He was looking a bit harried, as a new father will. "I can't say as I know him."

"You knew him as Colonel Hamish Mac-Hugh," Rosecroft supplied. "Is that jam on your cravat, Deene? Valentine has apparently started a new fashion."

"It's the blood of the last man who suggested I'd disgrace my marchioness with anything less than perfect turnout before her brothers. Keswick, shall you lead?"

Keswick tossed out a card. "Somebody has to."

"Hamish MacHugh was the fellow held by the French," Deene said. "Could not have been a pleasant experience, but then he probably wasn't a pleasant fellow to have as a captive, if the gossip is to be believed."

"What gossip?" Westhaven asked.

"Play a bloody card," Rosecroft muttered.

Westhaven flicked his wrist, and a card went sailing to the exact center of the table. *"What gossip?"*

Rosecroft set a card on top of Westhaven's. "The gossip that said MacHugh was of such a violent disposition even the French interrogators didn't want him underfoot. He had a reputation for acquitting himself well in battle, but then one hears he led his own men into an ambush at some godforsaken bridge."

Keswick collected the cards. "He was considered a brute. Witnesses saw him snap an unarmed man's neck without batting an eye. Not the done thing, even on the battlefield, and some say MacHugh's own brother was among those jeopardized by the colonel's disregard for orders. Others have suggested gossip is in error. Might we change the subject?"

"What flavor jam is that on your cravat?" Rosecroft inquired of Deene. "Raspberry stains worse than strawberry, I've found."

Deene glanced down at his cravat. "I don't know. Evie will lecture me into next week, but what's a fellow to do when he's acquired a lapful of smiling cherub, and nobody warns him the cherub has been at the jam?"

"Change his cravat?" Westhaven suggested. "Wash the cherub's little paws with one of the three handkerchiefs no self-respecting papa is ever without? Hand the cherub off to the nursemaids with a lordly scowl, muttering about decorum in the nursery?"

"Ha!" Lord Valentine chorused from across the table. "Decorum in the nursery is an oxymoron once you get past the first child, rather like a good night's sleep."

And thus, Keswick mused, did grown men while away an evening, alternately taking a respite from the rigors of domestic bliss, and wondering how their ladies and offspring fared at home. The gathering broke up promptly at midnight, with Rosecroft suggesting that pouring boiling water continuously on any evidence of raspberry preserves might rescue a cravat from a fresh stain.

"Walk with me?" Deene asked quietly as hats and gloves and walking sticks were parceled out.

"Of course," Keswick replied. "Rosecroft, you'll join us for a breath of fresh air?"

"Somebody has to see that Deene arrives home safely, or Evie will lecture *me* into next week."

Keswick had needed patience and subtlety, but he couldn't consider the evening wasted if the family's three veterans of the Peninsular campaign found the privacy necessary to discuss another former soldier. As they walked along, carriages rattled past, and linkboys and footmen held lanterns for

284

the fashionable parties.

"MacHugh was rumored to be only half-sane," Deene said. "War doesn't exactly bring out the best in a man, but is that the sort of fellow Megan ought to consort with?"

"We were all half-daft by the time we crossed the mountains into France, and matters did not improve at Waterloo," Rosecroft said. "MacHugh's record includes insubordination, disciplinary proceedings, absence without leave, conduct unbecoming an officer, and all manner of disgraces. Moreland must not be aware of Murdoch's military record."

They walked along in silence to the next corner.

"Keswick, your usual loquaciousness has deserted you," Rosecroft said. "What are your thoughts?"

"We could warn MacHugh off," Deene said. "Evie says Sir Fletcher Pilkington has been sniffing about Megan's skirts."

"I asked Keswick for his thoughts," Rosecroft said. "Any damned fool knows Sir Fletcher has been doing the pretty around Megan, but he's the next thing to a fortune hunter."

Had Rosecroft and Deene been ten years younger, they might have shoved each other, elbowed one another in the ribs, and otherwise masked an abiding affection with fisticuffs.

Keswick might have knocked their heads together too. "Doesn't it strike you both as odd that MacHugh's military record is a little too awful? Why wasn't he drummed out of the regiment? Why no court-martial? Why all that bad conduct, but no reduction in rank?"

Rosecroft waited for a carriage to pass, then stepped into the street. "Because MacHugh was brave. The French talked about him in whispers, and his men would follow him anywhere. Even the generals respect bravery."

"Our generals talked about him in whispers," Deene said. "Mad MacHugh, the Terror of Toulouse, or something like that. The French couldn't hold him for long. It's odd that his name comes up, though, because I overheard a discussion last week in which he was mentioned."

As had Keswick. Several discussions. "Speculation about his fitness to hold a title? Intimations of an unbalanced mind? Vague innuendo about ungovernable temper, dishonor, and violent impulses?"

Deene bent to toss a dead lily into the nearest flower-bed. They were outside Lord

Anthony's town residence, the house dark save for lamps lit on the front steps.

"Exactly that," Deene said, straightening. "What has the peerage come to, when a savage brute, a murderer of unarmed innocents, holds a ducal title? When a man of significant rank leads his soldiers into an ambush against orders and evades justice? If that's what happened."

"When a title ends up in an unlikely place, there's always talk," Rosecroft said. "One endures the gossip and goes back to Yorkshire at the first opportunity."

"Or Kent," Keswick said. "And one doesn't convict a man on the basis of talk. MacHugh served honorably, no matter that his record has some blemishes. I'm inclined to trust Megan's judgment where he's concerned." Particularly when Megan had confided in MacHugh rather than bring her troubles to her own family.

Deene swung his walking stick up to rest against his shoulder, as soldiers often carried their rifles.

"Why trust our Megs? She isn't the most outgoing soul, and MacHugh — Murdoch, rather — has come upon the scene suddenly. Sir Fletcher has been constant in his attentions since the season began, and while I don't care for Pilkington, he'll not disappear into the wilds of Scotland once the vows are spoken."

"Are the cock pits, bear gardens, whorehouses, and gaming hells preferable to Scotland?" Keswick asked. "For those are Pilkington's favored haunts when he's not swilling drink at his club or ogling some debutante's mama." Or chasing heiresses, or using a lady's correspondence to coerce her hand in marriage.

Keswick wasn't about to reveal Megan's epistolary mistakes to her own cousin, not when MacHugh had apparently taken that situation in hand.

Rosecroft muttered something foul in his native Irish. "If we disqualify as a suitor every bachelor who behaves as a bachelor, my cousins will all be old maids. Keswick, what do you know that you haven't told us?"

"Much, of course, but what's relevant is that in every case where somebody has brought up Murdoch's unfitness — his alleged unfitness — in my hearing, that person has recently been discussing the new duke with one Sir Fletcher Pilkington."

"Him again," Deene replied. "This will get messy, and there's Megan in the middle of it, with Their Graces intent on marrying her off, come fire, flood, or famine."

"Here's what I think," Keswick said. "If

Sir Fletcher is concerned for Megan, then he ought to bring his concerns to her family, most especially to us three. Spreading talk in the clubs is cowardly, and whatever else is true, I have not heard Hamish Mac-Hugh accused of cowardice, ever."

"Messy," Deene said again. "Damned messy, when all we have to go on is a lot of conflicting talk."

"So we learn what we can," Rosecroft said, "keep a sharp eye out, and alert the rest of the family to a potential problem. Gentlemen, I'll bid you good night and wish you pleasant dreams. My regards to your ladies."

He bowed and strode back in the direction of Westhaven's townhouse. Deene took off in the other direction, while Keswick remained where he was.

"Are you coming?" Deene asked. "The hour grows late and my marchioness will worry."

"Your marchioness, like my countess, is not worried," Keswick said, resuming their perambulations. "She's waiting for you in her most diaphanous evening ensemble, probably enjoying a cup of chocolate and planning your welcome. This is how large families are made."

"One is inspired, Keswick, to know a man

of your stalwart nature regularly surrenders himself to the charms of diaphanous nightwear."

Every chance I get. "As do you."

They came to another corner, at which their paths diverged.

"What shall we do about Murdoch?" Deene asked. "I can have a word with a few former officers, nose about at Horse Guards, look over whatever records might pertain. I'm not above sending letters to some of the men I served with or chatting up a few others."

Keswick was abruptly desperate for his countess's company. Louisa was the most sensible woman he knew, and her advice on the matter of Megan's suitors had been brilliant.

"You must do as you see fit, Deene, but all that chatting, corresponding, and nosing about will fuel whatever gossip Sir Fletcher has set in motion. I suspect that's exactly his aim, and I for one do not intend to oblige him."

"You can't stand by and do nothing while Megan waltzes into the arms of an unsuitable *parti*," Deene said. "I don't care if Murdoch is a duke. A man with an ungovernable temper or scandal in his past won't serve, Keswick."

"Scandal means little to a Windham in love," Keswick said, "and I never said I'd stand by and do nothing."

"Then what will you do?"

"I'll talk to Murdoch," Keswick said, "and if he doesn't call me out or beat me insensate for putting a few awkward questions to him, I'll listen to what he has to say."

CHAPTER THIRTEEN

Spring came to Mayfair, and to Megan Windham. She suspected the season was contagious, for the longer Hamish Mac-Hugh courted her, the more his blue eyes took on the sparkle of a peaceful loch and the merriment of bluebells.

"I've realized something," Megan said as she and her beloved tooled along a quiet path in Hyde Park. Hamish drove as calmly as he did everything else — almost everything else. On a music room sofa the previous week, he'd shown a lovely propensity for passion.

"You will give me the benefit of your latest insight, I trust."

He trusted, he never demanded. Megan wanted to kiss him for that.

"Cousins are not like brothers," she said. "Not quite. I have male cousins, but Edana and Rhona are your sisters. You're more fierce with them than my cousins are with me."

Hamish turned the vehicle down a shady side lane. He drove a team seasoned by the heavy draft work at the brewery, still quite fit and sound, but in his words, "retired from combat duty." Their names were Clyde and Angus, and they were shamelessly fond of their owner. Perhaps that was contagious too, for as unconventional a choice as they were for a carriage duty, Megan smiled every time she saw them.

"Fierce isn't always good," Hamish said. "Edana and Rhona can grow fiercely acquisitive at the milliner's or the modiste's, and then when the bills arrive, I'm reduced to shouting, all to no avail."

"Give them funds of their own," Megan said. "Be generous, but firm. When they've spent what they have, they get no more until the next quarter. They can borrow from each other, or have their maid sell what's become outmoded or worn, but give them their own resources to manage."

He bumped her shoulder gently. "Have I told you that you're brilliant, Meggie mine? Colin is actually quite good with money and has plenty of his own, though his common sense is lacking in other regards."

Colin was quite good with charm. "He'd

293

better acquire some common sense. If he's a duke's heir, prosperous, handsome, and a novelty in a kilt, then the young ladies will favor him with their melting glances because of those attributes, and not because of his finer qualities."

Melting glances could lie. Megan suspected most women learned that sooner than she had. Edana and Rhona, who had several brothers, doubtless knew it.

"Colin rarely considers the why's," Hamish said, "which is his besetting sin. He's brave, he's honorable, but he's not . . ."

"He's a hothead," Megan said, hearing the worry in Hamish's voice. "My cousin Bartholomew was too. Impetuous, to those who liked him. Those of us who loved him called him reckless."

The memory still hurt, of hugging Bart so tightly as he'd prepared to leave for the war in Spain. Willing him to be careful, to behave as if he might take a bad tumble or come to far worse grief with any incautious step. To *look* where he was going, and see the danger before the danger found him.

"Colin's reckless," Hamish said, signaling the horses to slow from trot to walk. "Though he's always sorry for his stupid wagers or rash words. He likes you, by the way."

"I like him. I do not like that your siblings trouble you so."

Megan *adored* that the path was deserted. She and Hamish drove out early in the afternoon, long before the carriage parade thronged the park with fashion and gossip. With Hamish at the ribbons, these outings became an interlude of greenery, fresh air, talk, and shared touches. Clouds were gathering above, making the day a trifle chilly, but that gave Megan an excuse to sit closer to her intended.

"Family is a joy," Hamish said, "and a worry. My grandfather was quite young when the Forty-Five happened, but he told me stories of his life as a boy. The land was owned in common, even if it was held by the laird. Fortunes rose and fell for the clan as a whole, and nobody was left alone with their troubles or their joys. We still have the miseries and joys, but much has changed."

He steered the horses to a patch of grass beneath a venerable oak, and told them to stand.

"You're a duke," Megan said. "That's an enormous change, and it can be a change for the better, Hamish."

"I'm to marry the woman I love," he said, punctuating the sentiment with a kiss. "That's the best possible change."

For a few minutes, they kissed and nuzzled and risked scandal beneath the quiet oak, though only a minor scandal. When Mama and Papa returned in a few weeks, an engagement would be announced, and the wedding plans would start in earnest. Megan did not much care where or how the ceremony took place, she cared only that Hamish spoke his vows with her.

Hamish had already told her he loved her, sometimes with his kisses, and sometimes with blunt words tossed at her in the middle of private conversations. Megan hadn't acquired the knack of tossing the words back, but she wanted to.

"I like when you say my name," he whispered, when they'd satisfied the immediate need for kisses. "Somebody greets this Murdoch fellow, and I look about to see who he might be. Colin thinks I ought to start going by James instead of Hamish."

"Don't you dare."

She'd pleased him. Hamish gazed off down the path, but by the curve of his cheek, she knew he was trying not to smile.

"You speak the Gaelic to me more and more, Meggie. Did you know that?"

"Don't start going by James, please. I know you as Hamish, and that's your name. Now tell me why you joined the army."

His posture shifted. Very likely, the smile had disappeared. "Why do you ask?"

Because she could ask him anything, and he'd answer honestly, not with cousinly discretion.

"You love your home, you're the oldest, the head of the family. I don't gather you enjoyed any part of being a soldier, and yet, you served for years. I can't reconcile what I know of you with your past."

He unwrapped the reins from the brake and asked the horses to walk on. "Would you rather marry a man who thrived on war? Some said I had an aptitude for it, when I wasn't disobeying orders, setting a bad example for my brother, or getting captured by the French."

Despite the smooth path beneath the horses' feet, Megan had somehow steered the conversation to boggy ground. The breeze had picked up too, and she smelled a shower coming their way.

"I *am* marrying you, and Wellington apparently had an aptitude for war, much to England's great relief. If war thwarted a French tyrant, then I'm glad somebody in Britain was proficient at it. The Portuguese, Spanish, Germans, Russians, Austrians, Poles, and Italians weren't having much luck without us."

Hamish was silent for a good hundred yards, while greenery went by in a verdant blur. Megan had little sense of her bearings, which would have alarmed her had she been in anybody else's company. Whether they were near the Serpentine or Park Lane, wandering Kensington Gardens, or about to come out along Rotten Row, she did not know.

Hamish was beside her, and Hamish would see her back to the Moreland mews. The heavens could open up, thunder and lightning shatter the skies, and Hamish would see her safely home.

"After the Forty-Five," he said, "many a Scottish family was put off the land they'd worked for centuries, particularly in the west of Scotland. They couldn't speak English, didn't know how to read or write in any language, and the whole notion of documentation making a land transfer legal and binding . . . they didn't grasp that. After Culloden, a Scottish lad was often promised land in exchange for taking the king's shilling. He didn't join up to fight for king and country, or even for the coin. He joined up in hopes he'd be rewarded with a few acres, so his family wouldn't starve."

An uneasy shiver prickled over Megan's arms. "But the Scottish regiments are among the bravest."

"The Scottish regiments have to be the bravest. They're always deployed where the fighting is expected to be the worst. The military is smart about it too. In the army, a Scotsman can strut about in his plaid, hear the pipes, march to the drums. At home, these were long forbidden, though they're fashionable now. So the Scots joined up, and to the horror of the French and the amazement of all the lordlings idling about with their purchased commissions, those farm boys and village lads fought like blazes for their own."

Megan wrapped her hand around Hamish's arm, for the shivery feeling had become a chill abetted by the freshening breeze.

"You fought like blazes for your own."

Hamish urged the horses to pick up their pace, from a walk to a trot. "I fought beside my men. I all but stole requisitions, argued with generals, mislaid orders, and waged a war within a war to see that as many of my subordinates got home to claim their patch of Scottish ground as possible. I keep Napoleon in my prayers, Meggie. Because of him, a few acres of Scotland got back into the hands of the families who deserve them."

This view of war was complicated and uncomfortable, also intimate — unique to Hamish MacHugh, which made it a precious confidence.

"I did not fight for fat, nancy George," he went on, "or poor mad George, or any of the damned Georges who came before them. Do you think me a traitor, Meggie?"

"Of course not."

They trotted along for few minutes, suggesting Hamish had driven them in a great, green circle. Hyde Park was hundreds of acres, but eventually, all paths revealed it to be exactly what it was — a bucolic oasis in the middle of increasingly dense human habitation.

Megan waited for Hamish to say more, but the silence stretched on. Had she given the wrong answer? Why had the discussion — much less the weather — become so bleak?

"Charlotte fancies herself a Whig," Megan said. "Mostly, she likes to argue. Charlotte is frightfully smart."

"Siblings tend to think that of themselves."

"Charlotte is a great supporter of radical notions, freedom, equality, and fraternity prominently among them. She will harangue you about the decline of the monarchy, and the philosophical weakness inherent in the

300

divine right of kings, until you want to leave the room with your hands clapped over your ears."

Thunder rumbled off to the north.

"I do love you," Hamish said. "Not only because you think leaving the room is a great rudeness."

Megan ignored his attempt to distract her, because she had the sense her next words mattered. A lot.

"I have often wanted to ask my brilliant sister, what manner of freedom is delivered on the end of a French bayonet? What sort of equality requires a self-crowned emperor to ensure it? What variety of fraternity is earned by forcibly conscripting, and violently ending, the lives of countless hundreds of thousands? You fought for something honest and real, Hamish, so families wouldn't starve, so your men would get home. Who has dared criticize you for that?"

Somebody apparently had. Maybe many somebodies.

A raindrop splatted onto the bench beside Megan, and Angus gave a shake of his harness.

"Ah, damn. Now I have you out in the wet," Hamish said. "Take the reins for a moment, will you, Meggie?"

Megan accepted the ribbons, though she

301

wasn't wearing driving gloves, and had only a general notion where the path lay. The horses were perfect gentlemen, and trotted along smoothly despite the change of driver.

Hamish shrugged out of his topcoat and draped it about Megan's shoulders. As more raindrops spattered down, she was enveloped in warmth, the fragrance of heather, and a lovely sense of rightness.

Talk of war had left her unsettled — Hamish hadn't told her the whole of his situation, she was sure — but they had time to learn each other's histories and each other's hearts. The war was over, after all. Hamish had given her what protection he could from the weather, and he'd see her safely home.

For now, that was enough.

Across the room, Megan Windham was chatting up the Duke of Quimbey.

Hamish had stood against cavalry charges, French bayonets, and the knowledge of impending torture, but he was helpless to defend himself against tenderness. A softening of the heart befell him every time he laid eyes on Meggie, an easing of all tensions, a lightness of spirit that moved him closer to the man he'd been before soldiering had made him a walking weapon.

302

When Megan Windham touched him, his insides sighed, his mind turned to mush, and peace stole over him. She *listened* to him. Paid attention to his words, to his silences. With her hands, she drew secrets from him he'd been keeping even from himself.

He liked when she took his hand, liked when she wrapped her arm through his. She had a way of half-hugging him from the side, a quick press of bodies and squeeze of the fingers that melted him into a puddle of adoring swain.

"My countess claims you're mentally composing poetry whenever you behold Megan Windham," the Earl of Keswick said.

"Lord Cowlick, good evening," Hamish replied, though he did not take his gaze from his lady. "Has anybody told you sneaking up on a man isn't polite?"

Keswick's countess probably loved his eyebrows, for they were dark and expressive. Now they said the earl was torn between laughter and indignation, a fine place for a prospective family member to be.

"When you have children, Murdoch, you either learn stealth or acquaint yourself with the dubious charms of celibacy. Besides, a regiment mounted on elephants could sneak up on you when you're watching Megan

Windham."

"Aye." And would Keswick please hush, so Hamish could get back to that pleasant pastime? Meggie was charming old Quimbey, who'd recently discarded avowed bachelorhood for the company of a formerly widowed duchess. Gossip said a shared love of dogs had brought them together.

"Have you and the fair Megan set a date?" Keswick asked.

"You're worse than a midge. The lady sets the date, usually after her parents have announced an engagement. There's the small matter of the settlements to deal with, and in case you hadn't noticed — or your omniscient countess hasn't pointed it out to you — a woman is entitled to a few weeks of courtship before plighting her troth."

A string quartet was tuning up over in the corner, this being a musical evening, courtesy of the Marchioness of Deene. Edana and Rhona were at the punch bowl, fans fluttering gracefully, and Colin was likely charming some widow or other on the nearest shadowed balcony.

Siblings accounted for. Beloved not five yards away. London wasn't so bad, once a man found favor with the right lady.

"You haven't set a date," Keswick said. "This suggests you're getting your courage together, for I have it on good authority you've been given leave to pay your addresses. Before you importune Megan for her hand, I'd like to put a few questions to you."

Keswick spoke casually — too casually.

Hamish knew better than to visibly react, but the back of his neck prickled disagreeably. "Ask all you like. If you're inquiring about matters that are none of your business, I might answer you with my fists."

His lordship fluffed the lace of Hamish's jabot. "There's talk, Murdoch. Not the sort of talk one wants to hear about a former fellow officer. I'm not suggesting the talk has any substance, but you should know what's being said."

Hamish left off visually adoring his beloved long enough to consider the man beside him. Keswick was no fool, and Colin's discreet inquiries had revealed a reputation in Spain for quiet competence.

"You're either setting me up for an ambush, or trying to warn me of one."

"Louisa claims you're a bright fellow. I'm reserving — Well, damn. I thought he was hiding from his duns."

Sir Fletcher Pilkington had joined the gathering, and was bowing over the marchioness's hand, another fellow at his side.

"Megan hasn't recognized him." Megan had nothing to fear from Sir Fletcher and never would again. The prickling sensation at the back of Hamish's neck skittered along his arms, nonetheless.

"Murdoch, good evening," the Earl of Rosecroft said from Hamish's right. "Keswick, greetings. I don't suppose either of you intend to favor us with a song tonight?"

"Who's that with Pilkington?" Hamish asked, because the man looked familiar. Lean, a shade above average height, something nervous in his bearing.

"The Honorable former Captain Garner Puget," Keswick said. "One of Lord Plyne's younger sons without prospects. Had aspirations as a portraitist, according to the artists in the Windham family. Murdoch, you will arrange your features into something resembling a civilized expression or Lady Deene will think a Scottish brigand has joined the company. Your sisters are glaring at you already."

Hamish's sisters glared at him out of habit.

"Better still," Rosecroft said, "get yourself out to the balcony off the family parlor down the corridor, where your younger brother is about to avail himself of the favors of a lady whose husband is the jealous sort."

306

Sir Fletcher had left off fawning over the marchioness's hand. His attention was on Megan, who'd parted company with Quimbey and was making her way to the punch bowl.

Hamish swore in Gaelic. Rosecroft's brows rose. Too late, Hamish recalled that Rosecroft's first language was Irish, a cousin to his own native Gaelic.

"Time might be of the essence," Rosecroft said. "Your brother appeared to be a man intent upon his goal, as it were."

"He was born intent on that goal," Hamish said. "I can't tend to Colin now with Sir Fletcher about to trouble Meggie." Though somebody had to tend to Colin. The damned fool would get himself called out or worse.

"See to your brother," Keswick said. "We'll keep an eye on Megan — a close eye."

"Keep a closer eye on yonder knight," Hamish warned. "Sir Fletcher means her no good. If I'm not back in ten minutes, please see my sisters home, and tell Megan I'll always love her."

Hamish bowed to them as genially as he could when battle rage threatened. Colin had a positive genius for getting into scrapes at the worst possible times, though at least reinforcements were available if Meggie needed them.

Based on Sir Fletcher's demeanor — brilliant smile, and a gaze that put Hamish in mind of hungry serpents — she needed them that very instant.

A man in a kilt moved differently from a man in standard London evening attire. He moved more freely, more dashingly. Megan could not make out Hamish's expression, but she knew her intended stood watch across the room. The Duke of Quimbey blathered on about puppies and married life, while Megan nodded, smiled, and pretended to pay attention.

"My duchess has chosen our seats," Quimbey said. "You will excuse me, Miss Megan — unless you'd like to sit with us?"

The old scamp well knew Megan had other plans. "Thank you, Your Grace, but I see Lady Rhona and Lady Edana signaling me. They expect me to join them for the second half of the program."

Quimbey bowed over Megan's hand and strode off. Megan hoped that was Edana and Rhona by the punch bowl — they favored bold hues, and rightly so. With their red hair and vivid coloring, greens, burgundies, blues, and browns all looked quite well on them.

Megan was determined to sit with Hamish for the remainder of the program, and thus she nearly didn't see the man she collided with halfway to the punch bowl.

"Miss Megan, I beg your pardon."

Sir Fletcher kept his hands on Megan's arms, his grip uncomfortable. He'd worn too much attar of roses again, and the threat underlying his greeting slithered about in Megan's insides like a cold draft.

"Sir Fletcher, good evening. How are you?"

"I've been desolated for lack of your company," he replied, one hand over his heart. "Might I hope you've missed me?"

Megan would have missed a megrim as much, provided it was accompanied with a toothache, a turned ankle, and dysentery.

"I'm sure Lady Edana and Lady Rhona would like to greet you," she said, "and they expect me to sit with them." Right between them, if need be, for Megan had no intention of spending one instant longer than necessary beside Sir Fletcher.

"Come," Sir Fletcher said, taking Megan by the arm. "I know the crowded confines here are difficult for you to navigate. Stay by me, and I'll not let you come to harm."

He was up to no good, attaching himself

too closely to Megan's side, and at a gathering where much of polite society would take note. Apparently, he'd yet to realize Megan's letters had been returned to her.

Sir Fletcher did the pretty with Rhona and Edana. All the while, Megan expected Hamish to join the discussion, though she didn't dare try to attract his notice. Instead, Keswick and Rosecroft appeared, declaring themselves parched for both a cup of punch and the company of lovely women.

Megan was thus ensconced between two of her male cousins when the string quartet opened the last portion of the program, while Sir Fletcher was flanked by Edana and Rhona.

And Hamish was nowhere to be seen.

CHAPTER FOURTEEN

Something about Megan Windham was different, though Sir Fletcher could not decide if he liked the difference. She'd been standing in the center of the room, flirting with a duke. An elderly, newly married duke, but still . . .

Megan typically stayed to the perimeter of a room — probably less chance of falling on her face that way — and she wasn't in the habit of smiling and beaming great good humor at all and sundry. Perhaps her poor eyesight meant she'd been at the men's punch bowl rather than the ladies'.

Sir Fletcher had certainly availed himself of the libation, and a decent offering it was too.

The music was also fine, and the program ended with Lady Deene's brother, Lord Valentine, dazzling the assemblage with his skills at the keyboard. His lordship was prodigiously talented, which fact he impressed upon all and sundry at tedious length.

"Where could our brothers have got off to?" Lady Rhona mused as the gathering began to break up. "They both enjoy music, and I was sure —"

"Some guests were listening from the library across the corridor," Rosecroft said. "More comfortable chairs, you know. Lady Deene's invitations are seldom refused, and the result can be a crowd."

"Exactly," Keswick said. "Comfortable chairs, access to the buffet. What fellow wouldn't be tempted? Murdoch won't mind if we escort you ladies home, I'm sure."

"Capital notion," Sir Fletcher said, affixing himself to Megan's side. "I was about to make the same suggestion."

Megan Windham — the most pleasant, boring, soft-spoken, biddable spinster in captivity — muttered something under her breath that sounded distinctly unladylike.

"I beg your pardon?" Sir Fletcher murmured, bending close. One could take liberties in public, provided one appeared solicitous while doing so.

"A megrim," Megan said. "I'm certain a megrim is trying to get hold of me. Perhaps the fresh air will help."

The fresh air would help, as would the

darkened streets, and a bit of privacy.

Sir Fletcher had been lax in his doting and adoring for the past week or so. Fortunately, a musicale was free food and drink, and not the sort of venue where he'd be harassed about his debts. The time had arrived to remind Megan Windham of a few salient facts.

Once on the street, Sir Fletcher refused to budge from Megan's side, while Rosecroft escorted Lady Edana, and Keswick took up a place at Lady Rhona's side.

"Why won't they leave us any privacy?" Sir Fletcher asked quietly. "You should have them better trained than this, when we're all but courting."

No matter how slowly or quickly Sir Fletcher walked, one of Megan's relations remained ahead of them and one behind.

"They are conscientious in their duties," Megan replied. "Why would I want privacy with you, Sir Fletcher? Affording you a few moments of privacy resulted in some of my most dreadful memories."

For Megan to be that honest, her head must truly be paining her, poor darling. "Fear not, dearest. In time, you'll learn to enjoy my attentions," Sir Fletcher said, though he kept his voice down. "When are your parents returning from Wales?"

For Anwen Windham had neglected to send Sir Fletcher the address she'd promised him.

"Whenever they please," Megan retorted, tugging her arm loose.

Sir Fletcher caught her hand and curled it around his forearm, then laid his own over her fingers in a firm grip.

"I'm all for the occasional show of spirit in a horse or a woman," Sir Fletcher said, "but sulks and pouts do not become you. We need to set a date."

"Tonight will do nicely," Megan said, sounding as if she spoke through clenched teeth. "Tonight you commence leaving me in peace, acting as a true gentleman ought. Do not for an instant think to charm Lady Edana or Lady Rhona into some linen closet or saddle room. Their brothers will kill you for going near them henceforth. You'll leave my sisters alone too, or I'll come after you myself."

Over the rattle and racket of passing carriages, the conversations of other pedestrians leaving the musicale, and the calls of the linkboys, nobody else would have heard Megan's outburst.

Sir Fletcher wasn't sure he'd heard her correctly either.

"My dear, are you sickening for something? I'm the fellow who has sampled your charms, if you'll recall. The gallant officer to whom you penned torrid pages in impressive quantity. I have proof that you've surrendered your innocence into my tender keeping, and with that proof, I can ruin you and your sisters."

Also get his hands on a decent sum, thank God. What else was an earl's younger son to do, but marry as well as he could?

Megan walked along in silence, while Sir Fletcher considered that perhaps a strain of weak nerves ran in the Windham family. The sooner he married Megan and got her out from under her papa's roof the better.

Or perhaps Megan wasn't the docile, bespectacled schoolgirl he'd singled out for his flirtations years ago. That could make married life interesting — or a damned lot of work.

"You've grown quiet," he said. Megan had also grown tense. "You're having a bad moment, probably that dratted megrim. I've been considering a special license — best five pounds a bachelor ever spent, according to some. Your papa would thank me for saving him the expense of a wedding, and marriage is said to settle a young woman's nerves."

"Heed me, Sir Fletcher," Megan said, very

quietly. "I have my letters back. Every one of them has been returned to me. Your hold over me has been broken, and I will make very, very sure every woman of my acquaintance knows what you tried to do to me, until there's not a ballroom or garden party where you will be welcome. If I were you, I'd develop a sudden urge to tour the Canadian wilderness or the jungles of darkest Peru. A sudden, protracted urge."

Megan extricated herself from Sir Fletcher's grip and attached herself to Keswick's free arm. "We should bid Sir Fletcher good evening," she said. "We approach the intersection at which his path diverges from our own."

The hell they did.

Sir Fletcher bowed nonetheless, because clearly, Megan Windham believed what she'd said. She thought her letters were again safe in her possession, and considered herself free to bestow her company on any presuming Scottish barbarian she chose.

"I bid the company good night," Sir Fletcher said. "My ladies, my lords, a pleasant evening. Miss Megan, until we meet again."

For Sir Fletcher's path had by no means diverged from hers, nor would she be indulging this sudden penchant for the

316

company of the Duke of Murdoch, of all the loutish, inappropriate, laughable specimens.

Sir Fletcher would, however, procure a special license.

"You should just beat me and be done with it," Colin said as he walked along beside Hamish.

"I nearly threw you over the balcony." This was not true, though Hamish had been tempted to leap over the balcony and leave his handsome, randy brother to the fate he deserved. "The lady has a reputation."

The words echoed quietly in the dim street, also in Hamish's heart. When would Colin learn some caution? What had the world come to, when Hamish was better informed about a wife with a propensity to stray than Colin was?

"I like the ones with reputations. They're friendly when a fellow is all alone and far from home. How was I to know the husband also has a reputation?"

For dueling at the drop of a bodice ribbon.

Papa had tried thrashing sense into his sons, but even he had given up on corporal punishment where Colin was concerned. *Let the army sort him out.*

"Think of our sisters," Hamish said. "If you're embroiled in a scandal, then they are too, and scandal has a way of becoming a permanent fixture in a family's reputation. I've done enough to tarnish the MacHugh escutcheon. But for this damned title, Eddie and Ronnie wouldn't be accepted into such refined company as it is."

"Eddie and Ronnie would kill me if I caused a scandal," Colin said, steps slowing. "I wouldn't enjoy that."

"You'd disappoint them," Hamish rejoined. "Fate worse than death, when they get disappointed in a man. Winters are long enough without that pair sighing and muttering."

"That's why you should serve me a sound thrashing," Colin said. "If I'm sporting a few bruises, then Eddie and Ronnie won't bludgeon me with guilt. A black eye is all it would take."

"You're daft, but then, we knew that." Hamish would never strike his own brother, would likely never strike another living soul.

Colin took out his flask, had a nip, and passed it over to Hamish. "If I asked you to meet me at Jackson's Salon, would you?"

Hamish took a whiff of the open container, because Colin's tastes were as unreliable as his common sense. Tonight, the brew on offer was slightly smoky, with a delicate roll of cedar and cinnamon beneath the fumes. Sipping whisky, as opposed to the ruinous variety.

"For God's sake, why would anybody pursue a sound pummeling on purpose?" Hamish muttered.

"Because you get to pummel some other fellow, and it keeps a man on his mettle, to put up his fives."

No, it did not. Premeditated pugilism put a man within closer reach of memories best left unvisited. Hamish's single post-war attempt at hand-to-hand combat — a bout with his former captor, the Baron St. Clair — had proved that.

"I won't beat you," Hamish said. "Your guilty conscience can spare my arm."

Colin accepted the flask back, taking another swallow before tucking it away. "Will you at least take a swing at me if I admit I worry about you?"

Well, hell. "I'll have a laugh. You're the hothead, the reckless fool about whom our parents worried the most. We all worry about you, Colin. You are not to trouble your pretty head at this late stage about me."

"You hate being a duke, just as you hated the army."

Colin was indeed feeling reckless. "How

much have you had to drink?"

"Not enough. Interferes with my ability to please the ladies."

Hamish had hated the army, but until now, Colin had spared them both that admission. "With the right duchess beside me, being a duke won't be so bad. Megan's people have been dukes for centuries. I expect a Scot new to the title of duke is a mere aristocratic corporal by comparison. Were you trying to goad me into beating you, Colin?"

The resounding silence was answer enough.

"Colin, don't inspire me into raising my hand against you. You love a good scrap, while I've had a bellyful of fighting in all its forms. After a bout of temper, you'll probably shake hands with the fellow who's bloodied your nose, whereas I might well bury my opponent. I would hate for that fellow to be you."

The flask glinted in the light of the nearest porch lamp, though this time, Colin stopped walking and drained the container.

"You left a part of yourself back in France," Colin said. "I don't know what part, but it was important, and you haven't been truly happy since you mustered out — since you joined up, in fact. I don't know what to do for you, and now this damned title has been slung about your neck. Somehow, that feels like my fault too."

Quite the confession from a man who loved to gallop breakneck across open country or across some merry widow's sheets.

Hamish laid an arm over Colin's shoulders and scrubbed his knuckles against his brother's crown.

"I'm a duke. Soon I'll be a husband. I do believe the one will be copious consolation for the other. Maybe instead of chasing widows and testing my temper, you ought to find a wife of your own."

Hamish expected Colin to laugh. Instead another silence rose between them, this one as thoughtful as the last one had been frustrated.

"I apologize for abandoning you at the musicale," Hamish said. "Colin got into a wee situation involving a lady and a darkened balcony."

"Let me guess," Megan said as she strolled the Moreland gardens with her beloved in the morning sunshine. "The Viscountess Rothergild. She's had her eye on him since he showed up at Aunt Esther's ball in his kilt. I should have warned him."

Hamish seemed tired, or perhaps burdened, but then, he typically called on Megan in the morning, when most of polite society rested and domesticated.

"I'm not courting you so you can take on the task of looking after my siblings, Meggie. Your family has done much for me and mine already. Getting Colin out of scrapes has been my job since he was born."

As, apparently, was looking after Edana and Rhona, managing the family wealth, keeping an eye on other brothers and relatives back in Scotland as well as various cousins in London, and otherwise being head of the family. Megan took Hamish's hand, because she loved to touch him, and because the way his fingers grasped hers and the attitude of his walk told her as much as his words.

"Sir Fletcher escorted me home."

"Did he *bother* you, Meggie?" Hamish's tone promised woe to Sir Fletcher if he had transgressed.

What a lovely man Megan's intended was. "I informed Sir Fletcher that he no longer had my letters, and told him to keep his distance from me, my sisters, your sisters, and polite society in general. He seemed to take it well, but then, Rosecroft and Keswick were nearby, and Edana and Rhona were

322

along as well."

Hamish drew Megan behind a hedge of rhododendrons that had yet to bloom. His arms came around her, secure and sheltering.

"Meggie mine, you took a risk."

"You took a risk, retrieving my letters. Putting Sir Fletcher in his place was marvelously gratifying. I couldn't call him out, but I could deliver a set down. As much as I'm grateful to you for getting those letters back, I'm equally grateful that I had the chance to confront him. He's a pestilence that wanted purging."

"You put up your fives," Hamish said, kissing Megan's brow. "Poor bastard was doubtless ambushed. Well done, Meggie, but you must promise me you'll be cautious now. Sir Fletcher doesn't deal well with being thwarted."

The hedge gave them privacy, which Megan would have liked to use plundering her beloved's charms. Hamish, though, did not seem in a plunder-able mood.

"Tell me the rest of it," she said. "You know something you're not saying, and we're to be married, Hamish. You're very much in my confidence, and I hope you'll return that honor to me."

He kissed her, and even his kisses could

convey a sense of weariness. "I don't like to talk about my time in the army."

Megan rested her cheek against his chest, the better to feel his heartbeat. "Rosecroft says he prefers living up north for many reasons. He has no patience with men who've nothing better to do than relive a few years of gore and glory over drinks at the club. Life is not meant to be an endless reminiscence, much less one that misrepresents the past as other than it was."

Hamish's hand settled on her nape, and everything in Megan relaxed.

"Your cousin told you that?"

"He told Emmie that, and Louisa and Eve say Keswick and Deene are of the same mind. I love the scent of you, Hamish Mac-Hugh." She did not love that his sporran came between them. "Let's sit, shall we?"

He went unresisting to the nearest bench, a plain, sun-warmed wooden seat amid potted delphiniums. For long moments, he was quiet, his hand in Megan's.

"While you're gathering your thoughts," Megan said, "may I explain something to you? I've only recently puzzled it out for myself."

He kissed her knuckles. "I like when you explain things to me. Not many people bother to try, but you have the way of it."

Perhaps because Hamish listened when she spoke and wasn't in a great hurry to be elsewhere, though by rights he ought at that moment to be lounging about some gentlemen's club.

"My eyesight is poor," Megan said. "Even so, with my spectacles, I can see better than many, and my cognitive faculties are in fine working order. I'm grateful for that. I see especially well early in the day, but then my eyes grow fatigued. In any case, there's also much I cannot do because of my bad vision."

"Stone blind you'd be four times the woman most ladies are on their most sighted day, Meggie Windham, soon to be Mac-Hugh, and I'll —"

She kissed his chin. "Put down your claymore, Murdoch. My family loves me. The people who fuss at me for imperfect vision don't matter, and I use my relative obscurity to ponder my surroundings.

"Why is Charlotte so restless this year," she went on, "and what is stopping Beth from making a suitable match? Why is Anwen so devoted to those orphans, and when can you and I be married?"

"You deserve to be thoroughly courted," Hamish said. "Also kissed."

As it happened, Megan agreed with that

last sentiment, and somehow ended up in Hamish's lap as a result. She climbed off of him, and instead of taking the place beside him, folded down to the paving stones at his feet, sitting with her back to his knees.

"You have a talent for distracting me, Hamish. Hear me out, please."

His fingers whispered across her nape, as softly as sunshine. "Of course. Always."

What a privilege, to nuzzle a man's bare knee, to acquaint oneself with the muscle and bone and strength of him. Megan looked forward to the day — or evening — when she could learn all of Hamish Mac-Hugh at her leisure.

"I think about things," she said, before the temptation to kiss his knee overcame the last of her sense, "and that means, I'm good at puzzling out what might not be obvious. I suspect Sir Fletcher is not his papa's son, for example."

Those fingers, which were distracting Megan in the best possible way, paused. "A cuckoo in the nest?"

"He's a fourth son, meaning his late mama had done her duty by the title, and he came along a good five years after the next oldest brother. He doesn't look anything like his siblings, his papa hardly takes notice of him."

"And he has the put-upon air of one treated unfairly from a young age. You might be right. That would shed light on his behavior in Spain, though it wouldn't excuse it."

Two thoughts coalesced in Megan's awareness. The first was silly and delightful: Even Hamish's knee tasted of heather, suggesting he was fastidious in all particulars.

The second was delightful and not silly at all: Perhaps Hamish talked to her and listened to her so well in part because her eyesight was poor. A reserved man, a *shy* man, one uncomfortable in London society, would be more at ease when free from endless visual scrutiny.

How *wonderful,* that a lack of keen eyesight could be such a valuable asset.

"Tell me about Spain, and about Sir Fletcher," Megan said, twitching Hamish's kilt over his knee.

The wool was soft, the sense of tenderness Megan endured nearly unbearable. She'd never have to pretend with Hamish as she so often did with her family, never have to make light of a moment turned awkward because she'd forgotten her spectacles.

Hamish's palm smoothed her hair in a slow caress. "Sir Fletcher was a great one for having his men flogged. Any pretext would do, and his superiors turned a blind eye. Army discipline is a curious thing. We were downright social with the French sometimes, then word would come down that any man caught fraternizing would be court-martialed. For a time, distance would be kept. Very confusing for the men, and sometimes they got caught in the spats and stupidities of their officers."

That was all preamble, of course, though enlightening. "Sounds like the social season with guns. I can't imagine a less appealing undertaking."

Hamish's thumb traced the curve of Megan's jaw. "Sir Fletcher was mostly competent, from what I could gather, but his tolerance for the Irish or Scottish lads when they got to scrapping was poor. He accused a fellow of stealing from regimental stores, which is viewed very dimly. The boy was barely shaving, none too bright, and probably starving. I intervened."

"With your fists?" What did it say about a proper lady, that she relished the notion of somebody pummeling Sir Fletcher?

"Meggie dearest, you have a bloodthirsty streak. My papa, God rest him, would approve."

"Sir Fletcher needs to be held accountable," Megan said. "I have memories of him I wish I could wash out of my mind, Hamish." She knew how Sir Fletcher breathed under intimate circumstances, knew the feel of him between her legs.

And abruptly, tears threatened. She hadn't cried, not when Sir Fletcher had ignored her upon mustering out, not when he'd decided to take notice of her weeks ago. Not when he'd explained, in blunt, disrespectful terms, what his plans were for her.

"Ach, Meggie, let me hold you."

She was back in Hamish's arms, beside him on the bench, tears spilling in hot profusion down her cheeks. From her middle, a wail was building, a cry of regret and outrage.

"I *prayed* for him," she said, pressing her forehead to Hamish's shoulder. "I promised to wait for him, and prayed for his safe return. I told myself all couples need time, and eventually, I'd have children and a home of my own. I assured myself he couldn't answer my letters without risking my reputation, not very often. Then he mustered out, and the first time we encountered each other, he treated me like . . ."

"Don't speak of it, if it pains you," Hamish said. "He can't hurt you anymore, Meggie."

Oh, but he could. Sir Fletcher was hurting Megan at that moment, haunting her with memories of rejection and humiliation.

"He acted as if he barely recognized me. I didn't have my glasses. For a moment, I wondered if I'd mistaken some other gentleman for my very own Sir Fletcher. Before half of polite society, he made a prodigious fuss about recalling a few dances with me, graciously greeting a besotted young woman who'd made a complete cake of herself. With every gossip looking on, I realized how great a fool I'd been. I've spent my seasons since avoiding him, and then, this year, he decided to make a greater fool of me still."

Hamish held her, let her cry and sniffle and regret, but the longer Megan remained in his arms, the more the hurt and anger faded.

"I wish him to perdition for all time," she said. "I was an idiot — I hate that I was such a blind idiot — but he was no gentleman."

"He was, and is, a scoundrel of the first water."

Something in Hamish's voice caught Megan's ear. She sat up, tucking herself against his side. Before too much longer, some helpful sister — or duchess — would come strolling along, inspecting the beds of roses that were still not ready to bloom. If

Megan was found in tears, all manner of meddling might result.

"You've foiled him," Megan said. "Thank God, you've put Sir Fletcher in his place once and for all. I suspect it's not the first time you've frustrated a scheme of his."

"I'm marrying a woman of discernment. Sir Fletcher got the worst of our encounter in Spain too, though I suspect that's why he later sent Colin off on a goose chase."

"As long as Sir Fletcher got the worst of it," Megan said, snuggling closer to her beloved. "May he always get the worst of it in the end, and I do want to hear the details. But first, Hamish, you must know that my sisters agreed I should have the last bedroom in the family corridor. It's the one overlooking that border of heartsease. Will you join me tonight?"

He took to studying the flowers Megan had mentioned, cheerful little purple and yellow blooms that tolerated cold and wet easily. Shading the heartsease was a maple whose branches made climbing to the balcony the work of a moment for a fit and determined suitor.

"Your cognitive faculties have turned to organizing my evening schedule?"

Well, yes. More or less, and Hamish hadn't offered an immediate refusal either.

CHAPTER FIFTEEN

Army life had taught Sir Fletcher all about suffering — how to avoid it, how to inflict it on others, and even how to endure it when necessary. He hadn't liked the enduring part *at all.*

"Poppet, might you practice your singing somewhere else?" Geneva's voice would shatter crystal at thirty paces, for the child had operatic aspirations. Her older sisters, damn them to eternal spinsterhood, encouraged the girl's musical fancies.

"Papa says I must practice in the library for it has the thickest walls. When will you take me riding, Fletchie? You promised."

The late morning sun made patterns on the parquet floor, though even reflected sunlight was so many daggers plunged into Sir Fletcher's pounding skull.

"I'll take you up before me when the weather's fine," Sir Fletcher said, pouring himself a tot of brandy. The housekeeper doubtless kept track of whose visits to the library coincided with a reduction in the sideboard's inventory — one of the many indignities Sir Fletcher would not miss when he set up his own household.

"The weather is fine today," Geneva said, climbing onto the sofa. "Papa said the day is lovely, but my beauty surprises even the sun."

When the girl smiled like that, the sun very likely was surprised. "Not surprises, surpasses. It means goes beyond. Jumping on the sofa surpasses the worst manners I've seen you display heretofore, Lady Geneva Louise Marie Hamilcar Pilkington. Little girls who hop about and make noise won't find themselves sharing the saddle with their favorite older brother."

Sir Fletcher *was* her favorite, which mattered more than it ought.

She kept up her gymnastics, blonde curls bouncing against her little shoulders. "Thomas didn't scold me for jumping on the sofa. I like him. When will he get his livery so he doesn't have to work in that skirt? Is that why I haven't seen him above-stairs? Because his livery hasn't arrived?"

Her questions hammered against Sir Fletcher's aching head, a counterpoint to her unladylike hopping about.

"Would you like a sip of my drink?" Geneva was his sister, at least in name, though he doubted they shared any blood. All the same, scolding him had never worked when he'd taken a childish notion to abuse the sofa cushions, so he didn't bother to scold her.

"Your drinks are awful, and you forget to use your toothpowder in the morning. When can we go riding?"

"Where's Harriet?" Sir Fletcher asked, lifting the candlestick on the left side of the mantel. "A lady typically rides out with her friends, and Harriet will be wroth if you don't take her along to the mews."

Harriet was the best distraction Sir Fletcher could come up with on short notice.

"Her name is Harold," Geneva said, leaping from the sofa with an athletic bound. She landed hard, the impact reverberating between Sir Fletcher's throbbing temples. "Harold has a megrim, like you. You didn't answer my question about Thomas. He talked funny."

The key to the desk drawer was exactly where it should have been, under the candlestick, but no amount of reaching about or rearranging of the drawer's contents turned up Megan Windham's letters.

Buggering bedamned hell. Sir Fletcher had stopped at home after escorting Megan from the musicale, and lo, she'd been telling the truth: Her letters were no longer where they belonged. He'd gone on to his club in search of a quiet place to think, and perhaps relax with a hand of cards.

Or two or three hands. After that, matters had got muddled. Yesterday had been spent mostly recovering from a bit of overindulgence. Today, Geneva's older sisters were off at the modiste's, meaning the library was finally — almost — deserted.

"Will you draw pictures with me?" Geneva asked, latching on to Sir Fletcher's arm. "You draw the best unicorns."

"Ladies shouldn't wheedle," Sir Fletcher said, ruffling her curls. "Pamela is the artistic genius in the family, and you are the budding soprano."

"I'm the surpassing soprano," Geneva said, climbing onto Sir Fletcher's lap. "Don't breathe on me or I'll tell Papa you've a sore head again. Pammy said your head must be harder than paving stones. I bet Thomas had a sore head too. He fell on the hearthstones and said bad words, because he got an ouchy-poo you-know-where. I couldn't understand his bad words, because he talked funny, but they sounded splendidly naughty just the same."

Geneva was opening and slamming the drawers one by one, while Sir Fletcher's aching brain tried to make sense of her chatter.

"You say this Thomas fellow wore a skirt?"

"Yes, and he talked funny, but he was nice. He didn't scold me, and he smelled like flowers. You stink like cigars."

"You came across Thomas here in the library?"

Bang! She'd nearly caught Sir Fletcher's fingers that time. "Yes. He didn't light the candles because that saves money. Papa likes to save money, Mama says saving money is tiresome and un . . . unbedumbing of her station."

"Unbecoming, which means it doesn't suit her. Stop prying into grown-up business, poppet."

Geneva wrapped her arms around Sir Fletcher's neck and squeezed. "I like you the best because you explain words to me. Being stuck inside is unbecoming of my station. May we go riding now?"

If he took the child riding now, she'd be that much more tenacious about her next request. She was a bright, determined little female who'd make some man miserable when she grew older.

"Tell me more about Thomas. I don't think I've met him."

Geneva scrambled about in Sir Fletcher's lap, nearly gelding him with a knee. "Thomas is tall, and he speaks softly. He talks like . . . not like you. Like Mrs. Belkins if she were a man. He wore a skirt because his livery wasn't back from the tailor yet, and he didn't light the candles because that wastes money. He hasn't tattled on me."

Sir Fletcher set her on her feet. "When was this?" Ada Belkins had been brought up in Aberdeenshire, an aspect of her history obvious from her accent.

"The night Pammy danced with Mr. Puget. She loves him, Alexa said so, and Pammy hit her with a pillow. Can we go riding now?"

"May we." In the past few weeks, Sir Fletcher had seen Megan Windham in the company of two tall Scotsmen, one being Murdoch, the other being Murdoch's younger brother. Murdoch favored the kilt, he spoke with an accent, and his gaze when he studied Megan was watchful.

The younger brother was a flirt, though he might retrieve a lady's letters on a gallant dare. Sir Fletcher vaguely recalled some pranks among the officers in Spain involving the dashing Captain MacHugh. For much of the campaign boredom had been a more formidable enemy than the French, and the Scottish officers had been so easy to make sport of.

Perhaps the captain was up to some retaliatory pranks of his own.

The situation wanted more thought at some point when seventeen jack-booted devils weren't dancing a jig in Sir Fletcher's brainbox.

"Well, *may* we go riding now?" Geneva asked, turning her question into a musical bellow. "The day is fine, you're awake, and nobody is home to play with me. May we *pleeeeeease*?"

"You are persistent," Sir Fletcher said. "Let me change into my riding breeches, and we'll tour the alley before your poor governess can sound the alarm. You must promise me one thing, though."

Geneva pirouetted before the hearth, but spoiled the charming effect by coming to a graceless halt.

"You'll take me riding right now, truly?"

"You're my favorite sister, of course I'll take you riding. About the promise, Geneva."

"Anything," she said, spinning again. "Anything at all, Fletchie."

"Thomas got tired of waiting for new livery, and has taken a position elsewhere. It would be best if you didn't mention him to anybody else."

She grabbed Sir Fletcher's hand and began towing him toward the door. "I won't say a word, as long as you take me riding all the way to the park and back."

As if he'd be caught dead indulging a child in public. "We'll have a turn about the alley, and you'd better hope your governess isn't watching from the windows when you're supposed to be napping or working at your French."

"You're supposed to be amounting to something," Geneva countered. "Papa says you never will, and Mama agreed with him. Will I ever amount to something?"

The pounding in Sir Fletcher's head was joined by a seething biliousness in his belly. He shook his hand free of Geneva's.

"You are already my favorite sister." Also a very good spy, praise heaven. "Please go to the mews and tell Jacobs to saddle Jupiter. I'll be along shortly."

Or perhaps not. The situation with Miss Megan Windham wanted immediate attention, while Geneva could entertain herself for hours chasing barn cats and getting her pinafore dirty. Sir Fletcher, by contrast, had a special license to procure, and an errant fiancée to bring to heel.

"Aren't you coming with us?" Colin asked.

Hamish rubbed tired eyes. "What time is it?"

Colin consulted a gold watch that went nicely with his evening attire. He wore the kilt well, with just enough dash and just enough decorum.

"It's late enough that Eddie and Ronnie will be down any minute, ready to terrorize the unsuspecting bachelors of Mayfair once more. They've taken to being ladies with a vengeance."

Hamish set aside the ledger he'd been working on and moved the stack of bills to the edge of the blotter. His library wasn't the grand public room the Duke of Moreland's mansion boasted, but the books here were well loved and the chair behind the desk comfortable.

"Our sisters have taken to bankrupting me," Hamish said.

Colin settled into the chair opposite the desk, one ankle crossed casually over the opposite knee.

"Are you being the tightfisted Scot, bemoaning the loss of every groat while you hoard up twenty in its place, or are you serious?"

"Mostly the Scot," Hamish said. "I don't begrudge the ladies their finery, but we've weeks of prancing about to endure yet, and I hope to negotiate marriage settlements before we leave here."

Colin snapped the watch closed. "Would you tell me if you needed help?"

"I'd tell you before I'd tell anybody else."

The watch was tucked away, the chain hanging just so across Colin's flat middle. "I'll take that for a no, even though I'm filthy rich and I love you better than I love my horse."

"Colin Andrew, you'll move me to tears." Or to drink. Hamish tossed a bill across the desk. "Is this your new bootmaker?"

"Puget and Sons? Never heard of them, and I know the bootmakers in London because Eddie and Ronnie have dragged me to most of them. The merchants probably don't expect you to be here come December, so they're settling with you as they go."

Poring over the ledgers had left Hamish's eyes stinging, which made him think of Meggie, though everything made him think of Meggie.

"I don't blame the trades for trying to prey on a new title," Hamish said. "I do expect them to provide goods for the coin they seek."

Colin studied the invoice. "Let me have a chat with this bootmaker. I don't recognize the direction, but I'll stop around at their establishment and see what I can find out. We've barely been here long enough to have many boots made."

Hamish was about to demand return of the invoice, but Colin was watching him, his gaze unreadable. Colin had a temper, though unlike Hamish's, it was a cold, calculating temper. A man who crossed the wrong line with affable, easygoing Captain Lord Colin MacHugh would never see retribution coming until it put out his lights with the first blow.

"Let's not be hasty," Hamish said, holding out his hand for the bill. "I'm convinced London runs as much on gossip as the army ever did. One unhappy cobbler and I'll find old Moreland doubting my solvency."

Colin passed over the offending invoice and rose as feminine chatter sounded from the corridor. "Now you're doing your impersonation of the dour Scotsman. Moreland has five daughters, and he knows what a London season costs. I'll tell the ladies you have a megrim, because you look as if you do. Courting is taking a toll on you."

Waiting was taking a toll on Hamish.

"I'll make my own excuses to the ladies," Hamish said, pushing to his feet. "If they don't scold me for something twice a day, they mope."

Too late, Hamish realized he'd blundered. Again. Colin wanted to be useful, but Colin's version of useful too often ended up in wagers, fisticuffs, or awkward apologies.

The door opened and Edana and Rhona stormed into the room.

"Hamish, you will please make yourself presentable in the next twelve minutes, or you'll cause us to be late," Rhona said.

"Not fashionably late either," Edana echoed. "Rudely late. We'll miss the opening sets, and I've promised the promenade to" — she peered at a slip of paper — "Mr. Cam Dorning."

"He's too young for you," Rhona said. "But I do fancy his eyes. Hamish, what are you waiting for? You can't go out dressed like that."

"I'm not —" Hamish began as Colin opened the door and swept a hand toward the corridor.

"The ledgers have given Hamish a megrim," Colin said. "A predictable result of trying to keep up with all the bills you two generate. While you have a lie-in until noon,

343

he's out and about, wooing the fair young maid. I hear the coach, so let's be on our way."

"But Ham is the *duke*," Rhona said, tossing her curls over her shoulder.

"How will it look," Edana chimed in, "if the head of the family can't be bothered to escort his own sisters, ladies in their first season, despite the fact that we're nearly old enough to describe Noah's ark? When a man acquires a title —"

"Speak for yourself, Eddie MacHugh," Rhona shot back. "I'm not that old. Many women don't make their come outs until —"

"That's *Lady* Edana, if you please."

"Enough!" Hamish snapped. "You comport yourselves like children rather than daughters of Clan MacHugh. Colin, I'll thank you to see the ladies around tonight."

An uneasy glance passed between the women. Hamish hated that glance, for he hadn't even raised his voice.

Rhona stuck her nose in the air and flounced out. Edana cast Hamish a fretful sniff, then did likewise. Colin remained in the doorway, an odd smile lurking in his eyes.

"The world doesn't come to an end because you occasionally have an evening at home," he said. "I'll keep them out of trouble."

"Keep yourself out of trouble," Hamish replied. "Lady Rothergild apparently enjoys making her husband jealous, and he's accounted a good shot."

Colin's smile died. "I'll take care of our sisters, Hamish, and I'm an *excellent* shot. Get some rest. You need it." He marched off, not bothering to close the door.

"I'll go straight up to bed when I've finished here," Hamish promised his brother's retreating back.

Colin waved a dismissive hand and continued on his way to the front door.

"That went well," Hamish muttered as he capped the ink bottle and stood the quill in the standish. He'd managed to offend three siblings in the space of five minutes, and also to tell a lie — two lies, actually.

For he'd not be finishing with the ledgers, nor would he be going straight up to bed.

CHAPTER SIXTEEN

"You're sure you'd rather stay home?" Aunt Esther asked, her gaze appraising. "You'll be missed, Megs dear."

Uncle Percy held up Aunt Esther's cloak. "My love, every young lady is entitled to the occasional evening at home. Let the dashing swains pine for a change. Serves them right for all the times they dodge off to their clubs — or worse."

Aunt and Uncle exchanged a look that included humor, a short contest of wills, and possibly a bit of flirtation — and at their ages.

"I'll be fine," Megan said. "I'll read some poetry and go to bed early."

Charlotte and Beth came down the stairs, resplendent in aubergine and raspberry.

"Megan has decided to sit out the evening," Aunt said, raising her chin as Uncle Percy fastened the frogs of her cloak. "She needs to rest her feet, should anybody ask."

Charlotte accepted the next cloak from Uncle Percy. "Megs is avoiding the watch. Those three leave a lady cousin no peace. My feet could certainly use a rest. Perhaps I'll stay home."

Damn Charlotte for her loyalty.

"And leave me to contend with our cousins *and* the bachelors?" Beth retorted. "I think not. At least our cousins dance wonderfully." She peered into the mirror over the sideboard and touched the tips of her fourth and fifth fingers to a coiffure that blended demure elegance with russet tumbling curls. Charlotte, by contrast, was sporting a chignon worthy of a dowager Methodist.

"My boys get their nimbleness on the dance floor from my duchess," Uncle said. "Ladies, I hear the coach. Shall we be on our way?"

Yes, please. "Have a wonderful time," Megan said, holding the door for them. "Bring me back all the gossip."

The ladies filed out, while Uncle Percy remained behind, tugging on his gloves. "You've never been interested in gossip, Megs."

Well, no. She hadn't, and she still wasn't. "Perhaps I'm growing more social."

Uncle kissed her forehead. "Perhaps

347

you're falling in love. Enjoy your evening at home." He winked and set off down the steps at a brisk pace.

Megan remained in the doorway, waving her sisters off. Charlotte blew her a kiss and climbed into the coach. Beth twiddled her fingers in Megan's direction.

"One has no privacy in this household," Megan muttered.

The butler, a stalwart old fixture named Hodges, cleared his throat. "Miss Anwen has often remarked similarly, ma'am. Shall I have the kitchen send up a tea tray?"

"No, thank you, Hodges. I truly am quite fatigued. An early night will be the salvation of my week." Or her sanity.

"I'll bid you good evening, miss."

Megan made her escape up the stairs at a dignified pace, when she would rather have taken the steps two at a time. Her bedroom beckoned, though in truth all this subterfuge was likely pointless. Hamish was not the type to climb to a lady's balcony or indulge in clandestine trysts.

Megan loved that about him, loved how honorable he was — truly she did.

"Are they gone?" Anwen had opened her bedroom door a mere crack and spoken just above a whisper.

"They're gone," Megan said. "My feet

ache. I hadn't realized you were also remaining at home this evening." Though Anwen was so naturally retiring, she'd probably keep to her rooms for the duration. "What excuse did you use?"

"My monthly," Anwen said. "The merest allusion and Uncle Percy is striding from the room, and Aunt is serving the cordial. Then too, we had buckets of rain this afternoon, and I'm prone to colds."

Which cousin had said the quiet ones bore constant watching? "This is your second monthly in recent weeks, Wenny."

"The upheaval of changing households, the social whirl, the excitement of seeing our cousins," Anwen said, opening the door enough to lean on the jamb. "It's all quite daunting."

Megan was desperate to return to her room, and yet, a revelation ought not to go unremarked. "You're better at dissembling than I am. How could I not have realized this?"

Anwen twirled the end of her braid, a nervous habit she'd had since her hair had been cut short during a childhood fever.

"That's not a compliment, Megs. I'm more desperate to protect my privacy is all. Were we playing piquet?"

Playing . . . ? *Oh.*

"Yes, I think we were, until about half eleven in the library. You won, though not by much, then I took Lord Byron up to bed with me — so to speak."

Anwen did not often smile, except at babies, puppies, kittens, and the boys at her favorite orphanage.

She smiled now. "Megs, the servants are in and out of the library all evening — tending the hearth, lighting lamps or dousing them. We were not in the library, and you never read in the evening because it makes your eyes hurt."

Gracious days, lying was a complicated undertaking. "Piquet in your room, then," Megan said. "And you did beat me."

"Right. Until half eleven," Anwen said, drawing back. "And Megs?"

"Yes?"

"I like your Scot. I like how he watches you. I like that his brother loves him fiercely. Murdoch is protective and respectful toward you, and he watches you the way Papa watches Mama."

"I hadn't noticed." Hadn't been able to see, in other words. "Thank you."

Anwen closed the door without another word, though as Megan crossed the corridor to her own room, she wondered what else Anwen had noticed, and what else about her own sister Megan had missed.

She opened her sitting room door and tarried to bank the fire in the hearth. The servants would not intrude unless Megan rang the bell pull, though for all the urgency she'd felt to return to her room, she'd probably spend her evening alone.

Hamish's sisters expected him to escort them to every function, and he was nothing if not dutiful. Then too, no engagement had been announced. An engaged couple was permitted a significant amount of latitude, but a couple merely courting . . .

It was one thing to retrieve letters by stealth, quite another to invade a ducal mansion by climbing over a young lady's balcony.

Megan finished with the fire, and was ready to retire early, the better to enjoy Hamish's company when he came to call in the morning. He'd said he'd come by, and he wasn't the sort to break his word.

She had closed her bedroom door and pulled a few pins from her hair when a movement in the shadows caught her eye.

How lovely, for Megan had been in error. Apparently, Hamish MacHugh was the sort to fall fast asleep in his intended's very bed.

Hamish had drifted off on anxious thoughts

351

of the trouble his siblings could get up to without him on hand to supervise, but he dreamed instead of bliss.

A gentle arm wrapped about his middle, soft caresses trailed over his back, a sweet kiss was pressed to his shoulder. No camp follower had ever smelled this delicious, no army cot had ever been this luxurious.

He sat up. "Damn it to hell. I fell asleep."

Megan remained beside him, *in the bed.* "You don't snore."

"You'll not be informing the world of that, please. I meant only to rest my eyes." And the bed had looked so inviting, all warm covers, fluffy pillows, and elegant velvet hangings.

"I know how that feels," Megan said, trailing a hand down Hamish's arm. "If my eyes get too tired, there's nothing else I can do but close them and rest, they sting and water so. Cuddle up, Hamish. I've missed you."

Cuddle up. He'd never heard that particular command before and he liked the thought of obeying too well.

"I shouldn't be in this bed with you, Meggie."

She hiked up on her elbows, which dipped the covers low enough to reveal a fetching décolletage embroidered with emerald vines and pink roses.

"You'd better not be sharing a bed with anybody else, Hamish MacHugh."

He flipped the covers back, but stayed where he was, felled by the sight of Megan with her hair in a single loose braid.

That braid begged to be unraveled. "Are you the jealous kind, then, Meggie mine?"

"Where you are concerned, I am. If you don't intend to be a faithful husband, we'd best part ways now."

Megan had surprised herself with that declaration. Hamish saw the hesitation in her eyes, the vulnerability and the resolution. Well, damn Fletcher Pilkington all over again.

Hamish crouched over his beloved. "Listen to me, Meggie. Firstly, when I make a vow, I keep it. Forsaking all others, means forsaking all others. Secondly, I suspect once we're wed, the effort required to show up at meals with a few clothes on will tax the limit of my abilities. I'm marrying a passionate woman."

That reply earned him a kiss on the mouth. "So make love with me, Hamish. We're in a bed, with a guarantee of privacy, and opportunities like this won't come along very often."

Opportunities like this ought to never

come along this side of heaven. "I thought we'd talk, Meggie. Cuddle a bit, visit, and get to know each other better."

Perhaps Hamish already knew his intended well enough, because he could tell by the way she tucked the covers around him, that she was humoring him. From her, humoring wasn't so bad, but Hamish wasn't a complete fool.

He climbed off of her and situated himself at her side. His cock objected mightily to the change of location, which was just too bloody bad. To take Megan in his arms would be privilege enough that —

Megan slid an arm under Hamish's neck and urged him closer.

"Meggie, my self-restraint is that of a mere mortal man. Don't expect me to —"

"Cuddle *up,* Hamish," she said, wrestling him into the position of her choosing. "Let me hold you for a change."

"If you insist." Thank heavens he'd shaved before embarking on this sortie. Her breast made the softest pillow beneath his cheek.

"I do insist," she said, stroking his hair away from his brow. "What would you like to talk about?"

He wanted to talk about her breasts, her kisses, and what they should name their first eight children.

"Do you miss your parents, Meggie?"

She caressed his ear, which resulted in a curious, shivering sensation. "Of course not. They just left. Do you miss yours?"

He had known she would be this type of wife — fierce, perceptive, brave — but the reality was still a challenge.

"I do. My mama especially, because I was a boy when she died. Part of my job as oldest is to keep her memory alive for my younger siblings, to tell the stories. My father hasn't been gone as long, though I fancy he'd have made a proper duke, given the chance."

"Was he stern?"

Megan's caresses were soothing, making everything in Hamish relax and his eyes grow heavy. Desire hummed through his lassitude, sweeter than the usual ache he felt when near Megan, but no less demanding.

"Papa was more stern than most of the generals I served under, but I suspect now he was mostly bluster. This isn't what I came here to discuss, Meggie."

She yawned, which had the effect of gently raising and lowering Hamish's pillow. "What did you want to discuss?"

Hamish owed Megan an explanation of how matters stood between him and Sir

Fletcher Pilkington. That explanation wasn't exactly urgent — he'd shied away from it earlier in the day — but neither had putting it off made the telling easier.

"This morning, you asked me about Spain."

Megan shifted, or rather, commenced an ambush. Hamish had been floating on the cusp of bliss and torment one moment, the next he was being rolled onto his back, his intended positioning herself over him on all fours.

"This morning I changed the subject," Megan said. "You weren't mentioned in the dispatches, you don't socialize with your fellow officers, and my soldier cousins haven't much to say where you're concerned. I have the impression that for some men, campaigning across Spain was the occasional inconvenient battle between taking out the hounds, flirting with the ladies, and playing jokes on fellow officers, but not for you."

How easy it would be to make love with her. How delightful and necessary to join their bodies and fall asleep in her bed, carried off by a tide of physical satisfaction and intimacy.

And how quickly Megan would see through that subterfuge.

"You cuddle up," Hamish said, gathering her into his arms. "This is not lovers' talk, Meggie, but neither is it a topic to air in public. Spain was hell. We did the best we could — all of us, the Scots, the English, the Hussars, the French, the Spanish, and the Portuguese. We all did the best we could, and now we do the best we can to forget the bad parts."

"Which is most of it, I gather. Go on."

Go on. What a soldier did best, a good soldier. "I stopped Sir Fletcher from having a fellow flogged, though at this point, I don't know if Sir Fletcher even recalls the incident."

"I don't understand flogging a soldier," Megan said. "Seems if a man's willing to risk death for his country, he ought to be thanked, not further threatened by his own officers."

"There you'd be trying to apply logic to the army, which is always a risky bet. Army discipline isn't as bad as it used to be. Soldiers are no longer flogged for having their hair in disarray, and Wellington frowned on anything more than fifty lashes."

Megan was sprawled on Hamish's chest, and her simple proximity had inspired the notice of his breeding organs. She didn't seem to mind — worse, she seemed to have no self-consciousness at all about Hamish's arousal.

Though if any topic ought to scotch a man's wayward thoughts, talk of military discipline should.

"So Sir Fletcher wanted somebody flogged for no reason?" she asked.

"Oh, I expect the fellow was about to help himself to regimental stores. We were frequently short of rations, and marching on an empty belly grows wearying after the first twenty miles. Sir Fletcher made an allegation against this fellow and then summoned the provost marshal, who acted as a sort of roving military police."

"You weren't around to put in a word for the accused?"

"My men fetched me as the drum-head court-martial was in progress, else it would have gone very badly for my fellow. I supplied an alibi, said I'd seen the boy elsewhere at the time the alleged crime was to have taken place. The provost marshal decided it had all been a misunderstanding — mostly because nothing had been taken and the charge was theft, not attempted theft."

"Sir Fletcher is like that — nasty but lazy, both. I am glad you stood up to him." Her kiss suggested she was very glad, indeed.

"The point, Meggie mine, is that Sir Fletcher has no honor. He'll lie, cheat, manipulate, and inveigle others into doing his bidding. In this case, he took out his pique on Colin with more foolishness between officers. Sent him into the hills knowing the French were scouting the area, though Colin got back to camp none the worse for his outing. I don't trust Sir Fletcher, and I'd like to set a date soon and whisk you off to the Highlands."

Megan ceased nibbling on Hamish's ear. His kilt had twisted to the side, and her nightgown had somehow got bunched at her waist, meaning paradise — or perdition — was one well-placed wish away.

"There can't be any whisking until my parents are back from Wales. Uncle Percy will negotiate the settlements with you, but Papa must approve them. Until Papa has given his assent to the terms, we shouldn't set a date."

Hamish knew that. He also knew that he'd once again not had the discussion with Megan he'd needed to regarding Spain, the military, and the havoc Sir Fletcher could wreak.

"I should be going, Meggie. If I stay here much longer —"

Megan kissed him to silence, then began

undulating her hips in a manner calculated to part an angel from his last scruple, and Hamish was no angel. He was, however, a gentleman.

"Meggie, you lovely, daft creature . . . If you keep that up, I won't answer for the consequences. I ought not to disrespect Moreland's hospitality by stealing into your bedroom this way —"

"Into my bedroom, into my heart," Megan muttered against Hamish's mouth.

"But I missed you, and I knew you'd be waiting, and I can't — dear God, Megan Windham."

She'd shifted, and in one brilliant, bold maneuver, gloved Hamish with her heat. He went from struggling to find the resolve to part from her, to struggling for breath.

"You were saying?" she murmured, moving on him.

"I was saying . . ." Something, something important, and honorable, and . . . damn. "Don't stop, Meggie. Not yet."

Her teeth gleamed in a smile, and she didn't stop. Not for a long, long time.

Love brought Megan insights, not all of them happy. Twenty-four hours after sharing intimacies with Hamish, she was still contemplating those insights from beside yet another dance floor in yet another ball-room.

Megan's beloved, for example, woke up as nimbly as a starving cat shifts from watching its prey to pouncing. Still one moment, in mid-leap the next. Hamish was not cheerful upon rising either. As best Megan had been able to decipher his expression the previous night, he'd awakened prepared to kill — or die.

Fortunately, she was learning to set less and less store by appearances. Hamish looked fierce, but his touch . . . oh, his touch. Hamish MacHugh's caresses were insight on top of revelation wrapped in wonderment.

"Megs, take pity on me and come for a turn on the terrace," Devlin St. Just, Earl of Rosecroft, said, extending a hand to her. "The noise in this ballroom is enough to give a stout-hearted fellow a bilious stomach."

Megan accepted her cousin's hand — he'd apparently been assigned guard duty this evening — and rose from her bench.

"A breath of fresh air appeals," Megan said, for she couldn't spend the entire evening watching Hamish dance with her sisters and cousins. "I'm promised for the supper waltz."

"If you weren't, I'd be having a talk with your duke."

"He's not my duke yet," Megan said as Rosecroft led her through the wallflowers, dandies, and dowagers milling among benches. Rosecroft comported himself in a crowd the same way he did everything else, with a decisive efficiency that brooked no obstacles.

He soon had Megan out in the lovely night air, where, indeed, quiet was to be had.

"I would never argue with a lady," Rosecroft said, tucking Megan's hand around his arm, "but I might quibble with a cousin. Murdoch is very much your duke. He makes you sparkle."

"Would that I could make him sparkle," Megan said. "Hamish is a private man and he carries shadows."

"We all carry shadows, Megan. What of Sir Fletcher? He was all set to be your swain of choice, and now he's least in sight."

Sir Fletcher was Megan's shadow, but he no longer had the power to frighten her. "Sir Fletcher is among the gathering this evening, along with two of his sisters. He and I are . . . civil."

For a moment Megan and her cousin strolled along the gravel walk in silence, the sound of the ballroom fading as they moved toward the back of the garden. The torches were spaced farther apart here, and the night air bore a teasing hint of lilacs.

A lovely evening, but last night had been lovelier.

"I don't like how Sir Fletcher watches you," Rosecroft said. "Westhaven has declared me overly protective, and Valentine says I'm anticipating the day when my girls make their bows, but I'm here if you need me, Megs, as are Westhaven and Valentine."

The reassurance was as lovely as it was disquieting. "Why would I need you?"

He patted her hand. "Maybe you don't, but we like to be needed. You will never, ever tell Moreland I admitted to that. He's smug enough as it is."

Uncle Percy was shrewd, or Aunt Esther and Uncle Percy were a shrewd combination. "My thanks for the concern, but it's not needed. Hamish is an entirely worthy fellow, and he has attached my affections."

Rosecroft snorted.

"What does that ungentlemanly rejoinder imply?" For it had been a cousinly snort, not a dignified father, husband, and respected titleholder snort.

"You're in the courting bedroom, I hear, and Murdoch looks like an athletic specimen. Scaling the maple and hopping the balcony shouldn't be too much challenge for him."

Gracious days — and nights. "I will pretend I did not hear that observation, and pretend I am not blushing fit to light up the night sky, Devlin St. Just."

"If Her Grace raises with you the topic of certain purchases one can send one's maid to make at the apothecary," Rosecroft went on — parenting girls had apparently given him entire arsenals of ruthlessness — "you will blush and stammer and look mortified but intrigued. The intrigued part is important. Ask me how I know this."

"I will not ask any such thing. We will please return to the ballroom now." Megan spun on her heel, and Rosecroft followed.

"I know this, because at some point, every young fellow must be taught a few basic facts."

"Devlin, I will disown you." Or burst out laughing, for he was very intent on this awkward display of protectiveness. "You could not have brought up these subjects in broad daylight, else your own blushes would be too evident."

"A soldier learns strategy, and I got the short straw, because Valentine likely cheats and Westhaven is in the confidence of the

Almighty. I was planning on setting Emmie on you, but I'm your cousin."

The short — ? "And the oldest and a former commanding officer," Megan said. "Thrice cursed, you poor lamb. Did it ever occur to you that I have female cousins as well, and that they are also quite protective?"

Rosecroft paused beneath a lamp, his expression confirming his consternation.

Megan wanted to be inside the ballroom in time for her supper waltz with Hamish, but the moment was too precious to ignore.

"In your haste to slay all dragons, Devlin, you and your dear, henwitted brothers forgot the existence of your five sisters. That should worry you, for they are unforgettable women."

He bowed. "As are you."

"Well done." Megan kissed his cheek, and indulged in the pleasure of swanning off after having had the last word with one of her male cousins. Her glee bordered on gloating, until in the gallery outside the ballroom, she caught sight of Sir Fletcher Pilkington.

And he was marching straight for her.

CHAPTER SEVENTEEN

Women were not very bright, but some of them had formidable instincts.

Sir Fletcher thus knew the moment Megan Windham caught sight of him, for her posture changed, from a lady displaying her ballroom finery, to *prey*. She did what any trapped mouse ought to do — looked for a way out — but Sir Fletcher had chosen his moment well.

"You are welcome to stroll with me in the garden," Sir Fletcher said, "or we can enjoy the offerings in the portrait gallery one flight up."

"I've strolled my last garden with you," Megan said, taking a step to the left.

Sir Fletcher blocked her, and because people were assembling for the supper waltz, this passage was temporarily deserted.

"I say we've many more moonlit gardens to enjoy together," Sir Fletcher replied. "Come along, Megan. You and I have matters to resolve. We can either make a nasty scene right here — a lovers' quarrel, let's call it — or we can have a civilized chat on the terrace."

Her frustration was some satisfaction for all the hours Sir Fletcher had spent nursing a sore head and a murderous grudge.

"I'm not going anywhere with you," Megan said.

Oh, she was very much on her mettle. "Yes, you are, *darling.*" He kissed her cheek, leaving her two options. She could scream, or she could give him an excuse to escalate their spat.

Another desperate glance canvassed the exits. At any moment, somebody might come by, in which case Sir Fletcher would bestow another kiss on her.

"We go no farther than the terrace," Megan said, ignoring Sir Fletcher's proffered arm.

"My dear, you wound me. I offer my escort knowing the limitations of your sight, and having many memories of you stumbling over carpet fringes and thresholds. Why must you be so disdainful of my attempts to protect you?"

They reached the terrace, though all the other traffic was headed inside. Devlin St. Just, Earl of Rosecroft, went through the

367

second set of doors, deep in discussion with Joseph, Earl of Keswick. They either did not see Megan or they were colluding in Sir Fletcher's courtship.

No family wanted too many unmarried females underfoot. They were expensive, petulant, and got up to the stupidest intrigues. Witness Pammy and her impoverished captain.

"What do you want?" Megan asked, stopping at the top of the terrace steps.

"What I want is to enjoy a stroll with my intended on a pretty evening," Sir Fletcher said. "In addition to that, I want a goodly sum of money so that my future is secure, and I would not mind the attentions of a devoted wife and a talented mistress, if you must know. Do you mind if I smoke?"

"Yes."

"My, you are in a taking. When we're married, in the manner of devoted husbands the world over, I will ensure that my wife's nerves are settled."

"Sir Fletcher, either get to the point or prepare to enjoy the evening in solitude, for I'm promised to Murdoch for the supper waltz."

She'd gripped her fan as tightly as some men gripped their swords. How gratifying.

Sir Fletcher took out a cheroot and ran it

368

under his nose. Lovely scent, though too dear in his present circumstances. Marriage to Megan would change all of that, the sooner the better.

"This will be your last waltz with the estimable Murdoch," Sir Fletcher said. "You really are not safe with him, you know. He turned on his own men, led them straight into a nest of French soldiers. His subordinates would mention that day only in whispers — those who survived — probably because he threatened to kill any who spoke against him. Murdoch *is* a killer. You can see it in his eyes."

Megan snatched the cheroot away and pitched it into the bushes. "I could slap you for spreading such talk. If I were a man, I'd call you out."

"If I were not a gentleman," Sir Fletcher said, "I'd have you on your back out in the mews. Here's what you need to know, Megan. You think you have your letters, because you had one of your pet Scotsmen steal them from my home. I'm prepared to publicize that larceny — the duke would be tried in the Lords, but the younger brother remains a commoner, gallows bait just like the rest of us.

"Regardless of which brother I accuse," he went on, "everybody will believe my ver-

369

sion. The sad truth is, to explain how upset I am that my dearest literary treasures have gone missing, I will leave a trail of delicate inferences about the contents of the letters."

He smiled, very much enjoying the transition in Megan's eyes from distaste to fear. "I'm not very delicate when in my cups," he mused. "I try, but often fall short of the goal."

The violins were tuning up, and Megan's hand was fisted at her side. Marriage to her would not be boring.

"I do have my letters," she retorted. "Say what you please, and I'll simply produce the letters without revealing their contents. Perhaps you've an entire catalog of letters from compromised young ladies. Why don't you advertise that fact and see how much longer you're welcome in polite society?"

Sir Fletcher's pleasure in the encounter dimmed. A bit of spirit was interesting, but when a man exerted his superior intellect and natural authority, the woman was to simper and fuss, then turn up biddable and contrite.

"Megan, do not force my hand," Sir Fletcher said, leaning closer. "I am a very good shot, and if your cousins, or your Scottish wolfhounds, want to call me out, I will at the very least wound them sorely and cause great scandal. I was in the army, my dear. When I wasn't perfecting my aim, I was learning to make copies of every document that mattered. You have your letters, and I have precise copies of each one, right down to a beautiful facsimile of your elegant signature."

Ah, finally. Her bravado faltered. "You *copied* my letters?"

"A man never wants such precious sentiments to leave his control," Sir Fletcher said. "The orchestra will start on the introduction soon. Best run along, darling. From now on, though, your supper waltzes are all mine, as are your good-night waltzes. Let's hope your parents don't tarry in Wales for too long, hmm?"

He bowed punctiliously over her hand, and sauntered off in the direction of the card room. Let Megan have her waltz with the charmless Murdoch. Even condemned prisoners were allowed a last meal and a final prayer.

Megan was too angry to be afraid, but she knew the anger would burn itself out, leaving only the timid, compliant nincompoop Sir Fletcher had charmed and duped several years ago.

"Miss Meggie, I've been searching for

371

you," Hamish said as Megan crossed the corridor separating the terrace from the ballroom.

The duke made a stunning impression in his Highland finery, and every time Megan's path crossed his amid the music and fashion of polite society, he looked more at ease, more a man at home among his peers, if not his friends. At this distance, Megan recognized her beloved by the swing of his kilt, his height, and his posture more than his features.

And she knew Hamish's voice. Knew the caress lurking within the burr, and the affection and loyalty lurking deeper still.

Damn Fletcher Pilkington.

"Your Grace." Megan curtsied. "Our waltz should be coming up. I've been looking forward to it all evening."

Hamish peered at her, and Megan could not muster a smile for all the kilts in Perthshire. "Meggie, what's amiss? Do your feet ache?"

Her heart ached. "I'm a trifle fatigued. Perhaps you'd rather sit with me?"

Though what was she to say? Sir Fletcher had copied her letters and was eager to create a scandal should Megan refuse his suit.

"Aye," Hamish said, wrapping Megan's hand over his arm. "I think a few minutes' peace and quiet with my darling would be lovely."

"Don't call me your darling," Megan snapped, dropping Hamish's arm. "I'm sorry. I didn't mean . . . We need to talk, Hamish." They needed to end their engagement before it had been announced.

"We most assuredly do need to talk. Something's wrong, and you are my darling."

He led her to a bench on the terrace beneath a torch that had been purposely left unlit, run out of oil, or been snuffed by an opportunistic couple.

Megan settled beside Hamish, not as close as she craved to be. "I've been a fool again."

Hamish's posture changed, like a cat hearing a rustling in the undergrowth. "I'll not let you cry off on me, Meggie Windham. Whatever talk you've heard, whatever rumors are circulating now, none of it matters half so much as my regard for you. Tell me who has upset my duchess, and I'll have a word with them they won't soon forget."

He rose as if to charge away in search of an enemy, and Megan had to move quickly to get her hand around the belt holding his sporran.

"Don't you dare run off on me, Hamish MacHugh. Sir Fletcher will be lying in ambush for you, and that's the last battle I want on my conscience."

"Sir Fletcher? Has Pilkington bothered you, Megan?" Such gratifying menace in that question.

"He has more than bothered me, Hamish. He has copied my letters, and will cheerfully call out anybody who thwarts his plan to marry me. He has deduced that you or possibly Colin stole my letters back, and he'll cause all manner of talk should I balk at marrying him."

Hamish sank slowly to the bench. "He *copied* your letters?"

"Sir Fletcher claims that army life taught him to have all important documents copied, and that not only does he have a record of the contents of the letters, he's taken care to replicate my signature exactly. He even mentioned that Colin could be tried for theft as a commoner, while you would be tried in the Lords."

Hamish was silent for a long moment, while the introduction to the waltz began in the ballroom. The waltz was one of Cousin Valentine's more dramatic pieces, and the dratted dance was in a haunting minor key.

"Say something, Hamish, please."

More silence, while Sir Fletcher was probably bowing and smiling at some blushing debutante or running up gambling debts Megan's settlements were supposed to pay. The anger Megan had expected to fade was only growing.

"Forgery is a felony," Hamish said. "And you're right. This is an ambush. I've been ambushed before. I don't care for it. Colin is safe enough from a conviction — he was dancing and flirting while I was retrieving your letters — but the threat of criminal charges brought against my brother is bad enough, and exactly what I should have expected from Sir Fletcher."

"I'm sorry, Hamish. I've dragged you into my battles, and Sir Fletcher has no honor. He doesn't fight fair. I knew that, and I still involved you."

Hamish said nothing, merely sat staring at the flagstones. He might have been a statue, Highlander Seated, while Megan wanted to screech and kick something — Sir Fletcher's breeding organs, for example.

The torchlights flickered as the Earl of Keswick stalked across the terrace. He'd been injured on the Peninsula, and when he was tired his gait became uneven.

"Her Grace has asked after you, Megan," Keswick said. "Murdoch, good evening. When one partners a lady for her supper waltz, one is typically found dancing with the lady when that waltz is played."

Hamish rose in an eruption of muscle and male dignity. "The lady did not care for the gloomy quality of the music, and I was unwilling to forgo her company."

Forgo it, he must. Permanently. Megan might eventually learn to bear that heartbreak, but not if she was also expected to bear Sir Fletcher's children.

"Joseph, you may report to Her Grace that I'm merely taking the air in Murdoch's company."

"Yes, Cowlick," Hamish said. "Report to headquarters that the pickets are all on sentry duty, as assigned. I suspect your countess is wondering where you've got off to, so you might as well report to her too."

Keswick's gaze snapped from Hamish to Megan. "Perhaps you'll join me for a hand of cards after supper, Murdoch."

The earl's invitation bore the quality of a glove hitting the flagstones.

"Perhaps I will," Hamish said.

The ensuing silence was considering on Keswick's part, unreadable on Hamish's.

"I'll find a footman to relight that lamp," Keswick said. "Megan, good evening. Murdoch, I'll await you in the card room after supper."

Keswick disappeared through the open

doors to the gallery, leaving Megan with little more to say to her beloved except good-bye.

"I don't expect you to share the buffet with me," she said. "In fact, it's probably best if you didn't. Sir Fletcher will remark it, and I wouldn't want —"

Abruptly, she could not force any more words past the lump in her throat.

"What don't you want, Meggie?"

For the past few weeks, Megan had been building a vision of her future in her imagination. Beautiful Scottish scenery, laughing red-haired children, music, and cozy evenings by the fire had figured prominently. Cozier nights under the blankets had figured more prominently still, but so had decades of affection, trust, shared dreams, and shared life. She'd felt her world opening up into a beautiful vista of new experiences and new sights.

That vision had crumbled in the space of five minutes, and was replaced by years of sorrow and misery as Sir Fletcher's wife. He wanted a wife *and* a mistress, make no mistake about that, and he already regarded Megan's dowry as his to waste on as many mistresses as he pleased.

"I don't want to trouble you further," Megan said softly. "I've already asked too much of you."

Hamish stood very tall in the shadows. "I could fight him, Meggie. For you, I could meet him."

That admission had cost him, clearly. "You are not a killer, Hamish MacHugh, and you are far too precious to me to be risked at Sir Fletcher's hands."

"So you'll sacrifice yourself instead?" The question was quiet, bewildered, and pained.

"If I must," Megan said. "Sir Fletcher isn't the worst husband I could have. He'll likely grow bored with me after a few years, and we'll live separately as most fashionable couples do. A few sons, and he'll lose all interest in his wife."

She prayed that was so. Prayed she didn't find herself married to a man who'd break her glasses and her spirit for his own entertainment.

"Megan, are you asking me to leave you to Sir Fletcher?"

She owed Hamish a resolute yes to that question. She couldn't even nod her head. "Don't make me cry, Hamish. Please, not now, not tonight. I can't have any talk, and I wouldn't want . . ."

"I'm precious to you, but you don't want me," he said. The words should have been bitter, but Hamish enfolded Megan in a gentle embrace. "You are daft, Meggie Windham, and brave and foolish — also a bad liar. Before you blow a full retreat, grant me a boon."

Megan sensed a trap, but she was too busy savoring what might be her last moments in Hamish's arms.

"You're trying to charm me," she said, her cheek against the wool of his jacket. "I have no defenses right now, Hamish. I can barely think, and any moment, one of my cousins will come strutting through that door, and I'll want to smack him with my fan."

"I'll encourage you in any displays of affection you care to aim at your family, but all I'm asking you for is a truce, Megan."

Hamish was up to something, and the waltz would soon end. "What sort of truce?"

"We neither advance nor retreat. We hold our ground, displaying neither a flag of surrender nor overt aggression. A ceasefire while we tend to our wounded and consider our options."

Megan was wounded, and being in Hamish's arms was the only relief for her pain. "I ought to find Sir Fletcher right now and tell him I'll marry him. You're contemplating something dangerous."

"You won't allow me to call him out, for which I'm honestly grateful, and I can't stomach the notion of you marrying him. I'd say a ceasefire makes sense right now."

Megan tried to think, to weigh benefits and burdens, but no great insights or stunning conclusions materialized.

"How long does this ceasefire last, Hamish? I don't trust Sir Fletcher one bit."

"We are agreed on that much. Give me a fortnight, and don't be sacrificing yourself to Sir Fletcher's schemes just yet. Give me a chance to ambush the man who's again trying to ambush you."

"A fortnight, then," Megan said. Little enough for Hamish to ask. "Two weeks *at most.* Sir Fletcher is not a patient man."

Fourteen days of liberty and longing for what could not be, and then she'd give Sir Fletcher her hand in holy matrimony.

Hamish spotted Colin in the corner of the card room, looking rakish and happy in a foursome of former officers playing whist. Very likely, they were more invested in their reminiscences and their hostess's brandy than in the card play.

"I cannot for the life of me fathom what Megan Windham sees in a man who's incapable of smiling," the Earl of Keswick said, standing at Hamish's elbow.

"Ask your lady wife what a man incapable

of smiling might have to offer that's worth a woman's notice," Hamish replied. "She's bound to have a few ideas."

"My countess is a font of creativity, while you have no wife at all."

"Who's the man partnering Sir Fletcher?" Hamish asked, rather than admit the sad truth of Keswick's observation.

"Captain Garner Puget. One of Plyne's spares and not quite a fortune hunter, according to —"

"Your wife," Hamish finished. Keswick was besotted, and Hamish could only envy him. "Why does Puget look familiar?"

Hamish had seen the two together previously — at the musicale? — but why did the sight of Puget rankle, was the more pressing question. Of course, everything rankled, given the broadsides Megan had fired. She had looked so damned brave and pretty and *lost* when she'd announced Sir Fletcher's latest perfidy.

"Puget," Keswick said, "was one of those younger sons who made a good soldier during the Peninsular campaign. Once the Corsican was vanquished, his choices were limited to India, Canada, or mustering out. I believe he served under Sir Fletcher for at least part of his tour."

And Puget still associated with an officer

who'd been neither liked nor respected by his subordinates.

"I'd bet my coach and team Sir Fletcher has blackmailed the poor sod somehow," Hamish said. "Is there somewhere we can talk?"

Keswick took a leisurely sip of his drink, which appeared to be lemonade. "We're talking now."

"Fine, then I won't tell you that the glowering lot of lords Megan calls cousins must stay by her side every moment for the next two weeks. Sir Fletcher has made a pest of himself, and I wouldn't put it past him to propose to my Meggie in public."

Keswick wrinkled a splendid beak. "Three doors down the corridor, there's a parlor without a fire. We'll not be disturbed there."

Hamish let Keswick lead the way. Though as for not being disturbed, Hamish was well beyond disturbed. Copying Megan's letters showed determination, cunning, malice aforethought, and all manner of alarmingly shrewd tendencies in a man Hamish wanted to dismiss as a lazy bully.

Keswick locked the parlor door, and while the fire hadn't been lit, one wall sconce flickered dimly. The room was more shadows than light, and after the chatter and hum of the ballroom, quiet as a tomb.

"Why must Megan Windham be protected from an eligible suitor?" Keswick asked.

"Because Sir Fletcher Pilkington is a damned scoundrel."

"He'd say the same about you, and has been doing exactly that in half the clubs on St. James's Street. He claims your violence knows no bounds, you betrayed your men, and you're half-mad on your best day. What I'd like to know is why Sir Fletcher is indulging a penchant for old gossip now?"

Keswick was inviting confidences, such as Hamish hadn't reposed in anybody, not even his beloved. Hamish could not entirely oblige.

"Sir Fletcher is discrediting a rival, of course, and if you were in Spain, you know well what was said about me."

"I was there," Keswick said, taking up a lean against the mantel. "Saw you snap that poor bastard's neck. Saw the French start to fall back immediately thereafter. I'd been frequenting battlefields for years at that point, and observing that one death nearly had me retching in the bushes."

Keswick pushed away from the mantel, and Hamish thought this little frolic among the battle ghosts was over.

Instead, Keswick took two steps closer. "I cannot imagine what that must have been like for you."

Hamish's idiot, stupid, useless brain formed words, and his hopeless, floundering mouth pushed them into speech, though abruptly, ambushes lay on every hand.

"I meant to shove the damned man aside, to get him the hell out of my way, but the bloody Frenchman wouldn't move. I could see a half dozen of the French infantry closing in on my brother from behind, and Colin was oblivious to the danger, focused only on moving forward. I had to get to my brother's side, or I'd be watching him die, not ten yards away.

"And there was the Frenchman," Hamish went on, more softly, "blocking my way. I put my hands on him, and then he was dead. I think he slipped. I never meant to kill him. I long to believe he slipped, and that his death was an accident."

Keswick's gaze was unreadable in the gloom. "War is a series of accidents, either miraculous or tragic. That ground was so damned muddy we were all slipping, the horses were going down, the artillery couldn't be moved into position quickly enough. Your *accident,* if that's what it was, turned the tide of a battle that wasn't going well at all for our side. That single death probably prevented many others on both sides, and yet, I feel you're owed an apology."

Hamish had never asked an eyewitness what that tragic, violent moment had looked like to an observer, but Keswick's recitation brought back memories.

The screams of horses falling in the mud, the cursing of the infantry when the artillery couldn't do its part as needed, the slippery frustration of boggy ground hampering an advance the French had been mortally determined to stop.

Keswick didn't offer a ready assurance that the worst moment of Hamish's life had been an accident, but he offered a reminder of evidence supporting that conclusion.

All of which Hamish would ponder when Megan was safe from Sir Fletcher. "Nobody owes me anything, Keswick — and you'll not bring this up with Colin, ever — but you lot owe Megan Windham your escort. Sir Fletcher is spoiling to create scandal by calling somebody out, and if that somebody is me, I'll have to choose between breaking my word to a lady and taking a bullet from a scoundrel."

Keswick wandered off to a comfortable reading chair. He produced a flask and offered it to Hamish.

Well, yes. A restorative tot was in order

after every ambush.

"Are you that poor a marksman?" Keswick asked.

His flask held a fine, smooth brandy. It wasn't whisky, but it would do. "Compared to Sir Fletcher? Probably. I also promised the Baroness St. Clair I'd not fight any more duels. The baron is a formidable man, but his baroness puts even him to the blush."

"I've had the pleasure," Keswick said, accepting his flask back. "Gave me considerable encouragement at the time, to think that if St. Clair could stumble into the arms of a good woman, there's hope for the rest of us."

"He cheated my secrets from me," Hamish said, something only St. Clair himself knew. "Drugged my drink, because he said it would have been too much trouble to torture the information out of me. I was supposed to be consoled by that."

"And guilt has tormented you since," Keswick said. "Maybe that's the greatest wound war inflicts — guilt for when we fight well, guilt for when we don't. Guilt when we leave our loved ones at home, greater guilt when we leave comrades on the battlefield. Here's to peace."

Keswick tipped the flask up, then passed it over to Hamish. Gentlemanly consider-

386

ation meant Hamish took another nip.

"To peace," Hamish said, "but not for Sir Fletcher. You'll keep an armed guard on Meggie?"

"We always do. I'll put her cousins on alert, though, while you do exactly what?"

Strategy mattered. Whatever else was true, Hamish must not underestimate Sir Fletcher again. He was desperate and cunning, and as Megan had said, would not play by any honorable rules. Another reason not to challenge him, or accept a challenge from him.

"Megan tried to tell me to walk away."

"And yet, here you are, moving your infantry into place, disobeying orders, for which you're also apparently notorious."

Hamish took the second armchair, a comfy place to ponder the rest of his life. "I didn't disobey orders any more than anybody else did. My men mattered to me, and for a time my commanding officer was some marquess's spare who cared more for gathering intelligence beneath the laundress's skirts than for invading France."

"I suspected as much."

An oddly comfortable silence blossomed, such as soldiers frequently shared around a campfire. Somebody might recite a poem, somebody else sing an old song, the flask would make the rounds, until each man drifted away to dream of home, childhood, or a new pair of boots.

"I could fight Sir Fletcher," Hamish said softly. "I realize that now. I'm ready, willing, and *able.* I hadn't been certain before." How awful to know that he was battle-worthy again, and what a relief too. A relief he owed to Megan.

"Pilkington would kill you, bat his handsome blue eyes, and claim he meant to delope," Keswick said. "His titled English seconds would support that fairy tale, regardless of what I claimed to the contrary. Don't turn your back on Pilkington. While he's been spreading gossip about you, I've been collecting intelligence on him. He's spoiled, mean, had a vile temper toward his own men, and flourishes his charm like a silk handkerchief before the debutantes and their mamas."

This entirely unnecessary warning warmed that part of Hamish that Megan's attempted dismissal had left chilled and furious.

"I'll not turn my back on him — not again." Hamish wouldn't let the bastard take Megan to wife either. If scandal erupted, Megan's family might deny Hamish his lady's hand — until he could spirit her away to Scotland — but scandal was preferable to knowing Megan had been coerced into a marriage she loathed.

"You don't turn your back on anybody," Keswick said. "I'm not complimenting your manners, Murdoch. This damned flask has somehow become empty."

Only Megan complimented his manners. "You need a bigger flask, and I need time."

Hamish passed over his own flask. Keswick had spent years soldiering. He'd be no stranger to the water of life.

"Time to what? I can have a pigeon sent to Megan's parents, if that would help."

A pigeon had brought England the first news of Wellington's victory at Waterloo. "No pigeons, Keswick. Megan can summon her parents if she pleases to, but I need time, and waiting for Lord Anthony and his lady to return will mean Pilkington's options are limited for the present."

Keswick took a respectable draught from the flask and passed it back. "I think I'll return to the card room and find myself a hand or two of whist. If luck is with me, I'll lighten Sir Fletcher's pockets, which ought to keep him from partnering Megan on the dance floor for the next while. You still haven't formed a plan, have you?"

"I have much to consider when coming

up with my strategy. Just as soon as you leave me in peace, I'll be about it."

Keswick snorted, rose, and squeezed Hamish on the shoulder. "Lock the door after me, lest you be scandalized by a parade of couples seeking privacy. If Sir Fletcher is determined to cause talk, the sooner you devise a way to thwart him, the better. Talk travels like a scent on the breeze, and this time of year, Mayfair is a veritable windstorm."

Hamish remained seated, though he wanted to find Megan and hie her away to Scotland. "Go lose your pin money just so your countess can console you on your losses. I'm apparently not without allies, for which any soldier knows to be grateful."

The double negative was a useful fig leaf when a man's dignity was imperiled.

"You're *not without* allies, family, resources, and a good dose of soldierly cunning. My countess has declared that should you find favor with Megan, you'd do. On that warning, I'll bid you good night."

Hamish rose to lock the door behind Keswick, for he did have much to ponder. He'd failed Megan — stealing the letters hadn't been enough — and for that failure, he might lose the chance to marry her.

He'd not fail her again.

"How can a man knighted for bravery, the son of an earl, and one in possession of damning — if forged — evidence be brought to heel without risking scandal to my Meggie?"

The darkened parlor had no answers, but Hamish did have one additional question, a query that had plagued him since Megan had told him of Sir Fletcher's copies.

Copying thirty-one letters, meticulously, in the author's own hand, right down to perfecting a version of her signature, took a significant amount of time. A man of Sir Fletcher's fundamentally indolent, self-important character would not normally make such an effort. A certain artistic ability was required to replicate a signature convincingly thirty-one times, and Sir Fletcher was no artist.

So how and by whom had the letters been copied?

CHAPTER EIGHTEEN

Colin had done the pretty for the past week, while Hamish had lurked in the gentlemen's clubs, gone out on errands of his own, and generally broken the heart of a young lady whom Colin had hoped would be his brother's salvation. When that young lady crossed paths with Colin in Hyde Park early one morning — nothing like a good gallop to chase the cobwebs from a fellow's brain — he wanted to keep on galloping, all the way to the Highlands.

"Lord Colin, good morning."

Colin's horse snorted and puffed and acted like an idiot, while Miss Megan Windham controlled her chestnut mare easily.

"Miss Megan, good day. Enjoy the park, and give my regards to your —"

The lady twitched at the drape of her habit over her boot. Her gesture bore an air of patience, as if waiting for Colin to get through his prevarications.

"How is he, Lord Colin?"

He being Hamish, of course. "I don't know. I haven't seen him since the last ball, not to speak of." Hamish ate breakfast long before the rest of the family, closeted himself with solicitors and bankers, and then disappeared into the clubs, most of which he'd only recently been admitted to.

According to extended family gossip, he'd also consulted with a MacHugh cousin who was a publisher, another who made saddles, a third who ran a fishmonger's stall in the Haymarket, and a fourth who owned a pub in Knightsbridge.

"One worries about His Grace," Miss Megan said. A hundred yards up the path, some gentleman on a sizable black gelding waited for her. Her groom tarried a respectful dozen yards back. Colin looked for Miss Anwen, but she apparently hadn't ridden out with her sister.

"I've been worrying about Hamish for years," Colin replied. "It doesn't do any good. Hamish will do as he pleases, and there's no stopping him. If he has toyed with your affections, I can only apologize on his behalf, and tell you that's not at all like him."

As much as Colin hated to see Miss Megan gazing at the door at one society gathering after another, he was equally troubled to have lost track of his older brother. London in springtime was probably Hamish's idea of a nightmare, and yet, Colin had had such hopes.

"Will you ride with me, Lord Colin? I'd like to put a few questions to you, and we have relative privacy."

She was a lady, Colin was a gentleman — or aspiring to become one — and he could not refuse her. He turned his gelding alongside the mare and prepared to dodge an awkward interrogation.

"I will tell you what I can," Colin said. "I won't violate any confidences." Not that Hamish confided in his siblings. Possibly in his horse, or their papa's headstone, but never anything so trifling as a mere younger brother.

"Tell me about growing up in Scotland," Miss Megan said as her mare ambled along in the sun's first rays. "Tell me about your home and your younger brothers."

On those topics, Colin could be effusive, and so he held forth for a good half hour, while the horses walked the bridle paths, the sun rose, and Megan's escort kept them in sight at all times.

"Hamish ought to be the one hacking out with you first thing in the day," Colin said, some while later. "I don't know what's amiss with him, Miss Megan, but if I were to ask him, he'd snap and growl and tell me to buy a new pair of boots."

Maybe not boots, given the expenses Rhona and Edana had been running up lately.

"He's not been right since Spain, has he?"

Abruptly, Colin realized that all the reminiscing about Perthshire and describing the family tree had been so much subterfuge on Megan Windham's part. She'd been earning his trust, letting him maunder on as if his every word were her greatest delight. Like the bumbling idiot he often was, Colin had obliged her.

"Hamish never wanted to go to war," Colin said. "I know that, and I tried to talk him out of it. Leaving Scotland was like parting with a vital organ for him, but more and more of the local lads were joining up, and I'd seen as much of Perthshire as any young man needs to. I was mad to buy my colors, and there was nobody to stop me."

"You were young, Lord Colin. We haven't much sense when we're young."

She spoke as if she — a perfect lady from a perfect family — had blundered badly at some point, which wasn't possible.

"Hamish did not want me to go," Colin

said, the words twisting a knife of guilt in his conscience. "I concocted stirring speeches about patriotism, and the Corsican monster, and doing my part, but the truth is, I don't care a bit for whichever George we're stuck with on the throne. Never have, which makes me a scoundrel, I suppose. I simply wanted adventure, new sights, new faces, and some glory of my own."

Other riders were coming toward them, a pair of fellows whom Colin recognized as more perfectly turned-out Windhams — still no Miss Anwen. Both men rode fine horseflesh, and while the smiles they aimed at Megan were affectionate, Colin rated only a scowling tip of the hat.

As it should be, because the wrong Mac-Hugh was keeping the lady company.

"Did you find new sights, new adventure, and a bit of glory of your own?" Miss Megan asked when she and Colin had resumed their progress down the path.

Colin gave her question some thought, because this was not a woman to be dismissed with casual gallantries. Without her glasses, she wasn't scrutinizing his expression, but she'd hear insincerity in his voice.

"I made wonderful friends, saw parts of the world a Scottish lad wouldn't have seen otherwise, and I fought well. I enjoyed most of army life, and I can say that honestly."

"Then Hamish is doubtless pleased for you, and your happiness means the world to him. Maybe you ought to be pleased for yourself?"

"How can I be pleased for myself, when I see my brother —" Colin couldn't speak as bluntly before a lady as he'd like to. Hamish was mucking up this courtship of Miss Megan, disappointing hostesses, aggravating Eddie and Ronnie, and generally fouling up the works.

And Colin didn't know how to intervene, didn't know how to be the good brother Hamish had so often been to every one of his siblings.

Was this how Hamish felt, when Colin got into scrape after scrape? Helpless, inadequate, frustrated, and nearly choking on the need to help and be useful?

"Are we letting the horses rest?" Miss Megan had brought her mare to a halt, and why Colin's gelding had stopped in the middle of the path, he did not know.

"Walk on, you," Colin muttered, and the beast complied. "I need to have a wee chat with my brother. Set him straight on a few things."

"Not on my behalf," Miss Megan said. "I esteem Murdoch greatly, and wouldn't have

397

you troubling him on my account. I did have one more question for you, Lord Colin."

Colin wanted badly to canter off in the direction of his brother's house, hunt Hamish down, and *thank* him. Not the grudging thanks of a young man toward the fellow who'd spared him the risk and stupidity of a few duels, but a brother's sincere thanks for a life saved, many times over.

"I think that fellow on yonder gelding might be ready to escort you home, Miss Megan."

"Keswick enjoys his privacy," Miss Megan said. "He's a conscientious escort, but it's not as if I'm prone to tumbling from the saddle. Not lately. The question I have for you is one I can put to you alone, and I hope you'll answer honestly."

Unease uncoiled in Colin's gut. "Hamish killed an unarmed man, Miss Megan. It was in the heat of battle, one among many other deaths, and that's all you need to know. Hamish was a good ten yards off my flank so I didn't see it. He told me he was growing desperate because the line wasn't advancing and the rain had started up again. He needs to leave it on the battlefield, a necessary violence on the way to an equally necessary victory."

Miss Megan waved a gloved hand and readjusted her whip. "I know all about that, Lord Colin. Strangled a man with his bare hands, or broke his neck, possibly both. Beyond awful for all concerned, and certainly regrettable. I do not pretend to understand what goes on in the midst of battle. I want to know what happened when Hamish was ambushed. I think that's the worse memory, and yet, he can barely allude to it. Won't you tell me what happened?"

She knew all about that awful day in Spain? Only Hamish himself could have told her, and yet, here she was, wanting to know more.

Fifty yards ahead, the Earl of Keswick sat upon his horse as if posing for a statue. He'd wait for Miss Megan until high summer.

"You love Hamish, don't you?" Colin asked, though he only dimly grasped what it might mean, for a woman this fierce to love his brother. Trouble for Hamish, but good, long overdue trouble.

"I love him with all my heart, and I always will. Bear that in mind if you refuse me a few simple truths now, Lord Colin."

"I think you'd best dispense with the lord business, and call me Colin when we're private."

Her ladyship petted her mare's shoulder. "Colin, then. So tell me what happened, please."

The sun rose higher in the sky, and the laughter of children joined the quacking of the ducks and jingle of carriage harnesses beneath Hyde Park's towering maples. As dawn stretched toward a lovely morning, Colin told Megan Windham about the time Hamish MacHugh had chosen death over dishonor and lived to regret it.

"The trades must be paid. The books must balance."

Hamish muttered those words, which had been among his father's favorite admonitions. Most of the afternoon had been spent tending to finances, and while Hamish's hand had been writing bank drafts, and his mind totaling figures, his heart had been aching.

How was Megan faring, and how could Hamish assure her that he'd been working diligently to find a means of thwarting Sir Fletcher? A hint of gossip, a thread of dishonor, a disgruntled tradesman, anything . . .

"Are you still at it?" Colin asked, appropriating the chair across from Hamish's desk. "I take it you're abandoning us again this evening? Leaving all the bowing and smiling to me, all the escorting and cavorting?"

"Cavort with caution, little brother," Hamish said, rubbing his eyes.

And that made him think of Megan too.

"Have you given up socializing forevermore?" Colin asked. "Half the matchmakers in London will go into a decline."

"While all of the fortune hunters will rejoice. Have you met any young ladies who catch your eye, Colin?" Hamish picked up the last of the tradesmen's requests for payment rather than study Colin's expression.

The bill was the one for an exorbitant amount of bootmaking, from Puget and Sons. Hamish had put off paying it, at first because nobody in the family had purchased nearly enough boots to justify this much expense. Moreover, no one in the extended family spread out over various London trades — not a second cousin, not an in-law, not a great-auntie — had ever heard of the establishment.

"I thought you were on the verge of offering for a young lady, Hamish." Colin's gaze held accusation and quite possibly pity.

"I was, Colin, but circumstances have changed. You're sure this isn't yours?"

Colin snatched the invoice away and set it aside. "I don't want to talk about pence and quid, Hamish. Megan Windham cares for you, and you've turned your back on her. Not well done of you, and no kind of example for me."

"You're scolding me?" *How novel, and how heartwarming.*

Colin rose, braced his hands on the desk, and leaned forward so his nose was inches from Hamish's.

"Yes, I am scolding you. All I can think is that you've found some other way to be a noble martyr, and I'm sick of it."

Colin looked like Papa just then. Nobody had done a better rendition of fierce and deadly than Papa.

"I'm not a noble martyr," Hamish retorted. "Not unless you're referring to the expenses I'm paying for my sisters. I'm a Scottish upstart cursed with a title, and I've got a wee bit above myself where Miss Megan is concerned. I treasure her dearly, and if I've abandoned escort duty it's to ferret out ammunition to use against those who'd trouble the lady."

Hamish hadn't meant to reveal that much, but Colin looked relieved. He sat back down and picked up the boot bill.

"Somebody's making trouble for Miss

Megan?"

"Not somebody, Sir Fletcher Pilkington. The lady has refused his suit, and he's trying to force her to reconsider." Accurate enough, as far as it went.

Colin brushed the folded invoice across his lips. "So that's why Sir Fletcher has been spreading all manner of talk against you in the clubs. I thought he was just jealous of your title."

"You didn't call him out. I'm proud of you, Colin. Let him say what he will, and eventually I'll find something to use against him. Give me back that blasted invoice, lest I'm hauled into debtors' prison because you've taken my payable for a bookmark."

Colin peered at the document in his hand. "This is the bill that makes no sense. I wonder if these people are poor relations of the Earl of Plyne? The family's huge, which is why so many Pugets bought their colors."

The back of Hamish's neck prickled, though the afternoon was mild and sunny. "There's a problem with that bill, Colin."

"I didn't buy any boots from this establishment and neither did you."

"Two problems, then. Look at the signature."

Colin had good eyesight, and yet he rose to take the bill over to the window. "This is not your signature. Close, but not yours."

"Sir Fletcher has forged letters that he claims are from Miss Megan, and now I see a forged bill among those I'm to pay. I realized shortly after lunch why I was reluctant to pay the damned thing, and now the coincidence — forgery creating difficulty for both me and Miss Megan — troubles me exceedingly."

"Something is rotten in Mayfair," Colin said, bringing the offending document back to the desk. "There's a direction on this bill. Now will you let me pay a call?"

Everything in Hamish rebelled against allowing Colin to take risks on his brother's behalf. "You'll follow me if I go alone, won't you?"

Colin gestured toward the door. "I never thanked you for getting captured by the French. Let me thank you now."

A month ago, Hamish would have fought, argued, blustered, and pulled rank to keep Colin safe at home. Across Spain, into France, and again at Waterloo, Hamish had kept Colin safe, but Colin was no longer a green Highland lad eager to see the world. He'd become a soldier and a brother to be proud of.

Days of solitary reconnaissance had yielded Hamish nothing in the way of leverage against Sir Fletcher, and now this forged invoice had fallen into his hands.

Colin had bested the French when they were intent on murder. Surely he'd be able to handle himself on one innocuous stroll around the neighborhood?

Megan had missed her friends and relations when they'd gone off to war. Worse, she'd missed Sir Fletcher and prayed nightly for his safety.

She should have been praying for her own safety.

And yet, none of that anxious, worried waiting for soldiers to come home compared with how badly she missed Hamish, even knowing he dwelled only a few streets away. He might as well have been on the far slopes of the Pyrenees, for all Megan had seen of him in the past week.

In part to avoid Sir Fletcher, and in part because Megan was weary to death of putting on a show of conviviality every evening, she'd given herself an evening to stay home. Anwen had hugged her and winked, and nobody had looked askance at her decision.

More than a week of Hamish's ceasefire had gone by, and Megan had heard nothing from him. Hamish would never desert, never waver in the face of enemy fire, but he was a fearfully practical man, and every commander blew retreat at some point.

She took herself up to her bedroom, though sleep lately had eluded her.

A difference was discernible before she'd even closed her bedroom door. The air was fresher, more scented with greenery, possibly because the balcony doors had been opened recently.

More likely because Hamish MacHugh had once again fallen asleep in her bed.

Megan undressed in silence, locked both the sitting room door and the bedroom door, then climbed into bed beside her beloved.

"You'd make an excellent intelligence officer," Hamish said, his arm coming around her shoulders. "Slipping about, stealthy as a cat. I didn't intend to do this again."

Megan didn't intend to let him out of the bed. "I'm glad you're here, and I've missed you awfully."

Lest he mistake that sentiment for a platitude, Megan rose up on her elbow and kissed him.

Already, their kisses had become a form of communication. Hamish had something to tell her, and yet, he'd missed her too. His kiss said all of that. His sigh said the news wasn't good.

"Tell me," Megan said, settling along his side, pillowing her head on his shoulder. "As long as Sir Fletcher hasn't started crying the banns, I'll bear it."

As long as Hamish kept stealing into her room and taking her in his arms.

"Sir Fletcher claims to have forged copies of your letters, though copying every letter word for word would have been a tedious and demanding task, if they're forgeries rather than copies."

Lying beside Hamish, Megan could apply her mind to her situation, not merely worry and fume.

"Sir Fletcher claims he's matched my signature exactly. I took that to mean he matched my penmanship as well."

"How?" Hamish asked, turning on his side to face Megan. "Forgery is an art, though a felonious one. I've asked myself that question over and over. An earl's son isn't likely to have dealings with felons, but then I received a bill from a bootmaker, Puget and Sons, and my signature had been forged on the documentation supporting it."

"The Earl of Plyne's family name is Puget," Megan said. "I've seen Garner Puget in company with Sir Fletcher on many occasions. Never looking very happy, but then, what impoverished —"

Hamish was absolutely correct. Forgery was an *art*. "Garner Puget is a talented artist," Megan went on. "He's done portraits of his parents that are worthy of the Royal Academy. He's not considered a fortune hunter, but neither is he highly eligible. Her Grace says the oldest Pilkington sister pines for him."

Hamish kissed Megan, lingering at the corners of her mouth. "I knew we needed to compare maps. Of course, you'd be familiar with the circumstances of every bachelor in every ballroom in Mayfair. You confirm what I've learned about the not-so-honorable Garner Puget."

Megan had to kiss Hamish back, though she also wanted to know what he'd learned. Several passionate minutes later, Hamish — who'd shifted over her and lost his shirt somehow — pulled back.

"I'll forget my name if we keep this up, Meggie, my dear, and I didn't come here to further risk your reputation."

Megan locked her ankles at the small of his back. Hamish was aroused, though he still wore his kilt.

"Tell me the rest of it, and then I'm taking you captive, Hamish MacHugh. I've missed you more than I can bear. Every time I walk into a ballroom and you're not there, I'm worried that Sir Fletcher will trap me with a public proposal. He'd love that, forcing my hand while all of polite society smiles and nods at his good fortune."

"Puget might well have forged your letters," Hamish said. "I received a fraudulent invoice payable to the address of Puget's landlady, right around the corner from the rooms he keeps in Knightsbridge. I sent a bank draft as payment, and when Puget picks it up, I'll have grounds to lay information against him. As I see it, that gives us options."

Us and *options* went very nicely in the same sentence. "Get your kilt off, Hamish, please."

He sat back and got busy unpinning his kilt. "One option is to wrest a confession from Puget, but Sir Fletcher will claim innocent dismay. There's another problem with pursuing a confession."

"I'm listening." Megan was also glorying in the firelit beauty of Hamish's bare chest, his arms, the join of his neck and shoulders. She could not see details, but she could make out contours, she could feel the warmth and shape of him, and she could watch his kilt go sailing to the floor in a flutter of fine wool.

"You're driving me daft," Hamish said,

bracing himself on all fours over her. "God, ye smell good, lass. I'll be the first man in Perthshire to have his own lemon trees."

Hamish smelled better, all clean and heathery.

"Is Puget planning to elope with Sir Fletcher's sister?" Megan asked. "Maybe that's why he tried to steal from you. In his shoes, I'd do nearly anything to get away from Sir Fletcher."

Hamish settled closer, resting his cheek against Megan's. "You count Puget as another of Sir Fletcher's victims, rather than a willing accomplice. Why?"

Fairly soon, Megan would not be able to count to three. "Because that's what Sir Fletcher does. He backs good people into bad situations, like your soldier boy who was nearly starving. *Like me.* I was inexperienced, infatuated, and heedless, but no worse than any other young lady unwise about the greater world."

Megan could see that, now that Hamish was willing to hold Sir Fletcher accountable. Her crime had been innocence, nothing more. Unless Hamish could find Puget and wring a confession from him — a confession implicating Sir Fletcher — she might pay for her folly with the rest of her life.

"You were too innocent for your own good," Hamish said. "More English foolishness, to bring up a young lady in ignorance. If I can find Puget, I'll make sure he implicates Sir Fletcher thoroughly. If Sir Fletcher was willing to use a forger to trap you, and bilk funds from me, then he's likely been using Puget in other capacities as well."

Megan arched up into Hamish's warmth, because she craved as much closeness with him as she could beg, borrow, or reave.

"What's the problem with wringing a confession from Puget?" Megan asked. "He should be relieved to be free of Sir Fletcher's schemes, assuming you don't alert the authorities."

Hamish gave her the first, gratifying hint of penetration and went still. "The problem, Meggie, is that I can't find Puget. He hasn't been seen at a polite entertainment since last you and I spoke. If he's on his way to Gretna with the lady of his choice, nobody is breathing a word of it."

Scotland was days and days of travel away, and Sir Fletcher's patience was at an end. All over again, despair swamped Megan.

For a moment, she didn't move. She remained not quite joined to her beloved, and endured the possibility that Sir Fletcher might win after all. He had forgeries of her letters, his accomplice was nowhere to be found, and Megan's choices were fast narrowing to either ruin for her and her sisters or marriage to a scoundrel.

And yet, Hamish had come to her. Hamish had not given up, and he would not. Megan wrapped her arms around him and completed their joining.

"We have another problem, Hamish."

"Meggie, my heart, right now, I haven't a problem in the world. I have the woman I love in my arms, and that's miracle enough for the moment."

The woman I love. How brave he was, how worthy.

Pleasure welled, welcome and luxurious. "I love you too, Hamish MacHugh, but we still have a problem."

"Tell me this problem, Meggie, though if you love me, and I love you, there's nothing we cannot surmount together."

Colin had told Megan more of Hamish's battle history. Standing resolute was Hamish's nature, while skulking and scheming was Sir Fletcher's. That she'd been duped by Sir Fletcher's charm and pretty looks was not her fault, but oh, she regretted it more with the passage of time, not less.

"Meggie?"

Megan cast the last bit of caution to the

wind, and cast the last of her heart into Hamish's keeping.

"My courses are late."

CHAPTER NINETEEN

Hamish lay in Megan's bed far longer than he should have, felled by emotions too complicated to name. Wonder coursed through him such as he'd never thought to feel, for he and Megan were very possibly to have a child.

Worry chased close on the heels of that mighty sentiment, along with determination. Under no circumstances would Hamish allow Megan, much less their child, to endure the future Sir Fletcher had planned.

Fear tried to wedge a foot into Hamish's thoughts, but he shut and locked all portals against that demon. Megan was counting on him, and though it might require all manner of ugliness on the battlefields of Mayfair's social season, Hamish would not accept defeat.

He stole from the bed, pausing to kiss his beloved's cheek and tuck the covers around her. The dear woman had loved him witless, and he'd responded as best he could. Never had tenderness and passion colluded so forcefully and well.

Love had not muddled Hamish, but rather, had allowed him to see clearly.

He eased over the balcony railing, while in the darkened streets beyond the garden wall, polite society was returning from its latest revels.

Hamish, by contrast, was going to war. He'd inspect every gambling hell, drover's inn, sponging house, and brothel in London to find Garner Puget, and he'd do it in the next few days.

The garden below was dark, but Hamish got to the ground easily. He blew a last kiss in the direction of Megan's balcony, said a silent prayer that Garner Puget hadn't left the country, and was halfway down the terrace steps when a voice stopped him.

"Steal off into the night if you must, Murdoch, but if you have stolen Megan Windham's virtue, you are a dead man."

The tone was pleasant, which made the menace all the more believable. Hamish turned slowly, hands at his sides, to face the Duke of Moreland. His Grace's hair glinted golden in the moonlight, and he wore evening finery that would have cost Hamish more than one of Eddie and Ronnie's rampages at the modiste's.

"Good evening, Your Grace," Hamish said, bowing.

"Murdoch." No bow, not even a nod. "Do you know why my children have dubbed that chamber the courting bedroom?"

"No, sir."

"Because whoever sleeps there is courting folly. The balcony is visible from the apartment I share with my duchess. My children, brilliant though they are, don't seem to have realized this."

His Grace gave away nothing — not ire, certainly not humor, and not forbearance — so Hamish kept his own counsel too.

"Please assure me, Murdoch, that your call upon my niece was at her invitation."

And get Megan in trouble with her uncle? Hamish remained silent, while Moreland snapped off an early white rose and twirled it in his gloved fingers.

"My duchess claims you're a decent man, for all you sport about in that ridiculous skirt. That you don't incriminate Megan will save me the trouble of calling you out."

"My apologies for abusing your hospitality, Your Grace. My thanks for your discretion."

Moreland's posture became militarily upright. "You presume to compliment me

416

on my discretion, young man. Allow me to instruct you on that topic. If you harbor any regard for Megan at all, you will not creep about in darkened gardens, but rather, limit your adoration to venues such as crowded ballrooms, well-lit terraces, and proper carriage parades. Half the purpose of courting a woman is to prove publicly that you hold her in the highest regard."

"Yes, Your Grace."

Moreland's visage was stern in the moonlight. As the silence grew, Hamish considered confiding all in the duke, but again, disclosure would reflect poorly on Megan.

"You've nothing more to say, Murdoch? Not 'Yes, Your Grace,' or 'It will never happen again, Your Grace'?"

"My sincere apologies, Your Grace."

Moreland snorted. "Be off with you, and don't let me catch you within ten feet of Megan unless you're in public and she's acknowledged you before others. Sir Fletcher has asked to speak with me privately, and that does not bode well for your suit, Murdoch."

The duke disappeared into the shadows, the white rose marking his progress back to the house.

How in the hell was Hamish to communicate with Megan now, when she'd have to risk Sir Fletcher's attentions at any social event?

Hamish helped himself to the only other white rose gracing the trellis, lobbed it onto Megan's balcony, then slipped away into the night.

"Esther, remind me never to question your instincts." Percival punctuated his sentiments by passing his duchess the little white blossom he'd retrieved from the garden. "Murdoch was stumbling around in the gardens, smiling the most fatuous, glorious smile. I regret to inform you that our Megan has been entertaining at unusual hours."

Her Grace took a seat at her vanity, laid the rose down, and began pulling pins from her hair. She had strong Teutonic features, and age had gilded her loveliness with wisdom. Her hair remained golden blonde, and her figure perfection — in her husband's eyes.

Percival stilled her hands and took up the task she'd begun.

"I like Murdoch," the duchess said. "I do not like Sir Fletcher. If you ever tire of being a duke, I will write you a glowing character as a lady's maid, provided you seek your first post with me."

"I like Murdoch as well. He refrained

from impugning Megan's judgment, and when I did my best impersonation of the Duke of Outraged Propriety, Murdoch knew enough to keep his mouth shut. He's canny, as the Scots say. I insulted his national dress, and still, he would not be goaded."

Esther beamed at her husband in the mirror. "You were naughty, Percival. I adore your capacity for naughtiness. At least you didn't threaten to call the poor man out."

"I've every respect for the faster reflexes and damnably good aim of the seasoned soldier. Have you always used this many pins, my dear?"

"My hair is in need of a trim," Her Grace replied. "So did you spank Murdoch's conscience and send him quivering and apologizing on his way?"

That was the standard response when an overeager suitor was caught in the garden, provided the suitor was the young lady's choice. Percival removed the last pin and started on the unbraiding. Esther had looked quite elegant this evening, but then, she usually did.

"Why doesn't Murdoch offer for her, Esther? Sir Fletcher has asked for an audience with me, and I must oblige him eventually. I can't think of a reason to refuse him, if he asks for permission to court Megan. Sir Fletcher's father would take it amiss if I discouraged Sir Fletcher, and the old boy is tedious enough as it is when I need his vote."

Esther's hair flowed in long, silky skeins down her back. She passed Percival the brush, and took up the rose.

"Why not consult our sons?" she asked, twirling the blossom. "Westhaven and Valentine move in the same circles as Sir Fletcher, and they have some acquaintance with Murdoch. If you cannot make sense of a situation, Percival, then you're not in possession of all the facts. Megan approves of Murdoch passionately, to all appearances, and she barely tolerates Sir Fletcher."

"Right or left?" Percival asked.

"Left, please."

He arranged her hair to accommodate a single plait over her left shoulder. "You've put your finger on the problem, as usual. I must not be in possession of all the facts. I did warn Murdoch that in future, his attentions to Megan will be limited to public venues and acceptable locations. One doesn't like to think that Gladys and Tony's first grandchild might be a seven months babe."

Her Grace sat very tall. "Our first child

was born seven months after the wedding. Gladys and Tony's was. Westhaven's heir was a seven months child, so was your late oldest brother. Have you no respect for tradition, Moreland?"

Percival had endless respect for his wife, and for the foolishness of young people in love.

"If I see Murdoch climbing our garden walls again, I'll turn you loose on him," he said, kissing his wife's crown. "I'm still considering your observation that I haven't all the facts."

"We'll alert the children," Esther replied, passing Percival a hair ribbon. Blue, her favorite shade because it was the same color as his eyes, she claimed. "If there's more to the situation than we know, we'll soon learn the whole of it. I must put this flower in water before we retire."

"I'll do it," Percival said, taking the blossom from her grasp. "Matchmaking is tiring work, and we have three more nieces to go."

Esther rose and put her arms around Percival. "But then, my love, we can look forward to starting on the grandchildren. Rose and Bronwyn will set Town on its collective ear, and Bridget is nothing short of beautiful. I can hardly wait."

Percival could wait. Young people got into

the silliest scrapes, and yet, something about Megan's situation didn't feel silly at all.

"Nothing," Colin said. "Not a whisper, not a peep. Not a hint or a suspicion. I'm sorry, Hamish."

Hamish tipped his hat to some countess or other — spending time in a few ballrooms had helped him sort the courtesans from the countesses — and paused on the steps of Lord Westhaven's townhouse.

"You tried," he said. "The men have tried, but I should have known a lot of former infantry wouldn't hear much about where an earl's son might lay low."

That Hamish's former subordinates would try, so long after mustering out, meant a lot.

"What are we doing here?" Colin asked, eyeing the potted heartsease adorning the steps.

"I sent a note to the Earl of Keswick asking for an hour of his time. He suggested we meet here."

"You'll ask a litter of titled Englishmen for help finding Puget?" Colin demanded, fists on hips.

Why were the MacHughs doomed to brawl in public? "I would beg Lucifer's climbing boys for help if it would secure

Megan's peace of mind. Any day, Sir Fletcher will call on Moreland and ask for permission to court her. Any evening, Sir Fletcher might announce to all of Mayfair that he's so hopelessly smitten he must go down on bended knee in the middle of some damned ballroom. I'm out of time, Colin."

But Hamish could not stop hoping. He'd thought himself immune to hope, beyond its sticky clutches. A life of responsible contentment punctuated by only an occasional nightmare had been the sum of his aspirations.

Then he'd been gifted with Megan Windham's trust, and his ambitions had multiplied like stars filling the night sky.

"So you'll turn to the English officers who ridiculed you?" Colin pressed. "The very men who made sport of us both, spread talk, and mocked your bravery?"

"Colin, I can't do this alone. We can't do this alone. Puget is the son of an English lord, and so to English lords I will turn. You can leave me here, and I'll understand."

Hamish didn't want Colin to go, though. In fact, if Hamish had been able to bring Eddie and Ronnie along, he would have.

Colin shoved Hamish hard enough to make him take a step back. "As if I'd leave my own brother to face this pack of jackals and no loyal henchman at his side."

Hamish shoved him back, for form's sake, and because embracing his little brother on the street would mortify Colin.

"I see we're treating polite society to a fine display of Scottish manners."

Hamish knew that voice, and yet, it wasn't Moreland's. The Moreland heir stood two yards away, turned out in finest morning attire, his walking stick in hand.

"Westhaven, good day. You know my brother Lord Colin MacHugh."

Westhaven bowed. "We can stand here showing off our tailoring, or join my brothers before my entire store of marzipan is decimated." He gestured toward the steps, and Hamish led the way into the townhouse.

The butler greeted his lordship with word that the gentlemen were in the library, and her ladyship had asked for trays to be sent along.

As if tea cakes and two sips of overly sugared gunpowder would solve the problems Hamish faced?

The gentlemen included Lords Keswick, Valentine, and Rosecroft.

"Look who I found on my front steps," Westhaven said. "Two titled, wealthy bachelors without the sense to take a sister or two along for safety."

424

"You're daft," Hamish said. "My sisters have acquired battalions of friends, all of whom are eager to marry. The debutantes lurk in doorways, and pop out of sweet shops if my sisters are along. If it's only Colin and myself, we're left in relative peace."

"He contradicted Westhaven," Lord Valentine said. "Her Grace would approve."

"That's *Worst*haven to you," Rosecroft replied.

"And that's enough out of you, *Rosebud,*" Westhaven shot back. "Shall we be seated? Keswick, you called this meeting, and if your formidable wife could not solve whatever problem plagues you, then it must be quite the thorny issue."

They took chairs around a circular table that would have sat eight comfortably. Westhaven got down a tin from the mantel and offered it to Keswick, who sat on his right.

"The sweets in this household are always fresh," Keswick said, helping himself, then passing the tin to Lord Valentine. "Never will you see grown men taking such delight in ruining their suppers as in Lord Westhaven's household. It's disgracefully juvenile."

"Have another," Lord Valentine said, waving the tin under Keswick's nose.

"Don't mind if I do. Leave some for our

guests. We needn't be entirely without manners."

Apparently consuming forbidden sweets in the library was some ritual known only to titled Englishmen. Colin took a sweet and passed Hamish a nearly empty tin.

"Keswick," Westhaven said. "You have the floor."

"My thanks. I'll be brief."

"That's not how Louisa describes you," Lord Valentine muttered. Rosecroft smacked his lacey lordship on the arm, and Colin took another treat from the tin Hamish was still holding.

"I will be succinct," Keswick said. "Murdoch must locate Garner Puget, one of the Earl of Plyne's younger sons. The matter is urgent. Puget has behaved badly, probably in service to Sir Fletcher, who might well have coerced Puget into forging documents of an unfortunate nature."

"I know Puget," Rosecroft said. "He was a regimental scribe, for want of a better term. Had a lovely hand, and was always willing to write a note home for the men incapable of doing it themselves."

"Which means," Keswick went on, "Puget might also have drafted the occasional dispatch, requisition, or meticulous facsimile of same. Has anybody seen him in the past week?"

A general discussion followed, of where Puget might be found, and who might best look for him. Westhaven made a list of gentlemen's clubs Puget belonged to, somebody volunteered the name of his tailor, somebody else agreed to chat with his landlady. To Hamish, that good woman would have been hard-pressed to spare the time of day. For the English aristocrats at the table, she'd dip her best curtsy.

Hamish put a piece of marzipan in his mouth without thinking, and was surprised at the richness and intensity of the flavor.

Rather like the surprise of finding out that Megan's titled cousins were, in fact, *gentlemen.* Aid was being rendered without a lot of questions, and the relief of that was tremendous. Hamish would not have known which clubs Puget frequented, or to whom he'd given his sartorial custom.

"Are you hoarding the last of the treats?" Colin asked.

Hamish passed him the tin, and the meeting broke up shortly thereafter. A footman brought Westhaven a note, which his lordship barely had time to scan before Rosecroft plucked it from his hand.

"Moreland has summoned us," Rosecroft said, passing the note to Lord Valentine.

427

"He wants to consult with us on a matter of some delicacy."

Westhaven snatched the note back. "Why he'd involve you two louts in a discussion of a delicate matter, I do not know."

"I'm likely the matter in need of discussion," Hamish said. "His Grace came upon me delicately prowling across his garden at an awkward hour."

Conversation stopped, and four English lords all found it necessary to study the molding, the wainscoting, the books shelved in abundance along two walls. Doubtless, their children would be born as a result of divine intervention, so delicate were their lordships' sensibilities.

"Moreland caught you beneath Megan's balcony, and yet, you lived," Rosecroft murmured, after what might have been a respectful silence. "His Grace is growing sentimental on us."

"Perhaps the delicate matter is what to tell Sir Fletcher regarding his matrimonial aspirations?" Keswick suggested.

"Regardless," Hamish said, shoving to his feet. "Ask the duke if he knows where Garner Puget has got off to. I have the sense Moreland knows more than God, and his duchess more than Moreland and God put together, at least about the doings of polite society — and their own family."

Westhaven stared at nothing for a moment, then shook his head. "Involving His Grace is like involving the heavy artillery. No telling exactly where the ordnance will land or upon whom the shrapnel will explode. We'll casually inquire if His Grace knows of Puget's whereabouts. Any more pointed questioning risks ducal meddling, which is about as helpful as an outbreak of plague, cholera, and typhus all at once."

Amid murmurs of agreement from the other Windhams, Colin rose, taking one last piece of marzipan. Hamish assayed a glower, but Colin popped the sweet in his mouth and winked.

Keswick joined them on the walkway, apparently spared from the ducal summons. "They'll find him, Murdoch. Between the Windham gentlemen, their in-laws, their friends, and the people who owe them favors, Garner Puget is as good as found."

No, he was not. "There's a ball tonight," Hamish said. "I want you and Lord Valentine to stay with Megan at all times, even if you have to alternate sharing dances with her."

"I cannot possibly dance half the dances," Keswick snapped. "I'd be lame for a week, and everybody would remark the spectacle of Megan Windham limiting her partners to her cousins."

"I can dance with her," Colin said.

"You'll be with me," Hamish replied. "If Sir Fletcher can't get to Moreland privately, he might try to accost the duke in the card room or the men's retiring room tonight. Westhaven and Rosecroft can stay with Moreland, and run Sir Fletcher off if that happens."

"I'll have Deene and the rest of the in-laws stand up with Megan," Keswick said. "But if Sir Fletcher asks her to dance, she'll have to accept."

"Why?" Colin asked.

"Because a lady either dances of an evening, or she doesn't," Hamish said. "She isn't supposed to pick and choose among the gentlemen, rejecting this one, accepting that one." Megan had explained that to him, which had made sense of a lot of die-away glances from the young ladies, and odd pairings on the dance floor.

"Damned silly if you ask me," Colin muttered.

"My countess uses stronger language than that," Keswick said. "She maintains if a man can't endure being turned down for a waltz, he's not much of a man."

Hamish was growing to like Keswick's

countess, sight unseen. He did not like that even the best informed scions of fashionable society hadn't heard a whisper regarding Puget's whereabouts.

He didn't like that at all.

Sir Fletcher didn't like being made to wait, but at least he was being made to wait by a duke. The Windham guest parlor was lovely, with bouquets of fresh lilacs in both windows, and plenty of light bouncing off mirrors, gold-flocked wallpaper, and gilded furniture.

The room was pretty, in other words, which tempted Sir Fletcher to put his boots up on a cushion or overturn the ink bottle on the escritoire.

"Sir Fletcher, good day." Elizabeth Windham offered him a curtsy and a smile sporting too much intelligence and not enough simper.

"Miss Windham," Sir Fletcher said, bowing over her hand. "I am awaiting a moment of your uncle's time, and perhaps a turn in the garden with Miss Megan. May I offer my compliments on your ensemble? That shade of chocolate is luscious."

"Thank you. Shall we have a seat? The footman will arrive with a tea tray shortly, and I'm happy to pour out for you. How are your sisters?"

The woman excelled at small talk. Sir Fletcher was compelled to recite at length regarding his sisters, his stepmother, his older brothers, and his plans for the autumn.

The butler interrupted and had a discreet word with Miss Windham by the door, leaving Sir Fletcher to the dubious comfort of shortbread and gunpowder. Because the clubs kept punctilious track of every morsel a fellow consumed and every drop he drank, Sir Fletcher did justice to the offerings on the tray.

"Sir Fletcher, I'm afraid His Grace is unavoidably detained on a matter of pressing business. He's closeted with no less than three of my cousins," Miss Windham said. "I'd be happy to inspect the roses with you."

Good God. The roses were barely blooming. Sir Fletcher knew this because Geneva had demanded he bring her a rose to apologize for not taking her riding.

"I'd like nothing better than to enjoy the fresh air in the company of a pretty lady," Sir Fletcher said, rising and offering Miss Windham his hand.

"To the garden, then." She ignored his glove before her nose, snatched the last piece of shortbread off the tray, and led the

432

way through the French doors. If this was the example Megan's older sister set, no wonder the poor darling had no idea how to go on.

When they'd marched past rows of thorny bushes, admired the lilacs, and otherwise wasted half an hour of Sir Fletcher's day, Miss Windham took a shady bench beside a small fountain. The sculpture in the center was a swan, trapped in a perpetually graceful progress across the water.

"Do you think you can make my sister happy, Sir Fletcher? Please do have a seat."

Sir Fletcher complied. If he tarried long enough, he was bound to catch sight of Megan. With Puget having gone to ground — and all sources of income having disappeared with him — announcing an engagement had become a pressing necessity.

"I hope I can make Miss Megan more than happy." He'd ensure she was obedient, with child, and kept busy making his home a pleasant, commodious place. What more could a woman want, after all, than children, a roof over her head, and the protection and guidance of a man who knew what he was about?

"How will you undertake the challenge of making her *more than happy*?" Miss Windham broke off a corner of the shortbread she'd purloined from the tea tray and crumbled it onto the paving stones before the fountain. Two pigeons were soon boldly pecking away at an unexpected feast.

"Married to me, Megan will have a household of her own, children if the good Lord allows, a place in society, and the protection of a well-respected name. I will cherish Megan to the best of my humble ability."

More crumbs were tossed to the mannerless birds.

"Just the usual, then," Miss Windham said. "You don't speak of love, Sir Fletcher."

Women and their infernal sentimentality. "Nor would I raise such a tender emotion in what is essentially polite conversation, madam. I esteem your sister greatly, above all other women. Many a sound marriage has been launched on less regard between bride and groom."

Sir Fletcher esteemed Megan's settlements and her ducal connections. She composed a fine love letter too, but her taste in sisters was sadly lacking.

"You're right, of course," Miss Windham said, rising. "Megan has a keen appreciation of the honor you do her, or will do her, assuming Uncle Percy gives you leave. I'm sure if you call again later in the week, he'll be more than happy to receive you."

Well, damn the luck. Fortunately, the Countess of Hazelton's ball was scheduled for that evening, and Megan would not miss an event at which one of her cousins was hostess. The countess was Megan's oldest lady cousin, and the entire Windham family — including His Grace of Moreland — would doubtless be in attendance.

"I'll bid you good day," Sir Fletcher said, again bowing over Miss Windham's hand. She dipped a curtsy and murmured something about wishing him luck.

He didn't need to rely on mere luck, not when he had forgeries of Megan's letters. By this time tomorrow, Sir Fletcher intended to be a happily engaged man.

"I'm inclined to burn London to the ground," Hamish said as he and Colin waited for a hackney to trot through the intersection.

"Somebody already tried that back in 1666," Colin replied. "You might flush Puget from his covert, but we'd not live to catch him."

They'd spent the day checking every club, shop, brothel, and park bench in Mayfair and beyond, and still they had neither word nor whisper of Puget, not even in the coffeehouse off Grosvenor that claimed his regular patronage.

"Let's try again tomorrow," Colin said. "I'll spend the evening at Jackson's, and that will put me on my mettle — and might yield us some gossip about our missing forger."

The streets were busy, the season reaching its peak, and the sun having sunk low. Hamish's mood had sunk low as well.

"Tomorrow could be too late. Tonight's ball is given by one of Megan's cousins, and Megan dare not stay home yet again. Sir Fletcher will know that, and seize his opportunity."

They tramped along past Bond Street establishments, most of which they'd visited earlier in the day.

"Then you ought to attend the ball too," Colin said. "Ronnie and Eddie will never forgive you if you show up dressed as you are."

Hamish was appropriately attired for poking about London in search of a scoundrel. To appear at a fancy gathering in his boots and everyday kilt would be the undoing of several weeks of good behavior, at least.

"We keep looking," Hamish said. "I have promised Megan —"

He halted, because the back of his neck was prickling, the same way it had when he'd been searching for his brother in the foothills of the Pyrenees years ago.

"You have that, 'I smell a French foot patrol' look in your eye," Colin said, glancing around. "Angelo was an Italian, though."

They stood across the street from the famous fencing establishment named for its founder. The grandson, Henry Angelo, operated the place now. Hamish had been inside occasionally on his way north on leave. Jackson's boxing salon, which sat next door to Angelo's, had never interested him.

"Puget might frequent an establishment such as Angelo's," Hamish said.

"If he were honing his skills in anticipation of a duel?"

Hamish was already crossing the street. "If he were looking for artistic commissions for sporting portraits, or simply seeking to stay out of sight for a while. The former officers tend not to frequent the place, but the dandies and younger sons do."

Those who could regard violence as entertainment, in other words, and those who fancied having themselves immortalized with an idealized portrait.

"Hamish, you can't just barge into a fencing salon, and —"

Hamish barged in. "Captain Garner Puget," he said to the attendant. "Fetch him to me now, if you please."

The attendant was a thin, blond fellow with delicate features. "Whom shall I say is calling, sir?"

"God almighty," Colin muttered.

The attendant looked from one brother to the other.

"The Duke of Murder," Hamish replied. "And company."

"Don't call yourself that," Colin said as the attendant scurried off. "Duke of Mayhem, I can believe, but not murder. Never that. Possibly the Duke of Manners, now that Miss Megan has got you by the sporran."

Hamish was prepared to commit mayhem at least. "You should leave this to me, Colin. What I have in store for Puget won't be polite at all."

Colin took up a lean against the paneled wall and crossed his arms. "Get as unmannerly as you like, Hamish. It's about time, if you ask me. I'm not going anywhere."

"My thanks."

Garner Puget, looking rumpled and the worse for lack of sleep, joined them in the foyer. His cuffs were turned back, and his right hand was streaked with yellow pigment. The attendant, wisely, had not escorted Puget to greet his callers.

"Your Grace, Lord Colin, greetings."

Hamish drove his fist into Puget's gut. "Greetings yourself, on behalf of a lady whom you've wronged. If you don't want the same sentiments conveyed to your face, you will accompany me now."

The blow sent Puget sagging into Colin, who kept the slighter man on his feet until he could stand upright unaided.

"I'm happy to meet you on the field of honor, Murdoch," Puget said, "but I'll delope. I have failed in my duty as a gentleman, and my only defense is that I was cozened by a greater scoundrel than I. Excessive fondness for the scoundrel's sister blinded me to honor's demands."

"Is this Drury Lane?" Colin asked nobody in particular. "I thought we were on Bond Street."

"You're not the first man whose cock ran off with his common sense, Puget," Hamish said, "but your foolishness has devolved to the misery of a woman I value greatly, and you will make amends."

Puget rubbed his belly with the hand bearing the yellow stain. "You'll not kill me?"

"You used the word *devolved,* Hamish," Colin said. "You sounded very ducal about it too."

"I'll do worse than kill you," Hamish said. "If you survive what I have planned for you this evening, then your sentence shall be to immure yourself in the north at the seat of a certain dukedom, and steward the damned property so I need not trouble myself managing English land. Lady Pamela's father ought to look with favor on your suit should you offer for his oldest daughter, for his family is about to be embroiled in significant scandal."

"You'd do that for me? Offer me a post?"

"I'd do that *to* you, assuming the evening doesn't see you drawn and quartered, but first we need pen and paper."

Twenty minutes later, they were back on the street, marching directly for the Countess of Hazelton's ball.

CHAPTER TWENTY

"He's here," Anwen said. "I'll stay with you, and Charlotte and Elizabeth will keep Sir Fletcher in sight at all times."

Everybody was in evidence at the Hazelton ball, including Megan's cousins, her aunt and uncle, the in-laws, and — drat the luck — Sir Fletcher.

But no Hamish, not even Colin and the MacHugh sisters, though they'd been sent an invitation.

"You can't stop Sir Fletcher from approaching me," Megan said. "I should leave."

Though Megan had hoped she might catch a glimpse of Hamish among the dancers. No less person than the Duchess of Moreland had made it clear that Megan had used up her entire season's quotient of evenings at home.

Megan either met Hamish here, or she had to risk another outing in the park, which Sir Fletcher might learn of all too easily.

"What is Sir Fletcher wearing?" Megan asked.

"The usual formal attire," Anwen replied. "His waistcoat is burgundy with gold embroidery."

"And have you seen Garner Puget, by chance?"

Anwen took the cup of punch Megan had been holding. "How many men are courting you?"

"Officially, none."

"Sir Fletcher is coming this way," Anwen said, setting the glass on the tray of a passing footman. "What should we do, Megs? Sir Fletcher has extricated himself from conversation with Elizabeth and Charlotte, and he's headed this way. Where is the watch when we need — ?"

"Megan, I believe your quadrille belongs to me." Not one of Megan's cousins, but Lucas Denning, the Marquess of Deene, a cousin-in-law, offered a bow.

"Deene, good evening. Is it the quadrille already?"

"Indeed it is. Anwen, do you await a partner?"

"Certainly not. When you conclude your quadrille, you will bring Megan directly back here to me."

"And then," his lordship said, wiggling blond brows, "I will partner you for the minuet. Try to contain your enthusiasm until that happy moment."

Deene escorted Megan to the dance floor, which afforded her an opportunity to look about for a tall, auburn-haired man in a kilt.

"Murdoch isn't here," Deene said. "Your duke is searching for one Garner Puget, whom I knew in passing on the Peninsula."

The other dancers were assembling as a string quintet and pianoforte tuned up. "Is Lord Colin MacHugh in attendance?"

"Haven't seen him. Relax, Megan. If Sir Fletcher approaches Moreland, then Westhaven will intervene. If Sir Fletcher approaches you with anything other than perfunctory civilities, I will kill him."

The introduction began, which meant all conversation would soon cease, for the dance required couples to form a square, and to dance both with and around each other.

"You will not kill Sir Fletcher," Megan said as she curtsied to Deene. "That privilege should belong to me."

Deene treated her to the smile that had won him a reputation for raking prior to his marriage, and then the dance began. The quadrille was relatively new, but Megan had danced it enough to be confident of the steps.

She was not confident of this plan to keep her from Sir Fletcher's company. He was wily and shrewd, and persistent as a rash. She dared not venture so far as the women's retiring room, or even the card room, lest he accost her.

"Smile," Deene murmured as he turned her in a circle. "Dance now, murder later."

Not murder, precisely, but as Megan chasséd, jetéd, and pliéd, she battled a growing impulse to seek Sir Fletcher out and confront him, come what may. Colin MacHugh had put Hamish's military career in perspective for her, and if anything, the information had increased her determination to thwart Sir Fletcher's schemes.

"Where is Sir Fletcher?" Megan whispered on the next turn.

"Two squares down."

Close enough that he was probably watching Megan's every step. She'd always regarded her poor eyesight as a nuisance, not a curse, but for once, she wished she had the vision of an eagle.

The never-ending quadrille eventually concluded, and Deene escorted Megan off the dance floor.

"Who is to partner you for the minuet?" Deene asked.

"I don't know. Anwen is keeping track for me. I'm partnering with only family tonight, though I've half a mind to approach Sir Fletcher and let him make a cake of himself."

"Not wise, Megs. When there's talk, it always redounds to the lady's discredit. If you don't care for Sir Fletcher, then leave it to Moreland to send the brave knight packing."

"Redound to a lady's discredit," Megan muttered. "What does that mean? That the talk haunts her, as Sir Fletcher has made a pest of himself to me? That gossip reflects upon her, as impetuous behavior has reflected on me, even years later?"

A flash of golden hair, dark evening attire, and burgundy went by on her right. Deene shifted so he blocked Megan from Sir Fletcher's view, and Megan wanted to shove his lordship aside.

If Sir Fletcher was to ruin her future, let it be ruin on her terms. Megan's sisters had agreed with her on that point, and as for what Their Graces thought . . . Megan loved her aunt and uncle, but she loved Hamish more.

And she was heartily sick of being held

prisoner by Sir Fletcher's threats.

"One forgets how fierce the Windham womenfolk can be," Deene said. "But now is not the time or the —"

A commotion erupted at the far end of the ballroom, when the dancers ought to be assembling for the minuet.

"What is it, Deene?"

"I can't tell. Perhaps a footman fell on the steps to the minstrel's gallery, or somebody's having an argument."

Deene was tall, but the Hazelton gathering was very well attended, so the crowd was considerable.

Megan unwound her arm from his. "Go assure yourself that your wife has not come to harm. I'll find Anwen, and you can meet us by the punch bowl." Megan would find Sir Fletcher first, and give him the set down of his handsome, arrogant, conniving life.

The stir and murmur from the corner of the ballroom hadn't let up. If an argument were in progress, the crowd would have gone silent, the better to catch every word.

"Anwen is right where we left her," Deene said. "Sir Fletcher's back is turned. Off you go, and I'll see what's afoot."

He loped away, very likely intent on finding his lady wife, or offering aid to the host and hostess in the event something untoward was in progress.

Megan scanned the ballroom one last time in hopes she'd catch sight of Hamish, then realized it might be better if he were absent. Sir Fletcher needed to know that Megan spoke for herself, and had made her own decisions.

Megan had needed to know that too.

In the next moment, Megan found herself staring at embroidered burgundy and white lace, the combination putting her in mind of a wound bleeding through its bandages. As if her thoughts had conjured him, Sir Fletcher — amid a cloud of attar of roses — stood before her.

"My dearest Megan, good evening. Your escort seems to have deserted you. How fortunate that I've come to your rescue."

He took her hand and brought it to his lips.

"Fortunate, indeed," Megan said, though the menace in his tone had her knees wobbling. "Shall we enjoy the terrace?"

The terrace would have to do — more private than the middle of the ballroom, though on such a mild evening, not deserted by any means. More to the point, half the Windham family would see Sir Fletcher escorting her there, and stop him from any scandalous behavior.

He kept her hand in his, his grip uncomfortable through Megan's gloves.

"The terrace? As I recall, you disdained to share the out of doors with me not long ago. For what I have to say to you, a crowded ballroom will do nicely. A moment, please, while I review the speech I've prepared. Do try to look pleased when I get to the business about until death do us part, won't you?"

Hamish had tried to be discreet, but none of the footmen were willing to ask the Duke of Moreland to step out of the ballroom. Colin had located Moreland up in the minstrel's gallery, which was only slightly less public than the middle of the dance floor.

"The talk will never cease," Puget said as Hamish led him to the steps in the corner of the ballroom. "This is the social equivalent of housebreaking, MacHugh. You insult your host and hostess —"

Hamish stopped on the steps, which put him appreciably higher than Puget. Behind Puget, all of polite society was gawking and whispering, simply because three guests had arrived underdressed to the ball. Meggie was somewhere in that crowd, but so was Sir Fletcher, likely with a damned ring in his pocket.

"Puget, you will address me as *Murdoch* or *Your Grace,* lest you insult *me.*"

Colin, whose presence prevented last minute attacks of cowardice from inspiring Puget to retreat, aimed a spectacular glower at the people gathered at the foot of the steps.

"Murdoch," Puget said. "I beg your pardon."

"Pardon denied," Hamish said, resuming their progress up the steps. "It's not me you've wronged, though not for lack of trying."

Puget had disclosed the whole scheme, and had — like the dutiful scribe he was — kept track of every party who'd been fleeced by a forged IOU. Fortunately for Puget, Megan was the only lady whose letters had been copied and Hamish was the only person to whom a forged merchant's bill had been sent.

Unfortunately for Megan, Puget confirmed that he'd made meticulous forgeries of each letter, with special attention given to rendering a perfect replica of the lady's signature.

"If you knew it was wrong," Hamish asked as they reached the minstrel's gallery, "why did you do it?"

Puget was disheveled, exhausted, and facing the social equivalent of a firing squad. Hamish had intended the question as an opportunity for the condemned to unburden himself.

"It wasn't wrong, at first," Puget said. "Sir Fletcher asked me to make exact copies, works of art to safeguard the sentiments of his intended. Traveling across Spain, the originals had become creased and tattered. He told me he wanted only to preserve the correspondence."

The gallery was less crowded than the ballroom, but all eyes turned to Hamish when he reached the top of the steps. Moreland was near the railing, looking every inch the duke — the displeased duke, flanked by no less than three family members.

His Grace aimed an unimpressed glance at Hamish, then turned back to Westhaven.

"So you made copies," Hamish pressed, "not realizing they'd be used for blackmail?"

"I would never — of course I hadn't realized what Sir Fletcher contemplated. One doesn't, until it's too late. He mentioned over a drink late one evening that somebody might get the wrong idea, given how exactly I had copied the lady's hand. He never used the word forgery, but the threat was strongly implied. I was a complete dupe who'd taken

450

artistic pride in — why am I explaining this?"

Hamish took him by one arm, Colin took him by the other.

"You're rehearsing the story you're about to tell the Duke of Moreland," Hamish said, "and it had better exactly match the tale you told us at Angelo's."

"Exactly," Colin said. "Word for word, not a detail out of place. Artistic pride and all that."

Westhaven looked resplendent in his evening attire, Rosecroft was intimidating, while Keswick's expression was unreadable.

Too damned bad.

"If I might interrupt, Your Grace?" Hamish said.

Moreland turned slowly, as if reluctant to acknowledge an unfortunate connection. "Murdoch. One does not attend a ball in less than one's best finery. Go home and change. Better still, go home and stay there. You are creating a spectacle at my daughter's ball."

"I will make a worse spectacle yet if you do not afford me a few minutes of your time, sir. Deny me Miss Megan's hand if you must, but you will hear what Puget has to say. In private would be best."

Moreland arched an eyebrow that probably set half the House of Lords atremble when His Grace was displeased.

"You have presumed on my patience for the last time, Murdoch. Be gone."

Perhaps this was where Megan got her determination. What marvelously stubborn children she and Hamish would have, assuming Moreland didn't see his prospective nephew-in-law drawn and quartered.

"I will leave," Hamish said, "once you've heard what Puget has to say."

Westhaven scanned the ballroom, his profile much like his papa's. "I'd like to hear this tale. One grows bored of waltzing, sipping punch, and chatting over cards."

"In other words," Moreland snapped, "we've already drawn the notice of every gossip in Mayfair, so I'm to appear graciously entertained rather than outraged by this folly."

Rosecroft aimed a look at Puget. "You were the regimental scribe in Sir Fletcher's unit, if I recall correctly. What brings you here?"

Moreland let the question stand, suggesting His Grace had been testing Hamish's resolve, probably not for the first time.

Puget tugged down his waistcoat. "I was the scribe, but I became the regimental forger. And then I became simply a forger, and worse than that, a fool."

"Which fate apparently still afflicts you," Moreland said. "Spare me the dramatics, and get on with the rest of your tale. I have every suspicion it does not end happily."

"That was the point, Your Grace," Puget said. "As far as Sir Fletcher was concerned, the only acceptable conclusion to the story was marriage to Miss Megan Windham. The young lady apparently divined that her happiness would be forfeit in that case, and Sir Fletcher used my skills to ensure she was coerced to the altar."

Moreland appeared to be studying the crowd below, but he'd gone ominously still. "My Megan, *coerced*?"

Puget's upper lip was beaded with sweat, his complexion as pale as the duke's cravat.

"Blackmailed," Hamish said. "By Sir Fletcher, using letters Megan desperately regrets sending him when he served in Spain. I did not expect you to take my word for it, but Puget has no reason to dissemble."

"Go on," the duke said softly. "Leave no detail out, and be very sure of your facts."

Puget's tale was simple and sordid, and he'd reached the part about forging a bill for boots when Colin touched Hamish on the arm.

"Megan needs you," Colin said. "I'll tend to matters here."

Puget fell silent as the duke joined Hamish at the rail. "That scoundrel," Moreland said, gaze focused on Sir Fletcher halfway across the ballroom. "I'll make him rue the day he stood up with my niece."

One floor below, with a hundred gossips and tattlers looking on, Sir Fletcher bowed over Megan's hand. He stood too close to her, he kept hold of her hand, and everything about Megan's posture confirmed that she loathed his touch.

"Excuse me, Your Grace," Hamish said as the noise in the ballroom faded. "I have a knight of the realm to call out."

A circle had formed around Megan and Sir Fletcher, as if a bare-knuckle match were about to start.

Megan broke free of Sir Fletcher's grasp, by the simple expedient of withdrawing her hand from her evening glove. Sir Fletcher was left holding a length of white kid, while Megan backed up two steps.

"You will leave me alone," she shouted. "You will leave me alone, and you will leave every decent young woman alone, do you hear me?" She snatched the glove from Sir Fletcher's grasp, smacked him across the face with it, and tossed it at his slippered feet.

"She's a Windham," His Grace said. "By God, she's every inch a Windham."

"Your Grace, Megan's nearly blind in close quarters," Hamish retorted. "She can't see that Sir Fletcher's enjoying her outburst." Worse, Pilkington walked around Megan in a slow circle, clearly calculating how to use her behavior for his own benefit.

Hamish knew what it was to be without allies, at the end of his resources, with nothing to lose. He could not bear to see Megan in the same position. He turned for the stairs, but Moreland stopped him.

"Wait," the duke said. "Megan is not finished with Pilkington, and I am not finished with you."

Megan could not see who all was standing by, eagerly watching this altercation with Sir Fletcher. Her family was among the crowd, likely scandalized by her actions.

If I'm to be ruined, let it be on my terms.

"Megan, dearest," Sir Fletcher purred. "You are overset. Perhaps a surfeit of her ladyship's excellent punch is to blame, or perhaps your nerves have grown delicate waiting for me to offer for you."

He circled Megan, as if she were some

inanimate sculpture, helpless even to move.

"No offer from you will meet with my acceptance, Sir Fletcher, unless it's an offer for you to leave the country permanently. You are a disgrace to your gender."

Sir Fletcher came close enough to whisper. "At least I didn't pen my torrid sentiments in lurid detail, madam. It's time for you to drop into a convincing swoon."

"Get away from me." Megan drew her foot back, which should have been undetectable beneath her skirts. Sir Fletcher, though, like most predators, had sufficiently sound instincts that he stepped away.

"Are you throwing me over for that kilted barbarian?" he asked — *loudly.* "I could tell you tales about the Duke of Murder, Miss Megan, that would give you nightmares."

Such scorn dripped from Sir Fletcher's words that Megan gave up her last hope that this encounter could be blamed on nerves, fatigue, female hysteria, or — society's favorite explanation for dramatic scenes — *a misunderstanding.*

"If Murdoch will have me," she said, raising her voice for all to hear, "I will gladly become his duchess."

Sir Fletcher guffawed. "You'd marry that, that beast in plaid? He disgraced his command by disobeying orders, got captured by the French, barely knows how to waltz —"

Megan could not see the expressions of Sir Fletcher's audience — for this was skilled performance — but she didn't need to see who believed Sir Fletcher to know the truth.

"Waltzing would not have saved Lord Colin MacHugh's life, when you told him there were fresh horses to be purchased five miles north of camp in the Spanish hills. There were no horses, but there were French patrols."

"You know nothing about it," Sir Fletcher retorted. "French patrols were a fact of life. We were at war with the French, hence, French patrols. We traded them bread for brandy between battles. Would you expect to find Egyptian patrols, for God's sake?"

Somebody tittered, then fell silent.

"When Lord Colin didn't return to camp," Megan went on, "Hamish MacHugh went after him, and because Hamish had left camp without permission, he went out of uniform. His men were excessively loyal, so a dozen of them went searching for Lord Colin with him."

The story had upset Megan when Colin had relayed it in the park, and it upset her now. "Your directions were the merest fancy," she went on, "the sort of practical joke with which you amused yourself when not avoiding actual combat. So you left a dozen good soldiers stumbling about under the noses of the French, and the French found them."

The silence in the ballroom was absolute, and Megan made sure her voice carried to every corner.

"Such is war," she said, "that soldiers captured out of uniform are subject to torture. Fortunately for Hamish MacHugh's men, they found Colin. Unfortunately for Hamish MacHugh, so did the French. There was a battle, and there was a bridge."

She had to fight for her composure, but in this, she would not fail Hamish.

"On one side of the bridge, we have the soldiers you sent on a goose chase in time of war," Megan said. "On the other, the French, who realize exactly what treasure they've come across, courtesy of your dubious sense of honor. A dozen British soldiers out of uniform, exhausted, on maneuvers against orders, and ripe for capture. The man you malign so easily, the man you call a *barbarian,* ordered everybody else to retreat and get back to camp.

"Hamish MacHugh held that bridge," Megan said, hurling her words at Sir Fletcher. "He fought against impossible odds, knowing his fate would be death or worse. He forbid his men to admit they'd disobeyed orders with him, lest they be court-martialed. Lord Colin and the others reached safety, while Murdoch was taken prisoner by the most notorious interrogator in the French army."

Megan turned to the faceless crowd surrounding her and Sir Fletcher. "Who is the barbarian? The officer who nearly gave his life for his brother and his men, or the scoundrel whose carelessness precipitated the danger? Or maybe" — she swallowed past a lump the size of a fist — "the worst barbarism is perpetrated by ladies and gentlemen who spread gossip and spite for their own entertainment. Who think because a man is handsome and charming and looks like them, he must be good, but if he's different, then he must be a stranger to honor."

Sir Fletcher backed away from her, his footsteps on the chalked dance floor the only sound. He tripped over Megan's glove, turned, and scuttled away. The crowd parted as if even touching his sleeve would have resulted in a dreadful contamination.

Megan swiped at her cheek with the one glove she still wore. The silence grew until movement on the steps to the minstrel's gallery caught her eye. The crowd turned as three men descended. One of them — a tall auburn-haired man — wore a kilt.

Hamish. Megan knew his bearing, knew his step, knew *him* — and he'd heard her every word. He stopped at that distance where Megan could make out his features clearly. Keswick and Rosecroft were at his sides, and his expression was thunderous.

Hamish was such a private man, and Megan had turned his worst nightmare into grist for the gossip mill.

"Don't be angry," Megan said. "Please, Hamish, don't be angry."

He propped his fists on his hips. "That is the most skillful ambush I have ever seen, Meggie Windham. And you lot" — he glowered at polite society — "don't you know it's rude to stare? Where are your manners?"

He held his arms wide, and Megan flew to him as if she'd been shot forth from Cupid's bow. Applause started from the minstrel's gallery and became a deafening thunder as Hamish whirled her off her feet and scooped her into his arms.

"You routed the varlet, Meggie mine," he growled. "Sent him packing with his tail between his legs. You are magnificent."

"You're here. I was so worried, and you were here all along."

460

"I am here," Hamish said, setting her on her feet, "with you, exactly as I always hope to be, but unless I want a certain duke — or a certain duchess — to skewer me where I stand, I have a bit of an ambush of my own to conduct."

"Don't kill Sir Fletcher, Hamish. I know he's a disgrace, but he's not worth —"

"Hush now. I had Puget pen a passionate letter in Sir Fletcher's hand to a certain lovely viscountess. Alas, the letter will be delivered to her jealous husband by mistake. By sundown tomorrow, Sir Fletcher will be on a packet to Calais."

"That was brilliant," Megan said, going up on tiptoe to kiss her beloved. "Noon would be better, though, or at first light. How early does the first packet leave?"

Rather than answer her question, Hamish went down on one knee, right in the middle of the ballroom. He bowed his head as if he were a knight in some medieval ceremony, and just like that, the ballroom was silent again.

"Hamish, what are you doing?" All the joy Megan had felt in his arms became muted with bewilderment.

He took her bare hand in his. "I'm ambushing you, more or less, which is only fair, because you ambushed me first. Miss

Megan Windham, you have not known me long, but you know my heart and have made that heart whole. I love you. I will always love you. Will you . . . Will you *please* marry me?"

"For God's sake, say yes!" somebody — who sounded suspiciously like Uncle Percy — bellowed. The rest of the gathering took up the chant, and resumed clapping and stomping, but none of that mattered.

What mattered was that Hamish was hers, and Megan was his.

"I'll marry you," Megan said, drawing him to his feet and bundling close. "Gladly, joyously, of course I'll marry you. I love you, and you have made my heart whole too. We'll have red-haired babies, and sing the lovely old songs, and on cold nights, we'll have a wee dram to ward off the chill. They'll call us duke and duchess of marital bliss."

"We'll have each other to ward off the chill, Meggie. Make no mistake about that."

As it happened, they were both right — except that often, they had more than a single wee dram, and some of the songs they sang were on the bawdy side of lovely — but Megan and Hamish MacHugh were, indeed, known as the duke and duchess of marital bliss.

To my dear readers,

To once again write stories for the Windham family, and to visit with some of my favorite characters, was an absolute joy. I'd been missing Westhaven, Lord Valentine, and St. Just, especially, as well as Their Graces.

In my mind's eye, Hamish bears a close resemblance to Jamie Fraser of *Outlander* fame, and his home is in the part of Perthshire where I've spent a lot of happy vacation/writing time. I've put some pictures up on my website (graceburrowes.com) on the Scotland with Grace page.

The Windham Brides series will continue with Anwen and Colin's story, and I am hearing rumors about a certain Welsh duke crossing paths with Elizabeth Windham in the story after that. If you'd like to keep up to date on all my releases, book signings, travels, and other adventures, please do visit the gracebur rowes.com website to sign up for my newsletter.

I hope you enjoyed Megan and Hamish's tale, but now that they're off honeymooning in the north, how about a sneak peek at Anwen and Colin's story?

Happy reading!
Grace Burrowes

The employees of Thorndike Press hope you have enjoyed this Large Print book. All our Thorndike, Wheeler, and Kennebec Large Print titles are designed for easy reading, and all our books are made to last. Other Thorndike Press Large Print books are available at your library, through selected bookstores, or directly from us.

For information about titles, please call:
  (800) 223-1244

or visit our Web site at:
  http://gale.cengage.com/thorndike

To share your comments, please write:
  Publisher
  Thorndike Press
  10 Water St., Suite 310
  Waterville, ME 04901